Vladimir Sollogub
The Tarantas
Impressions of a Journey
(Russia in the 1840s)

Translated with an Afterword by
William Edward Brown

Ardis, Ann Arbor

The frontispiece and illustrations on pp. 12, 18, 59, 81, and 174 are by Grigory Gagarin. They are reproduced from the 1845 edition of *The Tarantas*.

Vladimir Sollogub, *The Tarantas*
Copyright ● 1989 by Ardis Publishers
All rights reserved under International and Pan-American Copyright Conventions.
Printed in the United States of America

Ardis Publishers
2901 Heatherway
Ann Arbor, Michigan 48104

Library of Congress Cataloging in Publication Data

Sollogub, V. A. (Vladimir Aleksandrovich), graf, 1813-1882
[Tarantas. English]
The tarantas: impressions of a journey / Vladimir Sollogub;
translated, with a commentary by William Edward Brown.
p. cm.
Translation of: Tarantas.

ISBN 0-87501-045-8 (alk. paper)
I. Title.
PG3361.S7T313 1989
891.73'3—dc20 89-6623
CIP

To the Beloved Memory of "Misha"

Contents

* marks the 1840 chapters

Preface

Vladimir Sollogub's *Tarantas*, although scarcely a masterpiece, is a work of great interest from several points of view. This translation and commentary are focused primarily on its place in the national ideology of the Slavophiles, which some critics of its own time and subsequently have professed to detect in the utterances of its eloquent protagonist Ivan Vasilyevich. But this aspect of the work does not by any means exhaust its interest. For anyone concerned with the social history of nineteenth-century Russia *The Tarantas* affords fascinating, though fragmentary insights. Sollogub, whose other literary efforts are chiefly concerned with the frivolous upper-class society of Moscow and St. Petersburg, does not approach the lifelikeness of his contemporary Vladimir Dal in portraying the lower classes, but even so in his depiction of merchants, petty bourgeois and peasants Sollogub is a good deal more successful than most writers of his time. Indeed, it may be said that his picture of the "high society" of the two capitals, with which he was certainly most familiar, is more a caricature than a portrait, while he achieves a considerable verisimilitude with petty officials and peasants.

From a purely literary point of view, which has been pretty much ignored in the present commentary, *The Tarantas* deserves more consideration than it has received. It is an uneven work and shows marks of carelessness, but these are balanced by liveliness, sometimes even brilliance, sympathy and a pervasive good temper; best of all, Sollogub has a sense of humor which is not in any way at odds with occasional seriousness. A casual reader would be well advised to skip the chapter on the Pechersky Monastery in Nizhny Novgorod, which is at best not much above the level of a Baedeker account, and has the added disadvantage of dealing with a city (Gorky) that is inaccessible to present-day travellers; some of the material in Chapter XIX is similar, and there are tedious passages elsewhere as well—but such is the fate of all, or most, books. With all its faults, this one has much to ponder, and not a little to enjoy.

The Tarantas

I

The Meeting

Vasily Ivanovich was strolling one day on Tverskoi Boulevard.[1]

Vasily Ivanovich is a Kazan landowner of about fifty, of rather short stature, but of such rotundity that it's a joy just to look at him. His face is wide and red, his eyes small and gray. He is dressed in landowner fashion: on his head a white felt service cap with a long peak; a blue frock coat with shiny buttons, made in Kazan by a misshapen tailor whose sign has for forty years been proclaiming him as "newly arrived from Petersburg"; pantaloons of a pea-green hue, undulating pleasantly in picturesque folds around his boots. A necktie with an enormous buckle in the back; on his vest a string of beads of light azure.

Vasily Ivanovich was walking by himself along Tverskoi Boulevard and smiling slyly at the thought of all the delights with which Moscow so bounteously abounds. As a matter of fact, when you think of it, the English Club, the German Club, the Commercial Club—and all the tables with cards where one may sit down and watch how people play for large and small stakes. And there is lotto, at which landowners sit, and billiards with moustachioed players and humorous markers. What a breadth of choice!... And the gypsies, and the comedies, and the bear-baiting by the little bulldogs at the Mat-Weavers' Gate,[2] and the leisurely strolling through the city, and the theater, where such beauties dance and make such flourishes with their legs that you simply can't believe your eyes. At this point Vasily Ivanovich remembered his terrible and portly wife, left behind to look after things in their Kazan village, and positively beamed with the look of a desperate rake.

At the same time Ivan Vasilyevich also was walking along Tverskoi Boulevard. Ivan Vasilyevich is a young man just returned from abroad. He is wearing an English mackintosh without a waist, his pantaloons were made at Chevreuil's, the stick he is leaning on was bought at Vernier's. His hair is cut in the style of the middle ages, and on his chin are still visible the traces of a most frightful beard.

Formerly when a young Russian would return from Paris he would come back with the look of a hairdresser, several bright-colored vests, some vulgar witticisms, various unbearable grimaces and a decidedly intolerable boastfulness. Thank God, this is now all passé. But now there's another extreme. Now our youth has become infected with deep thinking, it studies political economy, worries about the Russian aristocracy, is concerned about the good of the state—and what do you suppose?—turns Russian while abroad, even Russian through and through, thinks only about Russia, about the greatness of Russia, about the defects of Russia, and returns to the fatherland with a kind of peculiar rapture, sometimes ridiculous and out of place, but at least excusable, and in any case more laudable than the former good-for-nothingness. A worthy representative of young Russia, Ivan Vasilyevich had travelled all over Europe, and in trying to understand the political babble of miscellaneous castes, he had become accustomed to party passions concealed under the resounding names of the public good, freedom and enlightenment, and had come to realize how great and beautiful his native land was in many ways; and from that time there was kindled in him a warm though ignorant love for the motherland, and from that time on he had begun to be proud before himself and before the whole world that he had been born a Russian. Quite apart from this feeling, however, like the rest of the youth of any state, he had brought back from abroad a burning rapture as regards the Paris opera, and tender memories of Parisian suburban balls.

And so Ivan Vasilyevich was walking along Tverskoi Boulevard, glancing with amazement at the bright costumes of the Moscow dandies and the fantastic liveries of their unshaven lackeys, and humming to himself "*nel furor della tempesta*," the wonderful aria from Bellini's opera *Il Pirata* [1827]. "Oh, Lord," he thought, "what a pity there's so little life and gaiety here... *Nel furor*... It's quite different in Paris... *della tempesta*. Oh, Paris, Paris! Where are your grisettes, your theaters and Musard's balls?[3].. *Nel furor*... How one remembers Labiche, Grisi, Fanny Elsler[4]—while here all they do is ask you what your rank is. You say: provincial secretary, and no one will even look at you... *della tempesta*."

At that moment he glanced at a strange mass in a white service-cap, pea-green drapes around its legs, which was rolling along towards him. The smiling red face seemed familiar to him. "Hullo! Why, it's Vasily Ivanych," he thought, "our neighbor in our Kazan village. His village is Mordasy. Three hundred souls! A good manager. He's afraid of his wife. At name-day parties he gets quite jolly and sings Russian songs and sometimes even dances. He must surely have seen my father!"

"Hello, Vasily Ivanovich," the young man said politely with a bow. Vasily Ivanovich stopped and looked at him mistrustfully.

"Well, well, well!" he roared at last in a thunderous voice. "Well, well, well! Johnny, little Johnny, Johnnykins!... By what chance?—" and seizing the frightened dandy with his enormous paws Vasily Ivanovich began to smother him with heavy kisses, paying no attention to the crowd of strolling on-lookers. "Well, fellow, what a tailor's dummy you've turned into! Turn around, please. Again... Now isn't that something! What is this, the fashion with you people, eh? A perfect sack, a flour sack! Fine, lad, very fine! Where have you been?"

"I've been abroad."

"Well, sir! And where, if I may ask?"

"Six months in Paris."

"So!"

"In Germany, in Italy..."

"Yes, yes, yes... Fine... and if I may ask, did you scatter a good deal of dough around?"

"I beg your pardon?"

"Did you squander a lot of money, fellow?"

"Quite a bit."

"There you are! And your father, my neighbor, what'll he say to this? Old folks, you know, aren't very agreeable to their children's prodigality. And the years are bad. You've heard, I suppose, that all your father's buckwheat was beaten down by hail?"

"Father wrote about it.—I'm on my way to him now."

"It's a fine thing to comfort the old man. Ah... May I ask what's your rank?"

"That's it!" thought the young man. 'Twelfth class," he answered hesitantly.

"Hmm!... Not very high... and you've already retired, I suppose?"

"Yes, retired."

"Just as I thought! You young people have got it into your heads that you have to look down on the service. You've gotten too clever, see! And now, if I may ask, what do you intend to do, eh?"

"Why, I'd like to have a look at Russia, Vasily Ivanovich, to get acquainted with her."

"What!"

"I'd like to study my motherland."

"What? What?"

"I intend to study my motherland."

"If you please, I don't understand... You want to study..."

"To study my motherland... to study Russia."

"And how, my dear fellow, are you going to study Russia?"

"In two ways... in regard to her antiquity, and in regard to her national character [*narodnost'*], which of course are closely connected. By investigating our monuments, our beliefs and traditions, by listening to every echo of our olden times, I shall succeed... pardon! We shall succeed—we, my comrades and I... we shall come to an understanding of the national spirit, character and needs, and we shall know from what source our people's education must come, utilizing the example of Europe, but not taking it as a model."

"As far as I'm concerned," said Vasily Ivanovich, "I've got the best way for you to study Russia—get married. Drop the empty words, fellow, and let's go to Kazan. Your rank isn't very high, but it's that of an officer, you have a gentleman's estate, you'll easily find a good match. And thank God, we have a good harvest of marriageable girls... Get married, that's right, and go live with the old man. It's time to think about him. Eh, fellow, that's right! You suppose, of course, that it's tiresome in the country? Not a bit of it. In the morning, out in the field, and then a snack, and then dinner, and then a nap, and then to the neighbors... And the name-day parties, and the hunting with hounds, and one's own music, and the fair... Eh? That's living, fellow! What's your Paris! And the principal thing, you'll be having babies, and your rye will be yielding eightfold, and there'll be so much grain on your threshing-floor that you won't be able to thresh it, and so much money in your pocket that you can't count it, and so, in my opinion, you'll learn to know Russia famously...Eh?"

"Of course," said Ivan Vasilyevich, "that wouldn't be bad."

"You know what? You're going to Kazan?"

"Yes, to Kazan."

"When?"

"The sooner the better."

"Excellent. And in what, if I may ask?"

"I don't yet know myself."

"I suppose you don't have a carriage?"

"No sir, I don't."

"Splendid. We'll go together."

"What?"

"We'll go together. I'll take you to the old man... You don't have, I suppose, any extra cash?"

"Beg your pardon... I don't understand..."

"Enough putting on airs... Tell the truth."

"I am a little pressed for money right now."

"Now, now, now! Now you see... It would be a long time... I'll take you, and settle up with your father..."

"Oh, please..."

"Now what?"

"I'd be ashamed, sir."

"What nonsense! We're Russians, my dear fellow. Stop acting the dandy, fellow! No ceremony with me! Shake hands on it, what?"

"I shall be very much obliged."

"Well now, that's fine, that's great! But listen now, do you know what we'll be riding in? Eh?"

"A carriage?"

"No."

"A barouche?"

"No."

"A trap?"

"No again."

"A kibitka?"

"By no means."

"Then what?"

Here Vasily Ivanovich smiled slyly and announced in triumph:

"A tarantas!"

2

The Departure

A few days later, in a little wooden house on Dog Square,⁵ an unusual turmoil was in progress. In the courtyard a coachman was fussing around the post horses. Maids were running and bustling up and down the stairs. On the floors of the rooms were dumped trunks, boxes, ropes, hay, and all sorts of truck. In an upstairs room Vasily Ivanovich was standing before a mirror and making himself ready for the road.

An enormous knit scarf with a rainbow play of colors—a precious token of husbandly long-suffering—was tied around his stout neck. White overshoes had been pulled on to his feet, and on his upper body a shaggy fur jacket with the fur outside lent Vasily Ivanovich a Homeric beauty. On each side of him stood in respectful poses the master of the house with his hand in his bosom and the mistress, a stout merchant woman, with a pie baked for the road. Both were bowing to the portly landowner, and repeating again and again with various grimaces:

"Permit us to see your worship off... and to wish you every kind of good fortune. We beg most humbly... we beg you most humbly to accept our bread and salt⁶ for the journey—what God has provided. We beg you not to scorn it, but to eat it for good luck. It may come in handy on the journey. If God brings you back to Moscow again, we beg you most humbly not to offend us, not to pass by our shack. We're grateful, very, sincerely glad of such important persons. We beg you most humbly."

"Thanks, mine host," replied Vasily Ivanovich benevolently. "Thanks, hostess. I shall remember you and remember you kindly. Hey, Senka! Take the pie and stow it well in the boot, d' you hear? Perhaps God will bring us together again... Look out that it doesn't break!... We've had a pleasant time with you... [to Senka] You rascal, it's all the same to you."

Vasily Ivanovich put his pocketbook together with his travel pass and purse in a side pocket of his Cossack trousers, cinched up his fur jacket with a belt, crossed himself before the icon, sat down for a moment,⁷ embraced host and hostess three times, and emerged outside for the last-minute travel preparations.

Outside the tarantas was displayed in all its prairie splendor. But what a tarantas, what an amazing invention of the human mind!

Imagine two long poles, two parallel shafts, endless and immeasurable. Slung between them, unexpectedly as it were, an enormous basket, rounded on the sides like a gigantic cup, like a goblet of antediluvian banquets. To the ends of the shafts wheels were attached, and this whole strange creation seems from a distance to be some queer product of a fantastic world, something half-way between a dragonfly and a kibitka. But what can one say

of the art by which in a few minutes the tarantas suddenly disappeared beneath small trunks, small valises, chests, big boxes, little boxes, baskets, casks and all sorts of things of every kind and description? First of all, in this chiselled-out vessel there were no seats; an enormous featherbed had been dumped into the expanse, the upper stripes of its coarse huck covering were level with the sloping edges. Next seven feather pillows in cotton cases intentionally dark in preparation for the dirty roads, towered up in a pyramid upon their soft foundation. In the boot were stowed the pie for the road in a pile of bast, a flask with anise-flavored vodka, various roast fowls wrapped in gray paper, cheese cakes, a ham, loaves of white bread, fancy rolls and the so-called cellarette [*pogrebets*], the indispensable travelling companion of every steppe landowner. This cellarette, upholstered on the outside with a sealskin, bristles uppermost, and bound with tin hoops, contains in it a whole tea service—an invention of undoubted usefulness, but by no means complicated manufacture. Open it: under the cover a tray, and on the tray before you in all her beauty a sleeping shepherdess under a tree, swiftly sketched in three rosy spots by the decisive brush stroke of a bazaar artist. Inside the wallpaper-covered chest majestically stands a teapot of a dirty white hue with a gilt edge; close beside this a glass carafe with tea, another like it, with rum, two glasses, a milk pitcher, and the little appurtenances of tea-time enjoyment. The Russian cellarette, by the by, is fully deserving of our respect. Amid the general changes and improvements among us, it alone has not changed its original type, has not been attracted by the allurements of a deceptive beauty, but has gone indifferently and untouched through all the upheavals of time... That's what a Russian cellarette is like! All around the tarantas were strung little sacks and cartons. In one of these was a cap and crimson turban from Mme Lebourg on Kuznetsky Bridge [a fashionable Moscow shopping street], for Vasily Ivanovich's spouse; in others were children's books, dolls and playthings for Vasily Ivanovich's children, and above all two lamps for the house, several vessels for the kitchen, and even some colonial provisions for Vasily Ivanovich's table: everything purchased in accordance with a list given him from the country. Finally, in the rear, three monstrous trunks, stuffed with all sorts of trash and tied around with ropes, towered like an Egyptian obelisk on the hind portion of our travelling chariot.

With a look of dissatisfaction the red-haired coachman began to harness three puny horses to the tarantas.

At that moment Ivan Vasilyevich drove into the yard in a hired cab. The collar of his mackintosh was raised above his ears; under his arm was a small valise, and he was holding in his hands a silk parasol, a little travelling bag with a steel padlock, a beautifully bound book in brown Morocco with steel stitching, and a finely sharpened pencil.

"Ah, Ivan Vasilyevich!" said Vasily Ivanovich. "It's time, my dear chap. But where's your duffle?"

"I have nothing more with me."

"Whew! Why, fellow, you'll freeze like that, in your sack. It's a good thing that I have an extra sheepskin coat with rabbit fur. And by the way, tell me please, what will you have under you, featherbed or mattress?"

"What?" asked Ivan Vasilyevich in horror.

"I'm asking you what you prefer, mattress or featherbed?"

Ivan Vasilyevich was ready to run, and looked desperately from side to side. It seemed to him that all Europe would see him in a sheepskin coat, on a featherbed and in a tarantas.

"Well, which is it?" asked Vasily Ivanovich.

"Mattress!" he said, scarcely audibly.

"Well, fine. Senka, put down a mattress for him, and get a move on."

Senka in a raw sheepskin coat busied himself once again with his Cyclopean labor.

Vasily Ivanovich continued with a satisfied smile:

"And what do you think of the little tarantas, eh?... A perfect cradle. You'll never turn over, and it never has to be mended—not like your carriages with springs—every step, repairs. And soft, just like a bed, just learn to roll from side to side, wrap yourself up warmly, and sleep the whole way!"

Ivan Vasilyevich looked quite sadly at his travelling companion, not in the least convinced of the possibility of the forthcoming delights. But there was nothing he could do. Having squandered his substance, as befits a Russian, while abroad, he had no idea, to tell the truth, of how to get to his father's village.

And behold, a beautiful chance had opened up for him. Vasily Ivanovich, his father's friend, was taking him along on credit.

On the way he could study his motherland. Everything would be fine. But this base featherbed, these cotton pillows, this horrible tarantas!

Ivan Vasilyevich heaved a deep sigh, and pronounced in a toneless voice, humming:

"*Nel furor della tempesta...* Shouldn't it be time to go?"

And quite so, it is time. The horses are ready. The mistress of the house, the shop boys and the maids are bustling around the tarantas. All are helping and bowing and wishing a prosperous journey. Vasily Ivanovich, with general assistance, with pushing and shoving, had finally clambered into place and lowered himself onto the featherbed. Ivan Vasilyevich climbed in after him and sank into pillows. Senka took his seat beside the driver.

"Well, all ready?"

"Ready."

"Well, look here now, watch the road. Hold back the horses going down hill. No galloping and no dawdling, but drive at a trot...pace, pace, pace... Senka, no dozing on the box. D'you hear, you bum? You could perfectly well fall off. Now, with God, at a good hour, the Archangel's hour... Go!"

The tarantas gave a start and dragged itself forward, lurching heavily from side to side.

"Good-bye, hostess!"

"Good-bye, little father Vasily Ivanovich!... Please don't forget us. We beg you humbly."

And the hostess, and the shop boys and the servant girls all emptied out of the gate to gaze after the tarantas until at last it was hidden from view. And the tarantas rolled along through white-stone Moscow and aroused astonishment in no one. Yet there was a good deal to be astonished at, as one looked at the enormous mass with its pillows, on which a shaggy landowner was lying like an effete bear; the dandy sticking up beside him, with mackintosh and discontented physiognomy, deserved not a little astonishment; and in his own way Senka on the box, in a sheepskin like some savage from the icy wastes, was no less remarkable. In other regions all this would infallibly have aroused general curiosity; but in Moscow the passers-by, inured to such scenes, paid not the slightest attention to the tarantas. Only some street boys, tugging each other by the caftan, said to each other in passing:

"Look, there goes some landowner. Boy, is he bloated!"

III

The Beginning of the Travel Impressions

When the travellers had ridden past the barrier gate, conversation started up between them.

"Vasily Ivanovich!."

"What is it, my dear fellow?"

"Do you know what I'm thinking?"

"No, my dear fellow, I don't."

"I'm thinking that since now we're getting ready to travel..."

"What, my dear fellow! What do you mean, travel?"

"Why, we're travelling right now"

"No, Ivan Vasilyevich, not a bit of it. We're simply riding from Moscow to Mordasy by way of Kazan."

"Well, but even that's travelling, you know."

"What do you mean, travelling, my dear chap! People travel off yonder, abroad, in the German region. But what sort of travellers are we? Just some gentlemen riding to our country places."

"Well, it's all the same. Since we're now heading for the road..."

"Yes, that's it, if you please."

"It seems to me that I can use the time... of our expedition, so to speak... with profit."

"What sort of profit, my dear chap? I don't understand you at all."

"Look! Abroad it's the fashion now to publish one's travel impressions. All sorts of things go in them: where you spent the night, whom you saw, what understanding you came to and what you guessed at, your observations on manners, education, the level of the arts, on the movement of trade, on antiquities, and on contemporary life—in a word, on a people's whole way of life. Afterwards all this is collected and printed under the title of travel impressions."

"Well, I say!"

"Unfortunately these impressions do not always bear the stamp of truth, and hence lose their merit. Moreover everything that can be said about the state of the West has been said and printed repeatedly. Conclusions have been drawn, opinions defined,—there's nowhere for an observer to wander."

"What are you getting at with all this talk, my dear fellow?"

"Here's what. Impressions of travel abroad are of no use to anyone anymore because there can't be anything new in them. But travel impressions in Russia can reveal much that is curious, particularly if they are to be guided by truth alone. Just think, what an abundant field for investigation: study of the ancient monuments, study of the Russian way of life, study of our beautiful and great and holy mother country. Do you understand me?"

"No, lad, you keep talking such strange stuff."

"My hope, my desire, my goal," Ivan Vasilyevich continued, getting carried away, "is to make myself in some way at least useful to my compatriots. That's why, Vasily Ivanovich, I want to write down everything that I shall see; I want to write without any sophistry, but holding to the truth only, nothing but the truth. I have with me a traveller's inkwell and a thick notebook of paper," he said triumphantly, pointing to the magnificent book resting on his knees. "This book must be of service to me and to all Russia. This is the book of my travel impressions. My friends will read it, God willing, and it will instill in them the desire to penetrate more deeply into these matters which I can mark only in passing."

"And what are you thinking of writing in it?" inquired Vasily Ivanovich.

"Everything that we meet with on the road that is genuinely curious, genuinely worthy of note. Everything that I shall be able to dig up about the Russian people and their traditions, about the Russian muzhik and the Russian nobleman, whom I love with all my soul, just as I hate the official with all my soul, and that monstrous, nameless class that has grown up in our land from the pursuit of filthy lucre into some sort of pitiable, misunderstood culture."

"But why, my dear fellow, do you hate officials?" inquired Vasily Ivanovich.

"That doesn't mean that I hate people who serve conscientiously and nobly. On the contrary, I respect them with all my heart. But I hate that miserable type of crude culturelessness which one meets with among both gentry and commoners and among merchants, and which I call accordingly by the altogether inexact name of official."

"But why, my dear chap?"

"Because those whom I so designate, for their lack of a solid foundation give themselves only the externals of culture, but in reality are a great deal more ignorant than the simple muzhik himself, whose nature is still unspoiled. Because there is in these people nothing Russian, neither the moral character nor the habits; because with their tavern culture, their self-satisfied ignorance, their wretched dandyism, they not only hold back genuine culture, but often set it on a harmful direction. This is a monstrous class which has sprung up on the nation's soil, but is perfectly foreign to the nation's life. Just look at them: what has become of the noble traits of our people? This class is dirty, it drinks itself drunk, but not on holidays, like the muzhik; it takes bribes, it tries to put down everyone else, and at the same time puffs itself up and puts on airs before the simple folk because forsooth it plays billiards and goes about in a frock coat! Such a tribe is a corrupted tribe, degenerated from a fine beginning. But take a look at the Russian muzhik: who can be more beautiful and picturesque than he? But by a prejudiced indifference in the highest class among us there is little concern for him, or else they look at him as at a savage from the Aleutian Islands; and yet in him is concealed the germ of the Russian bogatyr spirit, the beginning of our mother country's greatness."

"They're sly rascals," observed Vasily Ivanovich.

"Sly, but for that very reason intelligent, capable of imitating, of appropriating what is new, and consequently, of education. In other lands the peasant, whatever you show him, will just keep on plowing; but with us, we have only to show something once, and he makes himself into a musician, a craftsman, a mechanic, a painter, a supervisor—what you will."

"What's true is true," said Vasily Ivanovich.

"And besides," continued Ivan Vasilyevich, "in what nation will you find such an instinctive understanding of one's duties, such a readiness to help one's neighbors, such cheerfulness, such cordiality, such humility and such strength?"

"A sly folk, there's no denying!" observed Vasily Ivanovich.

"And yet we disdain him, we look on him with contempt as an article of quit-rent, and not only do we do nothing for his intellectual improvement, but we try in every way to spoil him."

"How so?" asked Vasily Ivanovich.

"Here's how. By the gentry's rotten system. A household serf is nothing but the first step toward an official. The household serf is shaven, he goes about in a long-tailed coat of home-made cloth. The household serf serves for the amusement of idle sloth and gets used to parasitism and debauchery. The household serf already gets drunk and steals and puts on airs and despises the muzhik who toils for him and pays the soul-tax for him. Then under favorable conditions the household serf becomes a clerk, a freedman, a departmental clerk; the departmental clerk despises both the household serf and the muzhik, and learns pettifoggery, and on the sly from the district police officer picks up chickens and ten-kopeck pieces for himself. He has a nankeen coat and pomaded hair. He is already learning stealing of a systematic sort. Then the departmental clerk descends a degree lower, becomes a copyist, a desk supervisor [*povytchik*],[8] a secretary, and finally a full-fledged official. Then his sphere is enlarged, then he takes on a different kind of life: he despises both the muzhik and the household serf and the departmental clerk because they, if you please, are uneducated people. By this time he has the highest of needs, and so is already stealing bank notes. His drink, of course, has to be wine from the Don, he has to smoke Zhukov tobacco and play 'little bank,'[9] and he rides in a tarantas, orders caps for his wife with silver spikes of wheat, and silk gowns. For this he assumes his post without the slightest twinge of conscience, just as a merchant enters his shop, and makes trade of his influence as with any ware. One gets caught, and another... It's nothing to him, say his confreres. Take, but take care."

"They're not all like that," observed Vasily Ivanovich.

"Not all, of course, but exceptions don't alter the rule."

"And besides," added Vasily Ivanovich, "provincial officals are chosen in our land for the most part by the gentry."

"And that's what sad," said Ivan Vasilyevich. "That which in other lands is an object of national solicitation, comes to us of itself. We must not, we cannot dare complain of the government, which has presented us ourselves with the choice of our own executives for the internal management of our affairs. There's no concealing our fault. We're guilty of it all, we the gentry, we the landowners, who joke and laugh over what should be an object of deep concern. In every province there are even now educated persons who in cooperation with the laws could give a beneficial direction to the whole realm, but nearly all of them shun election like the plague, leaving it to intrigue and calculation, to petty gossips and provincial loud mouths. And the great proprietors, strolling along Nevsky Prospekt, or after a spree abroad, almost never look in on their estates. For them the elections are a caricature. District police officer, assessor, are caricatures, beautifully taken off in *The Inspector General*. And they make fun of their bald spots, of their pot-bellies, not thinking that they are entrusting to them not only their own present well-being and the well-being of their peasants, but—it's dreadful to say it—even their own future fate. Yes! If we hadn't taken this wretched direction, if we weren't so unforgivably light-minded, how splendid would be the calling of the Russian gentry, a gentry designated to march in front and show a whole people the path to genuine enlightenment. I repeat: we ourselves are to blame, we landowners, we of the gentry. Russian noblemen could bring a great deal of profit to their fatherland, but what have they done?"

"Squandered their property, the dears," observed Vasily Ivanovich very much to the point.

"Yes," continued Ivan Vasilyevich, "squandered their property on holidays, on theaters, on mistresses, on all sorts of rot. All our old names are disappearing. The coats-of-arms of our princely houses have been rolled in the dust, because there is nothing to re-erect them on, and the Russian gentry, prosperous, cheerful, hospitable, has surrendered its ancestral patrimonies to resourceful merchants, who have made factories in luxurious palaces. Where is our aristocracy? Vasily Ivanovich, what do you think of our Russian aristocrats?"

"I think," said Vasily Ivanovich, "that there won't be any horses for us at the station."

IV

A Station

Unfortunately Vasily Ivanovich's premonition was justified by the reality.

The tarantas stopped at a low little hut in front of which a four-cornered particolored post designated the stationmaster's house. It was already dark outdoors. A dim lantern barely lighted the outside stairway, swaying beneath the door overhang. Behind the hut stretched a three-sided shed roofed with straw, out of which peered hens, cows, pigs and chickens. In the middle of the soft, damp yard stood a half-ruinous timber wellhead. At the very entrance of the hut huddled an ugly throng of beggars, who had come running from various directions—legless, dumb, blind, with withered arms, with repulsive sores, in rags, with dishevelled heads. Among them there were drunken old women and pallid young women, and children in nothing but little shirts, who had pulled their hands out of their sleeves and crossed them on their chests from the cold. It was a sad thing to listen to their voices, affected, learned by rote, amidst the bellowing, imploring and mutual abuse of the ugly crowd which rushed, shoving each other, toward the tarantas, exhibiting wounds and holding out hands.

Meanwhile, as our travellers, wearied by their first stage, were disentangling themselves from featherbeds and pillows, the stationmaster in a worn green uniform coat came out on the porch and took a look on the sly at the new arrivals.

"A tarantas," he said quite contemptuously, "a three-horse team—they can wait... And you, get out of here, damn you!" he yelled at the beggars.

Like a pack of frightened dogs the hideous crowd ran off in all directions, and the travellers went into the hut to the station. The stationmaster greeted them extremely coolly.

"As you please, but I haven't any horses. There's been such a run on them as may God save us from."

"What do you mean, no horses?" cried Ivan Vasilyevich.

"Be so good as to look in the book yourselves. In this establishment there are nine three-horse teams in all. In the morning a court councillor's wife came through; she took six horses, and the heavy post took three three-horse teams and a certain colonel for official requirements took four horses."

"But you still have eight horses left," said Ivan Vasilyevich.

"No, sir, not at all. Be so good as to look at the book."

"But what has become of those eight horses?"

"They're courier horses, and I don't dare let them out. Very likely a courier will come through—you can imagine for yourselves."

"We'll complain."

"Complain by all means, my good man. Here's the book. Be so good as to enter your names, but we have no horses."

"Between Moscow and Vladimir," observed Vasily Ivanovich, "there never are any horses at a single station, whenever you may arrive. Evidently there's such a great run on them.[10] It seems this is the thirteenth time I've been through, and it's always the same story. But what are we going to do?"

"You can hire 'free' horses," said the stationmaster in a more conciliatory tone.[11]

"Free horses!" roared Vasily Ivanovich. "I know those arch-rascals! Jews, riffraff, they skin you a half-ruble a verst.[12] I'll stay here three days before I'll hire 'free' horses!"

"It *is* well known," observed the stationmaster, "that they won't transport you cheaply. However, fodder now is expensive."

"Scoundrels!" said Vasily Ivanovich.

"Recently," continued the stationmaster with a smile, "a certain general played a fine trick on them. At my station as though on purpose two state messengers came through, and the post, and regular travellers, all very important people. In a word, not a single horse in the horse barn. Then suddenly in runs an orderly, such a tall fellow, with a little moustache... 'Get ready to receive the general!' says he. I just had time to button up my coat and run into the passage. I hear him yelling 'Horses!' Such a calamity! There's nothing to be done. I go up to the carriage. 'Pardon, your excellency,' said I, 'all the horses are out.' 'You lie you rascal!' he yelled. 'I'll have you drafted as a soldier! Do you know whom your're talking to? Eh? I suppose you don't see who it is that's travelling? Huh?' 'I see, your Excellency,' said I, 'I'd be glad so help me God, to do my best, but where am I at fault? It doesn't take long to ruin a poor man. First it's this way, then that way... There are no horses.' By good luck, here come squint-eyed Eremka and bald Andryushka—such reckless fellows, you know, everything's all the same to them; they go right up to the carriage and ask 'Wouldn't you like to hitch on some free horses?' 'What will you charge?' asks the general. Says Andryusha: 'Two whities,' fifty rubles in bank-notes[13] and the distance is only sixteen versts. 'Well, put them on,' yelled the general, 'and be quick about it, you double-dyed rascals!' They were overjoyed, my drivers, they made fast work of it, you know, they hitched up the horses at the first demand and rolled away grandly. Dust went up in a column. And folks are envious: such good luck for the fellows!.. Well, sir, in the morning, when they returned to the station, I congratulated them on the money. I see them scratch their heads. 'What money?' says Andryushka. 'You know, the general reckoned it at five kopecks a verst, and what's more, didn't even give us a tip. What a joker!' "[14]

"Ha, ha, ha!" roared Vasily Ivanovich. "There's a fine fellow! That's what I like! It's time to teach them a lesson, the robbers!"

Ivan Vasilyevich was engaged in mournfully inspecting the stationmaster's living quarters.

On the walls of the room, particularly on the stove, there were still noticeable here and there dubious traces of white paint, modestly hiding under a triple layer of soot and dirt. By the door was hung a white-painted cuckoo-clock with weights and a moving pendulum. In the left corner a shrine with icons, and under it a long bench beside a rather long table. On the wall the regulations of the postal department and a few cheap pictures representing moral and allegorical subjects. Between the windows were displayed representations of Malek-Adel on an infuriated horse, the return of the Prodigal Son, a portrait of Count Platov, and the lamentable countenance of Geneviève of Brabant, somewhat befouled by flies.[14] The master's private section lay on the right side. All his inclinations and habits were concentrated here. Beside the bed, which was covered by a piece of flannel that had seen some service, there rose proudly on three legs, but without locks or handles, the room's prime adornment—a dresser of real mahogany, covered with dust and various little trifles—but what kind of trifles? A half-pair of spectacles, and a pair of tweezers, some tallow candle-ends and a little jar empty of pomade, a small comb, and a glass swan for perfume, with a strange stopper, and some soiled fashion plates, and a bottle with dry Madeira, and a cigar box without cigars, and nails, and a snuff box, and some bills, and a whole collection of headgear. First, a green service cap, appropriate to the stationmaster's official position; then a black hat with white spots, which the stationmaster put on when as a society man he paid a visit to the liquor concessionaire or the woman who bakes the consecrated bread; then a white hat with black spots, which lends him particular fascination when he plays the rake and courts the rustic beauties; then two worn winter caps, and finally a skull cap originally of velvet, with a dangling tassel. Drawn up to the dresser was a little pyramidal stand adorned with three Turkish pipes with feather ornaments, and a tobacco pouch of canvas, once embroidered.

Ivan Vasilyevich examined it all attentively, and felt even gloomier. What he was thinking God knows.

Meanwhile the room was filling up with travellers. A teacher from the Tobolsk gymnasium came in with his wife, a rather pretty Englishwoman whom he had just married and was taking in a two-horse carriage from Moscow to Tobolsk. A student came in wearing an overcoat with a scarf tied around his neck, with a pipe and a dog. A cheerful major burst in, threw off his bearskin coat, bowed to everyone in turn, asked each whom he had the honor to be addressing, where he came from, where he was going and why, cracked jokes at the stationmaster's expense, had friendly words with the coachman who was asking him for a tip at the door. Vasily Ivanovich took a great liking to him.

From the stationmaster all had a single answer: "The horses at present are all out; when they return from the run, there will be no holding back on my part."

There was nothing to be done. Vasily Ivanovich, as an experienced and capable man, did not waste time. The boiling samovar was already bubbling in a circle of glasses and tea things. At his invitation the group crowded around the table, faces became animated, clothing was flung back, and tea—fragrant tea, the Russian's comfort for all life's chances—began to pass from hand to hand in cups, bowls and glasses. Little by little acquaintance was established. First the road was damned, then there was complaint over the lack of horses, then the talk shifted to extraneous subjects. The student told stories about duels and hunting hares; the major was already addressing everyone with the familiar "thou."[16] He let the whole company know that he was going into retirement, that he had so and so much money, that he had intended to get married but had been turned down, that he was dissatisfied with his life—in a word, without any question on the part of his listeners he communicated his whole history from the cradle to the present moment, with the addition of various jokes and popular sayings. Vasily Ivanovich laughed and slapped the major on the shoulder, passing his judgment that he was "an army brick" [*kostochka*—lit. "a (cherry-) stone"]. Ivan Vasilyevich questioned the Tobolsk teacher about Siberia. Only the Englishwoman was silent and looked expressively at her husband. Suddenly a noise was heard outside. The tea-drinking company began to listen. First of all some sort of heavy equipage approached the station; there was a turmoil outside, the sound of carriage bells, the trampling of horses, and in a few minutes the sound of wheels gave token of the travellers' departure.

"What's that?" asked Vasily Ivanovich of the stationmaster as he came in.

"A privy councillor going through."

All those present looked at each other in gloomy indignation.

"Where did they get horses?"

"You, gentlemen," answered the stationmaster, shrugging his shoulders and a little confused, "wanted to drink tea, but a privy councillor, gentlemen... a privy councillor—why, you know yourselves how it is."[17]

V

A Hotel

Between Moscow and Vladimir, as experienced travellers know well, there is not a single hotel in which one might lament at his ease the dearth of horses. Only the cramped quarters of stationmasters, who are protected from beatings by the flattering rights of the 14th class,[18] afford their benches for the sorrowful meditations of disappointed expectation. Vasily Ivanovich had occasion several times a day to take his cellarette out of the tarantas and regale himself with tea. Ivan Vasilyevich had occasion to meditate his fill on the fortunes of Russia and look to his heart's content at the beauty of the muzhik who, truth to tell, had already begun to bore him. There was nothing to note down in the book. Everywhere the same vexatious, wearisome, prosaic refrain: "All the horses are cut." Ivan Vasilyevich would look at Vasily Ivanovich, Vasily Ivanovich would look at Ivan Vasilyevich, and both would sit down to doze, one in front of the other, for several hours at a stretch.

Moreover, a staggering misfortune befell them between two stations. During a moment of sweet slumber, when worn out by the jolts of the tarantas on the wooden roadway Vasily Ivanovich was resting noisily from life's vanity, Ivan Vasilyevich was picturing himself at the Italian opera, and Senka was swaying like a pendulum on the box, skilled rascals cut two valises and several boxes from the tarantas. Vasily Ivanovich's grief was genuine. Among other objects the cap and crimson turban from Mme Lebourg on Kuznetsky Bridge were lost, and the cap and turban, as we know, were intended for the lady herself, Avdotya Petrovna.

Arriving at the station, he hurled himself on the stationmaster with a complaint and plea for assistance. The stationmaster answered him by way of consolation:

"You needn't worry at all: your things are lost. This isn't the first time; you drove through a village twelve versts from here which is famous for this: all the inhabitants are rascals."

"What do you mean, rascals?" asked Ivan Vasilyevich.

"Everyone knows, sir. On the highroad they play their tricks at night. If you fall asleep, they'll cut loose the rear most valises, you can be sure."

"But that's highway robbery."

"No, not highway robbery, just mischief."

"Fine mischief," said Vasily Ivanovich gloomily, as he set out once more. "And what will Avdotya Petrovna say?"

"I wish we might rest somewhere in a regular inn," continued Ivan Vasilyevich no less plaintively. "I'm so shaken up that all my bones are quite broken. You know, this is the third day we've been on the road, Vasily Ivanovich."

"The fourth."

"Really?"

"Yes. What's more, lad, we're travelling with post horses. Those 'free' rascals have made nothing out of us."

"We'll be coming pretty soon to Vladimir: with Vladimir I can make a fine beginning with my travel impressions. Vladimir is an ancient city; everything in it should have the breath of ancient Rus. In it, surely, one may look best of all for the source of our people's Orthodox way of life. I've already told you, Vasily Ivanovich, that I... and not I alone, there are many of us—we want to untangle ourselves from the vile culture of the West and devise a culture of the East of our own."

"Is that in your book?" asked Vasily Ivanovich.

"No, there's nothing in my book yet. Judge for yourself: has it been possible to write anything? Road, huts, stationmasters, all this is so uninteresting, so prosaically boring. Truly, there would have been nothing to make note of, even if my whole back hadn't been broken. But here we are, coming close to Vladimir."

"And we shall have dinner," observed Vasily Ivanovich.

"The capital of ancient Rus."

"A regular inn."

"The Golden Gate."

"Only they'll soak us plenty."

"Well, get along then, driver."

"Oh, sir, you see how I'm trying. You see, the road is just a mess. Come on, gray mare... Come on... pull us out, old girl... humor the gentlemen... Now, now..."

At last Vladimir appeared in the distance with its cupolas and bell towers, the reliable sign of a Russian town.

Ivan Vasilyevich's heart began to pound. Vasily Ivanovich smiled.

"To the hotel!" he shouted.

The driver put on a dignified air.

"Well now, grey mare... it's not far now, damn it!"

And the driver lashed each of the consumptive nags who, in that inexplicable inspiration which is the property only of Russian horses, suddenly jerked up their muzzles and tore off like the wind. The tarantas hopped over hummocks and ruts, tossing its smiling riders around. The driver, gathering the reins in his left hand and brandishing the whip with his right, did nothing but yell, standing in his place; it seemed as if he had forgotten himself altogether in the rapid gallop and was flying, reckless even of himself, not heeding either Vasily Ivanovich or his own danger of ruining the horses. Such is the Russian people's way of driving.

Finally windmills came in sight, there were stretches of board fences; peasant huts appeared first, then small wooden houses, then stone houses. The travellers were riding into Vladimir. The tarantas stopped at a large building on the principal street...

"The hotel," said the driver and threw down the reins.

A pale-faced waiter in a stained white shirt and stained apron met the travellers with various bows and tavern-style greetings, and then conducted them up a dirty wooden staircase to a large room, also quite unclean, but with large mirrors in mahogany frames, and a decorated ceiling. Around the walls chairs stood sedately, and in front of a broken-down divan rose a table covered with a yellowed tablecloth.

"What do you have?" inquired Ivan Vasilyevich.

"We have everything," replied the waiter haughtily.

"Do you have beds?"

"No, indeed, sir." Ivan Vasilyevich frowned.

"What have you for dinner?"

"We have everything."

"What do you mean, everything?"

"Shchi, sir. Soup, sir. Beefsteaks can be prepared. But here's a list on the table," added the waiter proudly, handing over a gray slip of paper.

Ivan Vasilyevich began to read.[19]

Diner

1. Soup—li potage
2. Beef—veal with lempon
3. Fish—crabs
4. Sauce—patisha
5. Roast. Chicken with race
6. Cereal dish. Jelly with arnjes

"Well, bring it on quickly!" shouted Vasily Ivanovich.

Thereupon the waiter busied himself with various arrangements. First he took the tablecloth off the table and brought another, equally dirty, in its place. Then he brought two place settings; then he brought a salt-cellar; then after half an hour, when the famished wayfarers had already seized their spoons, he appeared with a cruet of vinegar.

To all of Vasily Ivanovich's impatient demands he replied coolly: "at once," and "at once" lasted exactly half an hour. "At once" is a great word in Rus. The hoped-for tureen of shchi finally appeared. Vasily Ivanovich opened his enormous maw and began to feed. Ivan Vasilyevich began to fish out of his plate various substances not appropriate to shchi, such as hairs, wood chips and the like, and set about his dinner with a sigh. Vasily Ivanovich appeared to be satisfied, and ate enough for three.

But Ivan Vasilyevich, in spite of his hunger, was hardly able to touch the viands put before him.

At the "patisha sauce" and the "chicken with race," he looked with genuine horror.

"Do you have any wine?" he asked the waiter.

"Of course. We have all sorts of wine: champagne, semi-champagne, dry Madeira, Lafitte. Wines of the first quality."

"Bring the Lafitte," said Ivan Vasilyevich.

The waiter disappeared for half an hour and finally returned with a bottle of red vinegar, which he set triumphantly before the young man.

"Now," said Vasily Ivanovich, "it's time to turn in. Senka!" he shouted. Senka came in.

"Have you had dinner, Senka?"

"I had a meal of *sel'ianka*"[20]

"Well then, get things ready for me to sleep. Set the chairs apart, and bring me the featherbed and the pillows and my dressing-gown. You see, Ivan Vasilyevich, what a good thing it is to have everything with you. How are you going to make your bed?"

"I'll ask them to bring me some hay," said Ivan Vasilyevich, "Do you have hay?" he asked the waiter.

"No indeed, sir."

"Well, get some, boy, I'll give you a tip."

"If you please, it can be got."

The preparation of Vasily Ivanovich's travelling bedroom began. Half of the tarantas migrated to the hotel room. The featherbed was laid down between chairs set apart. Vasily Ivanovich disrobed to his underwear, and reclined quietly on his downy couch.

After a certain time the waiter returned, puffing, with a whole load of hay which he flung in the corner of the room. Ivan Vasilyevich began gloomily to prepare for the night. First he carefully laid on the windowsill the virginal book of travel impressions together with his watch and pocket book; then he spread his mackintosh on the hay and threw himself on it in despair. O horror! Beneath him sounded a hiss, and from among the tufts of dry grass sprang an enraged cat, which had apparently gone to sleep in the hay mow. With angry spitting she scratched the frightened youth a couple of times, then suddenly jumped to the side and leaping over the chairs and Vasily Ivanovich, slipped through the half-opened door.

"Holy saints! What was that?" yelled Vasily Ivanovich.

"I lay down on a cat," replied Ivan Vasilyevich plaintively.

Vasily Ivanovich began to laugh.

"Then, my boy, you won't be having mice in your bed. I wish you good-night."

There were indeed no mice... But creatures of another sort made their appearance, which made our wayfarers toss and turn restlessly from side to side.

They were silent and tried to sleep.

It was dark in the room and the pendulum of the wall clock ticked through the nocturnal silence. Half an hour passed.

"Vasily Ivanovich?"

"What is it, my dear fellow?"

"Are you asleep?"

"No, there's no sleeping off the road."

"Vasily Ivanovich."

"What is it, my dear fellow?"

"Do you know what I'm thinking?"

"No, my dear fellow, I don't."

"I'm thinking: what good is it to me that the ceiling here is painted with various bunches of flowers, peaches and Cupids, and that there are two big ugly mirrors on the walls, into which no one has ever had any desire to look at himself. A hotel, it would seem, is for travellers, but no one has any concern for the travellers. Wouldn't it be better, for example, to have simply a clean room without any least pretension to a dirty foppery, but in which there would be a warm bed with good linen and no cockroaches; wouldn't it be better to have a clean, uncomplicated Russian table than to serve 'patisha sauce,' regale diners with semi-champaign, bed people down on hay, and with cats besides?"

"Right you are," said Vasily Ivanovich, "In my opinion a good rest house[21] is better than all these German-style taverns."

Ivan Vasilyevich continued:

"I've said and will always say one thing: I hate nothing more than a half-culture. All the miserable, foul caricatures of a way of life not our own are not just offensive to me, but even as repulsive as an ugly mixture of tinsel and filth."

"Really!" remarked Vasily Ivanovich.

"Hotels," continued Ivan Vasilyevich, "are more important in a people's life than you think; they express common demands, common habits; they facilitate movement and the mutual relations of the various classes. This we could learn from the West. There the first thought is for comfort, for cleanliness, and last of all for ornaments and ceilings... Vasily Ivanovich!"

"What is it, my dear fellow?"

"Do you know what I'm thinking?"

"No, my dear chap, I don't."

"I'd like to build a Russian hotel according to my own taste."

"Well, old chap, what would that be for?"

"This is... an assumption, Vasily Ivanovich... but I'm convinced that my hotel would be good because I would try to unify with the original character of Russian life all the requirements of comfort and small-scale neatness without which a cultured person now cannot live. First of all, all those anemic, ragged, drunken waiters—the miserable spawn of household serfs—will be ruthlessly banished and be replaced by obliging young lads on a good salary and under strict supervision. Inside the rooms the walls will be of oak, varnished, with carved ornamentation. On the floor will be Persian rugs, and around the walls soft divans... Yes, it wouldn't be at all bad, you know, to furnish a large eastern divan in preference to a bed," continued Ivan Vasilyevich, tossing back and forth restlessly on the prickly hay. "I'm very fond of soft divans. In general, I think that the furnishings of our ancestors' rooms had a great likeness to the furnishings of the rooms of the East... What do you think of this? Eh? What?... How?... He's asleep," concluded Ivan Vasilyevich with vexation, "It's fine for him on a featherbed, but for me, until my hotel is ready, I must still toss all night on hay!"

VI

A Provincial City

Early in the morning, while Vasily Ivanovich was still shaking the walls with his bogatyr snore, Ivan Vasilyevich set forth to search out ancient Rus. Zealous lover of his fatherland, he desired, as the reader already knows, to put his native land back again into pre-Petrine antiquity, and mark out for it a new path for the transformation of the people. This seemed to him perfectly feasible in the first place because several of his friends were of the same mind as he, and in the second place because he did not know Russia at all. And so, early in the morning, with this cherished idea in his head, he set out to wander through Vladimir. First of all he made his way to a book shop, and assuming that in our country as abroad, learning is sold cheaply, he asked for a guide to the city's antiquities and noteworthy items. To this request the bookseller offered him a new translation of *The Milk-Maid of Montfermeil*, a work of Paul de Kock,[22] a most important book, in his words; but if this shouldn't suit, then *The Brigands' Cave*, *The Bloody Apparition*, and such like horrors of the most modern Russian literature.

Not satisfied with this substitution, Ivan Vasilyevich demanded at least *Views of the Provincial City*. To this the bookseller replied that he did indeed have some views, and that he would let them go cheap, and that the buyer would be pleased with them, only they were not of Vladimir but of Tsargrad [Constantinople]. Ivan Vasilyevich shrugged his shoulders and left the shop. The bookseller pursued him into the street, proposing without fail some new Parisian caricatures with Russian translation, *Rules for Playing Preference*, *The Newest Medical Guide*, and *Key to the Secrets of Nature*.

Poor Ivan Vasilyevich set out to inspect the city without a guide and was instinctively astonished at his own deep ignorance. It was in vain that he sometimes read history—he was unable to retain anything solid and definite from it. In his head was a sort of foggy chaos, names without images, images without color. He recalled Monomakh[23] and Vsevolod[24] and Alexander Nevsky[25] and the appanage period and the Tatar incursions, but he recalled them as a schoolboy recalls his lesson by rote. How did people use to live here? What happened here? Who can tell this now? Ivan Vasilyevich inspected the Golden Gate with its white walls and green roof, stood beside it, glanced at it, then stopped again and glanced at it and walked on. The Golden Gate told him nothing. Then he went into the churches, the Dmitrievskaya first,[26] where he marvelled at the inexplicable hieroglyphics,[27] then into the Cathedral.[28] He prayed fervently, made obeisance to the dust of princes... but the tombs for him remained closed and mute. He walked out of the Cathedral with a gloomy thought, with a distressing doubt... On the square there were crowds of people, gentlemen were walking about in top hats, ladies with parasols; in the merchants' mart, which was crammed with haberdashery rubbish, loudmouthed vendors would clutch at the passers-by; officials with quill-pens behind their ears were peering from the enormous courthouse; in every window there were two or three officials, and it seemed to Ivan Vasilyevich that they were all mocking him... He realized then, or began to realize, that what is done is done, that there is no power that can change it, that knowledge of olden times is not housed in some wretched book, is not sold for a shilling, but must be acquired by the unremitting study of a whole life time. And it cannot be otherwise. In a situation where so few traces and monuments exist, in particular where manners change and cut history into two halves, the past does not constitute the recollections of the people, but serves only as a riddle for the learned. Such a sad truth stopped Ivan Vasilyevich at the very beginning of his great exploit. He decided to throw out the article about antiquities from the book of travel impressions, and set out to relax on the city boulevard.[29] The setting of this boulevard is beautiful, on a high hill, right above the Klyazma; in the distance a plain is spread, which merges with the horizon. Ivan Vasilyevich sat down on a bench and began to gaze reflectively into the distance, indefinite and misty as the destiny of peoples. He mused for a long time and did not notice that some gentleman, with back turned toward him, was sitting on the same bench with him and also thinking and whistling some Italian tune.

"Ha! Why, that's from *Norma*," thought Ivan Vasilyevich, and turned around.

Both men exclaimed at the same time:

"Fedya!"

"Vanya!"

"How on earth!"

"By what chance!"

"So many summers, so many winters.!"

"Yes, ever since boarding school!"

"Yes, yes, six years."

"No, friend, eight years. How time does fly! How do you happen to be here?"

"As a transient; and you?"

"Why, I live here."

"In a provincial city?"

"Well, what can one do?"

"Oh, how you've aged!"

"And you, brother, have changed so that if it weren't for your voice, I simply wouldn't have recognized you. When did you get those side-whiskers?"

"Really now, we had a good life in the boarding school."

"It was a happy time."

"Do you remember Ivan Lukich, the Inspector, and the huckster-girl Sidorka, and the candy store on the corner?"

"And do you remember how we pelted Ivan Lukich with potatoes in the dark, and how we burned the arithmetic teacher's wig? To tell the truth, you were a lazy student."

"And you never knew your lesson."

"Do you still play the flute?"

"I chucked it. And do you still write verses?"

"I stopped long ago... Tell me... What are you doing with yourself nowadays?"

"I've been four years abroad."

"Lucky fellow! I suppose you found it pretty dull, coming back?"

"Not at all. I was impatient to return."

"Really?"

"I had a conscience about idling over the wide world without knowing my own native land."

"What! Is it possible you don't know your native land?"

"I don't, but I want to know, I want to learn."

"Eh, brother, take me for a teacher—that's all I do know!"

"No joking: I want to journey and examine..."

"Examine what?"

"Why, everything—people and objects... First of all, I want to see all the provincial cities."

"Why?"

"What do you mean, why? To see their life, their differences."

"There aren't any differences among them."

"How so?"

"In our country all provincial towns are alike. Look at one and you'll know them all."

"It can't be!'

"I assure you that it is. Everywhere one big street, one principal store, where the landowners gather and buy silk gowns for their wives and champagne for themselves: then the court house, the gentry assembly hall, the drugstore, the river, the square, the merchants' mart, two or three street lights, some shops, and the governor's house!"

"But the societies aren't alike."

"On the contrary, the societies are still more alike than the buildings."

"How's that?"

"Here's how. In every provincial city there's a governor. Not all governors are identical: police sergeants run ahead of some, secretaries fuss about them, merchants and the petty bourgeois bow, and the gentry sulk with a certain terror. Wherever he makes his appearance, champagne also makes its appearance, a wine beloved in the provinces, and everyone drinks, with bows, and wishes of many years for the father of the province... Governors are in general cultivated people and sometimes somewhat haughty. They love to give dinners and play whist beautifully with liquor concessionaires and wealthy landowners."

"That's something quite ordinary," observed Ivan Vasilyevich.

"Hold on! Besides the governor, in almost every provincial city there is a governor's wife as well. The governor's wife is a quite peculiar person. She has usually been educated by the life of the capital and spoiled by provincial kowtowing. In the beginning of her stay she is affable and polite; then she becomes bored with the interminable gossiping; she gets used to favored treatment and begins to demand it. Then she surrounds herself with hungry gentlewomen, quarrels with the vice-governor's wife, brags of Petersburg, takes on a contemptuous attitude toward her provincial circle, and finally attracts a general indignation, down to the very day of her departure, on which day all is forgotten, forgiven, and she is seen off with tears."

"But two people don't make up the whole city," interrupted Ivan Vasilyevich.

"Hold on! Hold on! In every provincial city there are also several personages: the vice-governor and his spouse, various presiding officers and their wives, and a countless number of officials serving in the several departments. Their wives quarrel with each other in words, their husbands on paper. The presidents, for the most part older people and busy, with big decorations around their necks, leave their offices only on the appointed days for congratulating the government [i.e., on the birthdays or other anniversaries of royalty]. The public prosecutor is almost always a single man and an enviable match. The commander of gendarmes is a dashing fellow. The gentry chief is a lover of dogs. Besides the people in government service, in every city there also live landowners, who are usually either skinflints or people who have run through their money. They have arrived at a comprehension of the great secret, that just as cards were created for man, so man was created for cards. So from morning to evening, and sometimes even from evening to morning they call trumps in spades or diamonds without the slightest fatigue. Do you play whist?"

"No."

"Preference?"

"No."

"Well then, there's no need for you to be uneasy; you'll be lost in the provinces. But perhaps you'd like to get married?"

"God forbid!"

"Then don't even give us a look. They'd get you married by force. We have plenty of young ladies. They all, by natural inspiration, sing Varlamov romances, and pass in solid ranks through drawing-rooms where the talk is about the Moscow assembly.[30] In almost every provincial town there is a widow with two daughters, who has been forced to vegetate in the provinces after an allegedly brilliant life in Petersburg. The other ladies usually laugh at her, but try nevertheless to get into her set because in the provinces young ladies are the only ones who don't play cards—and even they, truth to tell, play 'fools' for walnuts! Several retired officers, several parasites without fortune or goal, the provincial wit who composes verses and nicknames at everybody's expense, an old doctor, two young ones, an architect, a land surveyor and a foreign merchant constitute the town's society."

"But what about their manner of life?" inquired Ivan Vasilyevich.

"Their manner of life is quite boring. The exchange of ceremonial visits, gossip, cards, cards, gossip... Sometimes you meet with a kindly, cheerful family, but more often you run up against caricatural grimaces, as though in imitation of some high society that never was. Almost no general amusements. In the winter assembly balls are planned, but as a result of their strange mannerisms few people go to these balls because no one wants to arrive first. The person of model behavior sits at home and plays cards. I've observed in general that when you arrive unexpectedly in a provincial city, somehow this always happens on the eve of, or still more often, on the day after some remarkable occurrence or other. You are always met by exclamations: 'What a pity that you weren't here then, or that you won't be here then! At present the governor has gone to inspect the counties; the landowners have left for their country places, and there is no one in town!' Not everyone is fortunate enough to arrive during the happy moments of a noisy gathering. Such memorable events happen only at the time of elections and the dispatch of recruits, during the mustering of regiments, and sometimes in years of good harvest and at Christmas time. The pleasantest provincial cities, particularly in the opinion of the young ladies, are those where the military are stationed. Where there are officers, there is music and learning and dances and marriages and love intrigues—in a word, such freedom that it's a marvel!"

"All this is fine; only there's one thing I don't understand," said Ivan Vasilyevich. "Why is it you are living here?"

"Why? Oh, brother, my story is a simple and stupid one."

"Tell it, please."

"Almost all our gentry will tell you nearly the same thing as I... First wealth, then poverty; first life in the capital, then you're lucky if you can get along even in some provincial town."

"But why is this?"

"Because we are almost all light-minded to the point of madness; it is because from childhood on we are all infected by a single disease..."

"Really? And what is the name of this disease?"

"It is called simply: living beyond one's means."

VII

A Simple and Stupid Story

"When you and I parted at boarding school, where, by the by, we both got a very poor education, I set out for Petersburg, with the intention of course of entering the service there. To live in Petersburg and not be in service is just the same as being in the water and not swimming. All Petersburg is like one enormous department, and even its buildings look like ministers, directors, desk chiefs, with regulation walls and uniform windows. It seems even the very streets of Petersburg are separated in accordance with some Table of Ranks into Honorables, Right Honorables and Excellencies—really, that's so. When I arrived I was convinced that as soon as I appeared everyone would turn his attention to me and that in a short time I would make a brilliant career. You recall that in boarding school I used to write bad verses; consequently I supposed that I would compose business papers excellently. But imagine my astonishment: at my first attempt I wrote such rot that my desk chief guffawed and assigned me only to make fair copies of documents... And not only the minister, not only the director did not encourage my inexperience, but even the section chief never spoke a word to me, and my brilliant talents remained decidedly in the shade. I consoled myself with the thought that the envy of those in service with me was blocking my rise, while on the other hand I consoled myself that in the service everyone thinks only of himself. The service, brother, is a ladder. Up this ladder crawl and step, clamber and jump people of a green hue,[30] now jostling one another, now catching hold of the coattails of a hopeful balancing artist; few walk solidly and unaided. Few think of the general good, but each thinks about himself. Each has his mind on how to grab a little cross [i.e., a decoration] so as to put on airs in front of his fellows, and how to stuff his pockets more fatly. Don't think, however, that Petersburg officials take bribes—God forbid! Don't confuse Petersburg officials with those of the provinces. Bribe taking, brother, is a vulgar, dangerous business, and besides that, not very profitable. But there are plenty of roads to the same goal. Loans, swindles, shares of stock, obligations, speculations... In this way, with a certain influence in the service, with luck and sharpness in money dealings one gets along in exactly the same way. Honor is saved, and money is in the pocket..."

"What's next?"

"Disappointed in my ambition, I decided to shine in society. But in society I had just the same experience. I supposed that I was rich, but it turned out that I was poor. I supposed that I would astonish everyone with my carriage, with my way of life, but it turned out that all my property was beggarly in comparison with others. I was compelled, through stupid self-esteem, to imitate the luxuries of others, and not to conform in any way with my own means. This is a general Petersburg vice. Life in Petersburg is like fireworks... A great deal of glitter, a great deal of smoke, and then nothing. Everyone puts his head in a noose in order to outshine his neighbor before the world; everyone trails along after the others; fortunes after fortunes, the poor after the rich. He who is not rich gives himself the outward appearance of wealth and thereby ruins himself at last; he who is rich is already letting himself go into such luxury, is building such palaces that willy-nilly he ruins himself too. As a matter of fact it seems that our gentry are looking for poverty. In our land gentry luxury has devised a multitude of such demands as have become as much necessities as bread and water; for instance a horde of servants, lackeys in livery, a fat major-domo, buffet waiters and other riff-raff, from twenty to forty people; big apartments with drawing rooms, studies; four-horse carriages, theater boxes, costumes, cards—in a word, it may be said that in Petersburg luxury constitutes the prime requirement of life. There one thinks first of the unnecessary, and only later of the necessary. And for this reason every day gentry properties are being sold at auction. And if you knew what passions are awakened from the incompatibility of fortune and expenses, what dreadful scenes resulting from this are daily played out in families, what fatal consequences there are from this, how many people from this mad intoxication have lost both repose of conscience and self-respect and have smirched their honor forever! The life of the capital is like a torrent, it carries everything away, pulls everything along with itself, without leaving even time to think. But that's the way we were created. First of all we look for distraction and satisfaction, and we have, brother, neither firm rules nor a fixed purpose in life. In the first place, we're badly brought up, in the second place we're weak in the face of temptation, and although we see before us terrible examples, still we do not correct ourselves. Here's something to ponder... But you're a Russian gentleman, so I've no need to tell you how people squander their money. Maybe in our complete disregard for calculation there is some sort of Slavonic dash, some sort of distant requisite of our broad, sprawling natural environment. However that may be, Petersburg luxury has reached the point of vulgar folly, and yet no one dares to set an example of rationality and intelligence. Usurers get rich, fashion is lord, changing her whims every day, and everybody submits without fail to fashion and brings everything, down to the last penny, in tribute to her. Hence no one has any family momentos. Not in a single house will you find traces of the family's grandfathers: neither family furniture nor signs of respect for ancestors— everything is swallowed up for the satisfaction of fashion's fancies... And would you believe it, beautiful Petersburg seems to be a city let out for hire. As regards my case, I acted like my companions, that is, I incurred debts and ran through twice the amount that I had coming in. This, however, is nothing remarkable; I had friends who had exactly no income at all, yet spent three times as much as I. How they did it I don't understand to this day. I was received everywhere, I courted the fashionable ladies, listened to their drivel and replied with the same, and endeavored in every way to enjoy myself. But to tell the truth amid the obligatory everlasting round of pleasures I was completely unhappy. Like many of our young people I wanted something, I was dissatisfied with something. I craved some impossible activity; in a word, I felt myself to be useless, superfluous, and I reproached others for my own nullity. With us a great many people suffer from such a 'black impotence'.[32] Then I took the notion of getting married."

"What? You're married?" asked Ivan Vasilyevich.

"Yes, I'm married," answered his interlocutor with a sigh. "But it's all the same as if I were a bachelor. Again a simple and stupid story.

"There are beautiful girls in Petersburg. To look at them is a feast for the eyes. Their hair is so smoothly combed, their figures are so sumptuous, they dance so nicely and so much, that it's impossible not to fall in love with them. And I did fall in love. My love began with a waltz, my fate was decided by a mazurka. My fiancée was the daughter of a wealthy man who gave admirable dinners and played whist every evening, the so-called 'big game' [that is, a game for high stakes]. I prepared to be happy. But in Petersburg, brother, marriage is the half of bankruptcy. Nowhere else in the world, I presume, is it the custom while approaching happiness to ruin it in advance, and in preparing for repose to annihilate first the very possibility of being at rest. But in Petersburg such is the custom, such the law. However foolish the general example may be, one has to follow the general example. With us conventional rules have been created for everything, as indispensable as ceremonial visits and taking off one's hat when bowing. Thus a bridegroom is obligated to the most ridiculous extravagance, no matter what his fortune may be; here's even an augmentation of the Slavonic 'dash.' First of all the bridegroom is obliged without fail to give presents. A portrait painted by Sokolov,[33] a sumptuous bracelet, a 'sentimental bracelet,' a Turkish shawl, diamond accessories and a countless number of other glittering baubles from an English shop. Then the bridegroom is obligated to do someone else's house over again, to furnish the room with potted plants, to acquire dandyish carriages with beautiful horses and gleaming harness. He puts two enormous lackeys in livery with armorial gold-braid, he lays in table settings, bronzes, porcelain, he prepares himself to give dinners, and finds out once he is married that there is absolutely nothing to give them with. The bride's father, in his turn, fits up the bedroom splendidly, as though setting his son-in-law an example of insanity, as though he were a great deal more concerned for the sumptuous furnishing of rented walls than for his daughter's happiness and repose. To top it all he fills a host of armoires and trunks with assorted rags and trash, which, under the name of 'dowry,' demands his whole capital; and finally, the day after the wedding, he gives his new son-in-law his entire confidence. He admits with complete candor that Petersburg life is extraordinarily expensive, that his cook is ruining him, that he plays whist and loses, and in conclusion declares that his son-in-law will have to wait until he dies to receive the promised revenues. Not a little confused by such a strange prospect and such a charming bit of news, the son-in-law for his part confesses to the lamentable condition of his affairs, and then, after a few days, quarrels for good with his new family.

"So it was with me. I wanted to retire to the country; my wife wouldn't have it; this was not the way she had been brought up. She was accustomed to strolling on Nevsky Prospekt and to going to balls and the theater. There was nothing to be done. A real penal servitude began for me here, brother. In a life beyond one's means there are dreadful moments. Sometimes your wife, in all her finery, is exchanging compliments with some fop in a theater box, and at home there's no firewood; sometimes guests have been invited to dinner, and the cook refuses to provide provisions any longer on credit and is rude to you besides, and you don't dare fire him because you're deeply in debt to him. It's a terrible thing to say, brother, but in the present fashionable Petersburg mode of life it is not only impossible to maintain one's dignity, but it's hardly possible to remain in the strict sense of the word an honest man. Above all and at any cost one must have money, but it's sheer trash that the money's needed for. In the evening you dance, but in the morning the house is thronged with so-called 'cabinet guests,'[34] extortioners, swindlers, usurers. You pawn, you sell, you borrow; you give bills of exchange and notes; you return the diamonds and the Turkish shawl and your horses; you curse life, you're close to desperation. There are moments when you're ready to shoot yourself. And with all this you are laced tight and perfumed, and your hair is frizzled; you bow and scrape and return calls, and with it all you can be sure that decidedly no one likes you and everyone is laughing at you.

"In this way I struggled through two years. But then I noticed that in society they were beginning to look at me with a certain contempt and offensive pity, I was bowed to less often, I was overlooked in invitations, they stopped choosing me for the mazurka, and little by little all my friends began to leave me, passing on to each other the news, not altogether unpleasant to them, of my ruin. 'He has only himself to blame,' they would say, 'Why does he crawl after other people? Why does he live with us?' And even people whom I liked with all my heart, like brothers, turned their backs on me when they learned that they couldn't win from me at cards or dine well at my expense; and not only did I not see a single sign of sympathy from them, but I even realized that they proclaimed my calamity with a strange kind of avidity and made impudent jokes over my misfortune. This was the most vexatious of all for me. I grew to hate Petersburg and determined to leave. I sold everything I owned, settled up with everyone I could, put my affairs in the best order possible, and one fine morning my wife and I set out to make our residence in Moscow."

"You've lived in Moscow?" asked Ivan Vasilyevich,

"I have, brother. It was the same thing over again. Again a continuation of the simple and stupid story! My wife wanted to live, if not in Petersburg, then at least in Moscow. I wasn't allowed even to think about the country. So here I was, settled in Moscow. I love white-stone Moscow, with the age-old Kremlin, with the glorious native memories at every step. Moscow is the heart of Russia, and this heart beats with a noble feeling for everything that belongs to our native land. In the lowest class of the Moscow population straightforwardness is the rule; in the highest shine certain talented, loyal intellects animated by love for useful occupations, by a striving toward a beautiful national goal. But I learned this later. I fell into a kind of peculiar circle that in the huge city constitutes something of the sort of an irksome small town. This small town, brother, is a retired town, the native land of moustaches and Hungarian dances, the haven of the dissatisfied of every sort, a den of brigandage of the strangest kinds, a crucible of the strangest stories. In it dwell the discharged and the retired, angry, disappointed in their ambition, in general altogether indolent and spiteful people. Hence there prevails among them 'the spirit of idleness and of idle talk';[35] there is good reason why this little town is called 'an old woman.' Above all else, it prattles, prattles at all costs. It will tell you that a gray wolf saunters down Kuznetsky Bridge and looks into all the shops; it will whisper in your ear that the Turkish sultan has adopted the King of France; it dreams up politics of its own, a Europe of its own,—just so as to have something to prattle about. But this is still only a minor mischief; idleness has spawned more disgusting things. I'll tell you of my own debut in the white-stone city. Immediately upon my arrival I was taken to a charming society. This society is something of the nature of a ministry of idlers, a chamber of parasites. At my appearance all those present began to eye me askance as though I were some sort of wild animal, and started to whisper together. Then a certain gentleman with a great blond crest of hair came up to me and began to make my acquaintance, saying that he knew my father very well, had served with my uncle, and even remembered my grandfather a little. 'By this right,' he continued, 'allow me to give you some advice. Do you see yonder a gentleman with a big black moustache? Look out for him... He will invite you to a game of cards and he will clean you out for sure.' I thanked the friend of my family and went into the other rooms. Imagine my surprise: the gentleman with the black moustache runs after me and begins a conversation: 'Have you been long acquainted with that blond top-knot?' 'No, I made his acquaintance just now.' 'Well, look out for him: he wants to clean you out at cards. I considered it my duty to forewarn you, because your auntie was always very nice to me, and besides, we are, it seems, distantly related.'

" 'What's this all about?' thought I, and began with curiosity to listen to the conversations. But here I heard such words, such open acknowledgments, such trends of thought that my hair began to stand up. Some in a quiet voice were airing their free-thinking views, while bowing low to the chief of police; others were talking with freedom and rapture about tripe and pie; a third group were bragging about having been absolutely soused; one gentleman even related very amusingly how he had once been beaten up; finally, several were conversing about such remarkable Muscovite mysteries as Eugène Sue himself would not have brought himself to publish. They also talked about dogs and about women, with the only difference that they treated the dogs with respect. Old men were playing whist and loudly abusing each other, and after the game was over they would go sniff at the supper and then go home. Finally, in a chamber of hell, desperate players with pale faces and sunken cheeks were playing a game in which the stakes were in the thousands. The curious thronged around the table with a senseless avidity on their faces and a base rapture toward a blind stroke of luck. Piles of bank notes were scattered about on the green surface, and the terrible silence was broken only by the fateful sentence of the loser. And how much was lost there in addition to money! There were silent people who sat in a corner and shrugged their shoulders; and there were many others who, inured to such a manner of life and habituated to strange talk, through force of habit found nothing reprehensible about it, but rather something bold and dashing. Thus, they are on fraternal terms with people to whom, with a genuine appraisal of conscience, they would forbid entrance even to their servants' quarters. This has a simple explanation. Petersburg vices originate from tense activity, from a desire for self-display, from vanity and ambition. Moscow vices originate from the absence of activity, from the lack of a living purpose in life, from boredom and burdensome gentry indolence. But then, this applies of course not to the whole society, but to the small part of that society which gets itself most talked about. There are good and intelligent people everywhere... only they customarily shun turmoil and make new acquaintances with difficulty, whereas the city riff-raff strikes the eye at once and lures into various stupidities such characterless simpletons as I was, for instance. Little by little I began to become used to the strangeness of the circle into which I had fallen, I became acquainted with all, and thereby better disposed toward all. There's no hiding one's sin—I stopped being horrified at the outspoken stories, I acquired the philosophy of sterlet chowder and small pies, I avoided cultured and intelligent people, of whom there are so many in Moscow, but stayed in the circle of the notorious gang, so that finally one fine evening I sat down to play for small stakes with the blond top-knot and the black moustache. It goes without saying that they cleaned me out and immediately made themselves very familiar with me, patted me on the shoulder, called me pal, dumb ox, oaf—in a word, they showed me the kindest tokens of friendship. This was vexatious... When I took it into my head to stop them, they became angry and began to abuse me. Top-knot called me a spy and moustache took the occasion to abuse my wife's conduct in the vilest fashion. With my right hand I seized hold of top-knot, with my left of moustache, and a regular brawl began. We were parted; we agreed, as is customary, to shoot at each other next day in Maria's grove, and I went home in despair. And what do you think, brother? I suddenly realized that I love my wife with all my heart, and that if she and I had been brought up differently, we could have been very happy: our souls were uncorrupted, but our habits were corrupted; in a word, the lack of firm rules, the necessity of social amusement had thrown us into a dreadful abyss. My wife was not bad-looking, a Petersburg lady. She had been received in Moscow with rapture and envy, extolled to her face and torn to pieces behind her back. Somehow she had danced several mazurkas one after the other with a certain officer. Two or three ladies exchanged winks, two or three smart alecks cracked jokes at her expense, and lo, a mountain out of a molehill. Next day on Tverskoi Boulevard they were saying that my wife was living openly with a lover, that she had two lovers on Dmitrievka, and that she had three lovers on the Arbat. In a week this piece of news had reached even the trans-Moscow district and the Red Gate, but by this time my wife's lovers had grown to a fabulous number. Moscow ladies carried about with them forged letters, related with feeling and indignation perfectly impossible occurrences, each one inventing some saying or other. A saying, by repetition, became an anecdote, an anecdote a romance, and Moscow's monstrous gossip took to circulating broadly and with verve through our little white-stone mother city at my wife's expense. When I came to my senses after the disgusting brawl, my wife and I had a talk together. She wept and complained of the disgusting gossip; I wept too, because I felt that I was to blame for everything, that I had squandered everything to the last penny, and that we were left beggars. A strange thing: at that moment my wife and I made peace, forgave each other everything, came to understand each other and to love each other, but there was no possibility for us to live together. Suddenly there was a knock at the door. Who was it? The police chief and the gendarmes. There was an order to take me at once and dispatch me to Vladimir. A wagon stood at the door. They put me, poor sinner, in it and hauled me away. My wife departed to her father in Petersburg, while I've been living here, brother, under police supervision; I walk the boulevard, look at the view—and there you have the end of my simple and stupid story. But let's go to my place and smoke a pipe together."

"Impossible, brother. My old friend is waiting for me, and I expect is already getting angry."

"Come by just for a minute. Let an old acquaintance unburden his soul."

"Impossible, really... Better for you to accompany me back to the tavern. The old man, really, will be angry."

And as a matter of fact at the hotel Vasily Ivanovich was already seated in the rig and muttering something about young people. Ivan Vasilyevich jumped into his place in a moment, and the tarantas slowly descended the hill and set off once more into the misty distance.

VIII

Gypsies

Ivan Vasilyevich was sitting in a corner of a room at a rest house [*postoialyi dvor*] and gloomily meditating on something. The book of travel impressions lay before him in its pristine whiteness.

"Really," he thought, "why is it that in life our expectations and desires and hopes are never realized? You make plans for one thing, and the opposite turns out,—and not even the opposite, but something completely different. In the imagination everything is sketched in bright, vivid, attractive colors, but in reality everything merges in a sort of turbid chaos of tiresome actuality. For a long time I desired to wander around in the West, to breathe the air of the South, to have a glimpse of the wise men of our age, to have a closer look at European culture, at contemporary glory, at everything that people make a fuss over and brag about. So there I was, reeling around Europe; I saw a lot of inns and steamships and railroads. I inspected a lot of boring collections, and nowhere did I find the lively impressions that I had hoped for. In Germany I was astonished at the stupidity of the scholars, in Italy I suffered from cold, in France I was revolted by the immorality and uncleanliness. Everywhere I found a base greediness for money, a crass self-satisfaction, all the signs of corruption and ridiculous pretensions to perfection. And against my will I came to love Russia and decided to devote the rest of my days to getting to know my native land. It would be a laudable thing to do, it seemed, and not difficult.

"Only here's the question: how will you get to know it? At first I clutched at the antiquities—there are no antiquities. I thought to study provincial societies—there are no provincial societies; they are all uniform, so they say. The life of the capital is a life that isn't Russian, but one that has adopted from Europe small-scale culture and large-scale vices. Where is one to look for Russia? Maybe among the simple people, in the simple day-to-day course of Russian life? But here I've been riding for four days, I keep my ears open and listen, I keep my eyes open and look, and do what I will there's nothing I can note and write down. The surrounding country is dead—land, land, so much land that your eyes get tired looking; an abominable road... Strings of carts travelling on the road... the muzhiks exchange curses, and that's all... and at your destination: now the stationmaster's drunk, now cockroaches are climbing up the walls, now the shchi smells like tallow candles... Can a decent person be interested in such stuff?.. And the dreariest thing of all is that in the whole enormous expanse a sort of dreadful monotony reigns which fatigues one to the utmost, and gives no respite... There's nothing new, nothing unexpected. Everything is the same, over and over... and tomorrow it will be just as it is today. Here's a station, yonder is the same station again; and still farther on, the self-same station once more; here's a village elder asking for a tip, and yonder again to infinity there are village elders asking for tips... What am I going to write? Now I understand Vasily Ivanovich: he was in fact right when he asserted that we aren't travelling and that in Russia it is impossible to travel. We are simply riding to Mordasy. My impressions are a total loss!"

Here Ivan Vasilyevich stopped. Into the room came the proprietor of the rest house, a tall, handsome fellow, with his hair cut short all around, with blue eyes and a light brown beard, in a dark blue peasant coat belted with a red sash. Ivan Vasilyevich took an instinctive liking to him, his spirit was gladdened by the beauty of the Russian folk, and he immediately engaged him in an inquisitive conversation.

"Tell me, friend... is this a county town?"[36]

"Quite so, sir."

"What is there remarkable here?"

"What should there be remarkable, sir? Seems there's nothing."

"No ancient buildings?"

"No, sir.... Wait a minute... There was a wooden jail—there's nothing to be said about it, it wasn't good for anything. And even that burned down last year."

"No doubt it was built long ago."

"No, sir, not so long ago, but the rascally contractor cheated with the lumber. It's a good thing that it burned... really, sir."

Ivan Vasilyevich glanced despairingly at the proprietor.

"Are there many people living here?"

"Plenty of commoners of my kind, sir, otherwise only people in service."

"A mayor?"

"Yes, sir, of course: mayor, judges, county police chief, and so forth—the whole lot."

"And how do they spend their time?"

"They attend hearings, they drink punch, they amuse themselves with cards... wait a minute," the proprietor broke off, smiling, "now we have a gypsy camp outside the town, so they've got into the habit of hanging around the camp. Just like Moscow, gentlemen or merchants' sons. Such goings-on, you'd be amazed. The judge plays the fiddle. Artamon Ivanovich, the assessor, dashes off in a Cossack dance; why, when someone's drunk there, there's no looking out for dignity. They're having themselves a good time, and that's all. That's the kind of people we are, you know."

"Gypsies, gypsies!" exclaimed Ivan Vasilyevich joyfully, jumping from his chair. "Gypsies, Vasily Ivanovich, gypsies!... The first chapter for my travel impressions. Gypsies are a wild folk, nomadic,[37] who find it stifling in the city, who prefer it in the woods, in their camp, in the fields, on the steppe, in the open spaces. For them freedom is the prime good, the prime necessity. Freedom is their whole life... How did they happen to come here?"

"They were detained, sir, by order of the authorities. They say the secretary demanded a gold coin [a 2 1/2 or 5-ruble piece] from them for each cart, to let them leave. Evidently they were ordered not to stir. Whether out of stubbornness, or they simply didn't have the money, they didn't pay; and now, poor things, they've been sitting here, forgive me for saying so,[38] for six months under police supervision."

Ivan Vasilyevich's rapture subsided a little. He got his book ready, however, and began to sharpen his pencil.

In the neighboring room a heavy clatter was heard, and the smiling face of Vasily Ivanovich appeared in the doorway.

"Gypsies," said he, "ha, ha, little gypsy girls. Such scamps, you know. Just as at the fair, or in Moscow... We've got ourselves some gypsies, if you please... That's what! Are there some pretty little ones?" he asked, screwing up his left eye and smiling meaningfully.

"There are all kinds," replied the proprietor. "There are pretty ones too. There's Steshka, such a bold one, a marvel-woman, the way she drinks... The lawyer, whatever he takes [i.e., in bribes] in his position, he takes it all to her. He spends everything he has, they say. Then there's Matryosha, the police chief's girl; there's Natasha, loud-voiced, and such a touch-me-not. The judge, they say, offered her thousands. 'I don't need your thousands,' says she. That's the sort she is! And a voice like a nightingale. There's no use talking, they sing splendidly... Well, if you want, you can hear for yourselves. They're no more than a half-verst away... If your honors would like, I can guide you."

Ivan Vasilyevich looked at Vasily Ivanovich. Vasily Ivanovich looked at Ivan Vasilyevich.

"Let's go," said Vasily Ivanovich. "Let's go," said Ivan Vasilyevich.

They started out.

Half-way along the road Ivan Vasilyevich stopped.

"However," he said, "I hope we won't meet any of those officials here."

"Not a one," replied their guide. "There's a hearing today."

"Well, then let's go."

On the very edge of a wood, around a large field, the gypsy camp was sketched in picturesque disorder. Wagons with pieces of canvas stretched to trees by way of tents, tethered horses, dark-skinned babies on featherbeds, smoking camp fires, ugly old women in tattered mantles, brown faces, dishevelled hair—everything stood out sharply in this strange, wild picture. Ivan Vasilyevich was very pleased, and although he had to hold his nose from the gypsy odor, yet the lure of the unexpected adventure and the hope of at last beginning his book disposed his spirit to the pleasantest indulgence.

Vasily Ivanovich puffed and hurried.

"Hey, you swarthy ones!" shouted the guide. "Come on out, devils, and make it fast! Look, some gentlemen have come to visit you."

The whole camp began to bustle. The old women ran among the wagons and called the young ones together. The young ones hurriedly attired themselves behind the pieces of canvas, the babies jumped up and down, the men made low bows and tuned their guitars. "Make it lively, make it lively, you women, the gentlemen are waiting!," shouted the chief. And out from behind their curtains came a crowd of gypsy women, dirty, dishevelled, in soiled cotton dresses and tattered pink aprons.

Ivan Vasilyevich was dumbfounded. What! Have miserable European fashions become established even among the gypsies! What! Have even they been unable to hold on to their own original physiognomy! Gone are the Gitanas, the Esmeraldas, the Preziosas; Preziosa is dressed like a clothes-horse of the Smolensk market; Esmeralda is in a checked gauze dress stolen on Basmannaya Street. But that wasn't all. The gypsy women exchanged signals and suddenly, with various grimaces, struck up a song in a common mournful squeal—not a gypsy nomad's song, but a Russian vaudeville romance. Where is the originality and national character here? Where will you find them in Europe, if even the gypsies have lost them?

The book of travel impressions fell out of Ivan Vasilyevich's hands.

Vasily Ivanovich, on the other hand, was in ecstasy. He jerked with his shoulders, tapped with his feet, even chimed in with the song in a quite hoarse voice, and wallowed in pleasure. Gypsy women surrounded him on all sides. Those who weren't singing were calling him a charmer, a "little sun," were reading his palm and promising him incalculable wealth. Drunken Steshka was dancing, spreading out her arms, Matryosha was yelling as though she were being murdered—and all of a sudden they began clapping their hands and proclaiming many years for Vasily Ivanovich. And Vasily Ivanovich smiled, and forgetting all about Avdotya Petrovna, scattered twenty- and forty-kopeck pieces into the rapacious crowd.

"That's the way, that's the way!" he said. "Great! Now then sing... 'Hey, you uhlans'...or, you know, here's what: 'You won't believe, you won't believe'... Beautiful! Now then, I've a notion to dance... That's the way! Beautiful! Wonderful!... Bravo!... Great!... Well, you've given me a good time... Many thanks! Ivan Vasilyevich, Ivan Vasilyevich, why are you standing there as though you'd lost eight on trumps?.. Look to your right... D'you see the one in the red dress? What's her name—Natasha, is it? ... What do you think of her, eh?"

Ivan Vasilyevich was annoyed at first, and then sad. He took a look at Natasha.

Natasha, in spite of her ugly attire, was indeed good-looking. Big black eyes flashed like lightning; her swarthy features were delicate and regular, and her teeth, white as sugar, showed up sharply against her crimson lips.

Ivan Vasilyevich took the gold pin out of his necktie and approached the beauty.

"Natasha," he said, "you were born a gypsy; remain a gypsy, don't wear stupid aprons, don't despise your own people, don't sing Russian romances. Sing your own native songs, and to remember me by, take my pin."

The gypsy girl quietly fastened the pin to her dress, looked at the young man half-gaily and half-thoughtfully, and said to him in a low voice:

"I love our songs. I shall wear your pin. I shan't forget you."

Ivan Vasilyevich returned to the side, and I don't know why, but he became still more gloomy. Several minutes passed thus.

"How do you like their singing?" asked a voice behind him.

Ivan Vasilyevich turned around. Behind him was standing their guide, looking at him slyly.

"Isn't it true, they sing well? The gentleman seems to like it," he continued, indicating Vasily Ivanovich, who was standing benignly among the gypsy women, who were once more clapping their hands and chanting 'many years' for Vasily Ivanovich.

"They sing well."

Ivan Vasilyevich did not want either to talk or to stay. With difficulty he dragged away Vasily Ivanovich, who, amid wild exclamations, was hardly prevailed upon to leave his swarthy charmers, and in conclusion threw them with rapture a red bank note.

Finally both set out in silence for the guest house.

"Their singing isn't bad," continued the indefatigable guide, "only it's a pity the poor things are sitting in police custody. Still, to sit in the open air, in the woods... is not to sit, as I did, for instance, one may say, in jail..."

IX

A Ring

"You've been in jail?" asked Ivan Vasilyevich with curiosity .

"I have been, sir. There's no hiding one's sin. I was in jail, but innocent."

"How was that?"

The strapping young fellow stroked his brown beard, straightened his moustache and smiled. His blue eyes were animated with the fire of understanding and gaiety.

"It was on account of a district police chief's wife."[39]

"How do you mean, on account of a district police chief's wife?" put in Vasily Ivanovich, laughing with his whole frame. "Over the wife of a *chastnyi pristav?* Is this possible? Brother, you're a card. Entertain us, brother, and tell us how this happened. Let's hear about your pranks."

"If you want, sir, maybe I'll tell the story... Please note: I have my rest house for travellers, and there's a shed, and we keep hay. Anyone you please is welcome, the samovar is always ready, and such liquor [*nastoika*], I can tell you, to make you smack your lips. This, you know, is just for refreshment, it's forbidden to sell by the drink... Well, who's not a sinner before God and guilty before the Tsar? Good people, God give them health, don't forget me; so they do drop by my place. And downstairs, sir, please note, I have a shop with all sorts of odds and ends for peasant needs. There are all kinds of ground grains, and mittens, and sashes, and horse collars [*khomuty*], and twine, and prunes—in a word, whatever you need.

"Two years or so ago they sent us a new district police chief from the provincial capital. Such a little fellow, round as a barrel, not very young, and to tell the truth, a heavy drinker. 'Well, fellows,' said we, 'they've sent us a good-for-nothing for a police chief. But what are you going to do about it? No matter if he is good for nothing, he's still the police chief!' There was nothing to be done. We went to him to pay our respects: one took a pound of tea, another a loaf of sugar, another other goods from his shop. Impossible not to congratulate him on his arrival. So there we went, one in uniform, one in a new suit, as is proper, with bread and salt, and we take our stand along the wall. And the police chief struts around in a dressing gown like a peacock and goes over our presents. I remember to this day how Fyodka Sidorin nudges me in the side: 'Look at the doorway. It seems the police chief's wife is peeking out. Oh, what a bright-eyed beauty!' And why shouldn't one look, indeed? The police chief's wife was really, to tell the truth, a regular poppy flower! Such a ruddy complexion, and eyes that sparkled like live coals. The devil enticed me and I gazed at the beauty. I guess she noticed it, and slammed the door and was gone.

"From that time on—there's no hiding one's sin—an unspeakable folly fell on me. I didn't sleep, I didn't eat, the light was hateful... all I could think of was how to get to the police chief's. I'd run to him, and it would be: 'Your honor, my neighbor's hogs give me no peace; please order the owner to keep them shut up.' Or it would be: 'The town cops,⁴⁰ your honor, are quarrelsome and demand that they be served vodka free; they say that they're official people. What do you order me to do with them?' Or it would be: 'Your honor, a wheel is broken on the fire engine. How much money will you allot for repairing it?' I thought up a lot of things. And I'd arrange things besides when I knew the chief was lying dead drunk. I'd knock, knock. Maria would come out in a little fur-trimmed jacket [*katsaveechka*]. 'What do you want?' 'Is his honor at home?' 'He's not feeling well, he has a headache, he has lain down for a while.' 'Hm, of course. No matter. I'll drop by later. Tell him that Ivan Petrov Fadeev came by on business.'

"Well, sir, not long afterward Maria Petrovna began to stroll past my shop and start a conversation. 'What do you think, Ivan Petrov? Isn't it cold today?' 'It seems, ma'am, there was a frost last night.' Or: 'How's business, Ivan Petrov?' 'All right, ma'am, we can't complain.'

"Finally the chief himself began to drop in to my shop. He would come in and puff and say: 'How about it, brother? I'm frozen! Don't you have some vodka to warm me up a bit?' 'Of course. Your honor, please have a drink for your health.' And the vodka is really first rate... I'd serve him a glass, then a second. The chief would get so warmed up that he'd hardly get home. So in this way I became his bosom friend. All I'd hear would be: 'Ivan Petrov, drop in for a snack. Ivan Petrov, please come by this evening and let's try some punch.' From morning to night it would always be invitations to his place. And that was just what I wanted. The chief out of the gate... and I'm in the door... In a word..."

Here the narrator smiled and stopped again.

"In a word... Well, what's the use of saying more? A month went by, and another. I'm sitting in my shop and doing business as usual. I see the chief coming along, puffing. I call to Senka: 'Serve the anise vodka; here comes the chief.' The chief comes in. 'Greetings, Ivan Petrov.' 'I wish you health, your honor.' 'How about it, brother? I'm frozen. Wouldn't you have something to warm me up with?' 'Of course.' I was just taking a glass and presenting it to him with a bow and 'Drink for your health.' But he swells up of a sudden, goes all red, and his eyes are like spoons. Lord God, what's the matter with him? He's looking at my hand, and standing as though petrified. I look at my hand myself... Oh, what a mistake! I'd forgotten to take off the ring.

"I have to tell you, sir, the chief's wife had given me a little ring of red gold with a little blue flower, and asked me to wear it as a memento, only not to show it to her husband.

"As soon as he had left, I realized that this was a bad business, and I went as fast as my legs would carry me, by the back ways, over fences, to the chief's wife. 'Misfortune, Maria Petrovna, misfortune! Take back your ring!'

"I'd no sooner returned than three policemen seized me by the collar and dragged me off to jail. 'If you please, I'm a merchant's nephew, don't you dare touch me!' Not a bit of it: they tied my hands, and set me down in jail, in the dark, and put handcuffs on me. I'm a thief, they say.

"It isn't very jolly, sir, to sit in jail. It's so stuffy that you can't bear it. There are irons on your hands. You want to raise your arms—you can't. You want to lie down—there's no place. You want to eat—bread and water for you. May God never put you in jail!

"And now the rumor runs all over town that Ivan Petrov Fadeev stole a gold ring from the police chief. I'm well liked by good people, God give them health. They go and ask the mayor to make the investigation himself. Our mayor is a good sort, he used to serve as lieutenant in a regiment of musketeers. He goes himself to the police chief's and takes with him the administrative secretary and a lawyer. And the chief out of grief has got himself so soused that he hasn't even tied up his shoes. They send for me. They bring me with discharged soldiers [as guards], like a criminal. I was ashamed before the people, but there was nothing to be done.

" 'The district police chief charges you with having stolen from his house a woman's ring of solid gold with blue stones.'

" 'I've never stolen anything, your excellency,' said I. 'Has there ever been any talk among the people that Ivan Petrov Fadeev is a rascal and a thief?'

"The chief fairly bellows: 'Thief, thief! A thief, I tell you! Just yesterday I saw that ring on Maria Petrovna's right hand. Now please look for yourselves.' The chief called his wife and brought her to the mayor. 'Here,' he says, 'you may kill me... thunder strike me dead if just yesterday on that finger there wasn't... What the devil! How did it get back here again?'

" 'What ring?' asks Maria Petrovna. 'No ring of mine has been stolen. Here's the sardonyx one, here's the one with a little sapphire,⁴¹ here's the gold ring with the little blue flowers. Shame on you!,' she says to her husband, 'to drink till you take leave of your senses!'

"The chief's mouth fell open, he was completely confused, and the mayor, the lawyer and the secretary looked at each other and realized what had happened. And they started to laugh, they began to hawhaw, God bless them! They fairly burst their bellies.

"As for me, they sent me home then and there.

"That's the way it all ended. Only the mayor said to me: 'Let this be a lesson to you, brother. Not to wear little rings and not to philander with gentlewomen, but bring a good housekeeper into your house, who can look after everything for you.' 'Yes, sir,' I answered, and home as fast as I could go. And what rejoicing! Senka, Sidor, all the neighbors, all the Orthodox people caroused at my place till morning. Next day the police chief and his wife left town. And right after Christmas⁴² I took myself a wife, from neighbor Sidor, and it's now the third year," added Fadeev, "that we've been living, thank God... I can only say, in harmony."

X

A Little Something about Literature

The travellers are riding along the highway. The road is sandy. The tarantas is dragging along at a walk.

"I must admit," said Vasily Ivanovich, yawning and stretching, "it's a bit boring at times, and the views at the sides aren't very exciting."

"Flat on the left..."

"Flat on the right..."

"Everywhere the same... If one could only think of something to take up the time."

"Reading, for example," said Ivan Vasilyevich.

"Yes, perhaps, even reading. I like very much, sometimes, when there's nothing else to do, to read a little book. Sometimes there are very entertaining stories. Incidentally, if I may ask, are you yourself perhaps a writer?"

"No, sir."

"That's good, brother. It isn't suitable for a gentleman to be a scribbler... And besides," added Vasily Ivanovich, sighing significantly, "not everyone has been given *talen-t.*"[43]

"For present-day literature talent isn't needed," said Ivan Vasilyevich.

"Not everyone has been given ability."

"Ability isn't needed."

Vasily Ivanovich looked at Ivan Vasilyevich.

Ivan Vasilyevich looked at Vasily Ivanovich.

"Yes," continued Ivan Vasilyevich, "nowadays ability isn't needed. Only cleverness is needed. Nowadays literature is a craft, like the craft of the cobbler or the turner. Writers are nothing more than artisans who turn out literary products, and they'll soon be making themselves signs, just as on bakeries and confectioners' shops."

"Oh, come on now," broke in Vasily Ivanovich, "this is evidently just a figure of speech you're using."

"No, I'm telling the truth. Surely you must know what miserable and petty calculations are hidden beneath resounding names! Do you still believe it when they tell you that literature is the expression of a people's spirit and way of life; do you believe in its lofty calling to teach people, to correct vice and direct the soul toward pure enjoyment? All that is nonsense. Literature is one of a thousand ways to make money,[44] and all the fine feelings, all the profound ideas with which books nowadays are filled, can be calculated in bank notes and silver. Do away with the sale of books—and literature will disappear. In our venal age, poetry is decomposed into shares of stock and rapture is farmed out.[45] Soon they'll be putting up authorial factories, and ready-made feelings will be sold at fixed prices according to quality, just as coats and trousers are now sold at the tailor's."

"Last year," observed Vasily Ivanovich, "I bought myself a flannel frockcoat on Kuznetsky Bridge. And what do you suppose? It wasn't good for anything. The French rascal cheated me."

"And it's just the same way that these people cheat you when you, as a good, decent person, read for pleasure. You buy a coat with confidence, and your coat is stitched together of rags, and 'with red-hot needles' besides. Tailors or literary men nowadays have acquired a splendidly practical hand with a pattern. With them, everything goes into the business: politics, religion, morality, legal questions, philosophical tasks, and above all, love adventures of all possible kinds. Take a look at contemporary European literature; take a look behind the scenes at a popular theater. I warrant you, it'll make you sick. Everything before you is rouged up, prettified, false; everywhere are tinsel and tinfoil, everywhere a greedy desire to fleece the public. But the public isn't taken in, and goes its own way past literature, just as it does past beggars, and only occasionally throws them a rusty penny. As a matter of fact, Europe is so old and experienced that it can't any longer play at literature honestly. In Europe, honest feelings are smothered by vices and calculation. There are no more of those virginal appeals which are essential for the outpouring of virginal and unfeigned impressions. Here and there one still encounters perhaps a few people animated with a noble fire, but they can't revive what is dead, they can't make purple robes out of rags. That's why a country which is still in many respects virginal, a country which still has not entirely lost its holy of holies, its primal national character, a country both powerful and valiant, such as Russia is, should have springs of its own, pure, bright, uncontaminated with the filth of corrupted education."

"Yes, sir," said Vasily Ivanovich, who was listening pretty carelessly and understanding nothing. "You like our Russian literature?"

"God preserve me from it!" interrupted his companion with animation. "I said no such stupid thing. And besides, what literature are you talking about? We have two."

"How two?"

"Yes! One, a talented but tired one, that makes an appearance but seldom in public, and humbly, sometimes with a smile on its face, but far more often with heavy sorrow in its heart. Our other literature, on the contrary, shouts at every crossroads that it alone should be taken as the genuine Russian literature and hasn't been. This literature always brings to my mind the vociferous shopkeepers on the Apraksin Court,[46] who almost grab passers-by by the throat to palm off their rotten wares on them. I confess, I've never seen anything more ridiculous, more amazing, uglier and more repulsive than this spurious literature."

"What's the reason for this?"

"The reason is that there's really no literature in it, but only the name. The reason is that our talented writers have always shunned and shun to this day the very touch of it, afraid of getting mixed up in this strange activity; the reason is that, nowadays in particular, it is nothing but a miserable excrescence on the national soil; the reason is that it has neither purpose nor sense. Furthermore, if you please, we have a large number of such literatures: several belonging to Petersburg, several belonging to Moscow, several belonging to the provinces, and in each literature there are several parties, which move about and fuss and bustle in their anthills, like Gulliver's Lilliputians. Jealous members of a dismembered body, they regale holy Rus with verselets in the manner of Lamartine, dramas in the manner of Schiller,[47] stories—miserable parodies of stories from abroad, which are caricatural even without this; and finally, with that monstrous indecency which they call, if one may use the words journalistic criticism... But all this, thank God, is not Russian. The Russian will never recognize his own native genius in a miserable buffoon who tumbles and dances before him in rags, and believe me, in the flea market of collectors of foreign art, the Russian will not respond to a single voice that is unknown and unintelligible to him. He does not need to: give him his native sounds, his native pictures, so that his heart may begin to beat faster, so that the light may begin to dawn in his soul. Speak to him in his own language about the sage and simple customs of his realm, about its living needs... But alas, our popular beliefs and customs are disappearing. Everything that is still alive in the nation's memory, everything that could have been the basis of a national literature, is being lost every day with the alteration of our manners. The Russian genius is dying, suffocated by everything that has been heaped on him. Poor child, he wanted only to grow up and assume dignity so as to speak a firm word in his own way, so as to shout to the universe in our way, in our own language, with all his bogatyr's breast. But we have loaded him with a French peruke and a German coat and swaddled him in the tattered fabrics of a theatrical wardrobe, and we don't see, don't want to see, that the poor boy pines and wails inconsolably. But what can one do, you ask. It's not hard to answer. Set the child free, throw the theatrical trash into the stove, and return once more to natural, native principles. Culture has distanced us from the people: through culture let us return to it once more. Who knows: perhaps in a single peasant hut is hidden the germ of our future greatness, because in the peasant hut alone, and at that only here and there in the backwoods, is our primeval, uncontaminated national character still preserved.

"People of conscience! Do not seek native inspirations in the drawing rooms of St. Petersburg, where they dance and speak French. Believe me: you will find them more quickly in a poor peasant's hut buried in snow, on a warm couch where a blind old man in a singsong voice will recount to you wonderful traditions, full of fire and spiritual youth. Hasten to listen to the old man's stories, because tomorrow the old man will die with his tunes on his lips, and no one, no one will repeat them any more after him.

"Much has already perished thus without recall. Much is being lost with every day. Our past [*starina*] is disappearing and carrying our national character with it. And what are we receiving in return? Not fresh food, not

ruddy fruits, but spiritual rags, rotting offal. Say, wouldn't it be better to throw this literary rubbish out of the window and take to gathering patiently all of ours that is original, word by word, whatever it may be, not, like a fashionable countess, disdaining peasant simplicity, but cherishing, as a Russian, everything Russian that remains to us. Through knowledge of our past we shall reach knowledge of our language, our national spirit, our national need. And then we shall have a national literature, the expression not of an imitative, limp talentlessness, but of a useful, hard-working success, an object of national pride, national pleasure, national improvement... I've grown a little heated," continued Ivan Vasilyevich. "But aren't I right? Agree, you're thinking about it apparently?"

Vasily Ivanovich didn't say a word. Ivan Vasilyevich's eloquent extravaganza, as in general everything that pertained to Russian literature, had had its usual effect on him: he was sleeping the sleep of the just.

XI

A Russian Nobleman

The weather was overcast. Something not quite rain and not quite mist clothed the dead surroundings with a damp pall. Ahead the road wound like a dark brown ribbon. On a solitary mile post sat a jackdaw. On both sides stretched open fields with here and there a small fir tree. It seemed that even nature was bored.

Vasily Ivanovich, wrapped up in a dressing gown, fur jacket and long duster,[48] was lying on his back, trying by force of will to overcome the jolt of the tarantas and go to sleep in spite of the roadbed... Beside him squatted Ivan Vasilyevich in a sheepskin coat trimmed with rabbit fur borrowed out of necessity from his companion. He was looking with distaste now at the gray sky, now at the gray distance, and softly whistling "*Nel furor della tempesta,*" an aria which, as we know, he particularly liked. Never does time go so slowly as on the road, especially in Russia, where to tell the truth there is little to divert one's eyes, but a great deal to disquiet one's sides. Ivan Vasilyevich was vainly trying to seek out the slightest object that might give an impression; everything around was barren and lifeless. Only a single peasant with bast sandals slung over his back came walking toward them and took off his hat out of politeness, and two nags with their forelegs hobbled gave their greetings at the wickerwork rim of the tarantas with some quite peculiar capers. Ivan Vasilyevich was just about to seize his book and hurl it indignantly into a large puddle in which the tarantas almost halted, when suddenly he opened his mouth, began to stare, and stretched out his arm. In the distance appeared some sort of strange object like a black spot on the brown background. Ivan Vasilyevich gave a start.

"Vasily Ivanovich, Vasily Ivanovich!"

"Huh?... What is it, old man?"

"Are you asleep?"

"Yes, of course! Devil take it, how can you sleep here?"

"Look at the road."

"What is there that I haven't seen?"

"Someone is coming."

"Merchants, probably, for the fair."

"No, this seems to be a carriage."

"What, what?... Yes, in fact... It wouldn't be the governor?"

Here Vasily Ivanovich put the disorder of his travelling costume a little to rights, shifted with difficulty from a reclining to a sitting position, straightened the peak of his cap, which was over his left ear, and holding his palm above his eyes, he raised himself a little on the featherbed.

"Yes, it is in fact a carriage, and it's standing still. Probably something's broken: a spring has given out, or a tire has blown. In these spring carriages it's repairs every step. A good tarantas, you know, is quite a different matter: it doesn't break down, it doesn't turn over; if the road is a good one, it wouldn't even be bumpy."

Meanwhile, they were moving closer to the object of their curiosity. A carriage was, in fact, standing across the road, and indeed a dandified carriage, a travelling *dormeuse*.[49] Neither in the rear nor in front was there any sign of the trunks tied with rope or the boxes or the little bags used by Orthodox travellers. The carriage, except for the spatters of mud, was outfitted as though for a promenade. A gentleman with glasses and a Turkish skull cap was looking out of the window and cursing his men in the worst kind of terms, as though they were to blame that a spring had broken in the English carriage.

"Hey, you!" he bawled quite impolitely to the approaching conveyance. "Help, please."

"Stop!" shouted Vasily Ivanovich.

Ivan Vasilyevich gasped.

"Prince... How is it that you're here... in Russia?"

The prince looked mistrustfully at the unexpected acquaintance and asked through his cigar smoke:

"And how do you know me?"

Ivan Vasilyevich hastily threw off the sheepskin coat trimmed with rabbit fur, jumped out of the tarantas and ran to the door of the carriage,

"Greetings, prince. You don't recognize me: I'm Ivan Vasilyevich... You and I saw each other last year in Paris."

"Ah, so it's you! *Que diable*! Who the devil would have thought of meeting you here."

"And you yourself, how did you get here? I thought you always lived abroad."

"Sinner that I am, I'm a Russian in soul, but I can't live in my native land. You understand, one who has become used to civilization, to the intellectual life, can't live without it... Hey, you fools," he added, turning to his servants, "Get their coachman, and make it quick. What are you gaping at, you rascals? I'll give you rascals five hundred lashes. I'll have you flogged so that you'll remember it. Russian people! *Cara patria*," he added contemptuously, turning to Ivan Vasilyevich. "They don't understand any other language. You won't get anywhere without the stick. My own people stayed abroad, and the ones I have with me, you know, are some blockheads who were in service even with my father."

"Where are you going?" inquired Ivan Vasilyevich.

"Oh, please don't ask! Such a bore, such a frightful bore! I'm going to my country place. There was nothing else to do. The bailiff isn't sending the quit-rent; the devil only knows what all they write. Supposedly they've had a crop failure, the village is supposed to have burned down. But what business is that of mine? I'm European, I don't mess with my peasants' affairs; I let them live as they please, as long as they turn over the money punctually. I know them through and through... Dreadful rascals! They think I'm abroad, and so they can cheat me. But I know how to deal with them. The bailiff's sons to the army, the defaulters to the workhouse. I'll take the whole income for a year in advance, and winter in Rome... Well, and what are you doing?"

"I...uh... thought of traveling."

"What! in Russia?"

"Yes, sir."

"Well, that's an original idea. How does the saying go? 'Desire is better than... better than something'..."

"Better than un-desire."

"Yes, yes, better than undesirably.[50] What do you want to see here?"

"There's much you won't see abroad."

"Really! I wish you pleasure and success. In my opinion: die for your country, but live abroad."

"Of course," said Ivan Vasilyevich, "it's jollier to live abroad."

"So it is, but not everywhere. In Germany, for example, living in the winter is unbearable: philosophers, scholars, musicians, pedants at every step. Paris, yes, Paris for all tastes, In the summer, Baden, in the winter Paris, sometimes Italy. That's a life that is a life! Do you remember the little Duchess of Bainville?"[51]

"Why, yes."

"She's now with our Russian, Sergei."[52]

"Really! Our lads do get around!"

"But they're nothing to our young ladies. It's a caution what a gay life they lead. Do you remember..."

Here the prince began to say something quite softly into Ivan Vasilyevich's ear.

Ivan Vasilyevich interrupted in utter astonishment.

"What, she too?"

The prince smiled and continued in a whisper:

"She too; and what's more... and so-and-so and so-and-so and with so-and-so and so-and-so...yes, and what's more... what do you think of our ladies, eh?"

"Well! And what about you, prince?" asked Ivan Vasilyevich finally.

"Oh, I'm just the same. I'm bored. It's too late to get married, too early to settle down. I'm too old for the service, I'm no good for business. I like to live quietly. To tell the truth, there's little enjoyment, I kill time somehow... Tell me please, what is that strange figure sitting with you in your trap?"[53]

"In the tarantas," said Ivan Vasilyevich hesitantly.

"Oh! That thing is called a tarantas? Ta-ran-tas. Is that it?"

"Yes."

"Tarantas. I'll remember... Well, who is it riding with you?"

"That is Vasily Ivanovich. A Kazan landowner. He's a little awkward... and a great eccentric, but by no means stupid, and a reasonable person."

"Really, I haven't seen such a strange figure in a long time. Well, you've got it fixed, have you?"

"It's fixed, your highness."

"Well, so long, old fellow. I hope to see you again in Paris. Don't forget. Rue de Rivoli, 17 B. In a couple of weeks, I hope to return from Russia... Frankly, I've become completely unused to the manners here... Well, get going!" he yelled, sticking his head out of the window. "And you, Stepan, give the driver a good wallop in the back, d'you hear? In the back, the rascal, so that he'll whip on the nags till they drop."

Stepan's terrible fist descended on the driver and the carriage darted ahead like an arrow, covering with mud both the tarantas and our travellers.

"My dear fellow," asked Vasily Ivanovich, while Ivan Vasilyevich was clambering into his seat,[54] "tell me kindly, who was that?"

"An acquaintance of mine from Paris."

"A Frenchman?"

"No, a Russian. Only he can't live in Russia—it doesn't suit him. He's become completely unused to it."

"Do tell! Where's he going?"

"To his country place, to collect the arrears."

"And where is his country place?"

"In Saratov."

"For pity's sake, brother, this is the third year that there has been no real harvest there."

"What's that to him? He doesn't want even to hear about it."

"Really! And when he's robbed his peasants, then he's straight off for foreign parts?"

"Straight off."

"To live?"

"To live."

"The swine!" remarked Vasily Ivanovich with sudden eloquence, and once more settled down in his featherbed.

And once more the dead landscape stretched ahead; once more the damp mist wrapped the travellers in its folds, and once more the solitary mileposts began to flash past on the shoreless wilderness.

An hour passed, then another. The travellers, it seemed, were thinking of something. Suddenly Vasily Ivanovich broke the silence with a strange monologue:

"Really, what the devil kind of people are the Russian gentry? They get, if you please, a lot of money to spend, and they have to go squander it with the Germans, so that it won't by some chance fall into the hands of a Russian! It's just as though it were impossible to live in Russia, the way they all sneak away. Evidently there's some great curiosity there, that is, such a curiosity as we can't even have an idea of. Tell me, brother, do people abroad walk on two legs as we poor fools do?"

"Exactly the same way."

"You're fooling! Do they walk just the same, and get married, and even die?"

"They even die."

"You don't say! But at least there aren't any beggars, any oppression there, there isn't any hunger?"

"They all exist."

"Is it possible! Well, tell me at least, what is it was so remarkable that you saw abroad?"

"Russia," replied Ivan Vasilyevich.

"Well, what do you know! So it seems it wasn't worth the trouble of going so far!"

"On the contrary, it's possible to understand and value Russia only after one has had a look at other countries."

"Explain, my dear fellow."

"It isn't hard to explain. You know that truth is revealed only by means of comparisons; consequently, only by means of comparisons can we appraise the advantages of our native land, and besides, foreign example can point out to us what we should guard against and what we should adopt."

"What should we adopt, in your opinion?"

"Unfortunately, a good deal. First of all, the feeling of being a citizen, of civic responsibility, which we do not have. We have become accustomed to piling everything on the government, forgetting that it needs tools. We take government service not out of conviction, not out of duty, but for the advantage of vanity, and although we love our native land, we love her with a kind of youthful, irrational fire. The 'general good' with us is an empty word, which we don't even understand. With the feeling of being citizens we acquire an urge toward material and intellectual improvement, we understand all the sanctity of a solid culture, all the lofty usefulness of the arts and sciences, of everything that betters and ennobles man. Germany will lend us her sense of family, France her experience in the sciences, England her commercial knowledge and feeling of civic responsibilities, Italy will even send her divine arts to our frostbitten land."

"So!"said Vasily Ivanovich. "And what should we guard against?"

"Against what is destroying Europe... The spirit of self-satisfaction, of conceit, of pride. The spirit of doubt and unbelief, with which forward movement is made impossible. The spirit of dissension and restlessness, which destroys everything. Let us guard against German arrogance, English egoism, French depravity, and Italian laziness, and before us will be opened such a path as has never been opened to any people. Look at the measureless extent of our land, at the unity of its formation, at its gigantic construction, and awe will come over your soul... And then look at the people which inhabits this land, a people just, cheerful, intelligent, of unshakeable spirit and titanic strength, and your soul will be relieved, and you will take joy in the fate of a great land. But the best guarantee, the best token of the present and future greatness of Russia is her mighty humility. With us there is no empty shouting, no nonsensical to-do over trifles, as there is abroad, because we do not need to puff ourselves up before each other in order to lend ourselves dignity. We have quietness and a consciousness of strength, and hence we not only seem sometimes indifferent to our native land, but feel ashamed as it were before Europe and are inclined to apologize for our own advantages. Only don't you touch Holy Russia. Otherwise we will rise up without any noise and pelt the unwanted guests, if with nothing but our hats."

"Yes, yes," said Vasily Ivanovich. "So, in your opinion, what is remarkable abroad..."

"Is its past."

"And in Russia?"

"The future."

"Yes, yes... Well... Good. Only, to tell you the truth, I don't understand how they let you and your kind roam around the world... You get such ideas and talk such paradoxes that one doesn't even understand you right off."

"Ah, Vasily Ivanovich, traveling doesn't damage anyone. The intelligent person sees and becomes more intelligent, and just by this brings profit. And of fools there's no lack even in Russia. There are a good many left even without the travellers."

Conversing thus they moved forward, however slowly. The night passed somehow, accompanied by jolts and intermittent naps, and early next day they saw before them the wonderful panorama of the entrance into Nizhny Novgorod.

XII

The Monastery of the Caves of Nizhny Novgorod

If you happen to be in Nizhny Novgorod, go and pay your respects to the Monastery of the Caves [*Pecherskii monastyr'*]. You will love it with all your heart.

Even as you approach it, you will feel your soul becoming light and untroubled.

First your whole being will expand, as it were, and existence will become brighter from a single glance at the sumptuous picture of the Volga shore. To the left, at your feet, below a terrible steep incline, you will see the broad mother-river, beloved by the people, celebrated in Russian superstitions and sayings; she plays proudly, and glitters as with little silver scales, and stretches smoothly and majestically in the gray distance. To the right, on the slope of the hill, picturesque huts are piled in a friendly heap among bushes and trees, and above them on a precipice that juts out into the river, you will see the white ribbon of the monastery enclosure, within which rise the cupolas of churches and the cells of the monks.

Go around the hill, go down along a broad road to the monastery gate, and shake off all your trivial passions, all your worldly ideas: you are in the monastery enclosure.

Around you, long buildings stretch mournfully. In the middle of the open court two old churches are united by covered exterior passages. Here in these churches, the silent witnesses of our forgotten antiquity, under heavy vaults and carved iconostases, many tears and prayers have poured forth because of attacks by the Tatars and the incursions of the Poles, and for the glory and long life of the princes of Nizhny Novgorod.

The steps of the churches are overgrown with grass. All around, amid thick undergrowth, white monuments stand out and the crosses of graves bend gloomily down to the ground. Here all is wild and sombre. Here is the threshold of human vanity. Here all is quiet, all is silent, all dead, and only from time to time will a monk in a black robe dart like a shadow among the tombs.

The modest little house of the archimandrite clings close to the dwelling of the whole brotherhood. The little house is simple and unpretentious, but from its windows, from the decrepit balcony the most splendid picture unfolds; in the distance gleam all the riches of Russia.

On one side, on the hilly bank, the ancient citadel rises, and the scale-slated bell towers stand out loftily against the blue sky, and the whole city bows and stretches toward the slope of the Volga bank. On the other, low-lying side[55] the eyes take in a boundless expanse, settled with villages and watered by the mighty streams of the Oka and the Volga, which mingle their different-colored waters at the very foot of the city, and in mingling form a promontory, upon which seethes and rages a fair known throughout the world; on this spot Asia collides with Europe, the East with the West; the prosperity of peoples is determined here, here is the well-spring of our national treasures. Here all kinds of tribes appear in all their color, all dialects are heard, and thousands of benches are heaped with goods, and hundreds of thousands of buyers crowd in the shops, booths and temporary inns. Here the entire population crowds around a single idol—the idol of trade. Everywhere tents are set up, freight wagons are tethered, samovars are smoking. Persian, Armenian, Turkish caftans are mingled with European apparel; everywhere boxes, barrels, sacks, everywhere wares of whatever kind: diamonds and tallow and books and tar and everything whatsoever that man trades in. But more than this: the water does not lag behind the land. The Oka and the Volga stretch out beside each other like two huge armies, one before the other, with a numberless multitude of flags and masts. There are vessels of all denominations, from all the ends of Russia, with the manufactures of distant China, with our own abundant grain, with full burden, waiting for an exchange in order to proceed once more to the Caspian Sea or to insatiable Petersburg [i.e., downstream or upstream.] What a picture and what a contrast! Below, life in all the violence of the passions, above, the repose of the monastic cell; yonder changeableness, danger, fear, violence and passions; here, serene confidence and the word of forgiveness upon the lips. And every morning and every evening above the tumultuous marketplace [*torzhishche*: a Slavonic word] of the universe the peaceful shepherd quietly makes his prayer and instinctively thinks and begins to meditate on the nothingness of earthly vanity.

And at night, when the sky is strewn with stars, when the moon is reflected in the Volga and somewhere on the bank is the gleam of a forgotten little fire, and in the distance the mournful song of the Volga boatmen rings out sonorously, how beautiful it is on this spot, what spiritual refreshment is wafted there from above, what a quiet, bright happiness then fills all being. Believe me, if you happen to be in Nizhny Novgorod, go pay your respects to the Monastery of the Caves.

And moreover, in entering it, you are somehow involuntarily transported into another time, to other customs, another life. Before you is a sort of strange sketch of perished antiquity come to life. You are shown the ancient sacristy, ancient furniture, ancient synodics.[56] You stand amidst half-ruinous buildings; you live a life of the past, and the rare relics of our national art seem to reproach us for our inexcusable neglect.

And let not these words seem strange. The arts existed with our ancestors, and if not in external development, at least in artistic intelligibility and artistic direction. Our songs, icons, illuminated manuscripts serve as evidence of this. But architecture has left the most significant traces, and in such abundance and perfection that our present-day buildings, having lost originality, character and beauty, foreign to the Russian spirit and needs, seem perfectly worthless and out of place. But here arises a question: is a national architecture possible, and how shall we hunt out its principles, how create rules for it? It is possible only by means of the study and analysis of existing monuments. And however strange this may seem, from the very first glance we find two important indications in two kinds of building, which less than the rest have lost their original form: in churches and in peasant huts. And really, cannot the church and the hut be made the basis of Russian art, even as the national character and religion serve as the basis of Russian greatness?

Studying the kinds of buildings not in their totality but in details, we find almost the whole history of our native land: mouldings [*malichniki*], cornices, railings, roofs, windows—everything individually belongs to a certain epoch, to a particular occasion. And here, as in everything, Europe in our country collides with Asia, and eastern arabesques are often intertwined with Italian ornaments. It is significant also that the exterior of our temples has taken the form of Asiatic mosques, evidently from the incursion of the Tatars; but their interior has remained purely Byzantine. Doesn't this serve as a symbol that even if enemies did enslave our land, their power was only external, and that in the depth of her heart Holy Rus never changed her faith and never will be false to her calling? In general it may be said that in our national architecture three principles dominate:[57] the Byzantine or Greek principle, transported along with our religion in the time of Vladimir; the Tatar or corrupted Arabic principle, introduced with the Tatars; and lastly the principle of the period of the Renaissance, borrowed from the West in the time of Ivan the Terrible.[58] The study of these principles and their mutual interaction could serve as a foundation for our architects. They would have before them, it seems, a great and beautiful task, by means of shell-ornaments, individual parts, surviving details—in a word, by means of all the indications scattered up and down Russia, to recreate an art that has disappeared, without at all destroying the connection of the three different principles, consecrated by centuries, but by studying each principle in its genuine source. And why not once again give our buildings that marvelous original look which so amazed travellers: why destroy these strange, fantastic forms, these scale-slated roofs, these faience mouldings and windowsills, these tile cornices which in the north take the place of stone and marble, which are so picturesque to the sight and lend each building such an unexpected and original aspect? Let architecture establish a national art in Rus, and after it will follow painting and sculpture and music. The first two will immortalize our life and our glory, while the last will stir and elevate our souls by sounds close to the heart and with new bonds tie us to our native land.

But let us turn once again to the Monastery of the Caves. Its history is simple. Formerly it was rich. Now it is poor. Formerly it had eight thousand souls registered to it, and it had many donors who are all listed in the synodics so that prayers might be said in their memory. Now the patrimonies have departed to another ownership. Generous donors have disappeared. Only the prayers have remained unaltered, as before.

The most ancient synodic of the monastery has been maintained from the reign of Ivan the Terrible and includes name lists of many sovereign and noble houses, intermingled with modest donations for the repose of the souls of clerks of the chancery [*prikaznaia izba*], of court beadles [*sudovye iaryshki*], of merchants, officials and simple peasants. It is strange to view this enormous book of death, where all of dead antiquity is spread our before us in an endless memorial service. Here are named princes of Kiev, of Vladimir, of Moscow, of Nizhny Novgorod; here are encountered bishops and archimandrites, of whom there are thirty-four from this monastery alone. Here are encountered the names of the Russian nobility: the clans of the Godunovs, Repnins, Belskys, Vorotynskys, and many others; the family of Stolypin-Romodanovsky, the family of merchant Vasily Shustov, the family of the murza of the Mordvins, a certain murdered prince Simon, the family of boyar and Court Prince Alexei Mikhailovich Lvov, and many, many others who have disappeared forever, leaving only their names on the yellowed pages of the synodic. And in these mute appellations are concealed perhaps secrets lost forever, lofty thoughts, beautiful deeds, strong feelings, much happiness and much sorrow and much hope, and many deceits, entire events of importance, perhaps a whole vanished chronicle, a whole world forever perished.

In the *kormovoi* synodic[59] are preserved lists of donations, and among them one is struck by the following words: "Tsar Ivan Vasilyevich ordered to be inscribed in the synodic the princes and boyars and other disgraced persons[60] according to governmental charter. And he has donated for the remembrance of them in prayers 800 rubles and for the archimandrite with the assembled monks [*sobor*] to perform the memorial service." In 1620 for the slain Archimandrite Job was donated the sum of 70 rubles in coin, and in movable goods to the sum of 123 rubles 13 altyns and 4 dengi. In 1625 Great Prince Mikhail [I] Fyodorovich dispatched to the monastery treasury to Archimandrite Makary 30 rubles for memorial services for Tsaritsa Maria Volodimirovna. "And to memorialize such days," proclaims the synodic, "to establish for the brotherhood 'great feedings' [*kormy bol'shie*] with kalach [a kind of fancy wheaten bread] with fish and with mead" [or "honey": the word *med* means both things].

So stands the Monastery of the Caves ever since the fourteenth century, from the reign of Great Prince Ivan Danilovich Kalita [1304-1341], never intruding into secular matters, but only carefully listing in its chronicles of corruption the names of sinners for which it prays. In history it is only recorded that at the time of an incursion by the Tatars the monastery was laid waste, and in 1596 it suddenly slid down the slope of the hill 50 sazhens.[61] Such an unwonted occurrence was taken by all Russia as a presage of woe. But the royal generosity of Tsar Mikhail Fyodorovich reerected the monastery securely on a new foundation. The bell tower can be seen to this day, left intact on the spot where formerly the whole monastery stood. It is also well known that when Russia languished under the yoke of the Poles, Feodosy the archimandrite of the Monastery of the Caves was sent with officials and delegates to the Puretskaya district [*volost'*] to Prince Pozharsky and prevailed upon him to assume command over the army that saved Russia from the yoke that weighed upon her.

Since that time the Monastery of the Caves has been forgotten in Russian history. Since that time secular agitations have not any more intruded past its pious barrier, and it stands quietly and sadly above Nizhny, listening with sadness to the unstilled noise of the seething bazaar. It has seen everything in its time: internal dissensions and Tatar attacks and Polish sabres and boyar arrogance and the greatness of Tsars. It has seen ancient Rus, it has seen modern Rus, and as of old it quietly calls the Orthodox to prayers, and as of old rings its bells rhythmically and mournfully.

Trust me, if you should be in Nizhny Novgorod, stop by to pray in the Monastery of the Caves.

XIII

A Landowner

The tarantas was rolling slowly along the Kazan road.

Ivan Vasilyevich was gazing contemptuously at Vasily Ivanovich, and in his thoughts abusing him in the most unseemly fashion.

"Oh, you blockhead, blockhead," he was saying to himself, "you stupid samovar, you despicable being, you yourself are nothing but a tarantas, an ugly contraption, stuffed with rubbishy prejudices as the tarantas is stuffed with featherbeds. Like the tarantas, you have never seen anything better than the steppe, anything farther away than Moscow. The beam of enlightenment will not pierce through your thick hide. Art for you is concentrated in the windmill, science in the threshing machine, and poetry in cold fish soup and pie. You have no concern with the aspiration of the age, with contemporary European taste. Just so you have your shchi, and your bathhouse, and cellarette, and tarantas, and your country moldiness. You're a blockhead, Vasily Ivanovich! And my poor travel impressions are perishing on account of you; I asked you to stop in Nizhny, to give me time to run over everything, describe everything. Not a chance! 'The fair,' you said, 'hasn't begun yet. There are plenty of monasteries and churches in Moscow; you could have had your fill of them there. And now, my dear fellow—don't be angry—there's no time. Avdotya Petrovna is waiting. The muzhiks have long since been getting a welcome ready. The harvest is in the yard. Elder Sidor, though he's a sensible muzhik, one can't rely on him—he'll get to drinking of a sudden, the rascal: a Russian can't be left without supervision. Avdotya Petrovna, to be sure, understands how to run an estate, but sometimes, as everyone knows, it's necessary to yell and hit someone in the puss—and for a woman that's all the same a delicate matter.' In a word, take your seat, Ivan Vasilyevich. Get in, and no dawdling. The tarantas belongs to someone else. And besides, you're being carried on credit."

At such a painful memory Ivan Vasilyevich deemed it necessary to engage Vasily Ivanovich in a diplomatic conversation.

"Vasily Ivanych!"

"What is it, my dear fellow?"

"Do you know what I'm thinking?"

"No, my dear lad, I don't,"

"I'm thinking that you're a splendid farmer."

"Oh, a great farmer I am, my dear fellow! For two years now I haven't had any grain to grind."

"Indeed, I'm thinking, Vasily Ivanovich, it isn't easy to get to be a good farmer."

"Oh, yes. Just live in the country for thirty years and you'll get to be one, if you have the knack—but if not, don't get angry."

"Thanks for the advice."

"See here, if you please, my dear man, and I'll tell you such a truth as no German will understand. Give a Russian muzhik the choice between a good manager and a bad landlord, and do you know which he'll pick?"

"Obviously the good manager."

"That he will not. He'll choose the bad landlord. 'A littled teched,' he'll say, 'but he's ours; he's our father, and we're his children.' Understand that if you can."

"Yes," said Ivan Vasilyevich, "between the peasants and the gentry exists in our country such a lofty, mysterious, sacred bond, something in our blood, inexplicable and unintelligible to every other people. This echo of the patriarchal life, strange for our times, is quite different from the pitiful relation of the weak toward the strong, of the downtrodden toward the oppressor; on the contrary, it is a relationship which is expressed freely, from the soul, with a feeling of submissiveness but not of fear, with an involuntary consciousness of obligation, long ago consecrated with full confidence in protection and patronage."

"Yes, yes, yes," Vasily Ivanovich broke in. "You understand that in running an estate you won't get anything done that's worth while with a hired manager. The Russian muzhik has to see you and know that he's working for you, and then he will work cheerfully, willingly, successfully. After God and the Great Sovereign [i.e., the Tsar], the law bids him serve his master [*baryn*]. To work for outsiders is insulting and won't do at all, but for his master, God Himself commands it. They for you and you for them— that's the very Russian way of things, and the best sort of estate management."

"But what about the rules for management, Vasily Ivanovich?"

"What rules, brother? Habit, skill, and the will of God. Don't butt in looking for subtleties, but see to it that the muzhik is a first-class one, and don't allow any to be poor; introduce a description of all households, not for the sake of the binding, but for business—do you understand?[62] And see to both these things— so that the muzhik may have a full property, a complete outfit, so to speak."

"What is 'a complete outfit'?"

"Here's what. A first-class muzhik must always have in hand a good, well-roofed cottage with a shed, two horses, one cow, ten sheep, one sow, ten chickens, two wagons, a couple of sleighs, one plow, one harrow, one scythe, two sickles, one watering-trough, two tubs, one keg, one riddle, one sieve. Besides this, if he doesn't have a craft of his own, then he must own two planted desiatines each in the spring and the winter plantings, and a pasture for his stock. See, if you pleaase: if the muzhik has all this, then he's a first-class muzhik. If he has an extra horse and a couple of barrels of grain in reserve, he's a rich muzhik. If he lacks any of these things, then the muzhik is poor. A simple enough knack, it seems. My first rule, Ivan Vasilyevich, is for the muzhik to have everything in working order. If his horse founders—the horse is your responsibility; you'll pay for it little by little. If he has no cow, get him a cow: the money won't be wasted. The main thing is—don't neglect him. It doesn't take long that way for a property to fall into disorder, so that you won't be able later to put it right.

"If you're able and know how—no matter what the muzhiks may tell you—introduce for them a common tillage and a communal [*mirskoi*] reserve fund. Out of these funds pay the soul-taxes for them, and in general take care of the obligations to the treasury from your own funds, and of the obligations for road maintenance, for transport—as far as is possible, of course.[63] Even in furnishing recruits, take the expenses upon yourself. The muzhik is answerable to you, and you are answerable for him and yourself to the government, and to give him an example of obedience and the fulfilment of an obligation."

"But the communal business, apportionments, judicial sentences?" asked Ivan Vasilyevich.[64]

"Communal business, brother, leave to the *commune*. Do you know that with us in Russia an arrangement has been maintained from olden times in the rural districts such as neither German nor Frenchman, rack their brains as they will, have hit upon. Just see how every year they exchange fairly and equitably the parcels of land with each other, how they decide suits and disputes; try to understand properly how it is that they sometimes clam up and sometimes talk wisely."

"I think," observed Ivan Vasilyevich, "that the communal meetings must be the remote tradition of the old-time *veche* assemblies."

"I don't know about that, my dear fellow. That's not my business. My business is for the muzhik to be well-fed and healthy, only without any coddling. Pay the *obrok* [quit-rent] punctually, turn out as you should for the *barshchina*.[65] You've worked your three days and paid your respects—so go wherever you please and take care of your own work. I guess even in your 'abroad' for three days work there are no such privileges for the peasantry, eh?"

"Of course not," answered Ivan Vasilyevich.

"I thought not. The Germans and French feel sorry for our muzhik. 'He's a martyr!' they say, and you look, and that martyr is healthier and better fed and more contented than many other peasants. But with them, I've heard, the peasant really is a work horse: pay for everything—for water and for land and for house and for pond and for air—for anything you can fleece them for. Pay on time. Famine, fire—it's all the same. Pay up, you scum! You're a free man. If you don't pay up, you'll be chucked out on your ear, you can die with your children wherever you please—it's no concern of ours. Oh, those Frenchmen!" added Vasily Ivanovich. "They're always yelling that in our country people act inhumanly. But what's it like with them? It would be a good thing for them to think up something sensible, but as it is, the devil knows what sort of crazy stuff they talk. It makes a Russian fairly sick to hear. I suppose you like it?"

"Why?" asked Ivan Vasilyevich.

"Because, brother, you're a liberal. All you young people are liberals. Everything is not to your liking. This isn't right, and that isn't right, but if someone asks you, 'Instruct us, good people,' then you'll be stumped."

"Do you have many household serfs?" interjected Ivan Vasilyevich hastily.

"I'm a sinner, brother. A good many of the damned rascals have been bred. They're necessary, you know, for domestic service,—and Avdotya Petrovna has to have something to amuse herself with. They weave linen, you know, at home; beautiful rugs—truly something to brag about. Recently I sent a little rug of domestic manufacture as a present to the district police chief [*ispravnik*]. A splendid little rug, you know, with a landscape, and a hunter shooting at a bird. Would you believe it? The police chief says that it's the finest in the district. Well, Avdotya Petrovna was happy. It was nice for her, you know: that's a woman's way."

"But you don't have any factories?" asked Ivan Vasilyevich.

"And thank God for it! The Lord preserve you from factories based on estate economy.[66] In our country at present a passion for erecting factories in the domestic manner has become fashionable among landowners. An excellent calculation, it would seem. Your own muzhik must cut and prepare the timber, then do the building, then work in the factory, haul the firewood, make and mend the machines, and then with his own horses carry the wares from town to town. Your own muzhik does everything. It costs nothing, it seems, because, please note, *it is with your own peasants*. But what does it come to in reality? All this extra work takes just so much away from the agricultural work, which still, it seems, is the most important. Good muzhiks are turned into drunken factory-hands; their children become starveling household serfs, ragged, drunken, ungrateful rascals, whom you keep feeding for God knows what, and who are discontented with everything and become the foremost roughnecks in the village. The peasants' horses founder one after another. The peasants' strength is exhausted. Vice is introduced, and on top of that they'll deceive you and rob you all they please, no matter how careful you are, and everything on your estate will be turned upside down, such a chaos, such a confusion that you'll never find what's your own. That's a factory for you! No, in my opinion, if you have a place on communication routes and suitable for a factory, if you have an abundance of woods, water that isn't being used, and first and foremost, clear, available capital that doesn't depend on the estate and isn't provided by means of a mortgage, then introduce a factory, and God bless you, but introduce it on a commercial footing, as you would in Moscow itself, on Kuznetsky Bridge. Now you're a factory owner, not a landowner. Don't mix up these two businesses. Don't demand of your peasants an extra twig or an extra step, but bear firmly in mind, brother, that where a factory is introduced on an estate economy, the muzhiks are beggars, yes, and consequently even the landlord himself isn't far from being the same."

"I suppose," said Ivan Vasilyevich inquiringly, "that the account keeping must be very difficult?"

"Not a bit of it. With me this matter is handled by a woman, Avdotya Petrovna. First of all a separation is made in advance for the three-day work-period.[67] Then a record is kept in a field journal of what is accomplished in each three-day period. For the harvesting and threshing a special account book in two parts for intake and outlay; one for the grain, the other for the money. There you have all our great wisdom."

"But do you have a hospital and other medical facilities? Do you maintain shelters for the peasant children during periods of field work? Have you established a Lancaster school of mutual instruction?"[68]

"Hee, hee. hee! Brother, what do you want? At my place Avdotya Petrovna herself treats the sick with simple methods. Sometimes it even helps; and the sacristan teaches anyone of our people to read. Two boys themselves asked for it. Such bright lads, really—but the others weren't keen on it. 'Our fathers,' they say 'didn't know their letters, so why should we?' "

"Well, what do you do in famine years?" asked Ivan Vasilyevich.

"God is merciful. There haven't been any calamities for a long time, but I have reserves on hand. No one has an advance, thank God, and no one has asked for one from the day of his birth. Some fifteen years ago the estate was still, you know, a little weak, and there really was a bad year. Worms ate the winter planting right from the autumn. In the spring God sent no rain. In a word, neither ear nor grain, nothing at all. There were no reserves. What are you going to do then? The muzhiks came to me and wailed: 'Calamity, little father Vasily Ivanovich! We have nothing to feed ourselves or our children with. Evidently the last hour has come!' 'Well, lads,' said I, 'what's to be done? I have, thank God, grain in the barn. I could, of course, let it go at thirty rubles a quarter, but God won't send His blessing on any such deed. Take it as long as it holds out. Perhaps we shall be fed somehow or other.' Thank God, there was enough for all."

"Why, that's splendid !" exclaimed Ivan Vasilyevich.

"What's so good about it? You can't let them die of sheer hunger. But that's not all. Around me all the rich landowners, you know, are the kind that live abroad—how would they have any thought for the peasant? Do you know what it came to? A whole village will go out on the highway and waylay the traveller."

"What, rob him?" asked Ivan Vasilyevich.

"No, brother, they don't rob, but the muzhiks get down on their knees: 'Little father, you can see for yourself—don't let us die, but let us pray God for your soul!' They even came to me, and I gave them all that was left after my own peasants. I gave it, of course, as loans."

"And you never got it back again."

"You don't know the Russian muzhik! I got everything back to the last kernel. Of course, the price by that time was different... Well, on the other hand, one's heart was happy."

"And so they love you?" asked Ivan Vasilyevich.

"You'll see for yourself when we get home. The whole people will gang together. 'Our little father Vasily Ivanovich has returned.' Old and young, they'll empty everything out in the master's courtyard, one with a goose, another with some honey, another with whatever he happens to have. 'Greetings to you, little father Vasily Ivanovich,' they'll say, 'Why have you been away from us for so long? We've been so lonesome for your honor.' 'Greetings, Orthodox people. I guess you've remembered me?' 'How could we not remember you, little father? You saved my son from the recruiting draft, you built me a house, little father; you, little father, gave me a cow; you, little father, became my daughter's godfather; God grant you health, little father.' "

Vasily Ivanovich's eyes sparkled; Ivan Vasilyevich looked at him with respect... And the tarantas itself seemed to him almost better than the most dandified Jochim dormeuse.

XIV

Merchants

Around evening the next day the tarantas drove into a small but extremely queer little town. The whole little town consisted of just a single street, on both sides of which little buildings of grey boards bowed politely to those driving through. In the windows a large part of the panes were broken and replaced with oiled paper, from behind which here and there protruded worn uniforms, red beards and battered teapots. "A county town?" asked Ivan Vasilyevich, stretching himself.[69]

"No, indeed, sir." replied the driver "a town without a court house.[62]

Meanwhile in the movement of the tarantas something perfectly unusual was taking place. Its firm tread had suddenly become timid and irresolute, as though it had committed a folly of some kind. Surely it couldn't be that the tarantas, which never needs mending, never overturns—it, the pride and joy of the boundless steppe—had disgraced itself in the very middle of the journey and like some puny spring-carriage must submit to repairs in the town smithy? Sadly and timidly it halted at the post station. Senka slid down from the box, walked around the whole vehicle, looked under it, felt the central shaft,[71] shook the spokes, then shook his head, and taking off his cap, turned to Vasily Ivanovich with an unexpected speech:

"It's as you order, sir, but this way it won't go two versts. It'll all go to pieces."

"What!" demanded Vasily Ivanovich with wrath and horror.

If Vasily Ivanovich's head-man [*starosta*] was dead drunk, or Avdotya Petrovna had overeaten and fallen ill, such news would have grieved him, but still not as did the betrayal of the dependable, beloved tarantas.

"What?" he repeated with marked agitation, "What? It's broken?"

"It's all the same to me," continued Senka cruelly. "It's as you please, sir. You can look at it yourself. The tire on the front wheel has sprung.[72] And, you see, on a rear wheel three spokes have fallen out, and the whole thing is barely holding together. But all the same, sir, it's as you order, sir. It's all the same to me."

"So what, it has to be mended?" asked Vasily Ivanovich plaintively.

"It's as you order, sir. But evidently it ought to be mended."

"And didn't an apprentice from the carriage market in Moscow inspect it just a little while ago?"

"I wouldn't know, sir... It's as you please. But this here way, sir, you can see for yourself, this here way it won't get to the next station. At least, if just one more spoke falls out, it could all easily... Maybe it could make another stage, even two stages... But please see for yourself... Wheels like this ain't solid... The wood's all rotten. But then, it's all the same..."

"Oh, shut up, you fool!" yelled Vasily Ivanovich angrily. "Enough of this idle standing around with your mouths open... March off for a smith, and make it lively, d'you hear?"

Senka dashed away to the smithy, and the travellers mournfully entered the station. The stationmaster was drunk and asleep, having turned over the cares of government to his illiterate head man. The stationmaster's wife was away visiting the liquor concessionaire's wife.

They waited for the smith for half an hour. Finally the smith appeared, with a black beard, a black face, and a black apron. For the mending he demanded at first fifty rubles in bank notes, then after haggling agreed to three rubles in coin, and rolled the wheels off to the smithy.

The head man lit the splinter light in the storeroom, turned the travel pass meaningfully over and over in his fingers, and finally said with dignity:

"The horses for the carriage are ready, sir, as soon as your honor orders them to be harnessed."

"You and your horses!" roared Vasily Ivanovich in vexation. "Here you are at last, horses have turned up at last, just when there's nothing to ride in! The devil take you and your horses! Ivan Vasilyevich?"

"What are your orders, sir?"

"Shouldn't we drink a spot of tea for our sorrow? Hey, beard, d'you hear, have the samovar set up. I suppose you do have a samovar?"

"There's a samovar—of course there's a samovar! But there's no one to set it up. The stationmaster is ill. The mistress is off visiting, and has taken the keys with her. But there's a tavern not far from here. There you can get everything. If you like, you can be guided there."

"All right, let's go," said Vasily Ivanovich.

"Let's go," said Ivan Vasilyevich,

"Hey, you!" shouted the head man, "Sidorka, you bald devil, guide the gentlemen to the tavern."

They set out. The tavern, like all taverns, was a large peasant hut, once roofed with boards, with a large gate and a shed. Rickety and crooked stairs. Upstairs—like a walking candlestick, a waiter with a tallow candle end in his hand. On the right, the barroom, painted since time immemorial in the likeness of a sylvan bower, and still sticking out here and there, fantastic plant forms from under the soot and fallen plaster. On the bar, behind glass, an elegant display of tumblers, teapots, carafes, three silver spoons and a multitude of tin ones. At the bar two or three boys were fussing about, with bowl-style haircuts, in cotton shirts, with yellowed napkins on their shoulders. Behind the bar room a small room painted with yellow ochre, and adorned with three tables with piebald tablecloths. Finally, through a half-closed door peered a yellowish billiard table upon which was strutting a dignified hen. In the room painted with yellow ochre, around one of the tables, three merchants were sitting: red-bearded, black-bearded and gray-bearded. A copper samovar was steaming amidst their beards, and each of them, bathed in three-fold sweat and armed with a steaming saucer, was sipping, grunting, stroking his beard, and settling down to work once more.

"Well, how's the flour going?" asked red-beard.

"Oh, so-so," replied gray-beard, "This year we got it off our hands promptly. Can't complain. Not like last year, I may say. God help us! We had to put up with seven rubles a bag."

"Hee-hee-hee," observed red-beard.

"Well," added black-beard "it's not all profit. No bread without crumbs. You had to unload a lot, I suppose?"

"Yes, three times on the Volga alone, what? Such sand bars kept turning up as you wouldn't believe. But, truth to tell, we sold off a considerable lot."

"A horse-drawn boat load?" [*konovalnaia*]

"No, sir. A big canal-boat load[73] and three small tow-boats. Yes, but there's still the unloading charges, of course. They skin you, the rascals. They have no fear of God. But what are you going to do with them?"

"Well, who does run away from profit?" observed red-beard.

"That's right," added black-beard.

"Tha-at's so," was gray-beard's contribution.

"Well, I turned a neat trick last year. I'd bought, you see, from some Tatars around Samara, a little flour of, I may say, A-number-one quality, and five hundred bags or so I got from a landowner, of the most miserable quality, truth to tell.[74] That landowner, it seems, had lost at cards, so he really had to sell it pretty cheap. I looked at it—the stuff was junk, nothing but bran. You couldn't give it away. Well, say I, here's something to think about. I took it and mixed it in with the good stuff, and unloaded it all in Rybna on a liquor-dealer as first-class flour, if you please."[75]

"Well, that's commercial business," said black-beard.

"A well-known trick," added gray-beard.

Meanwhile Vasily Ivanovich and Ivan Vasilyevich were arranging themselves also around a little table, ordering themselves tea, and beginning to listen with curiosity to the conversation of the three merchants.

In came a fourth in a worn blue cloth coat and stood in the doorway. First he crossed himself three times before the icon in the corner, and then, with a shake of the head, bowed respectfully to gray-beard.

"Our respects to Sidor Avdeevich."

"Oh, greetings, Potapych. We humbly beg you to have a couple with us."[76]

"Much obliged, but no thanks, Sidor Avdeevich. Is everything good and healthy with you?"

"Thank God."

"And the missus and the children?"

"Thank God."

"Well, thanks be to Thee, O Lord. You're going to Rybna, it seems?"

"Yes, to Rybna. Do sit down, Potapych."

"No, please don't disturb yourselves. We can stand."[77]

"Have a little cup?...."

"Much obliged, but no."

"Just one little cup."

"Thank you humbly. I've drunk at home."

"Come on, brother, a little cup."

"So help me God, I've drunk at home."

"Come on now, have a drink of tea for your health."[78]

"I can't, truly."

Gray-beard held out a little cup to Potapych, and Potapych, after thanking him, drank the cup without drawing breath, after which he set it carefully on the table upside down on the saucer, and expressed his thanks again.

"Now that's more like it. Thanks, Potapych. Now, another little cup."

"No, really, so help me, I can't. Much obliged for your kindness and hospitality. I'm deeply grateful. I've got a favor to ask of you, Sidor Avdeevich,.'

"Something to hand over on a deal in Rybna?"

"Exactly, sir. To Trifon Lukich. I beg you most humbly."

"Quite a bit, is it?"

"About five thousand."

"All right, brother."

Here Potapych took out of the bosom of his coat an incredibly dirty piece of paper in which the money was wrapped, and with a respectful bow handed it over to gray-beard.

Grey-beard unwrapped the soiled roll, carefully counted the bank notes and gold pieces, and then said:

"Five-thousand two hundred seventeen rubles and fifty kopecks. Is that right?"

"That's it exactly."

"Very good, brother. It will be delivered."

Gray-beard lifted the tail of his long coat, quite carelessly shoved the roll into the side pocket of his trousers, and began an unrelated conversation.

"What kind of trading are you doing, Potapych?"

"Small scale, sir. Why anger God?" [i.e., by complaining]

"You deal in tallow, as I remember it?"

"In whatever turns up. We sell both tallow and potash [the ingredients of home-made soap]. Our business is small. A small capital, and it's all in circulation. However, we can't complain."

"Well, Potapych, one more little cup."

"No, no, really I couldn't, I'm heartily obliged. I can't do it."

In spite of his persistent excuses Potapych drank another little cup wih sugar, then after expressing his thanks again, he made a parting bow to gray-beard, black-beard and red-beard, wished each of them in turn bodily health, a good journey, every kind of good fortune, and finally disappeared through the doorway.

This whole scene aroused Ivan Vasilyevich's curiosity intensely.

"Please permit me to ask," he said, taking his seat next to the merchants, "he's evidently a kinsman of yours?"

"Who, sir?"

"Why, the one who just left, Potapych."

"Not at all, sir. I, thankful to say, know him hardly at all. He must be a *meshchanin* [petty bourgeois] from here."

"Then you do business with him by correspondence?"

Gray-beard smiled.

"Why, he's illiterate, I guess. But I haven't any dealings with him. Our business will be on a more important scale than theirs," added gray-beard with sly self-satisfaction.

"Then why doesn't he send his money by post?"

"Why, sir, evidently so as not to pay for the sending."

"Then why doesn't he ask for a receipt from you?"

Black-beard and red-beard began to laugh, but gray-beard flared up in earnest.

"Receipt!" he shouted. "Receipt! Why, if he had asked me for a receipt I'd have beaten in his mug with his money. Thank God, I've been trading now for fifty years, and never have I been shamed like that there!"

"If you please, gracious sir—I haven't the pleasure of knowing how to address you," said red-beard, "you know, sir, it's only among gentlefolk that there's such a usage as receipts and promissory notes. With us in the trading business, such a—so to say politic—isn't in use at all.[79] One's word alone is enough. If you please, we haven't time to bother with offices. That's all right for gentlemen in the service, but for our kind it's inconvenient. For example," he continued, pointing to gray-beard, "they [i.e., "he"] trade, maybe, up to a million silver rubles a year, and all the accounting is on certain scraps of paper, and that only as a reminder."

"I can't understand it!" broke in Ivan Vasilyevich.

"What is there to understand? It's just commercial business, without plan or facade. We're used to it from childhood. At first, if you please, as assistants or even as shop clerks, and later we get into capital ourselves. And then, truth to tell, there's no time for napping. You've set up a factory—then stay at the factory. You've opened a shop—then don't let a good buyer get away. If there's profitable business outside—then hitch up the kibitka, don't spare your bones, don't rely on anyone else. You'll see things better with your own simple understanding. Truth to tell, the work won't be easy. You're your own man of all work. And besides, you'll quite often suffer a loss. Well, there's an even chance, sometimes the Lord will bless you, and trashy goods will go for three times their worth. But, truth to tell, you mustn't be thinking of notions and foolishness. Here, sir, for example, the caftan that I'm wearing was made maybe eleven years ago, and in this caftan are hundreds of thousands and more; there won't be any less and there may be somewhat more."

"And you aren't afraid that you'll be robbed?" inquired Ivan Vasilyevich in amazement.

"Not at all, sir. God is merciful. Our kibitka, if you please, is a trashy affair. And the people here, thank God, aren't that venturesome. They'll steal a piece of rope or some old trace, perhaps, but surely no real criminal is going to touch that sort of money. It's now maybe fifteen years that we've been travelling this road. Thank God, we've seen no offense from anyone."

"You know, sir," put in gray-beard, "here's when it's bad business: when one of our kind begins to put on airs and crawls his way into the upper class, and begins to be ashamed of his calling, and shaves his beard, and starts to buzz around in the German way. He'll marry his daughter off to a prince, enroll his son as gentry. Then as a trader he's not a trader, and as a gentleman he's not a gentleman. He's dressed, it seems, like a man of rank, but he still smells of home-made liquor. Then his business goes to pot and debauchery begins, fast life, drunkenness... He begins not to fear God. Then's when his credit goes to pieces and no one among us will trust him for a penny, not only with a receipt, but even on a promissory note. 'If you haven't a soul, write [i.e., sign your name] on whatever you please.[80] So help me God, that's a fact."

Ivan Vasilyevich was pensive for several minutes. When pondering the destinies of Russia while he was abroad, he had of course not forgotten commerce, that important engine of national well-being. Only, for want of information, he had devised for himself a sort of Utopian notion of the direction of Russian commerce, not altogether resembling reality, not altogether conformable with possibility. And here, as always, in the transport of a restless imagination he sometimes came close to the truth, sometimes was carried beyond the truth, and sometimes out of ignorance and thoughtlessness decidedly missed the mark. On all subjects he expressed himself with heat and superficially, because he did not have the patience to study anything deeply.

"Permit me," he said with his customary warmth, "to say a few words. It seems to me that with us in Russia there are many people buying and selling, but that we have no real systematic commerce. For commerce there must be learning, there must be a confluence of educated people, a strict mathematical accounting, and not merely a lucky happenstance. You earn millions, because you victimize the consumer, against whom all deceptions are permissible, and then you add penny to penny, denying yourselves not only the pleasures but even the conveniences of life. You have only the profit of the present moment in view, and moreover, each thinks only of himself individually, endangering his comrades and without concern for the general good. You have only one thing in view, how to buy more cheaply and sell more dearly. In private life you won't take five kopecks from a stranger, but in a business deal you will mercilessly rob your own brother. Honesty with you is divided into two concepts: in the first you call deception deception, in the second you call deception profit. In this way commerce sometimes becomes pillage rather than exchange. The mass of consumers suffers from this, and consequently the whole realm is poor, to the profit of self-interest, illegal takings."[81]

"Please!" exclaimed red-beard, "we're not officials, for instance."

"Worse. Their takings are given voluntarily, but yours by compulsion. You still boast that you get rich by your own labor, and at the expense of your own sides in a wretched kibitka, in caftans full of holes. But this extreme in your condition, you know, is no better that the extreme of those of your fellows who go roistering with gypsies or, for all I know, achieve class and imagine themselves noblemen. You boast of your ignorance because you confuse vice with education. You despise culture because you see it in short coats, in German furniture and bronzes, the champagne that your sonnyboys drink—in a word, in stupid externals, in pitiful habits. Believe me, this is not education, not culture. Education doesn't shave your beards, replace your caftans; it has nothing to do with this. Education will show you that deceit, no matter how profitable, is still deceit; it will instruct you in the sciences that are indispensable for you, it will give you a knowledge of places and local needs, experience in calculations, in navigation, in acts based not on peaceable brigandage, but on reliable conventional accounting, which bring profit to all. Education will bring under firm rules that fine sense of trust which even as it is prevails among you in private life. Then you will not hide from each other, as you do now in business matters, but on the contrary, be subtly linked together, and by means of the joint handling of your capitals you will not only get rich yourselves, you will make your fatherland great. Great profits are won only by great means, by the pooling of strength—but what incalculable sources of wealth we have, which remain untapped for want of means! The mission of the Russian merchant caste, your mission—is to mine the ore of national wealth, to pour life and strength into the veins of the state, to be solicitous for the material well-being of the land just as the nobility must be solicitous for its moral improvement. Unite your efforts in the noble enterprise and do not doubt of success. In what is Russia inferior to England? Yet the English merchant class has hundreds of millions of people of property [*vo vladenii*], not to speak of treasures. Only understand your mission, illuminate yourselves with the light of education—and your indisputable love for the fatherland will lead you to the spirit of unity and community, and then, believe me, not only all Russia, but all the world will be in your hands."

This eloquent conclusion left red-beard and black-beard with their eyes popping. Neither of them understood a word, of course.

Gray-beard it seemed was pondering something.

"You, perhaps," he replied after a long silence, "are saying something true here, truth to tell, but a little too harsh. Yes, please see, we're illiterate people, not in a position to judge of all kinds of deals. It's only Frenchmen and swindlers who will turn up to set up companies, and there, sir, you've said good-bye to your capital. As like as not you'll fall in with the insolvents. No sir, this isn't right and proper according to the old way. Our way of doing things has been carried on in this way from olden times. Our fathers did it this way, and didn't squander, thank God, and left a capital for us. And here we've been toiling in our lifetime and we too, thank God, haven't squandered our fathers' blessing, and we've provided for our children. Let our children do as they please, they'll be free to... Won't you call, sir, for another little cup?..."

"No, thanks."

"Just one little cup."

"Really, I can't."

"With cream!..."

XV

Something about Vasily Ivanovich

It has long been time, it seems, to acquaint the reader more closely with the heroes of the tarantas. A reader is generally a curious person, fond of anecdotes. He doesn't care a whit for the idea that has given birth to a story, or the feeling that animates it. He seeks in a book not instruction, but for new acquaintances, new faces, that resemble that gentleman or that lady with whom he has a bowing acquaintance. Furthermore a reader likes fiery descriptions, an intricate plot, vice punished, love triumphant—in short, strong impressions. A reader in general is in this regard a little like Ivan Vasilyevich.

The author of this remarkable peregrination—there's no concealing one's sin—did think of humoring his spoilt judge by telling him some colorful cock-and-bull story. Unfortunately this was impossible. The tiresome truth was directly opposed to burning passions on the part of Vasily Ivanovich and entangled adventures for Ivan Vasilyevich, on the road to Kazan. Only one thing was left for the author to do for the reader's benefit: to present to him with all due respect two small, but as far as possible, detailed biographies of the two principal persons of his story.

He begins with Vasily Ivanovich.

Vasily Ivanovich was born in Kazan province, in the village of Mordasy, in which his father had been born and lived, and in which he also was destined to live and die. He was born in the '80s and developed peacefully under the shade of his father's roof. The child had plenty of room for growing. He would happily run up and down the squire's yard, driving three small boys with a whip; they represented a span of three horses [*troika*], and he would whip his harnessed team in quite proper fashion when they did not toss their heads sufficiently to the side. He also loved to amuse his endless leisure with *churók*,[82] knuckle-bones [*babki*], *svaika*,[83] and skittles [*gorodki*]; but the principal foundation of his educational system was contained in the dovecote. Vasily Ivanovich spent the best moments of his childhood at the dovecote; he would lure and catch the peasants' pure-blooded pigeons, and he acquired very extensive information regarding pouter and tumbler pigeons.

Vasily Ivanovich's father, Ivan Fedotovich,[84] had somehow the misfortune in his youth of ruining his stomach. Since no doctor was to be had in the neighborhood, a certain neighbor advised him, in order to put his health to rights, to resort to the constant use of herb-flavored vodka. Ivan Fedotovich became so enamored of this species of treatment, increased the doses to such a degree, that he presently acquired in the neighborhood the entirely unsurprising reputation of a man who drinks to excess. With time the squire's drinking became constant, so that every day, punctually at ten o'clock in the morning, Ivan Fedotovich with the exactitude of a good farm manager, would be already a little squiffed, and by eleven quite drunk. And since it's boring for a drunken person to be alone, Ivan Fedotovich surrounded himself with fools, male and female, who sweetened his leisure. He even indeed bargained for a dwarf, but the dwarf cost too much, and was thereupon shipped off to St. Petersburg to a certain magnate. He had accordingly to be content with home-grown fools and freaks, whom he dressed up in clothes of drill with red edgings and patches on the backs, with horses' tails, and other ridiculous adornments. Sometimes he would starve them for laughs, hit them on the nose or the cheeks, set the dogs on them, throw them in the water; in general they were used for every kind of entertainment. The whole day would pass in such pleasures, and when Ivan Fedotovich lay down to sleep, a drunken old woman had to tell him stories, ragged servant boys would lightly tickle his heels and chase away the flies around him. The male fools had to quarrel in a corner and on no account go to sleep or tire out, because the coachman would suddenly drive away their drowsiness and animate their conversation with a resounding application of the hunting-crop.

Vasily Ivanovich's mother, Arina Anikimovna, had also a female fool of her own, but more for propriety so to speak, and appearance. She was a serious and stingy woman, and did not like to concern herself with such trifles. She herself looked after the work, knew to whom to give a whipping, and to whom to offer vodka; she was present herself at the threshing, at the mill she witnessed the distribution of flour, she supervised the weaving shop, she ordered the men to be punished in her presence, and the women she sometimes pulled by the braid herself. It goes without saying that around her was found a whole herd of female household serfs of varying grades— hangers-on, tattle-tales, gossips, nannies, maids—who, as is customary, kissed Vasily Ivanovich's little hand, fed him honey on the sly, gave him small beer to drink, and coddled him in every way in the expectation of future benefits.

Vasily Ivanovich was even without this a chubby child, seldom washed, sometimes not combed, greedy, self-willed, without supervision or tendance. He grew up by himself in accordance with the simple laws of nature, as a cabbage or a pea-vine grows. No one bothered about his moral direction, about his intellectual and spiritual development. No one explained to him the beautiful symbols of the faith, no one told him that mere outward piety is not enough and that every person must create an invisible temple in his own soul, must glorify the Almighty not with words alone, but with feelings and life.

In his eleventh year Vasily Ivanovich began his course of education under the guidance of the parish sexton, and for some two years on end, with great repugnance, he put together the letters familiar to everyone, A-B-C. After which he even began to write, but no mention whatever was made of calligraphy or spelling, so that even now Vasily Ivanovich traces such queer goose-tracks, sometimes such outlandish words come to birth under his pen that one can't believe one's eyes. Then he was taught the catechism by question and answer and arithmetic in the same fashion. But here all efforts remained fruitless, it seems, because learning did not come easy to him. But then, it must be said for the complete justification of his parents, that they had also engaged a household teacher for their son's education. The said teacher was a Little Russian, a retired non-commissioned officer it seems, Vukhtich by name. He received as salary sixty rubles a year and two poods of measured flour a month, and the cast-off clothing from the squire's shoulders, and something in the way of footwear. Besides this, since there was but little clothing, inasmuch as Ivan Fedotovich customarily went about in his dressing gown, Vukhtich was also allowed by way of consolation to keep his cow at the squire's expense. Vasily Ivanovich showed little respect for his teacher, used to ride horseback on him, stick out his tongue at him, and frequently smack him right in the nose with a book. And if the long-suffering Vukhtich finally lost patience and grabbed the ruler, Vasily Ivanovich would run head over heels to complain to papa that his teacher was such-and-such—"He hits me with a stick and abuses me with bad words." Papa in a drunken state starts shouting at Vukhtich: "Oh, you so-and-so, you bald-headed dog, I feed you and clothe you, and you go and raise a row in my house. I'll teach you... I'll order you kicked out on your ear. No hay for his cow!" And the hangers-on and gossips surround Vasily Ivanovich and begin to comfort him: "Oh you, our darling, please let us kiss your little hand... Don't listen to that heathen Cossack [*khokhol*], our berry, our golden one; he's only a muzhik, one of us... How would he know how to deal with gentlemen of quality?"...

"Well, really," thought Vukhtich, "why not go with the world?"... The conclusion of it all was that Vukhtich gets married to a maid of the household, receives two desiatines of land as a reward—and Vasily Ivanovich's education was terminated.

However, to tell the truth, Vasily Ivanovich had by nature a good heart, a quiet and peace-loving disposition. The proof of this is that even his education did not spoil him. I say "education" for want of a word to designate a concept completely contrary to education. And it's strange, when you think of it... Almost all our grandfathers were taught as cheaply as possible [literally, "on copper coins"], were educated any old way, hit or miss, that is, they weren't educated at all, but grew up by themselves, as God willed. And our grandfathers were as a matter of fact illiterate; it was a rare person who knew how to write his own name correctly; but in spite of this they were almost all people of fine principles, with strong wills, and they resolutely kept a love for all the institutions of our native land, not from logical conviction, but from a sort of strange intuition. At present the ancient roughness is disappearing, being replaced by a spirit of vacillation and doubt. A deplorable advance, but perhaps necessary in order to proceed more hopefully and reliably to the truth.

When Vasily Ivanovich attained his sixteenth year he was sent to Kazan to the service... At that time, only a short while before, new arrangements had been formed in accordance with the decree concerning provincial institutions.

Vasily Ivanovich served for a short time in the governor's chancery, but as the saying goes even now in the provinces, only *pro forma*. As a matter of fact, a nobleman of high rank [*stolovoi*], even if illiterate, doesn't remain a minor.[85] Vasily Ivanovich had little inclination toward military service, whereas complete idleness coincided fully with his capabilities and habits. At that period he tasted the pleasure of society life and began to distinguish himself amazingly at balls. No one more nimbly than he went through the mazurka, the monimasque, the courante or the Daniel Cooper.[86] Sometimes in a small circle at the request of the ladies, he used to tear off in a Cossack dance[87] which was always accompanied by loud manifestations of pleasure. It was such an occasion that even decided his fate forever. Somehow at a name-day party at the procurator's he was asked to perform society's favorite dance together with the young daughter of retired second major Kryuchkin. The girl played coy for some time, but as is customary consented after lengthy persuasion. Modestly lowering her eyes and blushing red as a poppy, she put her arms charmingly akimbo, began so lightly to hop to the left and to the right that Vasily Ivanovich's heart began to tremble and his legs almost gave way. But he suddenly recovered himself and let himself go in the squatting-dance with such furious inspiration, began to play such tricks with his feet that the whole room shook with applause and several cronies who were somewhat in their cups even began to beat time and hum, smiling.

Vasily Ivanovich, panting, approached the young beauty, made bashful by the general rapture. "Oh," said he, "You were wonderful..."[88]

The young girl got redder still.

"Oh, sir, for goodness sake!" she replied in a whisper.

These words and this evening remained forever memorable both for Vasily Ivanovich and for Avdotya Petrovna.

Vasily Ivanovich had fallen in love in earnest. Whether Avdotya Petrovna had fallen in love will remain an eternal mystery. Subsequently, when Vasily Ivanovich, always a happy spouse, would ask her about this, she would only smile and repeat: "Oh, quit it, you clown!"

After the memorable Cossack dance, all the attractions of wedded life, all the charms of Avdotya Petrovna ceaselessly pursued Vasily Ivanovich with the most alluring pictures. A tender idea crept into his soul and at last took possession of him so thoroughly that he overcame his fear and shyness and made his way to Mordasy to ask his parents' blessing. But the attempt did not succeed. His father answered him briefly and clearly.

"What'll you think up next, you puppy! The milk is hardly dry on his lips, and he's already thinking of a woman! Send Matryosha here."[89]

Matryosha appeared, barefoot, in a *robe ronde* of drill, in a dirty gauze toque with feathers and flowers. With repulsive smiles she began to curtsey and mouth various mangled French words with an intermingling of a few that were Russian through and through.

"Here's a bride for you," said Ivan Fedotovich. After which he tossed off a tumbler of herb-flavored vodka and set out for the fields in a wagon.

From his mother Vasily Ivanovich received almost the same reception. Her husband's will was her law. "No matter that he's a drunkard," she thought, "he's still a husband." This is the way people used to think in the olden days.

Vasily Ivanovich returned downcast to Kazan.

Now the reader is fully entitled to expect a powerful incident—unhappy love, secret marriage, perhaps abduction, and a curse of some sort. Unfortunately nothing of the sort took place. In olden times children were slavishly subject to their parents. And besides Avdotya Petrovna was a clever girl, well brought up according to the ideas of the time, a hard worker—that is, she never went anywhere except to church, but sat the whole day long with her maids, knitted lace, strung beads, and listened to fortune-telling songs.[90] Furthermore, it need not even be mentioned that second-major Kryuchkin for his part would have given a proper cudgelling with his trusty walking-stick to any lawless person with designs on the heart and repose of his only daughter.

Vasily Ivanovich's position was most unfortunate. He did not even have the consolation of becoming a drunkard, since he did not feel any hereditary leaning toward strong drink. He was not of a violent disposition; he did not rail against fate, but grieved and resigned himself in simplicity of soul. Only he went rather frequently to church services at night, gazed at his beauty on the sly, sighed, panted, grew tender, and returned home. Not a single vicious thought, however, was roused in his blameless soul, not once did he even think of the possibility of disobeying the parental command or of inspiring an unlawful feeling in the object of his love.

In this way three years dragged gloomily by. Suddenly a new chance changed Vasily Ivanovich's life. One day he received a strange letter of ecclesiastical style and handwriting. The letter was from the village priest and informed Vasily Ivanovich that Ivan Fedotovich was ill and at the point of death. Vasily Ivanovich sent instantly for horses and galloped to Mordasy. He found a pitiful change, a sorrowful picture in his parental dwelling. The hangers-on and gossips were howling in various rooms, the male fools had suddenly become reasonable and thrown off their ugly attire. The dying man, victim of an unbridled appetite, was already lying on his deathbed, groaning pitifully and quietly repenting. The holy mystery of the terrible hour before death had awakened at last the voice of conscience and directed his soul to the right path, from which ignorance, parasitism, habit and example had diverted the sinner throughout his whole life. "Vasya," he said, "Vasya, something is burning in me... I'm stifling, I'm suffering, Vasya... I'm guilty before you! Forgive me, Vasya, don't curse my memory. I didn't bring you up as was my duty to God and the Tsar... You'll have children, Vasya—bring them up in the fear of God, teach them book learning, make them perform service... My heavy sin... Don't let your children, Vasya, abuse poor, weak people; don't turn your brothers into an object of mockery, don't draw the Christian blood from them... Everything comes to the mind in the last moment. Believe me,

Vasya, it is hard to die with an unclean conscience. I'm stifling, Vasya... Vasya, forgive me..." And Vasya, kneeling, sobbed quietly at the dying man's pillow, and the priest said a prayer over the bed of suffering, amid the benumbed servants. The struggle between life and death continued for a long time. The sick man was long tormented and worn down. He died at last. The house was filled with shrieking and moaning. The whole village accompanied the deceased to his last abode. The hangers-on and gossips with dreadful voices pronounced the speeches they had memorized: "Little father, our fosterer, our Ivan Fedotovich, to whom have you abandoned us?.. How shall we live without you?... Who will give us drink, give us food, who will provide bread for us orphans? All our lives we must weep for you, all our lives be unconsoled... Our dear little head has fallen!" All this was accompanied by screeching, and an affected, extremely repulsive frenzy... But at the final farewell on every face was the image of real sorrow. The muzhik's love for his master, an inborn and almost inexplicable love, was aroused in all its force. Great tears rolled down many a peasant beard, and in a scarcely understandable feeling of magnanimous self-restraint, even the poor fools, everlastingly mocked, everlastingly tortured by the deceased, wept inconsolably over his fresh grave.

The year of mourning passed. During the whole time of the period consecrated by custom, Vasily Ivanovich, having become full master of the property, did not even once think of the projects dear to his heart. But the year passed. A few more months passed. Vasily Ivanovich, in spite of his heart's pining, was becoming surprisingly fat. "It's time for you, little father Vasily Ivanovich," the old muzhiks would often tell him, "to provide yourself with a little mistress... Enough of your moping around as a bachelor."

"Well, Vasinka, really," said Arina Anikimovna to him one day, "I'm getting old, and what's a household without a housekeeper!"

That was all Vasily Ivanovich was waiting for. The tarantas was wheeled out of the shed, they said their prayers, ate breakfast, and were off for Kazan. Avdotya Petrovna was still unmarried, though there was no lack of suitors. On arriving in Kazan they sent at once for a matchmaker. A glib-tongued matchmaker with a kerchief tied over her head made her appearance. For several days on end the matchmaker plodded from Vasily Ivanovich's house to Avdotya Petrovna's house and back, brought with her the schedule [*riadnaia*], that is, detailed lists of the dowry, in icons, in kind, in money, in clothes, etc. Arina Anikimovna made annotations in her own hand on everything—too little of this, this not wanted, and enough of that. Finally the day was set for the young people to meet. At this memorable meeting Vasily Ivanovich and Avdotya Petrovna alternately grew red and grew pale, without saying a word. The matchmaker on the other hand joked incessantly and pleasantly, maliciously dropping various hints and equivoques at the expense of the bashful pair. The second-major laughed heartily and conversed familiarly with Arina Anikimovna about the price of wheat, the expected threshing, the worm that was damaging the winter wheat, and other subjects pertaining to rural politics. After a few days the young people were blessed, attended mass in the cathedral, and began to prepare for the wedding. In the years gone by preparations for a wedding were not accompanied, as nowadays, by total ruin; they did not order glittering carriages in which one is not supposed to ride, they did not send for hats from Paris, and they paid real money, not mortgaged villages. On the eve of the day designated for the wedding a huge van pulled up to Vasily Ivanovich's house, out of which were carried first several holy icons in settings, then they began to haul out pink featherbeds, pillows, chests of linen long since prepared for the wedding, a samovar, silver, and several dresses with extremely vile lace. The said lace Avdotya Petrovna herself had knit several years before, along with her maids, for the dowry, and probably she had meditated more than once over the work, involuntarily overcome with sweet terror at the thought of her own hazy maiden's fate. Arina Anikimovna counted everything and accepted it with her own hands, then signed the schedule and gave the matchmaker some Moscow silk material, quite light, for a dress. The wedding was celebrated with all possible pomp. An arch-priest of the cathedral performed the ceremony. The governor himself was the young bride's proxy father.[91] The whole town talked of nothing but the sumptuous supper magnificently given by Vasily Ivanovich. Seven bottles of champagne were poured and a military band played at table. Two weeks after the solemn day Vasily Ivanovich, after thanking all and sundry, making his bows and saying farewell to the whole town, seated his young wife in a new tarantas and set off for the village. At the boundary of the estate all the muzhiks were waiting on their knees for the young couple with bread and salt. Russian peasants do not shout 'vivats,' do not take leave of their senses out of rapture, but quietly and touchingly express their devotion; and he is to be pitied who sees in them only sly, unscrupulous slaves, and who does not believe in their sincerity. However this may be, from this time on, that is, Vasily Ivanovich's marriage, every muzhik was as happy as if he had got married himself. "Here's a mistress for us," they would say, "now we're not alone, thank God! May they live many years in health!" And old and young raced to the church to hear mass and have a good look at the young bride. The old priest with tears in his eyes took the cross from the altar, which the newlyweds kissed. On all lips a prayer was whispered, on all faces shone joy, joy unfeigned. And all this was simple, without preparation, without resounding declarations, without stupid speeches. Vasily Ivanovich led his wife into the little gray manor house. Arina Anikhimovna blessed them at the threshold with an icon—and Vasily Ivanovich began to live a new life.

And one must give him his due. Although he did not do away altogether with the order that had existed in his father's time, he at least changed it in many ways: he sent the jesters off to the carpenter's shop, he seated the coachman on his box, and as for himself, he drank no more than two wine glasses of herb-flavored vodka a day: one before dinner and one before supper. It should not be thought, however, that he had armed himself with

the rule of a terrible morality, and beat the drum with resounding words—
not at all. That which had interested and amused Ivan Fedotovich did not
seem detestable to him, only it did not interest or amuse him at all. He
understood that it is possible to be a drunkard, only he himself did not care to
drink. He understood that it was possible to be amused by fools, only he
himself did not find anything laughable in them. In a word, he became a good
person not out of conviction, but quite by himself, because otherwise he would
have felt awkward and uncomfortable. On the one hand he had a lively
memory of the last terrible precept of his dying father, and on the other hand
enlightenment, which is spreading imperceptibly everywhere, looking into
villages and hamlets, had not passed Mordasy by, but had begun gradually to
steal up to Vasily Ivanovich, speaking to him not in empty European
apothegms, but in a tongue he understood. Thus he came to understand that
his own well-being depended on the well-being of his peasants, and then he
busied himself with all his might in the good work which even without this
was dear to his soft-hearted nature. He began, indeed, to govern according to
the Russian method, according to the experience of the old-timers, without
any agronomical hocus-pocus, without philanthropical improvements, but
the landowner understood the muzhik and the muzhik the landowner, and
both strove without any violent jolts, but rightly and gradually, toward the
goal of improvement. Vasily Ivanovich was humane and just. The peasants
began to revere him no longer as a duty imposed on them, but out of holy
gratitude. Children were born to Vasily Ivanovich. He began to bring them up
not artfully, but no longer as he himself had been educated. A student from
the seminary was engaged for them, who taught them history and geography,
and a great deal about which Vasily Ivanovich had no conception. His eldest
son on reaching his eleventh year was sent first to the provincial gymnasium
and then to Moscow University. Vasily Ivanovich realized himself, not
knowing why, that in a good education lies hidden not only the moral embryo
of every man's life, but also the secret principle of the well-being and life of
every state.

With all of this, Vasily Ivanovich was one of the most prosaic of landowners. Old neighbors spoke of him as a crafty rascal, and young ones as a
vulgar fool. As a matter of fact he is simply even now what is called a man of
the old style. At assemblies of the nobility, at which he appears only on
unusual occasions, he does not speak extremely brilliantly, but he speaks to
the point, and in agreement with the understanding of the majority. The
proposition was made to him that he should run for office, but he rejected
such a proposal, first, as he said, on the grounds of his physical constitution,
which is clumsy through and through, and secondly because in the lower
duties he feared responsibility and did not feel himself worthy of higher ones.
He has been living now for thirty years in the country almost continually; he
grows fatter with every year; he is extremely fond of riding out for the
catching of fish, when he can lie on the bank while the fishermen cast the
seine with wishes for his happiness and for the happiness of all his children in

turn. He eats amazingly much and with amazing appetite, and Avdotya Petrovna every day thinks up some surprise for him: now a pie with *viaziga* [this delicacy consists of the backbones of cartilaginous fish], now some glorious ham, now a fish of enormous size, on which occasion a few neighbors are also invited. "Vasily Ivanovich invites you to eat a fish which one of his fishermen caught at his place." And the neighbors are enraptured by the fish, they measure it and compare it with other famous fish—and Vasily Ivanovich smiles and is satisfied with himself, the food, and life. After dinner they eat preserves with a common spoon, drink a wine glass of spirits apiece, then lie down to rest, then ride on a field wagon to inspect the winter or spring wheat, then they lie down again to sleep the night through at last. Vasily Ivanovich doesn't play cards. In the morning he checks the work, makes allotments, rides to the mill or the threshing machine, but he dislikes walking and decides on such a feat only on extraordinary occasions—at the time of the procession of the cross, for example, or when the dam bursts.[92]

Arina Anikimovna died long since, in extreme old age. For several years before her death she was blind, and she went peacefully to her grave, where she was buried beside Ivan Fedotovich.

Avdotya Petrovna has long since become fat and a quite loud-mouthed squire's wife. But then, she loves and respects Vasily Ivanovich, although not with her former unqualified submissiveness. She also has weight and a voice in management and the economy, and, to tell the whole truth, it must be admitted that Vasily Ivanovich is a little afraid of her. As a pleasant diversion for her, all care of the cattle yard, the poultry yard and the handicraft of the household women is turned over completely to her. Avdotya Petrovna likes to tell fortunes by cards, listens to the gossip of the old women of the household, and has acquired in the neighborhood quite a reputation for the peculiar art with which she salts cucumbers, by interlaying them with certain kinds of leaves.

For the rest, neither she nor her peaceable husband in the course of thirty years of married life has ever once regretted their choice, not once has their marital fidelity been broken, and not a single unpleasant thought, not a single venomous word has once troubled their constant harmony.

Thus has flowed, thus is flowing the impassive, peaceful life of the stout landlord. In the course of his thirty-year residence in the country he has been in Moscow a couple of times,[93] five times in the provincial town, and every year about St. John's Day [24 June] he sets out for the near-by fair.

This is all that, for the reader's benefit, can be drawn from the biography of Vasily Ivanovich.

XVI

Something about Ivan Vasilyevich

Thirty years after the birth of Vasily Ivanovich, Ivan Vasilyevich was born in a neighboring village.

Ivan Vasilyevich's mother was a Moscow princess, a princess, however, not of an old Russian family, but of some strange sort of name, and, it seems, of a recent eastern origin.[94] However this may be, she was a princess from head to toe, and flourished in Moscow in that blissful period when all young girls, and particularly princesses, had realized for the first time in Russia all the charm of French novels, customs and fashions. The reader must certainly know that there was a time when our ladies were ashamed to speak Russian and mangled our language most unmercifully—of which, let it not be said to their reproach, there are still some traces observable even now. At the time Francomania with us possessed all the first-rank nobility, which, following a customary secret weakness, used to think thereby to separate itself from the nobility of the second rank. But in accordance with the accepted rule, the second rank inevitably followed after the first rank so as to get itself into the same rank, and after these followed also the other grades. It is not known to which of these successive grades the princess belonged, but since no one disputed her primacy,[95] she assigned herself to the highest stratum of society, and in consequence of this wore unbelievably short waists, wore her hair in the Greek style, read *Grandison*,[96] Abbé Prévost,[97] Mme. Riccoboni,[98] Mrs. Radcliffe,[99] Mme Cottin,[100] Mme Souza,[101] Mme de Staël,[102] Mme Genlis,[103] and expressed herself no otherwise than in French with nurse Sidorovna and butler Karp [who, being Russian serfs, of course did not understand French!]. Sidorovna cried because the child had been bewitched with the evil eye and ruined; butler Karp answered every order with "Yes, ma'am,"[104] and the old princess [i.e., the mother], who, together with her pug-dog wallowed in immobile obesity, committed the French lexicon to memory and rejoiced that God had rewarded her with such an educated princess. But then, the influence of France on us at that time was quite understandable. Napoleon was shaking all Europe from one side to the other, and Russia, lover of every kind of daring, was marvelling from the side lines at the miraculous man. But when it became our turn, all our Frenchmen began to speak Russian... The feeling of nationality, the feeling of national love for Tsar and fatherland, this fundamental, ineradicable principle of Russian life, suddenly threw off the mask, and the whole realm rose up noiselessly as a terrible giant. The foe was met with fire and sword, and the burning of Moscow illuminated the feelings of Russians with red light. In that memorable year everyone sacrificed whatever he could: one his life, another his children, another his fortune, and it entered no one's head to ask recompense for this—something of which we have subsequently seen so many examples in the France that we glorified.

The young princess and the elder princess set out for Kazan in an enormous van, having stored in it the greater part of their movable property. All the rest burned in Moscow together with their house.

The French were chased away, but the elder princess decided that for her to return to the ash heap, acquire a new town house with damask drawing rooms and a filthy anteroom was too difficult and exhausting by reason of her obesity and declining years. Consequently she settled in Kazan, to the great displeasure of the young princess. The young princess put on airs, disdained provincial society and its awkward young people. Of course such a mode of thought provoked general indignation against her; the provincial wits launched the most amusing stories at her expense, the squires' wives were extremely unfriendly to her even though they slavishly imitated her clothes. The young princess was bored, and what is worse, she was getting older. To remain an old maid, even though a princess, however you may pretend, is never a cheerful prospect. The suitors who had been on the point of rushing to her, when they learned that she had six or seven brothers and that her dowry consisted of the French language, suddenly came to feel an aversion for her, and speedily consoled themselves in all directions. Finally there turned up a certain silent landowner who was numbered among the simpletons; blinded by princely glitter, he offered the princess his hand and village. The princess accepted the village, and of necessity also the hand to boot. The landowner did not resemble, as one can well imagine, either Malek-Adel or Eugène de Rathelin.[105] He did not even resemble a cruel tyrant, but was more like a marmot; he ate, slept, and dashed about the fields all day long.

From this marriage Ivan Vasilyevich was born.

Of course it was decided to give him a splendid education so that the son might not by any means be a dunce like his father, and as soon as he began to grow, they set about hunting up a French tutor. Everyone knows that the French have long since revenged themselves on us for their failure by leaving behind an incalculable number of sergeant-majors, surgeons' assistants and shoemakers, who under pretext of education have ruined almost a whole generation in Rus. These miserable locusts cannot, however, be compared with the émigrés, who anyway were somewhat better people and better educated, though they too did not give much return for Russian hospitality which has sheltered them from the horrors of the French Revolution.

To Ivan Vasilyevich's good fortune his tutor, Monsieur Leprince, was not among the meanest, most elementary of artisans. He belonged to a certain political party, and in his account, was the victim of important revolutions that had deprived him of a considerable fortune, without, however, explaining to anyone that his fortune consisted of a tobacco shop. He was not even altogether without education, but of course, as a Frenchman, his education was one-sided and boastful; he understood nothing and recognized nothing outside of France, and all discoveries, all improvements, all success he attributed to Frenchmen. Such a way of thinking, of course, can be extremely praiseworthy for a born Parisian, but not at all, it seems, the thing needed for a native of Kazan. Besides this M. Leprince was extremely pleasant to the ladies, he wrote smooth little verses with a witticism or a gallantry at the end, he talked very glibly and beautifully about everything which he did not know, he at times loved to utter pompously some profound word about the destinies of mankind, and with proud frankness he constantly repeated that he had become a tutor only out of necessity, but had by no means been born for such a calling.

Ivan Vasilyevich's mother was extremely delighted with such a splendid find. Evil tongues even launched rumors in the county at her expense that were not at all consoling for her husband. These rumors, however, were perhaps nothing but slander.

At his thirteenth year Ivan Vasilyevich knew that Racine was the world's foremost poet, and that Voltaire was such a multiplicity of wisdom that it was terrible even to think about. He knew that there was an age which had illuminated the entire world with its mighty literature—the age of Louis XIV; that after this age there was still another, the age of Louis XV, somewhat weaker, but still astounding. Ivan Vasilyevich knew all the scribblers of this era through and through. To give him his due, he often yawned reading these model compositions, but M. Leprince, jesting at his obtuseness, would predict to him that later, perhaps, he would come to understand the beauties that were now inaccessible to him. To cap everything Ivan Vasilyevich studied Latin by L' Homond's grammar,[106] but quite unsuccessfully; he memorized something from the "Universal History of Abbé Millot,"[107] sang Béranger songs, and described the sunrise in quite correct French. Subjects unknown to him M. Leprince touched extremely lightly, letting it be felt that though he had plumbed them to their depths, they deserved no attention.

Ivan Vasilyevich was a boy of a perfectly Slavic nature, that is, lazy but keen. Imagination and a keen mind made up with him for conscientious toil and tedious attentiveness. The pupil speedily exhausted the teacher's store of learning; but the teacher, like a true Frenchman, had not the least understanding of his own ignorance and kept right on teaching and stretching out all sorts of nonsense under the cover of resounding names. "First learn Cornelius Nepos really well," he would tell his charge "and then we will tackle Horace." But unfortunately M. Leprince himself did not understand Horace, and as a result Ivan Vasilyevich too remained all his life with Cornelius Nepos. For some two or three years Ivan Vasilyevich pored over French syntax, learning and forgetting by turns all the arbitrary turns of that garrulous language. Then for several years on end he studied French rhetoric, putting together various figures, tropes, amplifications, oratorical turns of speech, etc. "First learn rhetoric really well," said M. Leprince, "and then we'll go on to philosophy." But rhetoric stretched on to infinity, and for reasons easily understandable they did not reach philosophy. I have still forgotten to mention that Ivan Vasilyevich knew by heart the genealogy of all the French kings, the names of many African and American capes and towns, had got lost in fractions as in deep water, and had begun quite brazenly, following his teacher's example, to make judgments about many books and all branches of learning merely by their titles. Ivan Vasilyevich's mother, the born princess, went into ecstasies when her dear son presented her on a festival day with a congratulatory composition filled with rhetorical tropes, or, as like as not, sometimes even hammered into meter. M. Leprince, in respect for such services, was almost the master of the house, gave orders and made arrangements on all sides, kept horses of his own, went very often for diversion to the spinning-factory [where all the spinners were serf girls]; grew stout, became well-off, and finally began to trade surreptitiously in wheat, after which, having stuffed his pockets he made his bows in all four directions and rode off to France to tell all sorts of cock-and bull stories about us[108] and print brochures about the secret policy and the merits of our rulers.

No one, however, considered the fact that Ivan Vasilyevich would not be sitting in the Chambre des Deputes, would not be a Republican or Royalist, would not be walking all his life on the Boulevard des Italiens, but that he was destined to serve in the Ministry of Justice or Finance, that by God's will he should have possession of three hundred illiterate peasant souls who would place all their hopes on him and about whom he would probably not once think, excepting, of course, on the occasions when he was to receive his income from them. Everything was told and explained to Ivan Vasilyevich except what was under his nose. He saw a rather shabby master's house, some perfectly rotten peasant huts, a pretty decrepit old church, but no one explained to him how this house, these huts, that church had begun, how they had come to be, how they had reached their present condition. Russian history, Russian life, Russian law remained for him a kind of barbaric fable, and thanks to this muddle-headed direction a Russian child grew up French in the most Russian of backwoods. In the county this worthless fellow was set up as a real marvel, and his fortunate mother, in the pleasure afforded by her son, even forgot the boredom afforded by her husband.

One must not, however, reproach her too sternly for a weakness that is common to almost our entire nobility. Even now, when in our highest circle amid so many Russian names you will find so few Russian hearts, and especially, so few Russian minds, one thinks inadvertently of the education they have received, and instead of anger, pity is aroused in the soul.

One sad morning Ivan Vasilyevich's mother passed away, and the marmot found himself in a most difficult dilemma. What to do with the son? Since the youngster had not yet completed fifteen years, it was still too early to put him into service, but too late to engage another Frenchman. At a general conference with neighbors it was decided to send Ivan Vasilyevich to a sort of private St. Petersburg boarding school. And so it was done. The boarding school was notable for amazing cleanliness and order. The floors were polished with wax, on the desks there was not a single trace of an ink stain, and at lectures an incalculable number of different branches of learning were taught. Unfortunately among the pupils ignorance and carelessness were not counted as a vice; on the contrary, a sort of youthful swagger was the accepted thing, as giving proof of the independence of the years of approaching manhood. Led on by infantile vainglory Ivan Vasilyevich became completely 'one of the boys' [*molodets*]: he inhaled tobacco smoke in all corners until he was sick, he drank vodka, ran to candy shops, bragged of some imaginary drunk, devoted himself to the theatrical news, and at lessons learned certain dirty or free-thinking verses. In a word, he picked up a certain strange rebellious spirit, resented the name of student [*shkol'nik*], called the teachers asses, damned everything holy, and read with feverish delight those foul novels and poems which can't even be named. In this fashion he became a worthless scapegrace, a ridiculous and disgusting ignoramus, and even that meager store of trivial knowledge which M. Leprince had communicated to him disappeared in the fog of schoolboy's swagger.

Thus he ruined the best, freshest years of his life, when the soul is still so receptive, retains every impression so warmly and cleanly. The time for graduation and examination arrived. The examination consisted of thirty or forty subjects, not counting the fine arts and gymnastic exercises. Ivan Vasilyevich, of course, was extremely contemptuous toward the expected test, and, in the language of the boarding school, flunked from the word go. Such an outcome should have been expected. Ivan Vasilyevich, however, was unbelievably vexed, and even a little ashamed before others and himself. He was one of those people who want to know everything without studying anything. It was intolerably annoying to him to look at the two or three hard-working young people whom the whole class had always laughed at, who had never belonged to "the boys," and who had suddenly become objects of the involuntary respect not only of the teachers but even of the wildest, the most desperate of their comrades. Ivan Vasilyevich came to his senses and did some serious thinking. Shouldn't he begin again from the ABC's? Shouldn't he finally get down to business? He felt that he was gifted with a good understanding and a good memory; objects took clear shape in his imagination, even the most abstract ideas with an effort could take firm root in his mind. Finally he felt, even in his annoyance, that he was not born for unthinking dissipation, and that there was concealed in him something living, something noble, that was seeking for the light, demanding action, trying to rouse the soul. If he had followed the inner voice, if he had set about reeducating himself, he might still have become a useful person, and at the least, remarkable for firmness and persistence. But how should one begin to learn at the time when some of one's comrades are already titular councillors and leading a gay life in high society? Give Ivan Vasilyevich both service and society. He took a post in some ministry, bitterly lamented the folly of his school years, and began to serve zealously and assiduously. He made up for lack of the knowledge proper to the service by gumption and keenness of mind. He was used in the chancery and on detached assignments, he was zealous in the service as though wanting to make amends for the fault of his regrettable eclipse. In his zeal there was even too much ardor, because he could not keep it constantly at uniform strength. He even did much that was perfectly unnecessary and superfluous, not at all required of him. In a word he fell head over heels in love with the service, and in a short time the service bored him. It seemed to him that his merits were not being given their due, that he was not being singled out sufficiently, but was being passed over in presentations, that he should already be some important person. His ardor waned, and his ignorance, not concealed by caution, began to show through. His hard-working boarding-school comrades already mentioned, had passed him by in a short time because in the service as in school they were well grounded and consistent. Ivan Vasilyevich was on the point of becoming angry, but he speedily forgot even his anger because he suddenly stopped thinking about the service, and no wonder... He was in love. He was up to his ears in love with a certain young lady who was distinguished by a languid look and a passionate mode of speaking. At first they exchanged vague confessions, then they exchanged rings and finally mutual oaths to love one another forever. Ivan Vasilyevich for some time floated in the tempestuous heaven of passionate dreams, but this did not last long. The passion which lured him was all at once reaching its ultimate limit, and from its very strength was speedily weakened. But suddenly he noticed that his beauty was looking languourously at a certain hussar—and jealousy began to seethe. Vengeance, malice, blood began to rage in his head. Fortunately the beauty herself forestalled any tragic consequences by marrying such a wealthy monstrosity that it was impossible to be angry at him. For diversion Ivan Vasilyevich plunged furiously into society pleasures. But in these pleasures he did not find even a shadow of what he sought. Boredom, inactivity, deceived self-love, a sort of leaden weariness oppressed his breast. He began to curse the colorlessness of Petersburg life, not realizing that he was bearing this colorlessness in himself. Sometimes, in fiery bursts, he was carried away in the delightful world of poetry; he read Dante and Schiller and Byron and Shakespeare, and with a powerful hand pulled aside the curtain which separated him from the beautiful world so long hidden from his eyes. Sometimes he immersed himself in some branch of learning which attracted him, but all this was casual, without solidity, spasmodic. An open book would fall from his table, a written page would not be turned. And now, as before, he set about everything in a fever heat, but the fever soon passed; he tired, and sought for a momentary distraction, a stupid amusement. He realized then that education does not consist of words and dates, not in the number and details of learned subjects, but in a capacity for busying oneself profitably, in a strict criticism of life, in a strict and patient carrying out of every kind of action begun. He had become a truly pitiable person not because his position was unfortunate, but because he was unable to take part in anything for long, because he was dissatisfied with himself, because he had become tired of himself. Then he began to have intimations that there exists some lofty, beautiful purpose in learning, which pushes down to the soul's bottom the doubt, the distrust, the passions, the wearisome struggles unavoidable with human nature. Without beneficent learning all these hostile principles float to the surface of the soul and burn and rage and destroy the undefended life.

In such a comfortless position Ivan Vasilyevich consoled himself, however, with the comforting hope of going abroad, imagining that in foreign parts he would easily acquire the knowledge which he had been unable to acquire in his native land. In general the word "abroad" has among our young people a certain peculiar significance. It is just as though it were the key to all the good things of life. The sick man hurries abroad imagining that at the gates of Prussia he will become well. The painter is eager to go abroad in the expectation that as soon as he climbs Monte Pincio he will be a Raphael. The ignoramus who has loafed at home all his life and become ashamed at last of his ignorance, takes a seat in a *diligence* and thinks that lost time, enervating idleness, intellectual darkness no longer have any meaning: he is on his way abroad.

Ivan Vasilyevich set out for Berlin with letters of recommendation to all the notables of Berlin University. His first impression abroad was most unsatisfactory, although he could not himself give an accounting of what he had expected. The people were like people. The houses were like houses. The streets were like streets. And besides this, the people were even more tiresome than our Russians, the buildings worse than ours, the streets narrower than ours. The notables before whom he was prepared to be reverent produced on him the same impression as the cashier of his ministry or a billiard-marker at Isler's.[109] One notable had a fat nose. Another had a wart on his cheek. Ivan Vasilyevich raced to lectures, but once there observed with sorrow that he did not have the fundamental knowledge without which all that came after had no support. Besides this he had a poor knowledge of German, and although he would even discuss Hegel and Schelling, he didn't understand them at all, and became convinced, poor chap, that he must either begin from the gymnasium or stand waiting all his life before the lecturer's chair [*kafedra*] like a guest announced at the door of the temple. In Germany the secret of education was explained to him. He saw how there every person, from peasant to prince, revolved in his own circle of patience, and systematically, without trying to raise himself too high and without falling too low. He saw how every person chooses for himself a path of life and goes his way gradually along that path without looking to one side or the other and without once losing his goal from sight. Oh, how he then cursed his Frenchman-tutor, who had failed to give his life just this thing—a goal. He felt that in his spiritual life there was no connection, that he was nothing but a child alien to everything, a child which for pure playfulness passes suddenly from indifference to rapture, from rapture to despair. It seemed to him that he was rejected by the thinking and acting family of mankind, that he was condemned to wander eternally alone, forgotten, ridiculed, in a misty, impenetrable darkness. In order to console himself even a little, he began to make caustic fun of the Germans, of their tiresome and orderly life, of their wives' everlasting knitting, of their beer, their clubs and marksmen's associations. He didn't, however, live long with the Germans, but set out for Paris. Paris is so beautiful that it dispels any sort of spleen. Ivan Vasilyevich was wholly attracted by that eternally rushing crowd which is constantly hurrying after something and to some place, but never getting anywhere. He saw before him his own history on an enormous scale: everlasting noise, everlasting struggle, everlasting movement, resounding talk, loud exclamations, limitless boastfulness, a desire to show off and stand in front of others, and at the bottom of this seething life—an oppressive boredom and a cold egoism.

For a long time Ivan Vasilyevich idled about in all the offerings of Parisian play, beginning with the two chambers [i.e., the French Parliament]. He did not, however, fall in love with Paris. He was still too young. In defiance of fate, his soul craved something higher, more comforting, and the excursion into Italy has remained perhaps the brightest spot, the best memory of his life. There developed in him a feeling for beauty hitherto unknown to him. And not merely the poetical sensualism of art, like a bewitching woman, laid bare all her attractions before him. In Italy art has a kind of wonderful spiritual side which is impossible to express, but which permeates all being. In Italy, in Italy alone it is possible to stand for whole hours before a building, before a statue, before a painting. The soul is enlivened by the lifeless object and becomes as it were kindred to it, enters as it were into some sort of mysterious spiritual relationship with it. Only in Rome was Ivan Vasilyevich perfectly at ease in spirit. It would have gone against his conscience even to think about such an insignificant speck of dust as himself, in the presence of the classical monuments reared by the heroes of art over the corpse of human ambition. For the first time Ivan Vasilyevich even on the streets spoke in a low voice as though in the presence of the dead. And who indeed can look cold-bloodedly at the Apollo [Belvedere], at the Colosseum, at St. Peter's Square? Who can without pondering contemplate the peculiar combination of paganism and Christianity, of religion and art? In Italy every church is a sumptuous gallery, and the best products of artists of genius crowd humbly at the altar.

Wonderful, unforgettable Italy! Let them say that you have fallen, that you have perished, that you are buried—don't believe the perfidious words; you are living still, with the life of old, you breathe with the fire of old. You are still the queen of the world, and the nations flock to do you homage. And you have many treasures: nature and the people born under your sky have endowed you so richly that your largesse alone has enriched all Europe. Flourish, Italy, no longer indeed as a sportive beauty full of youth, but as an opulent widow who has seen the vanity of life and death close at hand, and with a bitter smile looks at people, demanding nothing of the present, but piously immersing herself in the sole and constant memory of past prosperity.

Meanwhile Ivan Vasilyevich was noticing that wherever he turned up, in whatever country he arrived, he was looked at with a sort of hostile, envious attention. At first he attributed this to his personal qualities, but then he divined that Russia occupied willy-nilly all minds, and that he was looked on so strangely solely because he was a Russian. Sometimes at the table-d'hote the most childish questions were put to him: will Russia presently take possession of the whole world? Is it true that next year Tsargrad [i.e., Constantinople] will be named the Russian capital? All the newspapers that fell into his hands were filled with observations about Russian policy. In Germany Panslavism occupied all minds. Every day there issued from the press the stupidest pamphlets and books at the expense of Russia, written with a sort of lackeyish resentment, and demonstrating absolutely nothing but the talentlessness of their authors and the fears of Europe. Little by little life abroad made Ivan Vasilyevich involuntarily begin thinking about his own native land. Thinking about her he began to be proud of her. In a word, that which in his native land had not been instilled in him in his education, stole little by little into his soul while in a foreign land. He began to remember all that he had seen and not taken note of in his village, on excursion in the provinces, at the times of the detached duties while in the service. Even though he felt that all these data did not add up to a general opinion, a genuine whole, yet certain traits he retained quite faithfully, while he filled in the rest with his imagination. Thus he put together for himself particular ideas about officials, about Russian commerce, about our education, about our literature. Then he decided to study his native land thoroughly, and since he undertook everything with rapture, love for his fatherland began to burn in him with a violent fire. Moreover he was delighted that he had given a meaning to his being, that he had found himself at last a goal in life, a noble goal, a beautiful goal that promised him an attractive occupation, useful observations. With such feelings he returned from abroad.

The reader already knows how he met Vasily Ivanovich on Tverskoi Boulevard, how he got into the tarantas with him, how he armed himself with a book for his travel impressions, and sharpened his pen.

But what will come of this? What will he write? What will he discover? What will he show us?

Nothing, it seems. Here too, as in all the other occasions of his life, Ivan Vasilyevich will not remain steadfast. First he is all fired up, then at the first obstacle he loses his strength. Not habituated to persistent work, he will meet impossibility where there is only difficulty—and his good beginnings will always remain without endings.

And he is not alone. There are many young people among us who suffer from a disease identical with his. There are many young people among us who faint under the burden of their own impotence and feel that their life is forever spoiled from a faulty, inadequate, half-way education. To be sure, they comfort themselves in their self-esteem with a mask of affected disillusion, of weariness of life, of hope deceived. But in reality they are merely worthless or half-way worthless, and so cannot but feel their own worthlessness. And yet there is perhaps hidden in them an inclination towards action, a love for beauty and truth, but they have not acquired the strength to actualize their inner urge. There is feeling in them, but no will. Passion seethes in them, but reason is forever deficient. Many for distraction sink themselves in the deep waters of wild pleasures, some become debauchees, others card-sharks, still others sacrifice their lives for a trifle, some imagine that they are free-thinkers, liberals, they curse the government under their breath, curse circumstances as though they were injurious. But even with other circumstances they would have been the same, because the evil lies in their very foundations, in the very root of their feeble vegetative life. Pitiful generation! A fruit that is spoiled while still in the flower! But thus it has been destined from above. In every improvement, in every transformation there must be victims. They have fallen in the struggle of past with present, of darkness with light. They will disappear without trace, without pity for their uncomprehended sufferings; but their sufferings should serve as an example. A luminous spot has floated for a long time on the dark firmament of age-old ignorance, and it is growing with every day and becoming constantly brighter and brighter. There will be people who will be burned by the unfamiliar fire; others, blinded by the radiance, will remain in perplexity between light and darkness, or chance into a mistaken path. But the truth is approaching closer and closer, and the day will come when the darkness will disappear completely and the whole earth will be illumined with a beneficent light...

XVII

A Rustic Holiday

Meanwhile Ivan Vasilyevich was in perfect despair. No impressions had turned up anywhere at all. Only his sides were under the influence of some very strong impressions. It was in vain that he peered intently to both sides of the tarantas—everything merged into a sort of muddy, monotonous picture. But then, he can't be blamed too much. In general, objects are defined in the mind not at all as in reality, but somehow more prominently, more sharply, more picturesquely. Besides, there are such people as will stand long in admiration of some lithograph and never notice in nature that which it represents. A muzhik done in oils, for example, or simply sketched with the pen, will make them stand for a long time before it, and even afford them considerable pleasure, but the real muzhik, uncombed and unwashed, in bast shoes and sheepskin coat, will never attract their attention, because there are so many such muzhiks that you never notice them at all.

Be that as it may, Ivan Vasilyevich was in a most sorrowful frame of mind. The untouched book was wallowing around under his feet next to the cellarette. Russia's instruction as regards her antiquities and national character had decidedly not been advanced. The business, it seemed, was not for the many. Ivan Vasilyevich divined that a good intention alone was not enough for carrying out a great exploit. Placards weren't hung all over Russia on which her life could be read, everything that was, that is, and that will be. One excursion to Mordasy was somehow too little for such a study. Something else was still needed. Everlasting tenacity was still needed, through the course of a whole life. And considerable of this, it seemed. It was necessary to penetrate into the very depths of every subject because from the smooth outer surface nothing was extracted. It was necessary to seek out, as the key to the riddle, the secret, sometimes lofty meaning of every prosaic phenomenon that turned up at every step. But as we know, Ivan Vasilyevich was a person of a weak nature. As he met with difficulties, he made no effort to overcome them, but changed his undertakings. Thus little by little he had renounced, as we have seen, the fine studies, the important discoveries for which he was preparing himself with such ardor for the good of humanity. However, although he had lost hope on many counts, yet he still hoped to penetrate into the soul of the Russian. "As a matter of fact," he thought, "we fuss and bother about Russia, but what we don't know is precisely this: what is a Russian, a real Russian, without the admixture of foreign influences. What kind of mental life does he have? What does he expect? What does he desire? Toward what is he striving? The pure natural principle is to such a degree muffled in our present way of life that we are unable to separate basic concepts from later accumulations. To define this principle, to search out these native concepts—

this will be a glorious task! We talk a lot about national character—but what is national character? What does it consist of, what are its component parts? Here's work for you, Ivan Vasilyevich. Investigate, define, exhort. Russia will thank you..."

As though on purpose the tarantas drove into a large, beautiful settlement, and Vasily Ivanovich declared that he was so tired of lying in the tarantas that he intended to rest in the stationmaster's house and lie down for a little while on the stove-couch.

The endlessly long village was resplendent in its most celebratory look. In front of the high peasant cottages, adorned with their carvings, peasant men and women were sitting on benches, cracking nuts. The holiday attire with its bright colors showed gaudily from far off. At the bridge which cut the principal line of houses in two a small building of civic architecture signified by its fir-bough sticking out above the door the public house beloved of many. To the right a whole throng of young women in red and blue sarafans with snow-white sleeves were watching while two barefoot wenches capered on a plank. Around them two fellows in red shirts and cloth coats thrown open were paying no attention, it seemed, to the expressive jeers of the comrades standing not far away. Some of the latter were whistling a little tune through their teeth. Others standing in a circle around a well were assiduously rattling a heavy iron pin [*svaika*] in an iron ring.[110] In the middle of the street a crowd of small boys surrounded a little wagon harnessed to an old nag, by which a cheerful pedlar was offering, with a medley of folk-sayings and popular jokes, gingerbread, carob pods,[111] pretzels, and all sorts of goodies. Beyond the bridge the silver spire and green cupola of a church rose high above the peasant cottages, standing out sharply against the gray background of the sullen sky.

"Well, now," said Vasily Ivanovich to the stationmaster, "what's going on here? A church holiday?"

"Just so, sir," replied the stationmaster.

"Best wishes for it, friend," continued Vasily Ivanovich.

"Our humble thanks."

"How about it, friend? Wouldn't it be possible to bring out a little samovar?"

"The samovar's ready, sir. We've been honored by a visit from guests from the neighborhood. My gossip[112] even came from town with her son-in-law... They came to see us for the holiday, you see. Well, everyone knows—of course you entertain dear guests. I guess we're putting out the fifth samovar."

"A kind act, a kind act," observed Vasily Ivanovich, after which he drank with relish three glasses of tea, sensed the pleasant warmth, and with not a little difficulty scrambled up on to the stove-bed, upon which Senka in good time had thrown a few cushions. In a few minutes Vasily Ivanovich declared to those present that he intended to sleep, and Ivan Vasilyevich set off to saunter a bit in the village—and incidentally, look for national character.

The whole population was on foot, crowding in picturesque groups around the buildings. At the public house two Orthodox "beards" [a somewhat derogatory slang for "peasants"] were kissing each other with heart-felt effusions and such furious oaths of mutual friendship that it was terrible to hear. A red-headed muzhik with a big jug in one hand and a bright green beer glass in the other was entertaining his comrades, pursuing them importunately with his offers, taking offense at their refusals, bowing to the waist, and not thinking at all that he was drinking up all at once the fruits of a year of toil.

A shrill-voiced, red-faced peasant woman was pushing her besotted husband toward home, shedding bitter tears, cursing him as a drunkard, reproaching him with leaving her and their orphan children to go begging— and she too was completely drunk.

Ivan Vasilyevich hurriedly turned away from this picture, so repulsive to a person of delicacy, and started to stroll toward the young women, to admire the beauty of our northern belles. It must be noted that at this point he set a little to rights the disorder of his costume, pulled his topcoat down, buttoned up, and assumed a dignified air. Following the secret weakness of incurable social vanity, Ivan Vasilyevich, although without particular consciousness of this, was convinced that his unexpected appearance in the motley throng would produce a powerful effect.

He was wrong, however.

A healthy, ruddy wench pointed at him quite insolently, addressing her companions: "Look at the slicked-up German coming!"

The young women began to laugh and a lad in a red shirt intruded into the conversation:

"What a sharp-tongued gal Matryoshka is! Look out that I don't hit you in the snout!"

Matryoshka smiled.

"Oh, you scare me terrible!... What a scamp! I'll give you such a crack that you won't ask for the change!"

Ivan Vasilyevich did not think it necessary to listen to the conversation that followed, and a little offended by the contemptuous designation of "German," took once more to his strolling. First he crossed the bridge, then found himself on a small grass-grown square. He skirted a small pond, on which ducks and ducklings were muttering, and finally found himself near the church. Here quiet settled down on his spirit, and his thoughts took a different direction. Around the church rose a high stone wall, beside which in the thick grass a few wooden crosses, painted dark red, were bending to the ground. At sight of these simple memorials of a simple life that has flitted by, his soul was humbled in a sort of pious silence. And it is just so: rural cemeteries produce a completely different impression from those of the city. At sight of the latter a sort of heavy, nagging feeling is involuntarily engendered; at sight of the former the soul becomes serene and bright. The closer life approaches nature, the less terrible does death appear; on the contrary, it appears as a peaceful transformation which is recompense for a great deal—not a comfortless deprivation, not a crushing rupture with all hopes, with all cares, with a person's whole being.

At the church wall the sacristan with a bundle in his hand was moving forward, and from the distance the priest was coming, in a long silken cassock, in a broad hat, with a tall staff in his hand. As he approached, the peasants stood up, took off their hats, and bowed respectfully to their shepherd. Some kissed his hand, others brought their children forward for his blessing. Only one pale, emaciated peasant with a black beard and sunken eyes did not take off his hat, and turned rudely away.

This seemed strange to Ivan Vasilyevich. He stopped in front of a husky householder who beside his gate was dandling his year-old child in his arms.

"Say, brother, why didn't that black-bearded fellow take off his hat before the priest?"

The muzhik first covered the baby with his sheepskin coat, and answered quite carelessly:

"From old belief."

This new idea flashed like lightning in Ivan Vasilyevich's head.

"Here's an impression! Here's a task!" he thought. "To define the influence of heresies on our people! To search out their beginning, development, and purpose!"

"Are there many schismatics among you?" he asked hurriedly.

"What?"

"Are there many schismatics among you?"

"Schismatics... No, not many."

"How many would there be?"

"How many... Who knows how many there would be."

"Tell me, brother, what does their doctrine consist of?"

"What?"

"What do their rites consist of?"

"Rites? Why, according to old books."

"But in what do they differ from you?"

"What?"

"In what do they differ from you?"

"They differ... Why, by the old belief, it seems."

"I know; but of course they have their own service, their own monasteries, their own priests?"

"Everyone knows—according to the old belief."

"Of what sect are they?"

"What?"

"Of what heresy?"

"What?"

"What are they? The Priestless [*bespopovshchiny*], Dukhobors [*dukhobortsy*, i.e. "spirit fighters"]?"

"Dukhobors... No, no, not dukhobors, I guess, but it's like this. They just don't go to church. From old belief, must be."

"Well, it would be a curious thing to know," continued Ivan Vasilyevich, thinking aloud, "does their creed differ from ours in form only or in substance? Is their defection from us civic or ecclesiastical?"

"From old belief," concluded the muzhik, after which he coolly turned his back on Ivan Vasilyevich and disappeared with his little son behind the wicket.

Ivan Vasilyevich walked meditatively on.

Although the peasant's explanations regarding the schismatics were a little obscure, even unsatisfactory, yet here was something to think about. Ivan Vasilyevich walked and thought... Suddenly loud laughter interrupted his ruminations right in the midst of their most significant development. Taken aback by the sudden noise, Ivan Vasilyevich raised his head, losing the thread of deep ideas, and stopped involuntarily. At the gate of a guest house a whole crowd of people were surrounding a sort of storyteller, in a short, uncovered sheepskin jacket, in a military service cap, beardless, but with a great gray moustache reaching up over his sideburns to his ears. On the sheepskin jacket on the left side hung two medals on faded ribbons, but by his firm posture alone, by his decisive movements alone, it was not hard to recognize in the storyteller an old discharged soldier.

"What a serviceman!" said someone in the crowd, "Oh, what a serviceman! Lord help us! He's been everywhere. Seen everybody."

"Yes," put in the storyteller, who had, it seemed, taken a drop too much at the merry church festival, "nothing like your sort. I haven't been sitting down all my life with the women behind the stove. And I've threshed peas, and a lot bigger than yours. God be praised, I've seen the Frenchy and I've gone after the Turk."[113]

"Did you now! Even went after the Turk?"

"I did. So help me God, I did. In the year '28 I did. And when we gave the heathen what for, it was just 'oi-oi-oi!' "

"And why was it, uncle, we had war with the Turk?"

"Why? Everyone knows why! The Turkish Sultan—that means like 'tsar' in their German tongue[114]—sent a letter to our Tsar. 'I want you to get out of the way or you'll be kicked out. And besides, please christen all your Orthodox people into our pagan faith.' "

"Oh, the godless rascal!" exclaimed a little old man in the crowd.

"Certainly he's godless and what's more, without any subordination.[115] He sent such a bold envoy. 'To your imperial highness I'm sent by the Turkish Sultan,' and that's all. But our boys also tell that he brought with him a handful of poppy seed. 'As many grains,' he says, 'as there are here, so many regiments we have, so won't you give orders for things to be our way?' "

"Well, what did our Tsar do?" asked a husky lad in the crowd.

"Our Tsar, thank God, had his wits about him. In answer he sent a handful of pepper grains, 'They may be a little fewer, but just you try to eat them.' "

The muzhiks laughed noisily.

"That's all right! So help me God, that's great! Well then, I guess the Tatar made peace?"

"The devil he made peace! The evil one confused him. Evidently the ammunition in his noddle wasn't in good order. He didn't take the business reasonably. Just see, what a blockhead! He's talked to, it seems, in good Russian, and still he makes trouble! And where should he go with his scurvy crew but up against some battalion of grenadiers! We didn't even really have a chance to have all the fun our hearts desired. Someone would come flying along pretty smartly, and you'd think: 'Let's play with him a little for fun,' and you'd give him a snap with your finger—and you'd look, and the dog, he's on his back already!"

"I guess they must be a long ways from here?" asked someone.

"Yes, a little farther than your garden. We walked and walked three months, I guess... We lost count of the river crossings. And such country as we went through—really, good for nothing: like nothing at all. All mountains and more mountains. Such a pity, truly. Evidently God doesn't love them on account of their heathen belief. That is, you might say, there isn't even room enough to line up a regiment! A miserable country! And nothing to get. So help me God, there isn't a simple shop. The gentlemen said that the climate was good. The devil it's good! Four kopecks for a needle!"

"Where did you get to?"

"The devil only knows what they call places there! We got to the Caucasus— into some—devil knows what—Avaria.[116] I mind me, in the year '14 we went to Paris, and then too we went through this Avaria. It's spread out, you see, like a sort of wedge. Well, from Avaria we came into the Turkland itself. I was still one of the bakers."

"I suppose you went through a lot?" the little old man asked again. "And you didn't get to take naps very often on loft-bunks.[117]

"A lot of loft-bunks there, old beard! Our night lodging was under the open sky; the commander will order 'to rest!' and it's arrange yourself as best you know how. Lie on your belly and cover yourself with your back and sleep till the morning drum. But that's nothing. A soldier is a healthy fellow; but there's nowhere to get kvass.[118] What a heathen people!"

Having said these words the old serviceman spat and waved his arm. For a little while all those present stood silent, filled with indignation. Finally the tall lad once more embarked on some inquisitve questioning:

"Tell us, uncle, how did you get wounded?"

"Oh, what a great thing that was! A paltry business, so help me, paltry. Y'know, they don't even know how to wound you properly. Bruised my knee a little, that's all."

"But how did it happen?"

"How did it happen? Here's how it happened. It was at the foot of a fortress, what?... Such an outlandish name that you can't get it out at once. We were halted, for example, about ten versts away. Suddenly we hear—they're firing. Wow! Seems they want to take the town by storm. The commander says 'Boys, here's no time to be dozing, but to give our lads a hand and show what we're made of!' We went on the double for perhaps eight or nine versts. The boys were beginning to puff. No joke, what? We ran right up close to the town. Well, they gave us a chance to catch our breath. They brought us each a glass. I remember it was here that gray-haired Tarasenkov made me laugh—what an old codger, he was already in service under Suvorov, and afterward he got into the drum corps.[119] 'Oh,' says he, 'that's annoying! And I was just getting warmed up!' He killed us, the old devil... When we'd caught our breath, the general asks: 'How about it, boys, can this fortress be taken?' And the fortress sticks up like the devil, no place to approach it for the life of you. 'No, your excellency, she's mighty strong, she can't be taken.' 'Well, and if those are the orders?' 'Well, if it's ordered, we'll take it anyhow.' 'Well then, the Lord bless us! Climb up, boys... And cheerfully... Singers, forward march.'[120] And from the fortress they're shooting from cannons and muskets at anything and everything. Such a din that you could scream... But no nonsense now, brother... Didn't you hear the command? We'll take her friendly-like. Hurrah, boys! We only just made it. I don't remember how we climbed up, but climb we did, and silenced the cannon and hauled down the flags and captured the fortress. Many, truly, were missing. Well, the kingdom of heaven be theirs; they died a good death. About vespers, eh, the sergeant says to me: 'Brother, it would be a good thing for you to visit Doctor Karl Ivanovich. I guess they've given you a pretty good scratch.' Well! So it was, in fact! And I hadn't even noticed it. There was nothing to be done. They took me to the hospital... But it was a paltry business. Didn't even need crutches. The only trouble was, it was inconvenient to march... Well, I guess I've served my time. Time to gossip a little with the peasant women... Stay happy, gentlemen. I've been invited to the police-chief's for beer."[121]

Here the old serviceman dropped his arms to his sides, and executing a left turn from long habit according to the rules of the drill-field, he made his way, limping a little, along the main row of houses, accompanied by small boys who now lagged behind and now raced ahead of him. The dense crowd of listeners began slowly to break up, shaking their heads and exchanging heartfelt exclamations: "Oh, the old dog!... just look, what a fellow! Oh, that soldier!... He didn't eat bread for nothing... Wow, what a fellow!"

Ivan Vasilyevich set out again on his way.

In places songs were sounding, half-sad, half-gay, expressing now an all-embracing feeling, now subtle, biting mockery. In places small boys would throw knucklebones under his feet, and then, stopping in front of him, would stare at him with wonderment. Frail, bent old men with silvered beards walked cautiously around buildings, supported by respectful grandsons. Young fellows took off their hats to them. Young men seated them solicitously on benches. At the police chief's the party was decidedly in full swing. Not only the cottage, but the porch and even the yard were full of guests. Pies, pancakes [*lepeshki*], dried fish and meat of various kinds, among which not the least part was played by a suckling pig, were spread out in an opulent pile on the recently improvised tables. Enormous buckets, full of home brew and beer, lured their devotees with tempting fragrance. A few drunken comrades were already seated on plank settles. The mistress of the house would bow every once in a while to her dear guests, begging them not to scorn the humble entertainment which God had provided. The master of the house from time to time filled up the drinking dippers and urged on his wife to bow more often and invite more urgently. Both were ready to spend on the festival not only what they had put away, but even what they might receive in the future, merely in order that their guests might be content, only in order that the honored guests might get drunk and then say: "Oh, what a police chief!"

Ivan Vasilyevich walked in sad perplexity. "A strange folk!" he reasoned, "an incomprehensible folk! There are so many contradictions in them that you can't make them out in a whole lifetime. And besides, a nation isn't national character. The different castes do not of themselves constitute a common spirit, a common demand. What is needed for this is a general merging in a single feeling. There's no doubt that in our land too all the nation's strata mysteriously form a brotherhood, but in external life this brotherhood appears so seldom that you sometimes think: Does it even exist in reality? Where is national character to be found?"

At this moment a dashing troika darted past Ivan Vasilyevich like an arrow. The driver, gaily brandishing his whip, was shouting: "Fall down!" as he stood on his box and winked at the beauties smiling at him in the windows. In the vehicle was seated a certain rather elderly gentleman in a gray overcoat with a red collar and a uniform service cap. Ivan Vasilyevich raised his head. "An official," he said involuntarily. "An official!" But the assessor was already far away. The equipage had dashed past. But for quite a while the bell continued to emit its sonorous jingling from far away, now dying away, now becoming louder, and for a long time it echoed in Ivan Vasilyevich's heart like some strange resounding feeling of sorrowful distance, of a plaintive spirit.

Ivan Vasilyevich returned to the guest house with the strangest and most unexpected conclusion.

"Oh, you officials!" said he, sighing and addressing himself. "Oh you officials! Isn't it you, who, out of the habit of thievery, have stolen our national character from us?"

XVIII

Officials

In the morning the next day the tarantas drove up to the poor little hut of a post-station master.

Vasily Ivanovich gave a loud grunt and began to scramble out with Senka's help.

"How about a spot of tea?" he said, "I'd like to have a spot of tea. Warm up a little, eh?"

Quick-witted Senka rushed for the cellarette. Ivan Vasilyevich at the same time jumped out of the tarantas and was about to run into the hut when he suddenly jumped three steps backward in fright. An *official* was approaching him—an official as an official should be, in all the pitiful majesty of full dress, in an old tricorn hat, an old worn uniform with gold edging on a black velvet collar, with an enormous paper sticking out between the buttons of his uniform. He was poking along slowly from old age and a sort of habitual timidity. His little face was shrivelled into little wrinkles. He bowed and seemed not to be surprised at Ivan Vasilyevich's unfriendly fright, but kept approaching closer and closer, and finally in a humble old man's voice uttered a few words:

"Beg pardon, sir... I ask you most humbly to forgive... I dare to ask... would you know, would you be so good as to know... Will his excellency be coming here shortly?"

"I don't know," answered Ivan Vasilyevich rudely' and turned away with annoyance.

"What?" exclaimed Vasily Ivanovich, "Is his excellency the governor pleased to be touring the province?"

"Just so, sir. Directions were received this week."

"And you're the county police officer?" inquired Vasily Ivanovich.[122]

"No, sir," the official turned to Vasily Ivanovich and bowed to him respectfully... "One performing the duties of the office."

"Here's the border of the county?"

"Precisely."

Vasily Ivanovich, like a true Russian, was very fond of new acquaintances—not, however to extract some profit from their conversation, but just to chatter a bit about all sorts of nonsense, and have a look at a new person.

"Wouldn't you like to have a cup of tea with us?" he asked invitingly, paying no attention to his companion's sour look.

The official bowed again to Vasily Ivanovich, then bowed to Ivan Vasilyevich, stepped aside for Senka who was dragging along the cellarette, and plodded on, coughing as quietly as possible, behind his new acquaintances.

It was quite dark in the stationmaster's room; an old cotton curtain indicated the bed in a corner, upon which from time to time a quiet rustle was heard. The travellers, without paying any attention to this, took seats on a bench under the icon, pulling up to them a longish table. Presently the cellarette disgorged glasses and saucers, the samovar began to boil, the glasses were filled, conversation began.

"Have you been serving in an elected post for long?" asked Vasily Ivanovich.

"Since 1804," replied the little old man.

"Why do you serve as an elected official?" asked Ivan Vasilyevich slyly.

"What's one to do, my dear sir? Poverty."

Ivan Vasilyevich smiled meaningfully. "Bribetaker!" he thought. "So it is." The little old man understood his thought, but did not take offense.

"Nowadays, my dear sir," he said, "times aren't like those when one used to get rich in these positions. It used to be, anyone who was made county police officer, it would be said at once that he had acquired a village of three hundred souls. The authorities now are strict, they keep a keen eye on such as us. Oh, oh, oh! Every year five or six people in criminal court. And besides," continued the old man in a whisper, "the common people, my dear sir, aren't the same. Very, very seldom, on a holiday, they'll bring a pound of tea or half a loaf of sugar by way of good wishes.[123] You know yourself, my dear sir, one won't get rich or go far on that."

"Then why are you in service?" asked Ivan Vasilyevich.

"Poverty, my dear sir, children: eight persons,[124] eleven souls all told—have to be fed. Living with me are two sisters and a blind brother. Well, you're always thinking of how to do the best for your children. Perhaps they could get into the cadet corps or an institute by the kindness of the authorities. But thank God and our little father the Tsar, we're now paid a salary that's not what it used to be, it is possible to feed oneself."

"But there are profits?" asked Vasily Ivanovich.

"What kind of profits, my dear sir! There are some, there's no use denying it, but not many. Now a sack of oats, now a little flour will be sent by some landowner, and that just out of acquaintanceship. Times, my dear sir, are different now."

"And you can't avoid a bit of trouble, I suppose?" asked Vasily Ivanovich.

"That goes without saying, my dear sir. There's no time to eat dinner. Here I am now, please see, I have to wait here for the governor, and meanwhile there are three dead bodies unburied in the county, and six investigations not finished, and some back taxes; it's describe this, look into that, I'll tell you, the devil's own misery. Every day confirmations from the provincial government, and reprimands, and threats of punishment, and special messengers just ride their rounds on our account. It's hard, my dear sir. All you can do is keep your eyes open so as to save yourself from court. And my office, my dear sir, you know yourself what that's like. I have one secretary,

Mitrofashka, and that's all. And besides, it's pay him out of my own salary and give him all kinds of clothes and cut boots.[125] He drinks a lot, the rascal, and he's a dog to write! There will come an unhappy time, he'll hand me some paper in a hurry, while he's drunk, I'll sign it, but it'll turn out to be the wrong one, and I'm done for!"

"But you must have an estate?" queried Ivan Vasilyevich.

"My dear sir, what an estate! There are four of us owners, and we have seventeen souls [i.e., serfs] all told, according to the last census. My share amounts to three families, and these almost all women and old men. And here's no paradise. There was one good young lad—he sprained an arm; and the women, so little and puny, they can't work in the fields or weave cloth—nothing."

"Yes," observed Vasily Ivanovich, "that's a real misfortune. A poor woman worker doesn't bring much profit."

"That would all be nothing," continued the poor official, "but here's the worst. I'm so far along in years that I'm becoming weak somehow through illness. Sometimes I'm sitting over papers, and suddenly everything will grow dark before my eyes, so dark that I can't make out either writing or paper—devil knows what it is! God's punishment—but what are you going to do? But the chief thing is that for journeying around—such as for instance to trot off to meet his excellency—I'm no good at all. Everything is just breaking up, but there's nothing to be done: trot off in a troika and have your horses ready."

Involuntarily Ivan Vasilyevich began to feel sad. He got up from his seat and approached the dark corner. Behind the curtain was heard a sigh. Ivan Vasilyevich hastily pulled it aside. On the bed was sitting the stationmaster dangling his legs to the floor. Ivan Vasilyevich, although he was a European person, a preacher of general equality, none the less found it extremely insulting that a simple stationmaster should dare not to stand up before him. He was minded to make the most un-European remark, but an observant look at the stationmaster stopped an outburst of gentry indignation. The imprint of grievous suffering was visible on the stationmaster's pale and sunken face, and a sort of strange lifelessness was expressed in his whole being.

"You're ill?" asked Ivan Vasilyevich.

"Yes, sir," answered a weak voice, "this is the second year that both arms, both legs have given out."

On a featherbed, upon which the ossified stationmaster was sitting, lay three children. The oldest boy was gazing at his father with a look of sympathy and pity, the others rolled in the feathers and begged pitifully for bread or wrapped themselves up in the fragments of a tattered blanket.

"Why is it so cold in your house?" asked Ivan Vasilyevich solicitously. "That's bad for a sick man."

"What's one to do, my dear sir? They don't give us firewood: this is a free [i.e., privately owned] station, the landlord is an estate owner, he gives orders not to give us good firewood... that's the way he'll have it. Please look in the stove—all brushwood and dried twigs. You get only smoke from them, they won't catch fire however much you try. I sent to him the other day to see if it would be possible to give us firewood— not a chance! He bellowed: 'I'll throw him out,' he says, 'here's a big highroad, a sick man's no use, go wherever you please!' But you can see for yourself where I can go! See," continued the stationmaster with an envious smile, "it's fine at the next station; a good landowner, firewood three feet long.[126] That's a very good place to live. As for me, I would have been chased out, but thank God the authorities intervened; my little son— here he is beside you—has been allowed to perform my duties. He's only eleven, but he writes already..." The poor sufferer looked with inexpressible tenderness at the fair-haired boy lying in a sheepskin coat beside him. "Now, Vanya, get up, enter in the register... Give me the road pass."

Vanya unfolded before his father's eyes the road pass, then drew a table up to the bed, armed himself with a pen, and waited respectfully for his father to tell him to write.

"Well, ready, Vanya? Write: 'From Moscow to Kazan...' Thanks to the authorities, I wasn't driven out, they intervened... 'According to the road pass of the civil governor of Moscow...' And thanks to the travellers passing through, no one complained, thank God. I've always tried... 'On the second of October...' Written already?... they were free to do as they pleased... 'Number 7273...' All kinds of courtesy. Thank God, they're sympathetic... 'For a Kazan landowner...' A doctor came through the other day, such a kind man! He advised me to go to the city to be treated. Me! Go with what? Where would I get the money? Go in what? I can't stir! I'll treat myself as it is somehow or other with simple means, but the best thing is to pray to God."

"A strange thing!" thought Ivan Vasilyevich reflectively. "When I came into this room I was inclined to be angry and contemptuous, or at least to mock my fill; but now, to tell the truth, I'm almost inclined to cry."

He glanced at his fellow conversationalists. They were diligently drinking each his fourth cup of tea.

XIX

The East

"Kazan! Tatars! The East!" exclaimed Ivan Vasilyevich joyfully as he woke up. "Kazan! Ivan the Terrible... turquoise, soap, dressing gowns... The tsardom of Kazan... The gateway to Asia. At last I'm in Kazan... Who would have thought it, but we really have arrived. We've come to the East; though not quite the East, still, in the neighborhood... Why, it's already a different kind of village we've come to on the roads, with mosques, window-less huts, women who hide from our tarantas, covering their faces with dirty pieces of linen... It's already rare for an Orthodox 'beard' to turn up on the road... It has already become more picturesque. Some little Tatar, with a shaven head, dressed in a *chibiteika*, comes walking along, or a stupid Chuvash, or a Mordvin woman in all her finery. Everything's better. Take up your pen, Ivan Vasilyevich! Take it up quickly! Wait for inspiration, but write in the meanwhile... Write your observations... Begin your impressions."

"A Tatar comes walking along, a Chuvash comes walking along, a Mordvin woman comes walking along... Well, what more?"

"I've seen a Tatar, I've seen a Chuvash, I've seen a Mordvin woman—Well, and what's there in this?"

"Here's what!" exclaimed Ivan Vasilyevich with rapture. "Here's what!... A gap in our history must be filled in. I must write a short but significant chronicle of eastern Russia... Cast an eagle eye upon the deeds and way of life of the nomadic peoples. This once was the Mordvin tsardom, which broke in two and threatened Nizhny with enslavement under the leadership of its chieftain Purgas. It once was the Bulgar tsardom with seven cities, and enormous commerce. A multitude of people lived here; they came from no one knows where, wandered away no one knows whither, and disappeared leaving neither trace nor memorial... What about that!"

At this point Ivan Vasilyevich's ardor cooled down some.

"But where are the sources?" he thought.

"Sources will be found somewhere. But how to find them?"

No, Ivan Vasilyevich, this task, it seems is not for you. You want to get to the goal faster. And indeed, who would be eager to sacrifice his whole life to something that might still prove to be rubbish.

"Shouldn't I write in a business-like style some sort of formal statistical article? 'Kazan. Width. Length. Topography. History. Quarters. Commerce. Manners.'

"Here it could be mentioned that I stayed in Melnikov's hotel, that so much is paid for a meal, so much for tea. In Kazan there are a hundred hotels, which indicates the flourishing condition of the town and its commercial importance. There are so and so many houses, so and so many baths.

"No, Ivan Vasilyevich, this would no longer be a living impression, but something of the nature of a report written under the compulsion of the service, or a note from the provincial newspapers. Then how should it be?

"Surely posterity mustn't be deprived of a fine work?

"It would be possible to say a word about the university and about all universities in general. The university here is famous in Europe for its observatory, for its mathematical faculty, and in particular for its study of oriental languages. But I don't know them.

"They say the library here is good. There are many manuscripts. I don't know how to read them, but still I like them.

"I remember the most important ones.

"Oriental ones with beautiful sketches and arabesques which can in time be borrowed for the adornment of our architecture. A Hebrew one: the Pentateuch of Moses, written on fifty skins and rolled up in an enormous scroll.

The Book of 1703, and in it a list of boyars, okolnichie and dumnye liudi and blizhnie liudi and striapchie and young dvoriane and clerks and zhiltsy.[127]

Travels of stolnik Peter Tolstoi through Europe in the year 1697.[128]

Order and accession of the Great Princes to the Tsardom. Marriages of Tsar Mikhail Feodorovich and of Alexei Mikhailovich.

On the arrivals of the holy universal patriarchs in Moscow according to the letters to them from Tsar Alexei Mikhailovich.

Register of who sat [as judges] *in the Department* [*Prikaz*] *of Justice in the year 1613.*

List of Departments.

Military Code of Tsar Vasily Ivanovich Shuisky.

Traité d'Arithmétique par Alexandre de Souvoroff, written in his own hand by Suvorov in childhood.

"Besides this, the whole library of the books of Prince Potemkin-Tavrichesky."

"Wow!" said Ivan Vasilyevich, "all this is undoubtedly important, but all this has to be read...

"It would be simpler to take Mr. Rybushkin's description of Kazan and copy something from it.[129] And in order to give a learned look, which will deceive only a few, but will deceive somebody, I shall lose myself in conjectures about the origin of the city's name.

"There are many among us who have a reputation for learning through the learning of others.

"Many, like myself, would begin their book with the following:

It is asserted that the name of the city of Kazan is derived from the Turkish word

$$خَازَن$$

which signifies an iron kettle.[130]

"Whatever you may say, this word, which neither I nor the reader will know how to pronounce," observed Ivan Vasilyevich, "will immediately contribute to my introduction a certain dignified and attractive color.

Not everyone will write

ذَا زِن

Not everyone knows that

خَا زِن

and an iron kettle are one and the same.

"But if you think about it, what does anyone care about this? Now the time for empty words and playing the charlatan is passing. And is it worth bothering about to know whether the servant of a certain Altyn-bek unintentionally dropped the kettle into the river while drawing water for his master? This will do nothing for him. This is pure nonsense. Even if khans did drink water out of kettles—on this we have no particulars."

Suddenly Ivan Vasilyevich smote himself on the brow.

"At last!" he cried with inspiration. "At last I've found my novel, profound, resounding outlook... I'm Russian. I've devoted myself to Russia. Whether she will thank me or not is not the question. I'm giving all my labor, all my thoughts to my native land, and accordingly other subjects can have for me only a relative value. And I shall study the influence of the East on Russia, in its relations toward Russia alone, an indisputable influence, an important influence, a threefold influence: ethical, commercial and political.

"First I shall begin with the ethical influence, which since ancient times has been carrying on a stubborn struggle upon our soil with the influence of the West. Both foes long ago flew into a fury and hurled themselves into hand to hand combat with one another, not noticing that between them they were squeezing the poor, emaciated Slavonic principle. Wouldn't it be better, it would seem, to make peace and from both sides take their innocent victim by the hands and bring her into the pure air and give her a chance to set herself to rights and regain her health. Let each one of them make confession of his heart to her, set her on the true path, pointing to the fatal consequences of its own errors, and the dazzling rewards of its own virtues. And in truth Russia does find herself in a strange position. Europe on the left, like a perfidious charmer, keeps whispering seductive words into her ear; the East on the right, like a gloomy gray-haired old man, drawlingly but threateningly, keeps repeating to her his eternally unvarying word. Which should she listen to? Listen to both. Turn to neither, but go ahead on her own path. Listen in order to make use of the experience of another, the misfortunes of another, the peculiar lessons of another, and thus more hopefully, more surely strive toward truth. In the East every conviction is sacred. In the West there are no more convictions. In the East feeling is master, in the West the idea dominates. But Russia's destiny is to merge in herself idea and feeling in the rays of enlightenment, as in the sky the colors of the rainbow merge from the bright rays of the sun. The East despises the vanity of the demands of everyday life—the West is perishing in their incessant collision. And here a mean can be found. It is possible to merge the desire for improvement with a peaceful, lofty quietude, with unshakable fundamental principles. We owe much to the East. It has given us the sense of deep faith in the destinies of providence, the beautiful custom of hospitality, and particularly the patriarchal character of our national everyday life. But, alas! It has also given us sloth, its aversion to the successes of humanity, an unforgivable indifference toward the obligations imposed on us, and worst of all, the spirit of a sort of peculiar, subtle slyness, which, as a national element, appears among us in all the ranks of society without exception. With a beneficent direction this slyness can become a good quality and even a virtue, but in the absence of spiritual education it leads to the most lamentable consequences. It leads to insincerity in mutual relations, to disregard for others' property, to a constant secret striving to disobey the law, not to carry out orders, and finally even to the most immoral rascality. We owe it to the East that so many muzhiks and craftsmen deceive us in their work, so many merchants cheat us with false weight and false measure in their shops, and so many noblemen destroy the name of an honest man in the state service. It is a terrible thing to say—but habit in us has brought it about that we remain indifferent when we are witnesses of the most illegal spoliations, so that even our original concepts are altered with the years and theft does not seem to us to be robbery, deceit does not seem to be a lie, but rather some kind of precautionary necessity. But then, thank God, here the East has been overcome by the West, and a vengeful torch has lit the abyss of trick and shame. For a long time the traces of the routed principle will still appear with us, but these traces have long since passed into the dregs of all classes, into the lowest strata of people of various denominations, for every class has its riffraff. Whatever you may say, whatever you may shout, whatever you may print, Russia is pressing forward in swift flight on the path of greatness and glory—toward the goal, unattainable on earth, of perfection. And more than all other nations Russia will approach it, because she will never forget that material well-being alone is exactly as insufficient for the life of a state as it is insufficient for the life of an individual person. With a broad and mighty heel she will crush the petty reptiles, the bloodthirsty vipers which would stealthily get to her heart, and she will gaily start back, full of love and power, toward the pure, illimitible Russian sky...

"Here," concluded Ivan Vasilyevich, "is a subject that is a subject! Ethical influence, commercial influence, political influence. The eastern influence merged with the influence of the West in the Slavonic character indubitably constitutes our national character. But how is each element to be recognized separately? This national character, it seems, is properly entangled. It must be unswaddled in order to get at it, but then how are you going to know what is swaddling and what is leg? Be a man, Ivan Vasilyevich! It's a great task! You've landed in the East for a reason; so study assiduously the influence of the East on Russia... Seek out, seek out your impressions now. Scrutinize the eastern peoples. Study everything to the last detail. Inspect every drop that has been poured into our national life—and then you will find the national character. To work, Ivan Vasilyevich, to work!"

The First Impression

"Master, don't you want a dressing gown, a real khan's dressing gown such as our khan wears?"

"Master, don't you want some turquoise? The very best. Not painted."

"Master, don't you want some Chinese pearls?"

"Chinese ink?"[131]

"Chinese *kashma?*"[132]

"Chinese mirror?"

"*Ergak*, best quality?"[133]

"Chinese ink, master, Chinese ink, master?"

"I'll sell cheap."

"I need the money."

Ivan Vasilyevich raised his head. While he had been preparing himself for his first impression, the room had been filling up with Tatars with expressive faces, who wore *chibiteiki* and carried goods under their arms. They were all talking together, all bowing and smiling; each clutched first at his cotton or red calico caftan, pulled out some yellowish folded paper from his bosom and then, throwing himself on the floor, began to unwrap bundles with dressing gowns and various wares.

Ivan Vasilyevich's eyes raced back and forth. In the first place he had become accustomed while abroad to revere Asiatic wares; secondly, he was of those Russians who can't look into a shop without finding the urge to buy everything in it. Every sort of gaudy trash in the way of wares has for such people a certain invincible charm. Ivan Vasilyevich forgot about the influence of the East and his beautiful researches. He was suddenly animated by a new feeling: he had taken an extraordinary liking to a striped dressing gown.

"What's the price?" he asked.

"The final price is 300 rubles. You won't find another... They don't make them any more... Oh, take it, master. You'll be satisfied... A prince came from Petersburg, took two such dressing gowns. Seven hundred rubles he paid. Don't be stingy, master. For you I'll let it go for 250... Master, I see you're a good man. Buy it, really. Just look, what a dressing gown... On both sides... You wear it this side out... Turn it inside out—a new dressing gown. Well, take it for 200 rubles... I need the money... Otherwise I wouldn't have let it go... What a dressing gown, and they don't make them any more... The final, really the final... Well, all right, 150. I see you're a good man... For a start, I'll sell it at a loss."

"And turquoise?"

"Give five gold rubles. You'll be getting it for nothing."

"And pearls, and a mirror, and Chinese ink?"

"Five rubles. Ten rubles. Twenty rubles. Buy, master, you'll be getting them for nothing. Mighty cheap. Buy for a start... Only for you, because you're a good gentleman. If you don't buy, you'll be sorry. Need the money."

Ivan Vasilyevich couldn't hold out against such temptation. He emptied his whole purse on the table, and the nimble Tatars, quickly dividing the money up among themselves, rushed, jostling each other, to the door and scattered in the corridor.

At that moment in the adjoining room was heard a resounding yawn, and Vasily Ivanovich began to stir, sigh quietly, and finally get up from his couch. Soon the door of his room was thrown open and he, in frank morning disarray, covered with nothing but his sheepskin coat, made his appearance at Ivan Vasilyevich's joyful invitation.

Ivan Vasilyevich was sitting in his new variegated dressing gown, with some greenish yellow turquoise in his hand. On the table in front of him were lying in yellow papers some kind of mutilated shells, two pieces of Chinese ink, and a tiny mirror.

"Vasily Ivanovich!"

"What is it, my dear fellow?"

"Do you see these things?"

"I do."

"Put a price on them, please."

Vasily Ivanovich looked with disdain at the alleged treasures.

"The dressing gown," he replied, "at the factory in Moscow where they make them, is worth thirteen rubles and a half. For that worthless turquoise even a ruble is a lot. The Chinese ink might be worth half a ruble. But why do you want Chinese ink, Ivan Vasilyevich? You don't sketch, it seems?"

"I don't sketch, Vasily Ivanovich, but still it's interesting to have such a thing."

"And, my dear fellow, what the devil are you going to do with it?"

"Well, what about the rest?"

"The rest I wouldn't advise you to take for a gift. And what did you give?"

"Everything I had in my purse," answered Ivan Vasilyevich ruefully. "My first impression," he added mentally, "I won't put into my work."

Vasily Ivanovich roared with laughter.

"Oh, those Tatars are rascals! That's the way they give babies like you a lesson. Ha, ha, ha! That's a fact. Don't buy turquoise another time!"

"Senka!" he yelled suddenly.

Senka entered.

"Have they greased the tarantas?"

"Yes, sir."

"Order it hitched up."

"What!" asked Ivan Vasilyevich in horror, "You mean to go?"

"What do you suppose? To buy dressing gowns, I guess?..."

"Put it off for just a day. Give me a chance to see Sumbeka's tower."[134]

"What for?"

"I want to study the East."

"You don't say! But this isn't the East, just Kazan."

"The faces here are eastern. A Tatar population."

"My dear fellow, I guess you've already learned to know the Tatars! That should be enough for you. Tomorrow we'll be in Mordasy. I'm lonesome for Avdotya Petrovna and my old men. I've got plenty to do. You can study the East, if you want to, another time..."

Willy-nilly Ivan Vasilyevich climbed angrily into the tarantas alongside his traveling companion... The tarantas lumbered out of Kazan along a broad road. And soon the city walls and the tall towers were lost from view, and the tarantas drove on and on into a broad, level plain... And now woods disappeared, and valleys, and inhabited places. The bare steppe opened up, spread out in all directions, like a fettered sea... Scraggly feather-grass barely swayed in the broad sweep of the unobstructed wind... Clouds raced like white waves across the sky... An eagle, spreading his wings, was soaring in the measureless height... In all nature there breathed a mysterious, sombre majesty. Everything was reminiscent of death and at the same time merged into a kind of obscure concept of eternity and life illimitible...

XX

A Dream

In the late evening the tarantas was rolling along over the broad steppe. It was growing dark. Finally night came on, covering the whole neighborhood with a dark curtain.

"What's this?" said Ivan Vasilyevich in agitation. "What has Vasily Ivanovich done with himself? Vasily Ivanovich! Vasily Ivanovich! Where are you? Where are you, Vasily Ivanovich?"

Vasily Ivanovich did not answer.

Ivan Vasilyevich rubbed his eyes.

"Strange, an outlandish thing," he continued. "It seems to me, you know, that we're in the dark, and now it seems that the tarantas is not a tarantas at all... A big cockroach, it looks like... It's running just like a cockroach... No, now it's like a bird rather... But nonsense, it can't be... But whatever you say, it is a bird, a large bird, I don't know what kind. There aren't any such birds of such enormous size. And has anyone ever heard of such a thing, that tarantasses only pretend to be vehicles, and are really birds? Ivan Vasilyevich, you aren't going out of your mind? This is what you've come to, brother, with your ravings. Pfui! I'm getting scared. A bird, decidedly a bird!"

And in fact, Ivan Vasilyevich was not mistaken. The tarantas really was becoming a bird. Out of the box was stretching a neck, feet were forming from the front wheels, the back wheels were turning into a thick, broad tail. The feathers had begun to crawl out of the featherbed and the pillows, disposing themselves symmetrically as wings, and now the enormous bird had begun to shuttle from side to side as though intending to rise into the air.

"No, nonsense!" said Ivan Vasilyevich, "To be left alone in the steppe at night—no, thank you! You, if you please, may pretend to be a bird, but you don't fool me, I know that you're nothing but a tarantas. I ask you to keep carrying me on whatever you please and as you please. That's your business."

Here Ivan Vasilyevich grabbed hold with his hands of the fantastic creature's enormous neck, and letting his legs down over the wings on both sides, he waited, not without some agitation of soul, for what would come of all this.

And lo, the strange bird—eagle but not eagle, turkey but not turkey—began to rise quietly. First it stretched out its neck, then it squatted to the ground, shook itself, and then suddenly, with a flap of its wings, it rose up and started flying.

"I've really got the impression I've been waiting for," he thought, "and of the vulgarest, stupidest kind. It just had to be this kind of misfortune! I look for a contemporary, national, living impression—and after long, vain waiting, what I get is some sort of ridiculous, fantastic story. As a general rule

I can't stand this imitative, warmed-over, fantastic genre... What an annoying thing! Have I been fated to search all my life for the truth, and all my life get nothing but nonsense?"

In the mean time the darkness was terrible and becoming ever more impenetrable. The atmosphere had suddenly become stifling. The dreadful sepulchral damp threw Ivan Vasilyevich into a fever. Little by little he began to feel that heavy vaults were closing over his head. It seemed to him that he was being carried no longer in the air, but in some sort of stifling cave. And as a matter of fact he was flying in a narrow, dark cave, and from the ground there was wafted to him a kind of cold as of the tomb. Ivan Vasilyevich was frightened in earnest.

"Tarantas!" he said plaintively, "good tarantas! Nice tarantas! I believe that you're a bird! Only take me out of here, fly out of here. Save me! I'll remember you all my life!"

The tarantas kept flying.

Suddenly in the yawning void of the cave a red fire began to glow, and against the dark red flame terrible shadows began to detach themselves. Headless corpses with the instruments of torture around their limbs, with their heads in their hands, were walking sedately, slowly, bowing to right and to left, and disappearing in the darkness; and after them were coming other shadows, and there was no end to the bloody procession.

"Good tarantas! Splendid bird!" cried Ivan Vasilyevich. "I'm scared! I'm scared! Listen to me. I'll honor you. I'll feed you. I'll put you in a barn. Only take me out of here!"

The tarantas flew on.

Suddenly the shadows became confused. The cave once more grew black with impenetrable darkness.

The tarantas still flew on.

Some time passed in stifling darkness. Ivan Vasilyevich suddenly began to hear a distant noise which became continually louder. The tarantas quickly turned to the left. The whole cave was illuminated in a moment by a pale yellow radiance, and a new spectacle struck the trembling rider. An enormous bear was sitting, squirming, upon a stone, and playing a dance tune on a balalaika. Around him ugly monsters, with whistling and guffawing, were dancing, with the Cossack squat, some sort of repulsive trepak. It was disgusting and terrible to look at them. What faces! What figures! Pokers in official uniforms, bats with spectacles, dandies attired in fluffy feathers with a visting card instead of a face beneath a hat worn at an angle; little children with enormous dried-up inkwells on their infantile shoulders, women with moustaches and wearing jack-boots, drunken leeches in long-tailed frock coats, powdered apes in French caftans, paper snakes with embroidered collars and fine little swords, asses with beards, brooms with aprons, ABC-books on stilts, peasant huts on chicken legs, dogs with wings, pigs, frogs, rats... and all this was hopping, turning, jumping, squealing, roaring, so that the very walls of the cave shook to their foundations and trembled spasmodically, as though frightened by the hellish revelry of the raging monsters...

"Tarantas!" wailed Ivan Vasilyevich, "I adjure you in the name of Vasily Ivanovich and Avdotya Petrovna, don't let me perish in the flower of my years. I'm still young. I'm still unmarried... Save me!..."

The tarantas flew on.

"Aha! Here's Ivan Vasilyevich!" shouted someone in the crowd.

"Ivan Vasilyevich! Ivan Vasilyevich!" took up the monstrous rout in chorus. "We've been waiting for that scum! Ivan Vasilyevich! Give him here! We'll give him what for, the villain! We'll teach the darling boy! We'll receive him with cudgels, we'll make him dance! Let him dance with us! Let him croak! Now we've got him. Hee-hee-hee! Brother! You've been mighty stuck up. You looked for light. We'll light you up in our own way. What a great figure!... And you don't like dirt and you disapprove of bribes, and you don't care for twilight. But we here are bribes ourselves, children of darkness and light, twilight ourselves, children of light and darkness. Hee-hee-hee! Tally-ho, get him!... Tally-ho, get him! Don't slack up, boys!... Get him! Grab him, grab him, grab him ! Bring him here for judgment, the villain! We'll show him! Hee...hee...hee..."

And the brooms and the pokers, all the disgusting, ugly monsters began to come on, to rush, to fly in pursuit of Ivan Vasilyevich.

"Stop, stop!" cried hoarse voices, "Get him! Grab him! We'll give it to him, the scoundrel! You won't get away now... We've got you!... Seize him, seize him!"

"Police!" roared Ivan Vasilyevich in despair.

But the good tarantas comprehended the danger. It began suddenly to ply its wings more powerfully, and doubled the speed of its flight. Ivan Vasilyevich closed his eyes and was neither dead nor alive, riding on his strange hippogriff. He was already feeling the touch of hairy paws, sharp claws, shaggy wings; the hot, poisonous breath of the hellish crowd was already burning his shoulders and back... But the tarantas flew on dauntlessly. And now it is ahead... And now at last the devilish pursuit is fainting, tiring, and storming and yelling and cursing... But the tarantas pressed ahead ever more dauntlessly, ever more powerfully. And now at last they have tired out altogether; and now their raging is already far in the rear... But for a long time still in Ivan Vasilyevich's ears resound the abuse, the mockery, the curses, and the squealing, whistling and repulsive laughter... Finally the yellow flame began to fade... The hellish uproar turned once more into a dull hum which became more and more distant and less and less clear and gradually began to disappear. Ivan Vasilyevich opened his eyes. Everything around him was dark, but a cool breeze was already blowing upon him. Little by little the vaults of the cave began to grow wider and wider and merged gradually with the transparent air. Ivan Vasilyevich felt that he was free and that the tarantas was rushing high, high across the steppe of the sky.

Suddenly in the vault of the sky a ray of sunlight flashed like lightning.

The sky passed gradually through all the rainbow hues of the dawn, and the earth began to be distinguishable. Ivan Vasilyevich, bending across the tarantas, gazed in wonderment: beneath him spread a panorama of a vast expanse which was becoming more and more clear in the first gleaming of the rising sun. Seven seas were heaving all around it, and upon the seven seas the dots that were the sails of countless vessels were tossing. A mountainous ridge, flashing with gold, forged with iron, stretched from north to south and from west to east [the Urals]. Enormous rivers, like life-giving veins, flowed in every direction, intertwining and pouring out everywhere abundance and life. Forests were set between them like a broad meadow. Fat fields burdened with the harvest were waving in the pre-dawn wind. Cities and big villages in the midst of these were as colorful as bright stars, and dense ribbons of roads stretched from them like rays in all directions. Ivan Vasilyevich's heart began to beat hard. It began to grow light. Suddenly the whole enormous expanse became illuminated with a friendly, uniform life; everything began to bustle and seethe. First bells began to ring, summoning to morning prayers; then solicitous farmers scattered over fields and cornlands, and on the whole earth there was not a place where prosperity did not shine, there was not a corner where toil was not in evidence. Upon all the rivers flew steamboats, and the treasures of whole kingdoms changed places with incredible speed and everywhere supplied wealth and repose. Strange carriages and tarantasses unknown to Ivan Vasilyevich began to fly and race back and forth from city to city over mountains and steppes, carrying whole populations with them. Ivan Vasilyevich held his breath. The tarantas began to descend slowly. The golden cupolas of the towns sparkled in the morning light. But one city sparkled brighter than the others, with its churches and royal palaces, and it spread out in proud expansiveness over a whole region. Mighty heart of a mighty realm, it stood seemingly as a bogatyr guard and protected the whole state with its strength and solicitude. Ivan Vasilyevich's soul was filled with rapture. His eyes began to sparkle. "Great is the Russian God! Great is the Russian land!" he exclaimed involuntarily, and just at that moment the sun began to play with all its rays over Russia beloved of heaven, and all the peoples from the Baltic to far Kamchatka inclined their heads and as it were merged together in a friendly prayer of thanksgiving, in a victorious triumphal hymn of glory and love.

Ivan Vasilyevich quickly descended to the ground, and as he descended the tarantas once more exchanged its bird-like exterior for a more seemly aspect. Its neck became the carriage box once more, its tail and feet became wheels, the feathers alone did not merely collect into the featherbeds, but were carried freely about in the air. The tarantas had become a tarantas again, not clumsy and dishevelled as Ivan Vasilyevich had known it, but polished, lacquered, graceful—in a word, a perfect, dashing youngster. The boxes and the cords had disappeared. The mattings and the bags as it were had ceased to exist. Their place was taken by small chests covered with hide, and tightly attached to the places designed for them. The tarantas has been as it were reborn, reeducated, and made young. In its firm tread there was no trace of its former slovenliness; on the contrary, on it was impressed a kind of confidence, a feeling of inalienable dignity, even of a little pride.

"Hey, Vasily Ivanovich made it," thought Ivan Vasilyevich involuntarily, "a long vehicle, it's true, but quite suitable for steppe travel. Moreover it's not devoid of originality, and riding in it is extremely pleasant... But where is he in fact? Vasily Ivanovich! Vasily Ivanovich! Where are you? Vasily Ivanovich is gone. Surely he isn't lost, disappeared completely? A pity for the old man! He was a good person. He's gone all right. He fell out somewhere on the road. Shouldn't we stop and look for him?" But it was impossible to stop. A dashing three-horse team was harnessed to the tarantas, the driver gave a merry shout, and Ivan Vasilyevich began to gallop along with such incredible speed as he had never yet experienced, even when in former times he had ridden around on official business with a courier's pass. The tarantas kept speeding ahead without a halt over a road as smooth as a mirror. The horses were changed imperceptibly, and the tarantas rolled on farther and farther past fields, villages and cities. The lands through which he was speeding seemed familiar to Ivan Vasilyevich. It must be he had often been there at some time, on business of his own and on official duties—but everything, it seemed, had taken on a different look...Places where formerly were immeasurable barren expanses, swamps, steppes, wildernesses, now were alive with people, with animation and activity. The forests were cleaned up and kept as national treasures. The fields and corn lands, like varicolored seas, were spread out to the horizon, and the blessed soil was everywhere bearing an abundant reward for the cultivators' cares. Herds are pasturing picturesquely on the meadows, and little villages, scattering cultivators around them like their own symmetrical shadows, are, as it were, watching over the saving of time and of human labor. Everywhere you look, abundance, everywhere enlightened care. The villages through which the tarantas was speeding were Russian villages. Ivan Vasilyevich had even often been in them. They kept their former, original exterior, only they were cleaned up and improved like the tarantas itself. The black huts, the straw-thatched roofs, all the ugly marks of poverty and neglect, had completely disappeared. On both sides of the road rose buildings with iron roofs, brick walls, colorful tile facings at the windows, and finely wrought railings and ornaments... On the broad oaken doors were fastened signs which gave token that in the long winter days the master of the house did not spend his time in drunkenness, did not toss idly on the loft-bed, but brought benefit to his brothers with a profitable craft, thanks to the Russian people's capacity for imitating and making everything, and thereby enhanced his own prosperity as well. On the streets there was no sign of either drunkards or beggars... For frail shelterless old people alms-houses were constructed at the churches, and there were also shelters for looking after small children while their fathers and mothers were occupied with work in the fields. To the shelters were attached hospitals and schools... schools for all children without exception. At the doors, shaded by trees, colorful crowds of little children were playing, and in their unconstrained gaiety was evidence that the hours of labor had not gone by for nothing, that they were constantly and patiently preparing themselves for a useful life, an honorable name, and praiseworthy labor... and the rustic shepherd [i.e., priest], sitting beneath a broom-bush, looked lovingly upon the childish games. Here and there among the trees rose the landowners' houses, constructed in the same taste as the simple cottages, only on a larger scale. These houses seemed to stand as guardians of order, as a pledge that the happiness of the realm would not be altered, but thanks to the wise solicitude of its enlightened leaders, all would still strain forward, all would develop still further, glorifying the works of man and the loving-kindness of the Creator.

The cities through which the tarantas was dashing also seemed familiar to Ivan Vasilyevich, although there was much in them which he did not recognize. The streets did not stand like sad wastes, but were alive with movement and people. And nowhere were there fences in place of houses, houses with a mournful exterior, with broken windows and a ragged rabble at their doors. There were no ruins, tottering walls, filthy little shops. On the contrary, the houses pressed together like friends, shone with gay cleanliness. The windows gleamed like mirrors, and the carefully wrought ornaments gave the beautiful facades a sort of Slavonic, national, original outward look. And from this outward look it was not hard to conclude in what good order, in what spirit the life of the citizens flowed—an immeasurable multitude of signs gave token on all sides of the region's commercial activity... Enormous hotels enticed travellers into their clean rooms, and over the golden cupolas resounding bells intoned blessing upon the brotherly family of the Orthodox.

And lo, before Ivan Vasilyevich gleamed a whole assemblage of shining cupolas, a whole region of palaces and buildings... "Moscow," cried Ivan Vasilyevich... and in a moment the tarantas disappeared as though it had sunk through the ground, and Ivan Vasilyevich found himself on Tverskoi Boulevard at the very same spot where only recently, it seemed, he had met Vasily Ivanovich and arranged with him to ride to Mordasy. Ivan Vasilyevich was amazed. Age-old trees covered the boulevard with broad, thick shade. At its sides palaces stood in beauty, of such a light, such a beautiful architecture that the mere sight of them filled the soul with a noble love for the beautiful, with a comforting feeling of harmony. Every building seemed a temple of art, and not a pretentious showplace of senseless luxury... "Italy... Italy... Have we not really outdone you in finery!" exclaimed Ivan Vasilyevich and suddenly stopped. It seemed to him that the prince was approaching him, the same one whom he had once met on the highway in a *dormeuse*, the one who always lives abroad and journeys to Russia with no end but to collect the quit-rent from his peasants.

"It can't be," he thought, "yet it does seem to be the prince... But he's surely abroad... and what's more, is he coming from a masquerade, in such an outfit?"

Coming toward Ivan Vasilyevich was in very fact the prince, only not in an aspect such as he had known him formerly. On his head was a beaver-fur hat, his upper body was tightly laced in by a light fabric jacket trimmed with sable fur, and on his feet the yellow morocco boots indicated, according to Slavonic custom, his noble rank.[135] He recognized his old acquaintance and greeted him politely.

"Greetings, old friend," he said.

"How is this, prince... So this is really you?... I would never have recognized you in this costume."

"Why so?... This costume is perfectly appropriate for our northern cold, and besides, it's our own, our national costume, and I wear no other."

"I didn't know, sorry. I didn't know this at all... But I supposed, prince, that you were abroad."

"What?"

"I supposed that you were abroad."

"Abroad where?"

"Why, in the West..."

"Why?"

"Just to be there."

"Please!... We have our own west, our own east, our own south and our own north... If you want to travel... Right here you won't get over all your own country in an entire lifetime."

"Of course, that's true, prince... However, you have to admit yourself that abroad we find not only satisfaction but also useful lessons."

The prince looked at Ivan Vasilyevich with wonderment.

"What sort of lessons?"

"Examples."

"What sort of examples?"

"Why, enlightenment and the freedoms."

The prince began to laugh.

"Please... These are nothing but words... We are not children, thank God. It's unseemly for us to concern outselves with charades and to take names for facts. I see, however, with satisfaction that you read history—praiseworthy occupation. You are talking about that time when uninvited loudmouths used to wail about the fate of the common people [*narodov*: not "nations" here], not so much for the peoples' good, as in order that their own voice might be heard. But the common people, you know, have themselves long since guessed that all this noise was a cover-up for petty calculations, private passions, personal self-love, or youthful fire. Believe me, if the common good has been advanced, this has been from our own strength, not from resounding proclamations. For every kind of human doing passion is not only destructive, but even deadly. History will show you this, but history is nothing but the past's lessons to the present, for the future. Our beginning was the latest of all, and for this reason we have not fallen into the former childish delusions. We have gone quietly ahead, with confidence, with submissiveness and with hope. We made no noise, we shed no blood, we sought no safeguards from lawful authority, but an open, sacred goal, and we have attained it, and exhibited it to the whole world... Through patience we have guessed the answer to a riddle that was simple, but guessed by no one up to now. We have explained to the whole world that freedom and enlightenment are one and the same whole, indivisible, and that the whole is nothing but each man's exact carrying out of the duties imposed upon him."

"You're joking, prince."

"God save me from it! People used to make a lot of noise about their rights, but they always played down their duties. But we Russians have done differently: we have kept a firm hold on our duties, and in this way our right [*pravo*: "justice, truth"] was defined of itself."

"But how did you accomplish this?"

"God blessed our humility. You know, Russia has never been carried away by a spirit of pride, has never desired to serve as an example to other nations, and for this reason God has chosen Russia."

"Is this really the truth, prince?... But still I don't understand how you attained to such happiness."

"We attained it simply, by submitting to the tendency of the age, but not running away with it at full speed. We sought the possible, and did not chase after the unattainable, we separated the human from the ideal. We were not enticed away by empty, inapplicable principles, because we knew that there is no principle which carried to its extreme could not become an absurdity, and worse, a transgression. That is why we have striven to harmonize diverse elements, and not destroy them, not crush them in irrational outbursts. We sought for equilibrium. It is equilibrium that keeps the whole world together, and we have found this equilibrium in love alone. In Christian love is hidden also civic repose and family happiness—everything that we can ask of earth, everything that we should ask of heaven."

"And you didn't meet with obstacles?" inquired Ivan Vasilyevich.

"Without obstacles there would be no success, there would be no human conditions. But in love we found also freedom and strength and victory over hostile principles, we found the unanimous influence of all classes for a great national exploit. The nobility went ahead, carrying out the blessed will of God's Anointed; the merchant class cleared the way, the army defended the land, and the common people cheerfully and confidently moved forward in the direction pointed out to it. And we have overcome both the western evil and the eastern evil, using them as examples, and now, thank God, Russia is sovereign over the universe not by her enormous powers alone, but by her spiritual influence, calming and of high morality."

"I see," observed Ivan Vasilyevich, "that you are still an aristocrat at heart."

The prince smiled and shrugged his shoulders.

"Words again... Empty names again... It's a good thing that you and I are old acquaintances and that I don't repeat your observation. But I'm warning you, you may lower yourself in public esteem if it's known that you still concern yourself with empty prattle about aristocrats and democrats. Now the whole is called by its real name and valued according to its deserts. The parasite who is puffed up with stupid arrogance is just as repulsive as the jaundiced envier of distinction and every kind of success. The hungry envy of beggarly mediocrity is not a bit better than haughty wealth. I am an aristocrat in the sense that I love lofty perfection, lofty genuine distinction, and a democrat because in every man I see my brother. But still, you see, these concepts are not at all at variance, but on the contrary closely tied together."

"Why, he's turned into a regular pedant," thought Ivan Vasilyevich in bewilderment. "He hasn't taken up German philosophy, has he? Philosophy is all the rage in Moscow... Evidently the prince has turned philosopher out of boredom."

Ivan Vasilyevich continued the conversation.

"How do you spend your time here, prince? It's a bit boring, I presume. Do you play lotto for big stakes, or 'drum-sticks' [another game of chance]?"

"What kind of joke is this!" retorted the prince, taking offense a little. "With us only servants play cards, and we sack them for such an evil waste of time. We have, thank God, plenty of occupations. The man who doesn't work is unworthy of the name of man. When we're tired from business, we go to the club."

"The English Club?"

"No, the Russian. There our bright minds congregate, and by listening to their conversation it is always possible to pick up either a new bit of knowledge or a pleasant impression. Would you believe it, all our enormous undertakings, all the improvements of which we are so justly proud, originated in the friendly interchange of opinions and feelings."

"So you live constantly in Moscow, prince?"

"Oh, no, I come to Moscow only seldom—I live for the most part in the county... The service takes a great deal of time."

"You're in the service, prince?"

"Yes... as an assessor."[136]

Ivan Vasilyevich burst into a hearty laugh.

"What are you laughing at?"

"Really, prince.... With your wealth, with your name..."

"That's just why I'm in service... In the first place as a citizen I am bound to give a part of my time to the public good; secondly my advantages as a landholder of distinction are closely connected with the advantages of my district. Finally, by being myself in service I am not taking away from the profitable occupation or craft of a poor man who otherwise might have to assume my office. Thus the government is not supporting penurious ignorance or conscienceless parasites. Safeguarding the laws is not made a source of law-breaking."

"Then you live in a provincial city."

"Sometimes... for the service, sometimes for pleasure. Come visit us.

You'll find much that's curious, many antiquities, many objects, not to mention enormous enterprises concerned with industry and commerce. Our society is serious, a foe of idleness with its pitiable consequences. Come visit us, or better still, come visit me in the country, in my old, ancestral castle. There is something to see."

"I can imagine," broke in Ivan Vasilyevich. "If luxury has become as perfected among us as everything else, what your rooms must be like. I suppose you change the wallpaper and the furniture every year?"

"Heaven forfend! My castle stands as it has been for several centuries. In it are respectfully preserved all the traces of our ancestors' life. It serves in some fashion as a reminder of their actions. Memory of them does not disappear but is passed on from generation to generation, instilling in the children a noble pride and the obligation not to lower the honor of our race. And besides, our grandfathers did not use up their money on trash, but on important local improvements, on books, on the encouragement of art, on grants to the sciences. And so every castle can serve with us as an example of the most interesting studies, the most elegant pleasures... We have a particularly significant collection of paintings."

"Of the Italian school?" asked Ivan Vasilyevich.

"Of the Arzamas school[137]... just imagine, I have a whole gallery of model productions of the famous Arzamas painters..."

"Well, what do you know!" thought Ivan Vasilyevich.

"My library too deserves no small attention."

"Of foreign literature, doubtless?"

"On the contrary. Of foreign literature you will find in my library only the small number of writers of genius, whose works have become the property of mankind. But you will find at my house a full collection of the Russian classics, an interesting collection of our fine journals, which with their useful and conscientious labors have encouraged the nation to take the path of real enlightenment and have become an object of general respect and gratitude. And so, if you can believe it, the reading of journals has become a necessity among all classes. There is not a cottage now in which one would not find the pages of *The Northern Bee* or the volumes of *Notes of the Fatherland*.[138] Our writers are the honor and glory of our native land. In their works there is so much honesty, so much native inspiration, so much usefulness, so much fascination, that one cannot but rejoice at their high and flattering importance in our society... I say, tell me, please... where is Vasily Ivanovich?"

Ivan Vasilyevich was confused. He had completely forgotten about Vasily Ivanovich, and his conscience began to reproach him for it.

"Do you know Vasily Ivanovich?" he asked hesitantly.

"I knew him in my youth... It's a long time since I've seen him. He is a person who is not sharp in conversation, but sensible in a practical way. If all people were as he is, simply without education, our nation would soon become educated. But as it is, we have long been hampered by half-educated loudmouths who have heard of something, but understood little of it... Give my regards to Vasily Ivanovich, if he is alive... And now good-bye... I've had quite a chat with you... Good-bye."

The prince pressed Ivan Vasilyevich's hand and quickly disappeared, leaving his interlocutor in a very thoughtful mood.

"Is not *this* our goal of civic virtue?" he thought.

"Vanya, Vanya!' cried someone suddenly from behind him.

Ivan Vasilyevich turned, and found himself in the embrace of his boarding-school comrade, the same one who had met him on the Vladimir boulevard.

"Vanya, how do you come to be here?" he said in friendly amazement.

"I don't know myself," replied Ivan Vasilyevich.

"Let's go to my house. My wife will be so happy to make your acquaintance. I've spoken to her so often about the happy time when in boarding school you and I sat on the same bench and paid such fervent attention, listened so greedily to the learned lectures of our professors."

"Are you joking?" said Ivan Vasilyevich.

"Oh, brother, how can one help being thankful to those people. I owe to them my soul's repose and my material prosperity. I'm rich because I'm moderate in my desires. I'm not fastidious because I'm always busy. I'm not distracted by the desire to seek distractions, because I find my happiness in family life. In this happiness is contained all my luxury, and thanks to strict order I am still able to divide my surplus with my brothers who possess nothing. Unfortunately there can be no equality on earth; one man can never be the equal of another man. There will always be rich men before whom others will consider themselves poor. Intelligence and culture also have their rich and their poor. But it is the duty of the rich to divide with the poor, and in this is contained their luxury. Let's go to my house."

They set out. Everything was simple in the modest dwelling of Ivan Vasilyevich's comrade, but everything had an air of beautiful elegance, a certain inexpressible reflection of the presence of a beautiful young woman. She smiled welcomingly to Ivan Vasilyevich, and he stood before her in mute reverence. It seemed to him that never before had he seen a woman. She was beautiful not with that foolish brilliant beauty which stirs up the passionate dreams of youth, but in her whole being was something loftily serene, poetically reposeful. On her face, radiant with tenderness, every impression was brightly distinguishable, as on a clear mirror. Her soul looked out of her eyes and her heart spoke from her lips. Upon her half-childish features was reflected such a kindly joyfulness, such solicitous submissiveness, such a high, holy, undistracted love, that every man, just by looking at her, was bound to be made better. In her every motion was an enchanting harmony... She smiled at the entering guest, and two rosy and playful children, confused at sight of a stranger, pressed their curly little heads against her knees. Ivan Vasilyevich gazed at this picture as at something holy, and it seemed to him that he was seeing in her the bright personification of quiet family happiness, that high recompense for all the labors, all the sorrows of man. And whether he stood before this wonderful picture for a short while or a long, he took no note; he did not remember about what he heard, about what he said—only his soul expanded more and more, his feelings became quiet in silent bliss, and his thoughts merged into prayer.

"There *is* a happiness on earth!' he said with inspiration. "There *is* a goal in life... and it consists..."

"Good people, good people help!... A calamity!... help... We're turning over, we're falling!..."

Ivan Vasilyevich suddenly felt a powerful shock, and smacking against something with all his weight, he suddenly woke up from the force of the blow.

"A... what?... What's this?..."

"Good people, help, I'm dying!" Vasily Ivanovich was yelling. "Who would have thought... the tarantas has turned over!"

In very truth, the tarantas was lying in a ditch, wheels up. Under the tarantas Ivan Vasilyevich was lying, stunned by the unexpected fall. Under Ivan Vasilyevich lay Vasily Ivanovich in the most terrible fright. The book of travel impressions was sunk forever at the bottom of a liquid abyss. Senka was hanging head down, caught with his feet on the box...

Only the driver had succeeded in disentangling himself from the traces, and was already standing quite nonchalantly by the overturned tarantas. First he looked all around to see if there were help anywhere, and then he said coolly to the yelling Vasily Ivanovich:

"It's nothing, your honor!"

Notes

1. Tverskoi Boulevard: present Gorky Street.

2. *Rogozhavaia zastava:* the obligatory check-point (*zastava*) on the principal eastern highway to Vladimir; Vasily Ivanovich would have been familiar with this, the route he would take to and from Kazan.

3. Musard (died 1859) was the leader of a large ball-room orchestra in Paris, for which he himself composed dances.

4. Luigi Labiche (1794-1858), opera basso; Giulia Grisi (1811-1869), soprano; Fanny Elsler (1810-1884), Austrian ballerina.

5. Dog Court: a square in the Moscow Arbat district, on Great Molchanovka Street (present Kompozitorskaia Street).

6. A gift of hospitality.

7. Traditional acts before starting on a journey.

8. *povytnik:* a court functionary in charge of correspondence.

9. A less devastating form of the card game "bank."

10. The author has a note here: "At the present time (1855) this accusation is wholly unjust."

11. "Free horses" is the term used for privately owned animals, not part of the government post system.

12. This would amount to about 24 rubles for the 16-verst run to the next station.

13. *belen'ka,* "whitey," is the slang of the time for a 25-ruble note.

14. The disappointed owners of the "free" horses must have received 2 rubles 8 kopecks, unless the general's carriage required two teams of three, in which case they would have had twice the amount.

15. Malek-Adel is the hero of the novel *Matilde ou les Croisades* by Marie Cottin (1770-1807); Count Matvei Ivanovich Platov (1751-1818), Hetman of the Don Cossacks, was a general in the War of 1812; Geneviève of Brabant was a legendary heroine of the French Middle Ages: falsely accused of infidelity by her husband, she was the subject of numerous sentimental tragedies. It should be noted that Sollogub in his description of the typical post-station repeats some of the items in Pushkin's tale "The Stationmaster," particularly the picture of the Prodigal Son on the station wall.

16. The second person singular "*ty,*" normally used only by members of one's family or very close friends.

17. A privy councillor, grade 3 in the Table of Ranks, held a rank equivalent to that of Lieutenant General in the army.

18. The 14th is the lowest grade in the Table of Ranks—that of "collegiate registrar," to which stationmasters were assigned; but it still protected the official from physical assault.

19. The menu is written in a pretentious "foreign" style filled with misspellings and garbled foreign words. The translation attempts to give the general effect of these: *obet* [vow] for *obed* [dinner]; item 1—*li potage* [garbled French]; 2—*tsindron* [garbled German for *zitron,* "lemon"]; 4—*patisha* [this doubtless represents some well-known sauce, not yet identified]; 5—German *reis* [rice, but the Russian *rys'iu* has the ridiculous meaning of "a trot"]; 6—*sapel'sinov* [Russian *s,* "with," with garbled German *Apfelsinen,* "oranges"].

20. *selianka* is defined in an old Russo-German dictionary as "a more or less thin dish of various sorts of meat, with cabbage, onions and cucumbers."

21. *postoianyi dvor*—a private establishment offering travellers a warm place to rest for a few hours, with benches and drinks available.

22. A translation of *La Laitière de Mont-fermeil* of the prolific novelist Charles-Paul de Kock (1793-1871) appeared in St. Petersburg in 1832. *The Brigands' Cave* and *The Bloody Apparition* are now unknown ephemera of the *école frénétique* introduced by such authors as Eugène Sue and Jules Janin and briefly popular in Russia. *Key to the Secrets of Nature* appears to be a translation of a work by Karl von Eckartshausen (1752-1803), a German mystic.

23. The city of Vladimir was named for Vladimir Vsevolodovich Monomakh (1053-1125), Great Prince of Kiev.

24. Vsevolod III Yurevich (1154-1212) built (1197) the Church of St. Demetrius; see note 26.

25. Alexander Yaroslavovich Nevsky (c. 1220-1263), grandson of Vsevolod III, was originally buried in the Church of the Nativity of the Virgin in Vladimir; his body was removed by Peter the Great to St. Petersburg in 1774.

26. Church of St. Demetrius, erected in 1197 by Vsevolod III Yurevich; the Cathedral of the Assumption (Uspensky Sobor) was erected in 1160 by Andrei Yurevich Bogoliubskii (c. 1111 1174).

27. The "ecclesiastical script," containing several letters not found in Peter's civil script, and using a great deal more ornamentation than Ivan Vasilyevich would have been used to, seems to him as incomprehensible as Egyptian writing!

28. i.e, the Uspensky Sobor, see note 26.

29. The boulevard is probably the Nizhegorodskaia, which has a fine view of the river Klyazma and its valley.

30. Alexander Yegorovich Varlamov (1801-1848) was a very popular composer of sentimental songs and romances.

31. A reference to the green uniforms of the civil service.

32. The term *chernaia nemoch'*, literally "black disease," ordinarily means "epilepsy," but a short story of Pogodin's with this title conveys rather the notion of "black despondency," the hopelessness resulting from an inextricable situation, which is evidently the meaning here.

33. Pyotr Fyodorovich Sokolov (1791-1848).

34. That is, people who are ushered into the owner's private "cabinet" or study, not into the drawing-room.

35. A reminiscence of a famous passage in the Orthodox service, "The Prayer of St. Ephraim the Syrian," utilized by Pushkin for a beautiful poem.

36. *uezdnyi gorod*: "Provinces were divided into smaller units termed districts (*uyezdy*), each with a district capital (*uyezdnyi gorod*) as its administrative center. There might be about eight districts in a typical province. Districts did not have governors, but came under the general administrative control of a chief of police, the so-called *ispravnik*." (Ronald Hingley, *Russian Writers and Society 1825-1904*, New York, McGraw Hill Book Co., 1974, p. 193).

37. "Gypsies are a wild folk": A. Nemzer (supplement to the facsile edition *The Tarantas*, M.: 1982, p. 50, note 91) detects reminiscences of Pushkin here: "the constraint of stifling cities (*The Gypsies*) and "I'm stifled here... I want to get away to the woods" (*The Robber Brothers*).

38. Literally, "Don't get angry with me for saying so." The word "sitting" which the proprietor has just used is the term ordinarily employed for spending a while in jail (see examples in Fadeyev's later narrative—, and is a rather too bold term to apply to the gypsies' detention.

39. *chastikha*: the authority in a district (*uchastok* or *stan*) a subdivision of the *uezd* (county) was in the hands of an appointed official called *uchastkovyi* or *stanovyi pristav*; *chastikha* means the wife of such an official.

40. *desiatskie*: local police with beats covering about ten (*desiat'*) households each.

41. Ivan Petrov evidently isn't quite familiar with the stone, and makes it *supirochik* instead of *sapfirchik*.

42. Literally "at the beginning of the meat-eating period," that is, between Christmas and Lent, fasting periods for the Orthodox during which marriages could not be celebrated.

43. Vasily Ivanovich doesn't know much French: he uses the French word *talent*, but sounds the final "t", which would be silent in French.

44. "Literature is one of a thousand ways to make money": Sollogub, through Ivan Vasilyevich, is here expressing the views of the aristocratic circle of writers which had formed around Pushkin, and in 1845 was represented among others by Prince V. F. Odoevsky. The chief representatives of "commercial literature" in 1845 were F. V. Bulgarin and O. I. Senkovsky.

45. *beretsia na otkup*: "let out on concession," like liquor licenses or some taxes.

46. A market district in St. Petersburg frequented by small traders.

47. "Dramas in the manner of Schiller": probably those of Nestor Vasilyevich Kukolnik (1809-1868) are intended here.

48. *shushin*: defined in an old Russo-German dictionary as "In eastern Russia, a colored sarafan, or a smooth sleeved jacket."

49. A *dormeuse* (French "sleeper") is a carriage which rides so easily that one can sleep in it.

50. The prince doesn't remember the common Russian saying *okhota pushche nevoli*, "desire is better than un-desire," which is more or less equivalent to "where there's a will, there's a way." But the uncommon word *nevolia*, "un-desire," in the genitive case to boot, is too much for our Russian prince, and he falls back on the word *nevol'no*, which he substitutes, making nonsense of the saying: "Desire is better than involuntarily!"

51. "Duchess" here is the German *Herzogin*, not the French *Duchesse*: *benvil'skuiu*, however, is obviously a fictitious title: Duchess "of Bathtown."

52. "Our Russian Sergei (Serezha)": A. Nemzer (op. cit. p. 51, note 122) notes here that Sollogub is using the hero of his tale "Serezha" as a character in the background of *The Tarantas*! For the story, see V. A. Sollogub, *Povesti i rasskazy*, M.-L.: GIKhL, 1962, pp. 17-37.

53. *brichka*: the prince, in his complete ignorance of Russian rural life uses a term meaning a light two-wheeled carriage in referring to Vasily Ivanovich's ponderous four-wheeler.

54. Sollogub uses a very archaic and formal word—perhaps "throne"—for a very informal and uncomfortable seat.

55. The Volga, because of a geological tilting of the Russian plain, has a low, marshy (*lugovoi*) left bank, and a steep, hilly (*goristyi*) right bank.

56. *sinodiki*: lists of the dead who have left money to have masses said for their souls.

57. "In our national architecture three principles dominate." The notion that Russian pre-Petrine architecture is a synthesis of elements from Byzantium, from the East via the Muslim Tatars, and from the Renaissance West was a contribution of the artist Gagarin, and is embodied in some of his drawings for Sollogub's work, e.g. the ornamental initial at the beginning of Chapter IV, which shows a Russian *izba* holding with two stout arms a facade consisting of a four-pillared portico with pediment of the Roman Corinthian style. It is also very interestingly illustrated as presumably perfected in the future world of Ivan's dream on page 271 of the facsimile text.

The sketch shows on the right an Italianate church reminiscent of the Pisa cathedral, in the center a church with the characteristic five Byzantine-style cupolas but otherwise looking very much like a central Asian or Indian mosque, and in the right foreground a fantastic spire reminiscent of the style of the Moscow Church of Basil the Blest! In later life Gagarin elaborated his ideas in serious works on architecture.

58. Sollogub is somewhat in error here: it was in the reign of Ivan III rather than in that of his grandson that the influence of Italian Renaissance architecture began to be felt in Russia—e.g. Aristotele Fioravanti and the Uspensky Sobor on the Moscow Kremlin.

59. *kormovoi sinodik*: a listing of donations made for the "feeding" (*korm*) or maintenance of ecclesiastics engaged in prayers for the dead.

60. *opal'nykh liudei*: "people under *opala*, that is the disfavor of the Tsar"; with Ivan the Terrible this is equivalent to "executed."

56. About 300 feet: the 1914 Baedeker of Russia records the event (p. 343): "The Petcherski Convent was originally erected in the reign of Grand-Prince Alexander Vasilyevich, by St. Dionysius, Archbishop of Suzdal and Nizhni-Novgorod (1329), on the spot where the old Petcherskaya suburb now lies, 1/3 M. below the convent. Part of the walls of the old convent, the remains of which are still visible, slid down the slope of the hill in 1596. The reconstruction on the present site was begun by Tzar Feodor I Ivanovitch and completed under Mikhail Feodorovitch Romanov."

62. Vasily Ivanovich is probably hitting here at his companion's elegantly bound but empty "book of travel impressions"!

63. The "common" or "general tillage" (*obshchestvennaia zapaska*) is a plot taken from either the landowner's or the peasants' lands, and assigned to the peasant community as a whole, to be cultivated as a communal obligation, the proceeds to go into a communal chest for such purposes as e.g. buying substitute recruits for the army.

64. Each peasant community was organized as an *obshchestvo*, often called a *mir*: this elected its head man, or *starosta*, periodically reapportioned the communal lands according to the needs of each family, and decided what young men should be sent as recruits to the army. In the matter of recruitment, a peasant who was wealthy enough could pay to have his son exempted from the draft, or funds for this purpose could be taken from the communal chest, where this existed.

65. *barshchina*: obligatory work on the landowner's fields; at this date, this amounted to three work-days a week.

66. *s khozhaistvennym ustroistvom*: small factories engaged for example in making sugar from beets raised on the estate, or linen cloth from home-grown flax, or the like, and with peasants as the work force.

67. *trekha*: the three-day-a-week period of compulsory service owed by the peasant to his landlord.

68. "Lancaster schools": a system devised by the English Quaker Joseph Lancaster (1771-1838), in which better educated boys taught elementary literacy to those with no schooling. In Russia the system was widely used in the army, especially by officers imbued with "Decembrist" principles.

69. *uezdnyi gorod*: see note 36.

70. *zashtatnyi gorod:* a town with no court jurisdiction, but the administrative center of a district—*stan* or *uchastka*.

71. *droga:* the wooden "connecting rod" tying together the front and rear axles.

72. The *shin*, "tire," was of course not pneumatic, but a metal band fastened with nails to the rim of the wheel.

73. *tikhvinka*: a boat capable of carrying from 14 to 82 tons.

74. The phrase *priznatel'no skazat'*, which may be supposed to be a typically lower-class mannerism, recurs in the merchants' speech both where it is appropriate and where it is quite the opposite.

75. Rybna, a popular form from Rybnaia sloboda, the official name at this date for the great grain-trading center, modern Rybinsk, on the Volga between Nizhny Novgorod and Uglich; the 1914 Baedeker of Russia describes it thus: "The capital of a district in the government of Yaroslavl, [it] is a brisk river-port situated on rising ground opposite the mouth of the Tcheksna. It carries on a trade in grain, and is the centre of the caviar industry. It contains 31,500 inhabitants, a number raised in summer to 100,000 and even more." (p. 349) The whole low-lying area north of Rybinsk is covered at present by the huge Rybinsk reservoir. From the port lead the most direct water routes to Moscow and Leningrad.

76. The verb *vykushat'* would usually imply solid food, but *parochka* here seems to mean "cups of tea."

77. Note that the merchants usually use the *plural* even where, as here, the meaning implies the singular.

78. *vprikusochku* means a draft of tea drunk through a lump of sugar.

79. Apparently the speaker is trying to use upper-class language without being quite sure of himself; *zavedenitsa* is an unexampled formation from *zavedenie*, and *politika* seems a rather odd word in this context!

80. A popular saying, with the usual chiming rhyme-words: *dushi—pishi*.

81. *vziatka*: "takings," usually means "bribes," hence the next remark.

82. A game "in which each player tries with a cudgel to knock his opponent's small block of wood out of a pile heaped up in a marked square."

83. *svaika*: a game in which the object is to toss a large bodkin with a big head in such a way as to stick in the ground inside a metal ring.

84. A. Nemzer (op. cit., p, 52, note 175-176) points out that the picture of Vasily Ivanovich's father seems to have been taken from a neighbor of Sollogub's Simbirsk estate.

85. *nedorosl'*: by a law of Peter the Great a nobleman remained legally a minor and was disqualified even for marriage until he leared to read and write—cf. Fonvizin's comedy *The Minor*.

86. These are all old dances, evidently still fashionable in backwoods Kazan; Vasily Ivanovich was born about 1785; his period of service would thus have been about 1801-1810. Curiously, the War of 1812 is never mentioned in connection with his biography.

87. *kosachek*: an exceedingly athletic dance that involves what is called *prisiadka*, or rapid squatting movements.

88. The deferential quality of the second plural and the verb *izvolit'*, always used from inferior to superior, is impossible to convey in English.

89. Matryosha was one of Ivan Fedotovich's coterie of female fools. The implication is clear that "papa" expects his son to satisfy his sexual urge with her.

90. *podbliudnye pesni*: literally "under-the-saucer songs," that is, songs in which one after another various symbolic objects, interpreted by the fortune-teller, are pulled from under an inverted saucer.

91. It was customary to have distinguished people stand in for the bride's parents at weddings.

92. The *krestnyi khod* was the occasion on which the clergy of a rural church carried the cross throughout the village, blessing each household and receiving small gifts of food and drink; cf. Ilya Repin's painting of such a procession.

93. "He has been in Moscow a couple of times": in Chapter VI Vasily Ivanovich remarks: "This is the thirteenth time I've been through."

94. The lady was evidently the scion of one of the numerous petty nobles of Georgia.

95. *siatel'nost'* means literally "radiance," but is used here with its secondary meaning in mind as well, i.e. "Her Highness" or "Her Grace," used of persons of high rank.

96. *Sir Charles Grandison* by Samuel Richardson (1689-1761).

97. Antoine-François Prévost d'Exiles, known as Abbé Prévost (1697-1763), author of *Manon Lescaut*.

98. Marie Jeanne Laboras de Mézières Riccoboni (1714-1792), actress and novelist, author among many other works of *Lettres de Miladi Juliette Catesby* (1758).

99. Ann Radcliffe, nee Ward (1764-1823), English writer of Gothic novels.

100. Mme Sophie Cottin, dame de Risteau (1770-1807), French novelist, author of *Malek-Adel*; see note 15.

101. Adelaida Souza-Bothelo (1761-1836), French author of the novel *Eugène de Rathelin*.

102. Anne-Louise de Stadl-Holstein (1766-1817), author of the novels *Delphine* and *Corinne*.

103. Mme Stéphanie Félicité de Genlis (1746-1830), educator and novelist.

104. *slushaius'*, literally "I hear [you], ma'am."

105. See notes 100 and 101.

106. Charles-François l'Homond (1727-1794), rector of the Université de Paris and author of a famous Latin grammar.

107. Claude-François-Xavier Millot (1726-1785).

108. "All sorts of cock-and-bull stories about us." A probable reference to the notorious book of Marquis A. de Custine, *Russie en l'an 1839*, which enraged Russian nationalists of all parties.

109. A well known confectioner's shop in St. Petersburg.

110. See note 83.

111. *strachek sladkii*: St. John's bread, or carob, has a flavor slightly reminiscent of chocolate, and is widely used in Mediterranean lands in lieu of candy.

112. *kuma*: a woman whose position as godmother of a child has made her "god-sib" [gossip], i.e., "God-kin" to the child's *kum* or "godfather."

113. The speaker uses the illiterate *khrantsus* instead of *frantsus* for "Frenchman," and *turka* instead of *turok*.

114. *nemetskii* as usually in the illiterate language of the time means "foreign" rather than "German."

115. A big foreign word that the speaker had doubtless heard officers use in connection with military discipline, but which he doesn't really understand.

116. "Devil knows what—Avaria": The reading of V. A. Sollogub, *Povesti i rasskazy*, p. 271 is "Aravia"; the facsimile edition, however, has "Avaria," the name of a genuine district in the

Caucasus, which is undoubtedly correct. A. Nemzer in a note on the passage (op. cit., p. 53, note 227) writes: "The soldier... 'unites' the names Avaria (a district in the Caucasus) with Bavaria," a state through which he would have had to go in the 1813 expedition to Paris.

117. *polati*: a broad bed of boards in the warmer upper part of a peasant hut, right under the rafters.

118. *kvass*: the peasant's usual drink, a sour, mildly alcoholic brew made of black bread soaked in water and fermented.

119. Illiterate *barbony* for *barabany*.

120. The army was certainly not provided with a special corps of singers to lead an attack! The general's meaning is: Strike up a lively song as you attack.

121. The *sotskii*, literally "hundred-chief," was the principal official of a peasant *selo* or large village, elected by the community.

122. The *ispravnik*, "corrector," headed the county police force, and together with two assessors (*zasedateli*) constituted the county judiciary. He and the assessors are "elected" to this office "by the gentry," and have to be of gentry rank themselves, though in this case the "little official" is the proprietor of only three serf families.

123. *poklon*: literally "an obeisance," that is, the greeting of an inferior to a superior on a feast day.

124. Apparently the speaker, his wife and six children.

125. This probably means footwear cut to fit, not like the peasant's bast shoes, which could be used on either foot.

126. *trekhpolenye*: a *poleno* was a measure of firewood length equivalent to 12 *vershok*: three of these would come actually to between 4 and 5 feet.

127. *okolnichie*: the second grade of the old nobility after the boyars; *dumnye liudi*: members of the Tsar's crown council; *blizhnye liudi*, "close people," i.e., non-official persons close to the Tsar; *striapchie*: lower officials managing various household matters; *dvoriane* : military holders of state-assigned lands or *pomestiia*; *zhiltsy*: a minor grade of Muscovite service personnel.

128. Peter Andreevich Tolstoi (1645-1729), later ennobled to "Count" Tolstoi by Peter the Great, the first of his line to hold this title, was Peter's ambassador to Turkey in his later years.

129. Mikhail Rybushkin, *Kratkaia istoriia goroda Kazani*, Kazan, 1834.

130. An actual quotation from Rybushkin's book. The Arabic script in which Turkish was written before Kemal Ataturk's reform, conceals the word *kazan*, as it is written in modern Turkish, which signifies "cauldron."

131. What we call "India ink." It was sold in solid bricks and diluted piecemeal for later use.

132. Apparently some kind of seashell.

133. An *ergak* is a warm overcoat, worn by the Cossacks.

134. Sumbeka was the wife of the last khan of Kazan, who committed suicide when Ivan the Terrible took the city. The tower from which she is said to have thrown herself is, according to the 1914 Baedeker, in seven stages and 250 feet high.

135. The last clause of this sentence, with its "yellow morocco boots," was so ridiculed by Vissarion Belinsky that the author omitted it in the 1855 edition of *The Tarantas*.

136. Note that the prince holds the same position as the first of the officials of Chapter XVIII, for the *ispravnik* is only *locum tenens*—his actual rank is that of an assessor!

137. "The Arzamas school": There really was a short-lived and not very distinguished "Arzamas school" of painters, founded in 1802 by A.V. Stupny; it lasted until 1861.

138. "*The Northern Bee... Notes of the Fatherland*": note that *The Northern Bee* was the organ of the ultra-conservative Bulgarin-Senkovsky alliance, while *Notes of the Fatherland* was at this time under A.A. Kraevsky one of the two leading liberal periodicals.

Translator's Afterword

Literary and Ideological Aspects of Sollogub's *Tarantas*

Count Vladimir Alexandrovich Sollogub (1813-1882), while not exactly a *homo unius libri*, is so firmly linked with *The Tarantas* that few people associate him with anything else. He did, however, contribute to Russian literature a number of prose tales ("The Story of Two Galoshes," 1839, a sentimental tear-jerker, was at one time the favorite of romantic maiden ladies), and quite a repertory of clever, superficial, but very "well made" comedies and vaudevilles. *The Tarantas*, however, stands out in his production, not so much for its literary quality—it is a very uneven piece—as for the views on Russian life in a wide variety of manifestations which constitute its principal matter. These views, chiefly attributed to the more vocal of the two protagonists, Ivan Vasilyevich, were associated by some of Sollogub's contemporaries with those of the Slavophiles, although several avowed Slavophiles indignantly repudiated Sollogub's hero as a spokesman for their cause. Indeed the views expressed, whether by Ivan Vasilyevich or by the author himself, seemed to many more akin to the abhorred 'official nationalism' of S.S. Uvarov, Nikolai I's minister of education. It will be the task of this essay to examine the work in some detail to determine, if possible, the true place of *The Tarantas* both as a piece of literature and in the ideological controversies of the time.

The genesis of *The Tarantas* goes back to the autumn of 1839, when Sollogub and Grigory Grigoryevich Gagarin made a journey together from Moscow to Sollogub's Simbirsk estate by way of Kazan. Prince Gagarin (1810-1892), a friend from boyhood of Vladimir Sollogub, was a distinguished artist, a pupil of Karl Bryullov and of Horace Vernet (1789-1863). He ultimately became vice-president of the St. Petersburg Academy of Art, and was particularly well known for his studies of Byzantine architecture and its influence on the medieval architecture of Russia. Apparently the two young men undertook the expedition to Kazan for much the same reason as Ivan Vasilyevich did his—to get to know Russia. The artist had only recently returned from western Europe, and the writer knew little of his own country beyond the social life of the two capitals, which had formed the subject of most of his early stories. Grigory Gagarin's cousin Ivan Sergeevich Gagarin wrote to Prince Peter Vyazemsky on 30 Sept. 1839: "Sollogub is setting out today or tomorrow with Grigory: a union of novelist and artist for utilizing *couleur locale* ."[1] The idea for the book must have been settled on early in the trip, if not even before, for Gagarin's sketches were composed *pari passu* with the writing of the text, even to the inclusion of such secondary additions as ornamental initials, chapter colophons and the like. By the date of the travellers' return to St. Petersburg in January, 1840, all must have been quite completely sketched out, if not entirely written in preliminary form.

Friends and acquaintances of Sollogub testify to having read—or heard—parts of *The Tarantas* early in 1840. Thus E. A. Baratynsky writes to his wife in a letter which editors date "in the winter of 1840":[2]

> I forgot to say that before the Karamzins' we had heard at [Fyodor] Odoevsky's Sollogub's tale *The Tarantas*, which is adorned with the vignettes, full of art and imagination, of a certain Prince Gagarin. The vignettes are a delight, but the rest is mediocre. Everyone criticizes it. I too joined the others, but I was more moderate than the rest. The dispute, which had been unleashed at Odoevsky's, was continued at the Karamzins' and was the principal topic of conversation.

Prince Vyazemsky in a letter to his family dated 13 February 1840 reports: "Sollogub travelled through Russia with Grigory Gagarin, and they are preparing to publish their *impressions de voyage* under the name 'The Tarantas.' They say that Gagarin's illustrations are a marvelous delight. I haven't as yet seen them."[3]

It is not clear from this evidence how much of the work was available for discussion at the Karamzin and Odoevsky salons. The first publication of any part of *The Tarantas* consisted of seven chapters which came out in issue 10 of *Notes of the Fatherland* in 1840. These chapters—1-3, 5, 8, 9 and 18 of the final version—may have been all that was ready in 1840. After the publication of this partial version there is a hiatus of five years before the entire work made its appearance in the spring (March?) of 1845. The collaborators' personal affairs doubtless explain the delay: Gagarin's military service (1841-1845) and marriage (1843), and Sollogub's marriage (1840) and travels. Sollogub may well have utilized the time to do some revising of his tale. He was in western Europe in 1843 and spent some time in Nice where he met Gogol, who had just published Part I of *Dead Souls*. Gogol's influence is quite evident in the final version of *The Tarantas*, e.g. in the transformation of the vehicle into a bird in the last chapter, which one critic describes as a "realization of the metaphor" in the famous troika passage in the last chapter of Gogol's work.

As Baratynsky's letter indicates, the reaction of the literary salons toward the first version of *The Tarantas* was rather negative; the general opinion seems to have been that the author was treating important questions rather lightly. Perhaps Sollogub himself had misgivings on this score: in any case there is a notable increase in seriousness in the later portions of the work, especially in the "educational chapters" XV and XVI.

The existence of this partial first version complicates any consideration of the author's intentions. Seven of the chapters which make up the final text of *The Tarantas* were published separately in 1840, as noted above; these chapters were considerably augmented in the 1845 version, and one (the final XIII) transposed to a new position from its original place immediately following I-III. It is hard not to believe that these changes do not indicate a degree of change in the author's intentions, particularly as regards the characterization of his "hero," Ivan Vasilyevich,

The 1840 chapters in their original order but final numbering are as follows: the first three ("The Meeting," "The Departure," "The Beginning of the Travel Impressions"), XIII ("Officials"), V ("A Hotel"), VIII ("The Gypsies") and IX ("A Ring"). In this portion of the work Sollogub's characters are perfectly consistent, but rather different from their final aspect. Vasily Ivanovich is a fat rustic, "afraid... of his terrible and portly wife" Avdotya Petrovna, and delighted at the chance of having a fling with some gypsy women out of his spouse's reach. Ivan Vasilyevich is a young dreamer, enthusiastic over his project of "studying his native land" and writing his "book of travel impressions," into which will go all that he can find out about Russia's "national character." This will include animadversions against the stupid Western innovations which have displaced native ways of life, and a glamorized view of the Russian muzhik, the true representative of the land. Ivan has been disillusioned by the West, but is disappointed by the monotony and lack of color which he finds in his own country. He has an obsessive hatred of the official class in theory, but the two specimens whom he encounters in reality depress him and fill him with pity. He has a roseate view of the gypsies as a wild, natural, unspoiled folk, for whom freedom is the greatest good, and is horrified to find them not only dirty and smelly, but wearing the worst kind of "western" clothes and singing cheap vaudeville songs instead of their native airs. Nowhere in all this is there an intimation of what we find later (in Chapter XVI) that Ivan Vasilyevich's superficial and un-Russian education has rendered him unfit for any serious task, that he is doomed forever to take up projects with fervent enthusiasm only to drop them because they involve the background knowledge and dogged persistence which he does not have. As for his companion, there is a glaring inconsistency between Vasily Ivanovich's marital relations as hinted at in the seven chapters first published and the charming picture in Chapter XV of his first meeting with Avdotya Petrovna, their old-fashioned wedding, and the couple's idyllic life together. In the 1840 chapters Vasily Ivanovich is no admirer of the muzhik: "A sly folk," is his grudging comment to his companion's rhapsodies, and his attitude toward his servant Senka is brusque and contemptuous, quite at variance with the enlightened treatment which he accords his peasants according to his dissertation on estate management in Chapter XIII. The whole tone of the seven earlier chapters, moreover, is quite different from what was put out in 1845. It is light and ironic: Ivan's exaggerated views, whether of the extraordinary virtues of the Russian peasant or of the vileness of the half-educated, half-cultured class which he lumps together as officialdom, are presented as very evidently those of a very ill-informed youngster fresh from the West. There is even a good deal of humor in these chapters—e.g. the hilarious episode in the dirty and pretentious provincial hotel or the detached narrative "A Ring." In the rest of the work there is satire— e.g. "A Simple and Stupid Story" or "A Russian Nobleman," but little real humor. It seems quite clear that what started out as a light, whimsical tale with strong affinities with the "physiological sketch" has been transformed in five years' time into a somewhat tendentious document with a serious, if satirical purpose. What this purpose is we shall consider later. In the process the characterization of the two "heroes" of the piece has suffered considerable change.

The question can hardly be avoided: do the two protagonists of *The Tarantas* represent portraits from life or are they abstract literary constructs? It is a question which cannot be given a decisive answer, but one which we shall have occasion to deal with in more detail a little later in this essay. For the present it may be noted that A. Nemzer, in the chapter "Vladimir Sollogub and His Principal Book,"[4] presents good evidence that the visionary ideas attributed to Ivan Vasilyevich, and ironically treated by the author, correspond largely with those actually held at the time by the Gagarin cousins, Grigory Grigoryevich and Ivan Sergeevich, who like Ivan Vasilyevich had had a prevailingly western upbringing and had spent most of their youth in France and Italy. Nemzer rejects the idea, however, that Ivan Vasilyevich is in any sense a "portrait" of the Gagarins; some at least of his features seem to come from Sollogub himself; it is perhaps not without significance that Grigory Gagarin's sketch for the frontispiece of the book, consisting of portraits of its two heroes, shows Ivan Vasilyevich with the features of Vladimir Sollogub! There seems to be no candidate, however, to furnish a model for Vasily Ivanovich. Gagarin's sketch of him, although lively and individualized, doesn't correspond to the features of any known person of the time—but obviously this does not preclude the possibility that a real person whom we shall never know may have sat for the portrait. Samarin's suggestion that Vasily Ivanovich is only a modernized Prostakov or Skotinin is not convincing: Sollogub's creation is too attractive for such an ancestry!

Toward the beginning of his extensive critique of *The Tarantas* Vissarion Belinsky[5] has a few words to say on the work's genre definition:

> "We have said that Count Sollogub's *Tarantas* is an artistic work; but to this must be added that it is at the same time a contemporary work, a fact which constitutes one of its most important merits and is responsible for its unusual success. *The Tarantas*, then, is an artistic work in the contemporary meaning of the word. Into it have entered therefore not only discussions between its actors, but also entire dissertations. Hence it is not a novel, nor a tale, nor a sketch, nor a tract, nor a piece of research, but all of these at once. Let each reader call it whatever he pleases: what matters is the substance and not the name.

Whatever Belinsky may say, there are very few true discussions in *The Tarantas*: one of the characters (Ivan Vasilyevich) is prone to express himself in lengthy monologues, while the other (Vasily Ivanovich) replies in the briefest possible way, or doesn't reply at all because he is sleeping. When he does reply, his remarks are unlikely to have much bearing on what his companion has been saying. Thus when the enthusiastic Ivan Vasilyevich in Chapter III breaks off his denunciation of the shameful decadence of the westernized Russian upper class with the query: "What do you think of our

Russian aristocrats?" the reply is characteristically: "I think that there will be no horses for us at the next station." Of "entire dissertations" there are several: Ivan Vasilyevich delivers one on Russian literature in Chapter X; he treats the astonished merchants to one on commerce in Chapter XIV; Vasily Ivanovich, moved to unusual eloquence when the subject is one that he understands, gives his friend an extensive disquisition on proper and profitable estate management in Chapter XIII. As for the accepted genre classifications that Belinsky enumerates, "novel" is a term that it would be very difficult to apply to *The Tarantas*, although like some novels, it is held together by the external framework of a journey, and the author is at pains to develop the characters of his two protagonists by describing their bringing-up—two novellistic procedures. Two "tales" formally unconnected with the work's narrative structure are inserted: Chapter VII, "A Simple and Stupid Story," related by Ivan Vasilyevich's boarding-school friend whom he meets during a stroll in Vladimir; and Chapter IX, "A Ring," related by Ivan Petrov Fadeev, the young proprietor of a resthouse and village shop.

The term "sketch" (*ocherk*) at this date in Russian literature inevitably brings to mind the "natural school" and its favorite literary medium, the "physiological sketch." And indeed the early chapters of Sollogub's *Tarantas* exhibit many features of both the style and the genre. Physical descriptions of persons and places are detailed and objective, e.g. of the post-station and the stationmaster's belongings in Chapter IV, of the "hotel" and the travellers' meal there, in Chapter V, of the gypsy camp and the entertainment there put on for Vasily Ivanovich in Chapter VIII, and of the drunken village festivities in Chapter XVIII. In Belinsky's discussion of *The Tarantas* the author is unhesitatingly aligned with the writers of the "natural school," and specifically with Gogol. This, in fact, is what Belinsky means by his words in the passage quoted above, about the "contemporary" element in Sollogub's "artistic work." The narrative framework of *The Tarantas* is almost wholly in the "contemporary" naturalistic style, and such a chapter as XIV, "Merchants," could well pass for a "physiological sketch" up to the point of Ivan Vasilyevich's intrusive speech.

Finally, Belinsky speaks of "tract" and "piece of research." Chapter XII, "The Monastery of the Caves in Nizhny Novgorod" occupies a unique position in the work, since it is the author's own description of a place on the fictional journey which Ivan Vasilyevich, to his regret, was not given the opportunity of visiting; and in the description Sollogub even quotes, in the original 16th- and 17th-century Russian, excerpts from a precious historical manuscript kept in the monastery. A similar bit of "research" is the list in Chapter XIX of important manuscripts kept in the library of the University of Kazan—a list rather improbably presented as recalled by the poorly educated Ivan Vasilyevich. As for the "tract," probably the entire last chapter (XX: "A Dream") should be assigned to this category. Ivan Vasilyevich sees in his dream first a brief allegorical picture of Russia's grim past (the headless shades silhouetted against a lurid fire): of the disgusting present (a grotesque *danse macabre* of half bestial creatures readily identifiable as representatives of Russia's "upper classes"), and finally a glowing picture of a Russian future, where all is peace and quiet and harmony, and both the "prince" and Ivan's boarding-school friend, the hero of the "simple and stupid story" have been transformed into happy, useful citizens.

Two further episodes have to be mentioned, for which Belinsky provides no name: they may be best described as biographical sketches—Chapter XV, "Something About Vasily Ivanovich" and Chapter XVI, "Something About Ivan Vasilyevich." In each is contained an account of the background and early "education" of the two protagonists, in the author's own words. Both contain savage satires on the manner of life of Vasily's and Ivan's parents, and of the kind of up-bringing which this manner of life has imposed upon the children. In the case of Ivan Vasilyevich, indeed, this kind of education, which the author bitterly condemns as entirely responsible for his hero's uselessness, is subjected to a diatribe which may well be regarded as a "tract." It is rather hard to accept the plausibility of the picture, particularly in view of Ivan Vasilyevich's often mentioned intelligence, and powers of self-analysis and self-criticism.

It scarcely needs to be pointed out that such a diversity of genres as *The Tarantas* presents must result in a medley of styles and language. Two strikingly dissimilar styles are sometimes intentionally juxtaposed for ironic contrast, as in Chapter XIV, between the strikingly lower-class colloquial idiom of the merchants and the high-sounding rhetorical outburst of Ivan Vasilyevich which follows. A similar contrast is afforded by the young hero's meditations as he strolls through the holiday village in Chapter XVII and the tipsy old veteran's illiterate tale to his enthralled peasant audience. Of course it goes without saying that the contrasted characters of Sollogub's protagonists must result in a corresponding contrast in their styles of speech. Vasily Ivanovich says little, but what he says is usually to the point; it is always concrete and practical (in Belinsky's otherwise ridiculous parallel he represents Sancho Panza as against Ivan Vasilyevich's Don Quixote). As Yury Samarin in his critique points out, Vasily Ivanovich seems to be positively afraid of any sort of abstract idea, while his companion has a regrettable tendency to turn the most ordinary matter into theory. Thus in Chapter XIII, to Vasily Ivanovich's remark that the muzhik will say of a feckless landlord: "He's a little teched, indeed, but he's ours; he's our father and we're his children," Ivan replies with a paragraph of high-falutin nonsense about the "lofty, mysterious, sacred bond" which is in the blood of the Russian people, uniting the peasantry and the gentry.

On a larger scale the several chapters of *The Tarantas* are arranged with evident purpose so that such contrasts may be particularly striking. Thus, following immediately after "The Ring" (IX), told in the sub-standard language of the *meshchanin* Ivan Petrov Fadeev, comes "A Little Something About Literature," in Ivan Vasilyevich's most pretentious and metaphorical style. A contrast not only of styles but of theory with reality is to be found in the original order of the 1840 chapters, where Chapter III, ending in Ivan Vasilyevich's brilliant, exaggerated characterization of what he imagines the lower-class official to be like, is followed immediately by the present Chapter XVIII, his encounter with two real officials of low rank, whose humble and touching stories told in their own words, reveal them to be nothing like his stereotype.

In a work constructed as Sollogub's *Tarantas* seems to have been, inconsistencies in point of view are not surprising. As we shall see, there are not a few even in matters of ideology, but for the moment we are concerned only with the author's characterization of his two heroes. In the case of Vasily Ivanovich, who is given less to say and is a more conventional character (Yury Samarin sees him, rather unflatteringly, as modelled on the Prostakovs, Skotinins and Sobakevichs of Russia's classic literature), the inconsistencies are less glaring, and may be in large part explained by the shift, already noted, in the author's intentions between the partial version of 1840 and the full publication in 1845.

With the more prominent and original Ivan Vasilyevich the shift in the author's point of view is more substantial and perplexing. Frequently in his tirades Ivan Vasilyevich exhibits knowledge which is justified by nothing that has been said about his background. An instance is his polemic in Chapter X about the commercialism of Russian literature. How did he come by his knowledge of Russia's "two literatures" and their characteristics? As far as we know, his childhood was spent, under M. Leprince's tutelage, with Cornelius Nepos and French rhetoric, in a household which obviously knew nothing and cared nothing about Russian literature of any kind. The rather extensive curriculum of his pension may possibly have included some attention to this subject, but we know Ivan Vasilyevich's success in that institution. After leaving the service he plunged into desultory study in an effort to make up some of his deficiencies, and he read literature: "Dante and Schiller and Byron and Shakespeare!" He vehemently disclaims the idea that he might himself be a writer, and indeed, proves his point neatly by his total failure with the "book of travel impressions." And yet he knows not only that there are "two" Russian literatures, but that every province has its own, and that in the capitals there exist numerous warring literary cliques. Remarkably detailed knowledge for one who as far as the author gives us to know has never had the least interest in the subject!

Much the same may be said about his amusing picture of the "rake's progress" from household serf to official. Here is a young man who has left his father's country estate at the age of something under fifteen, after a childhood of which we know nothing except for his French studies—yet this is the only period when he could have gathered impressions about household serfs. And on what basis can he so confidently assert to his companion that the majority of the provincial gentry, who alone are eligible for election, as assessors or *ispravniki*, avoid such service like the plague? It is a true accusation, of course—Vasily Ivanovich himself is an example of such evasion (see Chapter XV), and we have evidence on the subject in complaints from Tsar Nikolai himself in some of his edicts. Yet Ivan has left his village at age 15, spent perhaps another two years in the pension, another six years in the service and in idle socializing, all in Petersburg, and finally two more years abroad (Ivan's friend reminds him that it is eight years since they left boarding school). So where has Ivan acquired his knowledge of what goes on at provincial gentry assemblies? Perhaps in the service, for he has been chiefly employed, we read, on detached assignments, that is, on missions outside the capital—but the short time that he has served would not have given much opportunity for observing elections, for these were held only every three years.

What is the explanation for this kind of inconsistency? I think it is mere carelessness. Sollogub himself knows a great deal about these matters and has some pertinent ideas about them which he is eager to impart; he is simply not concerned that he has failed to provide his hero with the means of sharing his knowledge.

But there is another aspect of this inconsistency that is rather more serious. Ivan Vasilyevich makes a long journey, probably of a couple of weeks, through the heart of Russia, encountering representatives of most of Russia's various castes, and demonstrates an almost unbelievable myopia: not a single "impression" to record in his notebook! Is this the same man who has observed the typical freedman on his way to officialdom, who knows that this quondam house serf now has to drink "wine from the Don, and smoke Zhukov tobacco," and who buys hats for his wife trimmed with silver ears of wheat? What has happened to his powers of observation? He notes the peaches and cupids painted on the ceiling of the hotel room, and the dirt-clouded mahogany mirrors along the walls, and he concludes from these items the nature of Russian hotels in general. Why can't he do the same thing with the other scenes that he witnesses on his trip? From his encounter with the Russian grain merchants and their talk he extrapolates to a picture of the totality of backward Russian commerce. Isn't this an "impression?" Of course it is, but the author will not have it so because it is his purpose to show us the awful results of Ivan's foreign up-bringing, and so at the story's end the still virgin "book of travel impressions" must find its final resting place in a mud puddle. Many times in *The Tarantas* Ivan Vasilyevich demonstrates psychological traits, in particular a power of self-criticism, which completely belies the author's picture of a worthless, helpless nincompoop. Whether this too is carelessness is hard to say. It looks as though, as sometimes happens, the author's creation has simply got out of his hands and taken his own course in defiance of his creator's intentions. Don Quixote is such an independent creature. Perhaps there is something of the Don in Ivan Vasilyevich after all!

Sollogub started out his *Tarantas* with abstract, schematized characters. Note the dearth of proper names in the work. Neither protagonist has a surname; one character is "the prince," and another is "the little official," the three merchants are "red beard, black beard and grey beard," etc. Ivan's friend from the boarding school is almost completely nameless. Ivan exclaims "Fedya!" at their first meeting, but even this nickname never reappears. But as the work progressed this abstractness, at least as regards the two protagonists, is gradually eroded. Vasily Ivanovich develops less of a personality, probably because he is given less to say; but Ivan Vasilyevich, the author's favorite, becomes, by the penultimate chapter, a real and likeable person—and one who does not at all match the author's tendentious sketch in Chapter XVI. Sometimes an author doesn't know as much about his characters as he pretends! Ivan Vasilyevich started his book life in the 1845 chapters, as a cold embodiment of a bad education, but by the book's end he has escaped from this stereotype, and the reader simply does not believe in his total worthlessness. The author has wrought better than he knew—or intended. Even Vissarion Belinsky, who takes a very dim view of most of Ivan's opinions, wonders why Vasily Ivanovich, with no education whatever, should have been saved by his "good heart" to be a solid and useful citizen, while Ivan Vasilyevich, endowed, it would seem, with a heart equally "good," is doomed to remain a sterile nonentity. It is useless, of course, to ask such a question: the author manipulates his puppets' strings as he pleases, and can provide their lives with any outcome, psychologically improbable though it may be. But a reader is not obliged to believe him!

In the complete published form of *The Tarantas* the author has made an evident attempt to present a panoramic picture of contemporary Russia, both of the various classes of a very class-conscious society, and of some of the leading aspects of Russian economic and social life. In many cases even the chapter headings indicate these types, e.g. "Officials" (XVIII), or "Merchants" (XIV) or "A Landowner" (XIII). A brief consideration of these may facilitate our attempt to find a "leading idea" in the work.

To begin with the highest class in the Russia of Nikolai I, exclusive of royalty, which of course does not appear in person or even in discussion, we have Chapter XI, "A Russian Nobleman." On a barren and monotonous stretch of road the travellers in the tarantas overtake an elegant English carriage which has broken down on the rugged country highway. Ivan Vasilyevich recognizes the vehicle's occupant as an acquaintance of his from Paris, a Russian "prince" (*kniaz*), that is, a scion of an ancient pre-Petrine aristocratic family. In the conversation between Ivan and the prince, and in Ivan's brief explanation later to his companion, we learn that the prince lives permanently abroad, but has returned to his native land on the present occasion to collect the quit-rent (*obrok*) which his bailiff has reported that the peasants are unable to pay because of a bad harvest and a disastrous fire. For the prince the peasants exist only to support him. He is convinced that their excuses are only a means for cheating him, and he intends to extort the whole amount of the quit-rent for a year in advance. The prince curses his servants in the most outrageous fashion because, through no fault of theirs, his carriage has broken a spring. He informs Ivan Vasilyevich that he spends all his time abroad because having become accustomed to civilization and the intellectual life he finds Russian ways intolerable. He doesn't even have a complete command of the Russian language, as his conversation demonstrates.

Both Vasily Ivanovich and Ivan Vasilyevich, after the prince has driven off in his repaired carriage, discuss him and his kind with some indignation over his heartless treatment of his peasants. He is presumably a typical specimen of his caste, at least in Sollogub's opinion. It may be noted that Yury Samarin in his critique considers this picture quite out of date.

It is evident that not all of the aristocracy live abroad: a great many, both in and out of government service form part of the society of the capitals as Ivan's boarding-school friend describes these societies. In most descriptions of the society of St. Petersburg the young noblemen who make up the officer caste of the Guards Regiments play a conspicuous part in that society. Sollogub has little to say of this element—Ivan's inamorata casts languishing looks on a certain hussar—but no doubt it plays its part in the cold, extravagant, conformist society that "A Simple and Stupid Story" depicts so graphically. Petersburg society seems to be infected chiefly, according to Ivan's friend by "the disease called living beyond one's means," and by the vice which in other societies is sometimes known as "keeping up with the Joneses." As for Moscow, where Ivan's friend retires after bankruptcy in Petersburg, it seems to be notable chiefly for gambling, for tight and exclusive cliques, for wildly eccentric people, and for the most malevolent gossip. The principal victim of the society life of the capitals in "A Simple and Stupid Story" is the narrator's marriage: his wife, a high-born society lady, refuses to stay with her husband when he is obliged to leave her world for good.

The upper class of nineteenth-century Russia had several components. The descendants of the old boyar class of the Kievan and Muscovite periods. such as Sollogub's prince, formed the highest stratum; below these came the descendants of the high functionaries ennobled by Peter the Great, and such later accretions to the nobility as the Georgian princes of Ivan Vasilyevich's maternal line. This stratum is otherwise unrepresented in *The Tarantas*, although the author himself, with his German title of Graf, "Count," belonged to it. At the bottom of the gentry class were the *dvoriane*, a class which in their economic aspect are called *pomeshchiki*, that is, holders of *pomestiia* or landed estates cultivated by enserfed peasants. This class had its origin in the days of Ivan the Terrible, who awarded extensive tracts of state land (including lands confiscated from the boyars) to his adherents, who bound themselves and their descendants to serve the state in war for as long as they held these estates. In theory such grants were revocable—the Tsar could reassign the land if the holder did not or could not fulfill his obligation; but under the Terrible Tsar's weaker successors this provision fell into desuetude until finally under Peter III the *pomeshchiki* were freed from obligatory state service, which by this time had come to include civilian as well as military and naval branches. Most *pomeshchiki* did in fact serve for a short time; when they resigned they retained the rank (*chin*) which they had attained in the service, as defined by Peter the Great's "Table of Ranks," but of course forfeited the state salary. They usually then returned to their estates and lived thenceforth in the country, supervising the cultivation of their *pomestiia* by their peasants, or, as was often the case, entrusting this supervision to a bailiff. Both Vasily Ivanovich and Ivan Vasilyevich belong to this class, and apparently have estates of about the same size—"three hundred souls." Ivan's father and Vasily both live on their estates, Vasily is a very model of a landowner (see Chap. XIII); of Ivan's father all we know is that his buckwheat crop has failed! He must, however, have been affluent enough to have maintained his son for several years in idleness in Petersburg and abroad. Ivan, after flunking at his pension, has been in the civil service for a time, and resigned with the rank of "provincial secretary," eleventh class. "Not a very high rank," observes Vasily Ivanovich, implying perhaps that his own is higher. He had served "a short time" in the chancery of the Governor of Kazan before his father's death called him back to his village.

After Vasily Ivanovich's refusal to linger in Nizhny Novgorod long enough to permit his companion to start his "travel impressions," the two continue their journey and Vasily Ivanovich launches into a lengthy dissertation on proper estate management. The pomeshchik's right relationship with his peasants is, or should be, one of enlightened self interest. Keep the peasants contented and busy, and they will work well and productively. Vasily grudgingly tolerates a few household serfs, largely for his wife's use, but most of his muzhiks work the fields. He inveighs strongly against what he regards as the entirely mistaken fad of trying to combine serf-run small factories with agricultural work. It may be noted that most of Vasily Ivanovich's recommendations in this chapter run counter to the actual practice of the landowners of the time. The picture which Sollogub paints of the estate of Mordasy is an unrecognizably idealized one.

In the travellers' first conversation on the road (Chapter III) Ivan mentions incidentally his hatred and abhorrence of "officials." To justify his attitude he resorts to the usual accusation of bribe-taking. Ivan's friend from boarding school corrects him on this score, at least as regards the upper ranks of officialdom: bribe-taking is beneath these gentlemen, and besides is dangerous. But there are other, less obvious but just as satisfactory ways of capitalizing on one's position. Bribe-taking really belongs only to the lowest ranks in the hierarchy. In *The Tarantas* none of the upper ranks appear, except in the background of "A Simple and Stupid Story;" two specimens of the lower ranks appear, however, a provincial assessor performing the functions of *ispravnik*, an office filled by election from the local gentry, and a stationmaster—"collegiate registrar," fourteenth class, the lowest of the Table of Ranks. This pair of real-life officials make a rather different impression on Ivan Vasilyevich than his preconceived prejudices led him to expect. The acting *ispravnik* gets a miserable salary from which he has to pay his drunken copy clerk and maintain a family of eleven persons. He confesses to accepting bribes on occasion, but only such things as a pound of tea or half a loaf of sugar—"and one can't get rich on that!" He lives in mortal dread of making some mistake that will get him sacked, and worst of all, he is old and infirm and often suffers from blackouts when he can't even see what he is writing. The second "official" is truly pitiable; he is not only old but half-paralyzed. His station is privately owned and the owner refuses to furnish him with the proper kind and amount of firewood, and threatens to have him ejected from the service altogether. Fortunately compassionate travellers have intervened, and the government permits him to let his eleven-year-old son do the actual recording of travellers' passes which justifies the title of "collegiate registrar." In his position the question of bribe-taking doesn't even arise. There is no service that he could perform that one would facilitate. Inevitably these pictures of humble lower-class officials bring to mind Gogol's Akaky Akakevich, who is usually regarded as the classic example of the down-trodden official. Akaky, however, was a "perpetual titular council-lor" (class IX), and moreover was in general perfectly contented with his lot until the unfortunate loss of his overcoat. Sollogub's stationmaster has himself and three children to support; it is unthinkable that he could ever have saved up enough money to buy himself an overcoat!

Another representative of the official class is the district police officer (*chastnyi pristav*) of the incidental tale "A Ring." One of the perquisites of his office is the custom-obligated presents which he receives on entering upon his duties; and thenceforth he makes a practice of cadging free drinks from the obliging teller of the story, who endures the imposition for ends of his own. Doubtless under other circumstances the officer's wife would have helped herself to some of the notions kept in Fadeev's store. This petty kind of graft seems to have been so universal that exception to it was looked upon as not only abnormal but positively eccentric. Ivan Sergeevich Aksakov, who had a very high concept of his duties as an honorable and useful citizen (he was a provincial judge in the Orel district) complains in his letters of the constant attempts made to bribe him. Sollogub's comedy *The Official*[6] has as hero a high-minded nobleman like Aksakov, who dumbfounds the rest of the cast by failing to conform in any way with the stereotype. Although Ivan Vasilyevich's prejudices against the official class are not borne out in *The Tarantas*, they appear to have had some foundation none the less.

Bribe-taking, however, is not the only item of Ivan's indictment of officials. He acknowledges that the term he uses is inexact—what he means by "officials" is the as yet nameless class from which officials mostly come. Ivan's eloquent and amusing characterization of this class (Chap. III) portrays what later in the century would be generally known as "the miscellaneous caste" or *raznochintsy*. Sollogub sees them all as metamorphosed household serfs; actually, of course, their origin was much more diverse—merchants' sons, priests' sons, the sons of minor officials, even perhaps some scions of ancient but impoverished noble families, like Pushkin's poor Eugene of *The Bronze Horseman*, as well as the uncultured freedmen whom Ivan describes. These people would naturally find employment chiefly in the lower ranks of the civil service. Ivan brands them as half-educated, pushing, vulgar, subservient to those above them and contemptuous of those below. They have lost their native Russian character and not replaced it with a full Western acculturation. A hint along the same line is given by the gray-bearded merchant in Chapter XIV when he describes what happens when one of his class tries to "crawl into the upper class." Ivan's characterization is evidently a very one-sided account of the matter. It may be noted that Vissarion Belinsky in his commentary and critique of *The Tarantas*, points out that while the first generation of peasants and merchants may be as boorish and uncultured as Ivan describes them, their sons, who will have had a wholly Western education, would not be distinguishable from the children of the "upper classes" in a cultural regard. Belinsky was himself a *raznochinets* of the second generation.

Chapter XIV is headed "Merchants." Sollogub presents three grain-dealers conversing in a tavern somewhere between Nizhny Novgorod and Kazan, and overheard by Ivan Vasilyevich at a near-by table. Another member of the class makes a brief appearance to ask a favor of one of the three; this man is a trader of the town, and on a much smaller scale than the three "beards." Potapych deals in tallow and potash, and the transaction which he arranges with "gray-beard" involves only about 5000 rubles, while the grain-dealers handle vastly larger sums. They go far afield to buy grain, evidently even to the mouth of the Volga, and having bought it, transport it in large, cumbersome river boats upstream to the great grain market at Rybinsk, north of Moscow, where dealers from all the cities of northern Russia congregate. Ivan Vasilyevich witnesses the primitive transaction between Potapych and gray-beard and is utterly bewildered by the absence of any of the commercial usages to which his Western upbringing has accustomed him— receipts, banks, letters of credit and the rest. The merchants carry great sums of money about with them, but are protected from brigandage, it seems, by their shabby, threadbare clothes and wretched vehicles. They never use banks, indeed are almost if not quite illiterate (they seem to be able to keep memoranda of figures on scraps of paper), and with each other they are scrupulously honest. A buyer, however, is fair game, and cheating one is considered just "accepted commercial practice." Ivan is shocked and lectures them on their backwardness and lack of civilized social principles. They admit their failings, but defend themselves with the plea that "this is the way it has always been done," the way of their fathers and grandfathers.

Another *meshchanin*, or member of the petty bourgeoisie who appears in *The Tarantas* is the young guest-house keeper, Ivan Petrov Fadeev, narrator of the incidental tale "A Ring." He keeps a small shop in the lower floor of his guest house, where he sells all manner of small items, from needles and thread to flour and prunes, to the lower-class townspeople. We learn nothing, however, of his practices or degree of commercial success.

The largest of all the Russian castes, over eighty percent of the total population, were peasants. This caste, however, was by no means homo-

geneous. The largest body of peasants, and the only one which Sollogub
introduces into his tale, is that belonging to the *pomestiia* or landed estates of
the gentry. Peasants on government lands, on church lands, and those
assigned to state-run industrial operations, such as mining, constitute other
subdivisions of the caste. All peasants were legally un-free and liable to the so-
called "soul tax," which in the case of the manorial peasants was collected
from them (or paid by a benevolent landowner out of his own funds.) The
peasant was bound to the land, and could be sold with it, or even, at the
landlord's discretion, without it. In regions where there was a surplus of
hands for agricultural labor, or where the landlord for his own reasons
wanted immediate cash (e.g. the prince, in Chap. XI), peasants could be
released from their estate to find work for wages in a factory, as boatmen on
the Volga, or the like. Such peasants paid their landlord the *obrok* or quit-rent
in cash in lieu of agricultural labor. In the more productive agricultural
regions of southern Russia most of the peasantry were engaged entirely in
field work; three days of the working week were by custom assigned to labor
on the landlord's private land—the so-called *barshchina* or corvee. Theoreti-
cally the rest of the week could be devoted to the cultivation of the peasant's
own allotment of land—much smaller, but usually, for obvious reasons, much
more productive than the landlord's. Many, perhaps most landlords,
however, were less ready than Vasily Ivanovich to release the peasant to do
his own work, and since no legal bar existed to prevent such exploitation, only
custom, and in any case the only enforcer of law for the peasant was the
landowner himself, there were cases when the peasant was forced to perform
barshchina even six days of the week. Narezhny, in his novel *Aristion*, even
notes the custom of a particularly miserly *pomeshchik* who imposes what he
calls "Christian taxes" on his muzhiks, which they must pay in cash or kind if
they want to go to church on Sunday!

Vasily Ivanovich's relations with his peasants, as he describes them in
the chapter "A Landowner" (XIII) are an idealized vision, perhaps very
exceptionally realized by some enlightened members of the gentry class in
nineteenth-century Russia; far more common, it would seem, are the
relations of the "prince" with his hapless peasants, who seem to be held for
obrok as well as *barshchina*, and, if the prince's intentions are carried out, are
going to be obliged to pay a whole year's quit-rent in advance, in spite of fire
and crop failure.

Peasants appear incidentally throughout *The Tarantas*, usually as
background figures: e.g. the smith of Chapter XIV who mends the wheels of
the tarantas, or the illiterate *starosta* of the same chapter who manages the
affairs of the drunken stationmaster. Nowhere in the work do the peasants
appear at their daily labor. Chapter XVIII, "A Rustic Holiday" describes a
large village (*selo*) on a spree, celebrating a church holiday. Two main themes
appear in this chapter: the wildly improvident behavior of the intoxicated
peasants, who are willing to sacrifice a year's earnings on lavish hospitality;
and the gulf between the gentry, represented here by Ivan Vasilyevich, and

the peasants. The two literally do not speak the same language; when Ivan attempts to quiz a peasant about the Old Believers in the village he is met with utter incomprehension, since the peasant not only does not understand his questioner's learned vocabulary, but is entirely unaccustomed to dealing with such abstractions as "beliefs" and "rites." This incomprehension of the two classes is, of course, an important item in the thinking of both Slavophiles and Westernizers: for the former, it is the fatal effect of Peter the Great's vaunted reforms, which introduced a new, non-Russian element into the lives of the upper class and so alienated them from the peasantry. The Westernizers while acknowledging the existence of this gulf, insisted that the way to eliminate it was not regression to pre-Petrine days, but an energetic re-education of the peasantry.

In connection with the village holiday the figure of the discharged soldier and his account of his adventures in the service must be mentioned. Like all private soldiers he was himself a peasant, drafted in his youth for the obligatory 25-year term of service. His experiences have broadened his horizon and given him a self-assurance which his stay-at-home fellows lack. He has seen France and Turkey in the wars of 1812-14 and 1828-29, but he has only the haziest notions of the geography of these regions, except that not being Russian, the countries are good-for-nothing. He has supreme contempt for these alien lands where a thirsty Russian can't even get a drink of kvass! As his folk-lore version of the origins of Tsar Nikolai's quarrel with the Sultan shows, his notions of the world of politics are equally hazy. He impresses the muzhiks with his experience of the larger world which is unknown to them, while Ivan Vasilyevich is impressed by his ignorance.

Of the aspects of Russian life which Sologub's *Tarantas* ignores entirely or touches upon too lightly to give an adequate picture, industry and religion are the most outstanding. The Russia of the 1840s was not an industrial nation, but factories did exist, and they were not all of the make-shift variety that Vasily Ivanovich inveighs against, attempts by landowners to utilize their peasants for a work force and home-grown products for raw material. These are the only industrial enterprises which Sollogub even mentions, and this with reprobation: they take away from agricultural productivity and they spoil the peasants. As for religion, except for the chapter on the Pechersky Monastery in Nizhny Novgorod, which is the author's own interpolation, unconnected with the journey of the tarantas, and the brief mention of the priest and the sexton in the "procession of the cross" at the rustic bacchanalia of Chapter XVII, the only mention of the subject comes in incidental references to prayers, the "beautiful symbols of the faith" (Chap. XV), and the like. The omission is certainly deliberate: any attempt to depict the reality of the rural priesthood, for example, would have been inevitably eliminated by the censors; the best that a realist writer could do was to be content with the vaguest generalities. Russia would have to wait for such satirists as Saltykov-Shchedrin with the written word and Ilya Repin with the brush in the 1880s to depict such subjects realistically.

In general, however, Sollogub's picture of Russian life in the 1840s must be credited with verisimilitude (except for the idealized portrait of the enlightened landlord) and impartiality. Some parts of it, e.g. the depiction of Petersburg and Moscow "high life" in "A Simple and Stupid Story" are obviously exaggerated and one-sided, but in fundamentals they agree well enough with other less distorted portraitures of the period to be accepted with perhaps a grain or two of salt. In any case they are not openly tendentious; the author is not avowedly and obviously propagandizing a point of view. He is indeed surprisingly impartial, and as we shall see, much of what might be interpreted as authorial expression of views proves on closer inspection to be ironical in its association with Ivan Vasilyevich. *The Tarantas* is a great deal more objective than it appears at first sight.

Intellectual Russia in the period represented by *The Tarantas* was beginning to be divided between the two ideologies usually referred to as Slavophilism and Westernism (*zapadnichestvo*). The question inevitably arises, as it did in 1845, to which of these alignments is Sollogub to be assigned—or is he "uncommited," a neutral, uneasily poised between the two camps? To attempt an answer to this question will require us to devote some time to a consideration of the history of the ideologies themselves, as well as a rather close inspection of the ideas put forward in *The Tarantas*: are these ideas those of the author and seriously meant, or do they belong only to one of his characters, i.e., Ivan Vasilyevich, and are meant to be taken as absurd and inapplicable to Russian reality, the wild chimeras of a young dreamer remote from the facts of Russian life?

We shall begin with a brief consideration of what is meant by "Westernism." Such a consideration does not need to be lengthy because the leading ideas of the *zapadniki* are simple and readily intelligible, and among them there is a great deal more unanimity than among the Slavophiles.

The polarization of Russian social thought may be said to date from about 1830 and the publication in Nadezhdin's periodical *The Telescope* of the notorious *Philosophical Letters* of Peter Yakovlevich Chaadayev (1794-1856). The *Telescope* in this instance showed remarkably short sight, for it was promptly suppressed, its editor exiled, and the author of the *Letters* officially declared insane. Although Chaadayev's extreme views were never accepted by the Westernizers, his general thesis that Russia's future lay in alignment with the West and abandonment of her Byzantine heritage became the basis for Westernism. Chaadayev repudiated Orthodox Christianity and called for submission to the Roman church as the true representative of the Christian faith; and with Orthodoxy he repudiated Russia's entire past. "We are living," wrote Chaadayev, "without either past or future, in dead stagnation."[7] The country's only hope, and that a very slim one, is to start all over again, as a humble pupil of the West.

None of the Westernizers accepted Chaadayev's religious views. Most of them repudiated religion altogether, and based their thought on philosophical materialism and atheism. Their chief focus was on social and political questions: they execrated serfdom and demanded its total abolition, and they rather naively admired the bourgeois social structure of the West. Alexander Herzen (1812-1870), however, who may be regarded as the leading ideologue of the movement, was early disillusioned with the western bourgeosie and in his later writings advocated socialism on the model of Charles Fourier. More conservative Westernizers were for retaining the monarchy in Russia, but with a limiting constitution of a western type.

The very influential and widely read literary critic Vissarion Belinsky (1811-1848), who wrote from within Russia while Herzen and his friend and coadjutor Nikolai Ogaryov (1813-1877) enjoyed the freedom of London, passed through several phases of philosophical discipleship, and carried much of Westernizing thought along with him. In his student years he, along with one of the future leaders of the Slavophiles, belonged to the "Stankevich circle" (Nikolai Stankevich, 1813-1840) who were at the time mostly followers of the German idealist philosopher Schelling. Belinsky's articles in the 1830s preach the duty of self-perfection for the good of "neighbor, native land and humanity." In 1837 he became rather imperfectly acquainted with the philosophy of Schelling's one-time friend and rival Hegel, and was particularly struck by the Hegelian saying that "whatever is, is right." During this phase Belinsky advocated, to the scandal of other Westernizers, a reconciliation with the Russian status quo. His break with Hegelianism in 1840 was violent and brought him into a final period of liberalism of western type. In this period, which is that of his lengthy critique of *The Tarantas*, he proclaimed the writer's duty to use his talents in so far as possible to combat social evils and preach a new order. In his article Belinsky rather disingenuously interprets *The Tarantas* as an ironic expose of conservative crypto-Slavophile doctrine.

Although there was never universal agreement among the Westernizers on matters of doctrine, any more than among their opponents, certain general positions may be noted: human civilization is one and indivisible, and the form it has taken in Western Europe is its highest form to date; it is a perversity to foster separate 'national' forms of this civilization; the marks of this universal Western civilization are humanism as against supernaturalism, freedom as against bureaucratic or autocratic constraint, and progress as against stagnation in the ways of the past. The Westernizers recognized the unfortunate effect on Russian life which Peter the Great's reforms had created, the vast gulf between an educated and westernized upper class and a stagnant lower class; the solution to the problem, in their belief, lay in educating the masses and bringing the whole population to the same level.

Slavophilism, which we shall examine in more detail, may appear at first glance to be but a mirror-image of Westernism. Where the one repudiates Christian Orthodoxy and would even substitute Catholicism, the other makes Orthodox Christianity the foundation of its structure. While the one proposes a universal civilization in which all particular national characteristics are lost, the other posits the preservation of 'national character' as its principal good.

Where the one demands progress and the abandonment of the outgrown past, the other would retreat into that past, even undoing as far as possible the injurious changes wrought by the "Great Reformer." Nevertheless, as we shall presently see, the two ideologies are by no means opposed in everything. Autocracy and the repressive bureaucratic police state of Nikolai I were equally detested by both, and the institution of serfdom, with the concomitant moral and economic degradation of the peasantry was deplored by the Slavophiles and vociferously denounced—from a safe distance—by the Westernizers.

Slavophilism is one of the most puzzling and misunderstood movements in Russian history. It is often regarded as an almost direct antithesis of the "Westernizing" movement; it is not infrequently, even by Russians, confused with the "Official nationalism" of S.S. Uvarov, and it is regularly regarded by historians of all varieties as a coherent, unified body of doctrine evolved by its principal spokesmen, Alexei Khomyakov, Ivan Kireevsky and Konstantin Aksakov. It is none of these things. As we have seen, Slavophiles and Westernizers were at one in their abhorrence of serfdom and rejection of an unlimited autocracy. "Official nationalism," consisting of the trinity *Pravoslavie, Samoderzhavie* and *Narodnost'*, or "Orthodoxy, Autocracy and Nationality," shows a verbal simiarity to Slavophilism, but the concepts behind the words are completely different. For Uvarov, Orthodoxy is summed up in the state church, embodied in the Holy Synod, which is practically a "ministry of religion." Nothing could be farther from the Slavophile concept of a mystical, free unanimity of all true believers, altogether divorced from institutional enbodiment. For the Slavophile the arbitrary, class-dominated tyrany of the actual autocracy was an offensive caricature of the true kind of monarchy which should be the simple executor of the "general will" of the entire people. The monarchy should have no interests discordant with the interests of the people as a whole. And finally, although *narodnost'* was one of the key words in Slavophile ideology, its fundamental character is that of a harmony among all classes of the country, with no encroachment of one on another, all being alike free and united in brotherly unanimity. With these glaring differences from the "nationalism" of Nikolai I, it is easy to see why Slavophilism was subjected to continual harassment and persecution. And as the third element of misunderstanding, the notion of a coherent and universally accepted body of dogma in Slavophilism is totally false. Certain basic principles there are, of which the above are examples, but beyond these there are constant and vociferous disagreements among the movement's ideologues, and details even of the fundamentals are often in dispute. The very name "Slavophilism" (*Slaviano-fil'stvo*) is the first element of misunderstanding. It was not chosen by the movement's adherents, but conferred derisively by its opponents. The adjective which is Englished as "Slavophile" first appears in Konstantin Batyuskov's satirical poem "Vision on the Shores of Lethe"; in this the shade of Admiral Alexander Shishkov, originator of a particularly conservative linguistic theory, is made to introduce himself thus, in pure Slavonic: *"Az esm' zelo slavianofil,"* "I am very much a Slavophile."[8] The word is of course a barbarism, compounded of the tribal name *Slaviane,* from the *Primary Chronicle,* and the Greek *philos,* "lover of." Moreover, in its context, the term has no reference to the Slavs as a people, but only to the Old Slavonic language, which Shishkov erroneously identified as the ancestral form of Russian, and advocated for literary use. The first element of the word, moreover, would seem to imply a fondness for the entire Slavic race, whereas the thinkers characterized as Slavophiles were interested only in the Russian branch. The founders of the movement themselves came up with various alternatives for the unsatisfactory term "Slavophilism": "Russian direction" (Konstantin Aksakov); "Moscow direction" (Yury Samarin); "Slavo-Christian direction" (Alexei Khomyakov); and *Samobytniki,* or approximately "followers of our own way of life." None of these awkward possibilities caught on, however, for obvious reasons: the Slavophiles had to be content with their name.

The Slavophile movement has complex roots. It is part of the general European romantic fashion, with its glorification of national as well as individual *differences* as against classical assertions of the uniformity of human characteristics in all times and places. It is indebted for a good deal of its character to the German idealist philosophers, Schelling and Hegel especially, themselves also romantics. And of course it would be absurd to deny it Russian roots as well, although its vision of the Russian past is founded more on philosophical theory than on close study of historical sources. To these components must be added, mostly for Alexei Khomyakov, a great deal of Orthodox Christian theology.

The leading Slavophile ideologues, moreover, although of one mind as regards essentials, were often at odds about matters of detail, and there was a considerable range in their thought even on essentials. Konstantin Aksakov, for example was the most radical; he disavowed Yury Samarin's rather objective critique of *The Tarantas* because it did not denounce sufficiently the reforms of Peter the Great. Aksakov was for rejecting Western influence altogether and going back to the traditions of Muscovite Russia. In token of this he grew a beard, in defiance of the law that forbade such an adornment to a nobleman, and dressed in seventeenth-century Muscovite costume. The result was predictable: people on the street took him for a Persian, and he was subjected to a personal reprimand from the Tsar. On the other extreme was Ivan Vasilyevich Kireevsky, whose first literary venture was a periodical, launched in 1831, which he named *The European,* in token of his conviction of that date that Russia's salvation lay in reinforcing, not abolishing, European influence. His article "The Nineteenth Century," published in his periodical, was so extreme in its Westernizing views, that *The European* was suppressed after two issues, and the editor forbidden for a time to publish anything. Kireevsky's conversion to Slavophilism, which may have been in part due to the influence of his brother Peter, a student of history, was never so thorough as to allow the idea of totally eliminating Western influence in Russian life. "Can it be supposed without insanity," he writes, "that sometime, by some power, the memory might be obliterated in Russia of all that which she has received from Europe in the course of a hundred years?"[9] The true course, as he wrote in his 1839 treatise "An Answer to A.S. Khomyakov," is not one thing or the other, as Khomyakov's essay "On the Old and the New" put the matter, but a synthesis of the two things, native Russian tradition and Western borrowings.

In other basic theses the Slavophiles show more unanimity. They all agree on the general proposition that Orthodox Christianity is the irreplaceable foundation of Russian life. Khomyakov, as noted, devoted most of his publicistic efforts (which had to be published in Czecho-Slovakia) to the religious question. He and Ivan Kireevsky do not differ widely in their interpretations here. They see Western Christianity as based on the principles of rationalism and individualism, both antithetic to true (Orthodox) Christianity. Catholicism has borrowed Graeco-Roman rationalism and applied it to religion, creating thus a body of scholastic theology typified by the *Summa* of Thomas Aquinas. Symbolic of this rationalism is the principal dogmatic difference between the two branches of Christianity, the disputed insertion into the Creed of a phrase not authorized by the Council of Chalcedon (A.D. 450): the authentic reading in the so-called "Procession of the Holy Spirit" is: (I believe)—"in the Holy Spirit... who proceeds from the Father." Some Roman rationalist, feeling that this wording implied an inequality among the members of the Trinity, added the phrase "and from the Son." But Christian doctrine, in Orthodox belief, was fixed for all time by the Seven Ecumenical Councils, which were divinely inspired. Therefore the Roman emendation, though it might sound logically more satisfactory, was contrary to the revealed truth, and a heresy. As for Western Protestantism, it is based on the theory that every man is free to interpret the faith by the light of his own reason. This individualism is equally at variance with the Orthodox doctrine of *sobornost'*. The Roman church possesses unity without freedom, the Protestant churches possess freedom without unity; only the Orthodox church possesses both in harmony. This harmony is a mystical unanimity, resulting from the humility of the Orthodox people, who have not attempted to assert individual opinions contrary to the received tradition, nor permitted the formation of a hierarchy headed by one man (as e.g. the Pope) empowered, contrary to tradition, alone to interpret the faith. The Orthodox church thus remains the sole repository of the Christian doctrine, embodied in the unaltered and divinely inspired traditions.

It may be asked: if this reading of history is right, how then was it possible for Peter the Great to do what he did? Kireevsky blames the *Stoglavyi Sobor* ("Assembly of a Hundred Chapters"—a compilation of church practices), promulgated in 1551 under Ivan the Terrible, and rescinded in 1667 under Tsar Alexei, by the Nikonian reformers. This initiated the schism in the church in Russia which has thenceforth divided the faithful.

In political history the story is rather similar. Viewing the state of Russian society of their own day, the Slavophiles see a wholly Westernized upper class, a gentry class (the *pomeshchiki*), retaining some features of ancient Russian tradition, but corrupted by superficial Western elements, and a peasantry scarcely if at all affected by the Petrine reforms (see Samarin's analysis in his *Tarantas* critique). It is in the peasantry, then, that the Slavophiles profess to find the principle that once prevailed in all Russian institutions, and which should be reintroduced and made to harmonize with imported Western ideas. This principle of *sobornost'*, or spontaneous unanimity, is embodied in the peasant commune, the *mir* or *obshchestvo*. In early nineteenth-century Russia peasant communes still existed everywhere, still independent of government interference (after the "Great Reforms" and the Emancipation of the 1860s, they were made the organs of state control of the peasantry). In their original state they performed two principal functions: a meeting of all the family heads of the *mir* carried out the periodic reassignments of communal land according to the needs of its members; and it decided the ticklish question of what young men should constitute the village quota for the military draft. In addition the *mir* assembly, headed by its *starosta* or "elder," maintained law and order in the commune and imposed sentences for minor infractions. The ultimate authority, of course, remained with the landowner, who could, but seldom did, interfere. In this system, according to Kireevsky's formulation, "the man belonged to the *mir*, and the *mir* to the man."

The foundation of all Western law and of the Western concept of individual "right" is the individual proprietorship of land; but in Russia the "ownership" of land is vested in the commune. It goes without saying that gentry proprietorship represents a breach in this system. The original *pomestiia* were, like the peasant allotments, temporary assignments, made with military service as an obligation—and these took form before Peter the Great. But such an anomaly the Slavophiles could readily ignore. The originally free peasantry who cultivated such *pomestiia*, could with some logic be restricted in freedom of movement, since only by their labor was their landlord in a position to perform his obligated service. This was the origin of *krepostnoe pravo* or serfdom. The restriction was not at first absolute: the peasant could leave a tyrannical landlord on one day a year—St. George's Day in late autumn. Restrictions were put upon this liberty by Boris Godunov in the early 1600s, and the *ulozhenie* or law-code of 1647 abolished it altogether. When Peter the Great imposed his "soul tax" on all members of the lower class, eliminating thus the former distinction between the wholly unfree "slave" and the half-free "serf," serfdom had reached its final form.

The Slavophiles were familiar with some of the historical facts relating to the peasantry and serfdom, but their understanding of the matter was founded more upon logic than research. The history of land tenure in medieval Russia is a very complex and difficult one, and any such simplicistic picture as the Slavophile theorists evolved is bound to be wrong. In general the Slavophile reconstruction of the Russian past is a mental construct, backed by no painstaking research into sources. As such it incurred the derision of its opponents, and constitutes the most vulnerable part of the body of Slavophile doctrine. The notion that communal ownership of land in medieval Russia was the universal norm is simply false.

How does the theory of a "general will" accord with the history of Russian monarchy? As everyone, including the Slavophiles, knew, Prince Vladimir "the Saint" had united the various eastern Slavic tribes under his rule; this united princedom had broken up through successive divisions among mutually hostile heirs, until the Kievan monarchy had fallen at last to the Tatars and Russia had suffered a two-hundred-year humiliation under "the Tatar yoke." During this period the princedoms of the northeast—Suzdal, Vladimir, Tver, Moscow and others—had taken advantage of alternating times of Tatar weakness or favor to build up their power. It was Moscow that emerged strongest in the end and suppressed all the other princedoms, and under Ivan IV even put an end to the last major Tatar state, the Khanate of Kazan. Clearly "unanimity" had been attained in the end by sheer force; under Ivan III and Ivan IV the last independent republics, Pskov and Novgorod, which could be imagined as still retaining some characteristics of an original "liberty," were incorporated with bloodshed into the Muscovite realm. Shutting their eyes to much of this history, the Slavophile theorists pointed out that in the Kievan era some cities, Novgorod in particular, were still independent enough to throw out an unwanted prince. Kireevsky's conclusion, correct of course, but scarcely novel, was that it was only possession of military force in the form of a *druzhina*, that made such encroachment possible. But military force had been the basis of the monarch's power from even before the reign of Prince Vladimir, and it is inconceivable that there was ever a time when it did not exist and did not dominate policy. The Slavophile picture, however, in defiance of history, is that this force was always originally used to impose not the individual will of the prince, but the will of the community embodied in the "Assembly of the Land," the *Zemskii Sobor*. This is perhaps the most visionary part of Slavophile doctrine. Historically the institution is unknown in the Kievan period: it dates only from the middle of the sixteenth century; in the reign of Ivan the Terrible the first Sobor was called in 1551, and then in 1566, 1575 and perhaps in 1580. In 1598 a Sobor offered the throne to Boris Godunov, and another in 1613 after the "Time of Troubles" elected Mikhail Fyodorovich Romanov to the throne. In the Romanov period Sobory were convened frequently in Tsar Mikhail's reign, and occasionally in that of Tsar Alexei. They ceased altogether with Peter I. These assemblies are perfectly parallel to the Estates General of Western history: occasional meetings called by the Tsar for consultation on such matters as new taxes, war, proposed legislation and the like. They consisted of representatives of the nobility, the clergy, the service gentry, sometimes the merchant class, and once (1613) of the peasantry. These consultative assemblies have no history before the reign of Ivan the Terrible, and no certain history as a Slavic native institution. They may well have been an idea borrowed from the West, e.g. from Poland. In Slavophile theory, however, they are envisioned as the ultimate authority, of whose will the Tsar is only the obedient executor.

Such are the tenets of Slavophile doctrine as it concerns past history. What are its implications for the future? These concern chiefly serfdom and autocracy. Both institutions are wrong because they are contrary to ancestral usage. In theory the peasantry should be liberated from the tyranny of the landlord—but not from their position as agricultural laborers. The autocracy should return to its position as executor of the people's will as expressed by the Assembly of the Land. But neither of these desirable objectives should be attempted through armed force. If serfdom is to be abolished, it can only be done by action from above—a decree by a benevolent Tsar. It is significant in this connection that several Slavophiles, notably Yury Samarin, had a considerable part in planning for the eventual emancipation. Exactly how such a reformation of the autocracy by itself was to have been accomplished is far from clear. It is difficult to imagine a Tsar voluntarily stripping himself of an authority sanctioned by centuries, in obedience to some quite questionable theory. On both these matters of practical action Slavophilism was diametrically opposed to Westernism, even though the ends envisaged were identical.

As was natural, the sumptuous publication in March (?) 1845 of Sollogub's *Tarantas*, accompanied by the lively and beautiful woodcuts made from Gagarin's sketches, brought forth prompt reviews in most of Russia's leading periodicals. As early as 31 March F.V. Bulgarin, editor of *The Northern Bee* noted its appearance and set the tone of most of the reviews by praising the artistry of the vignettes and condemning the text. Nekrasov in the *Literary Gazette* (12 April), although an ally of Belinsky, who admired Sollogub and considered him an adherent of the "natural school," wrote negatively of Sollogub's (or Ivan's) rejection of commercialism in literature, an attitude which he declared was a prejudice of the aristocratic circle of Prince Odoevsky and his allies. Nekrasov also noted very correctly: "In general, two sides must be distinguished in *The Tarantas*: a side copied from nature, and another the opposite of this. In the first everything is alive, faithful, witty, an abyss of superlative observations; in the other much is superficial, even quite unfaithful, because it is impossible to guess without making mistakes."[10] Pletnyov wrote a review for *The Contemporary* in which he criticized the contradictions in the viewpoints of the hero of *The Tarantas* and by implication of its author, and deplored what he considered the numerous borrowings by Sollogub from the works of Pushkin and Gogol. In general Pletnyov reproached the author for cynicism and an effort to achieve an easy success. Diverse as the literary positions of Bulgarin, Nekrasov and Pletnyov—and several less prominent writers of early reviews of Sollogub's work—may have been, they all represent straightforward attempts to deal with the tale as a work of literature, with its shortcomings, especially the want of a consistent point of view, and occasionally its success, e.g. Pletnyov's praise of the detached "Simple and Stupid Story." When it came Vissarion Belinsky's turn, however, to review *The Tarantas*, the approach he took was decidedly different and raised an issue that properly speaking is irrelevant to literary values.

Belinsky was at this time the critic on the important periodical *Fatherland Notes*, which in the hands of its editor Kraevsky had come to rival *The Contemporary* as a champion of liberal views. As has been noted, the seven 1840 chapters of *The Tarantas* had appeared in *Notes of the Fatherland*, and Kraevsky was pleased to have secured for his journal such a popular author as Sollogub's early society tales had made him. Belinsky, who in these last years of his life had come philosophically to rest in a kind of liberal socialism of a distinctly Westernizing variety, considered Sollogub to be a follower of Gogol and the "natural school," the headship of which he had assigned to Gogol. Beginning in 1839, as we have seen, the first Slavophile tracts made their appearance: Khomyakov's essay "On the Old and the New" and Ivan Kireevsky's "Answer to A.S. Khomyakov." The views set forth in these works seemed to Belinsky reactionary and dangerous, and since some of the rhetoric which Sollogub put in the mouth of his hero coincides with ideas championed by Khomyakov and Kireevsky, the critic turned his long "review" of *The Tarantas* into a polemic against Slavophilism. Taking advantage of the probably fortuitous coincidence of names ("Ivan Vasilye-vich" and Ivan Vasilyevich Kireevsky) he professed to believe that Sollogub held views on Slavophilism identical with his own and was holding his hero's utterances up to ridicule by exhibiting them as those of an ill-educated young visionary totally devoid of knowledge of the realities of his country. It is doubtful if Belinsky could have really been ignorant of the degree to which Sollogub shared Ivan Vasilyevich's ideas, but it suited his purpose to portray the author as ironical throughout. He does seem, however, in his review to detect a real sympathy on Sollogub's part for the earthling Vasily Ivanovich and his patriarchal way of life, an attitude which to Belinsky is at least as reprehensible as the one he is chiefly combatting. Since he is not really reviewing *The Tarantas* with reference to its literary qualities, but using the work as a shield for attacks on Ivan Kireevsky, it suits him to begin his tract with an equation of Ivan Vasilyevich and Vasily Ivanovich with Don Quixote and Sancho Panza—a comparison as superficial as it is ridiculous. Unfor-tunately the great prestige of "the furious Vissarion" was such that *The Tarantas* has ever since his review been associated with Slavophilism, whether or not either Sollogub or the Slavophiles acknowledged the association.

Written during the same months as Belinsky's ostensible review, but not published until 1846 (in an obscure Slavophile collection called *Moskovskii literaturnyi i uchenyi sbornik* or "Moscow Literary and Academic Col-lection"), is the Slavophiles' only riposte to Belinsky's attack—a review of

The Tarantas by Yury Fyodorovich Samarin, one of the younger Slavophiles and a particular friend of A.S. Khomyakov. Since a translation of this review is printed here with Sollogub's work, as being the most serious and pertinent contemporary treatment of it, it will be unnecessary to discuss this in detail. Samarin does not attack or even mention Belinsky directly, but confines himself strictly to the work he is reviewing, and by so doing obliquely deals his opponent a decisive blow. He takes the position that Sollogub's purpose in writing *The Tarantas* was to demonstrate the irreparable damage which a foreign education can have on a Russian. He ignores the possibility that it is any part of the author's purpose to advocate a "tendency" such as Slavophilism or Westernism. He decisively rejects the assumption that Sollogub is using Ivan Vasilyevich only as a spokesman for ideas which he himself rejects. For Samarin, as for any careful reader, there are numerous instances where the author's own views, expressed in explanatory passages, coincide perfectly with those given to Ivan Vasilyevich. In his review Samarin quietly returns the discussion of *The Tarantas* to a literary level, and condemns the author finally for failing in the final chapter to provide the summing up which the rest of the work calls for. His final verdict is much like Pletnyov's: Sollogub's all-pervasive ambivalence, which leaves the reader in perpetual doubt as to his intentions, reaches its climax in "A Dream" and leaves possible only one conclusion: he has not meant his tale seriously at all. At no point in his discussion of Sollogub's work does Samarin even mention Slavophilism. His own views and those of his circle appear in his review, but only in the account which he gives of the history of the social process which has, in his belief, resulted in the alienation of Russia's upper classes from their national roots. This alienation he finds responsible for Ivan Vasilyevich's profound ignorance of Russian reality. In sum, Samarin interprets Ivan Vasilyevich's character in Slavophile terms, but finds the hero's views almost everywhere ridiculous and inadequate, those of a rootless visionary. Ivan Vasilyevich's rhetoric does not express satisfactorily any Slavophile views.

Turning now from contemporary views of *The Tarantas*, how does the work appear to a twentieth-century critic without ties to either Slavophilism or Westernism? From a dispassionate modern point of view how do the ideas aired in the tale compare with those we know as Slavophile? Of the interlocutors of *The Tarantas* Vasily Ivanovich clearly is not a spokesman for any kind of ideology; he is the representative of an instinctive, unreflecting acceptance of "the way things have always been." He is no more a Slavophile than the three merchants of Chapter XIV who reject any Western innovation for themselves, while leaving their sons free to choose whichever way of life they please. Since, however, as we have seen, Ivan Vasilyevich was in Belinsky's view intended as a spokesman for Slavophile views, his case must be examined in some detail.

As we have seen, for Ivan Kireevsky and the Slavophiles generally, Orthodox Christianity is the foundation stone of Russian "national character." A serious treatment of this serious subject would of course have been highly inappropriate in such a frivolous work as *The Tarantas*, while a frivolous treatment would have been unthinkable; and yet one might have expected the subject to have been at least mentioned, as it is not. Ivan prays in the Vladimir cathedral, he hears in his dream the bells summoning the faithful to morning worship, and he shows some curiosity about the differences between the Old Believers' doctrines and "ours"—i.e., those of the Orthodox church. The last mentioned item is the only hint in the work of Orthodoxy specifically as against religion in general.

It is not surprising that the very touchy subjects of serfdom and autocracy should be avoided altogether. Relations between peasant and master are discussed (and idealized) in Chapter XIII, but only an oblique hint that the Russian muzhik is not a free man comes in Vasily Ivanovich's impatient remarks, evidently aimed at Western—or Westernizing—criticism: "The Germans and French feel sorry for our muzhik. 'He's a martyr,' they say, and you look, and that martyr is healthier and better fed and more contented than many other peasants." A little later he has the French or German landlord saying to his peasants: "Pay up, you scum! You're a free man!"—and can therefore be evicted if you don't pay up: but the Russian side of this implied comparison has to be mentally supplied: the muzhik is unfree, but he can't be evicted and told to go hang if he doesn't pay up. That he *can* be sold is discreetly left unnoted.

As for autocracy, *The Tarantas* of course has numerous mentions of "the Tsar," often in mere popular sayings, and in Ivan Vasilyevich's dream the prince explains the success of the Russian transformation by the words: "The nobility went ahead, carrying out the blessed will of God's Anointed,"—a phrase that recalls "official nationalism" much sooner than Slavophilism.

Slavophile theorists, as we have seen, were not unanimous in their attitude toward Peter the Great and his reforms. Konstantin Aksakov was for rejecting all the reforms and turning back the clock to the sixteenth century, while more moderate thinkers insisted on the necessity of a compromise between "the old and the new." Sollogub once (Chapter VI) remarks of his character Ivan: "Zealous lover of his fatherland, he desired, as the reader already knows, to put his native land back again into pre-Petrine antiquity and mark out for it a new path for the transformation of the people." The author has slipped here, for nothing has ever been said earlier in the work to give the reader such information, and there is nothing in any of Ivan's rhetoric in the body of the work to confirm this statement. Ivan's dream, however, does confirm it, for in the transformed Russia that Ivan sees and the "prince" describes, Western influence appears to be virtually eliminated, even to costume (e.g. the prince's fur hat and "yellow morocco boots"). Here then we do see a clear evidence of Slavophile doctrine embodied in Ivan Vasilyevich. But it is equally clear from the rest of Chapter VI that the ardent theorist is disillusioned. He realizes the superficiality of his own knowledge of the antiquity he idealizes, and concludes: "What is done is done, and there is no power that can change it."

Even in the 1840 chapters of *The Tarantas* Ivan Vasilyevich is presented as an ardent admirer of the Russian muzhik, about whom he knows nothing in reality. His "travel impressions" are to include: "everything that I shall be able to dig up about the Russian people and their traditions, about the Russian muzhik and the Russian nobleman, whom I love with all my soul, just as I hate the official with all my soul..." Later, in Chapter XIII he rhapsodizes: "Between the peasants and the gentry exists in our country such a lofty, mysterious bond, something in our blood, inexplicable and unintelligible to every other people. This echo of the patriarchal life, strange for our times, is quite different from the pitiful relation between the weak and the strong." etc. The muzhiks whom Ivan encounters in their crass reality, however (XVII, "A Rustic Holiday") are drunkards, reckless spendthrifts and ignorant boors. And it is certainly not without significance that neither muzhik nor agricultural labor appear at all in Ivan's dream, except at a very great distance: from a bird's-eye (or "tarantas-eye") perspective he sees cultivators going out to their morning's work in the lush fields, but there is no hint of how they may be transformed.

The principle of *sobornost'*, which plays such a key role in Slavophile theory is barely hinted at in *The Tarantas*. Of course, since there is no discussion of religion in the work, its theological aspect is wholly ignored. The peasant *mir* and the remarkable fairness of its operations in reassigning communal land, picking draftees and the like is mentioned by Vasily Ivanovich, but in his mouth of course without any metaphysical theorizing. Significantly, Ivan Vasilyevich does not comment on the topic beyond the casual observation that perhaps the communal deliberations may be a far off echo of the Veche of the free cities of Ancient Rus.

Although it plays no major part in Slavophile theory, a corollary of the idealization of pre-Petrine Russia and of the peasant as its survivor, uncontaminated by Western ideas, is the notion that the arts, particularly literature and architecture, should go back to peasant sources for renovation. Folk song, folklore, even folk superstitions are idealized. Ivan Vasilyevich's tirade on Russian literature (Chapter X) ends with exhortations to the would-be writer to seek out the vanishing vestiges of folk literature before they disappear with the death of the last popular bard. The Slavophiles did in fact attempt some such rescue operation, e.g. in the collection of popular songs taken down from the lips of illiterate peasants by Ivan Kireevsky's younger brother Peter. The utilization of such popular sources, however, was no Slavophile monopoly, but a phenomenon of general European romanticism. Non-Slavophile examples of the period are Gogol's Ukrainian stories in *Evenings at a Hamlet near Dikanka,* Orest Somov's tales of witches, werewolves and buried treasure, or some of Vladimir Dal's "Russian Folk Stories." As for architecture, Sollogub himself theorizes on the subject in his chapter on the Pechersky Monastery (XII), and it recurs in Chapter XX, where architecture, as well as art and literature, appear to be exclusively of the native Russian variety. The houses of the nobility are larger replicas of peasant huts, the prince's collection of paintings are "of the Arzamas school," and his library contains only Russian works.

So Ivan Vasilyevich expresses some Slavophile attitudes—idealization of the muzhik, repudiation of Peter's reforms, a desire to return to the patriarchal past, etc., but entirely without any of the philosophical foundations of Slavophile theory—Orthodoxy as the only true Christianity, *sobornost'* as the Slavic leading principle in both religion and social life, etc. He also expresses, of course, a general recognition that certain Western borrowings must be accepted and amalgamated with native traditions. This conciliatory attitude is typical of the less extreme Slavophiles, but hardly compatible with Ivan's reported desire to return his motherland to "pre-Petrine antiquity."

But now arises a most crucial question: does Sollogub mean us to take Ivan seriously? Belinsky, perhaps disingenuously, professed to see the whole picture of Sollogub's hero as ironical, intended to ridicule Slavophilism in a gentlemanly way. Samasin queries: Why is it that even the truest and most intelligent of ideas in Ivan's mouth becomes caricatural.? and answers that Ivan's essential hollowness, lack of a grasp on reality is the reason. But even Samarin excepts certain passages, e.g. the "pedigree of the official," as representing the author's own sincerely held ideas. I think other examples could be cited in this line, as for example the discussion in Chapter XI on "what should be and what should not be borrowed from the West." Moreover, there are several coincidences between Ivan's ideas and those expressed *in propria persona* by Sollogub in the "educational" chapters (XV and XVI) and in authorial remarks elsewhere. Evidently Sollogub does not intend everything that his hero says to be rejected as the idle dreaming of an ill-informed and perversely educated youngster. But how to separate what is meant seriously from what is ironical? I think such a separation is quite impossible to make—and by intention. For some reason the author meant to leave his intent ambiguous. What could be the reason for such a desire? Perhaps it is because his real and serious message has nothing, or very little, to do with the hostile ideologies.

To conclude, what *are* we to make of Sollogub's intentions in *The Tarantas*? Was he taking sides in the ideological struggle between Westernizers and Slavophiles? Was he attempting to convey any "message" to the Russian people, and if so, what was it? The answer to the first question must be quite definitely "no." Neither of the author's two spokesmen represents decisively either of the two ideologies. Vasily Ivanovich is the intuitive, natural man, almost totally devoid of education, who, like Topsy, "just growed." Every kind of abstract idea is foreign and suspect to him. As for Ivan Vasilyevich, with his wholly foreign upbringing, one might suppose he would be sympathetic to the Westernizing fashion. On the contrary, as the author repeatedly points out, foreign experience has engendered in him an ardent patriotism and love of all things Russian. So he is a Slavophile? By no means, for he knows nothing about the country he loves. The author makes it clear from the very first chapter that Ivan Vasilyevich's ideas are all half-baked, with a kernel of good sense and a vast deal of moonshine spun out of his own head. And in his discourses, even as they stand, there are undigested elements of both ideologies, as we have seen. He would advocate substituting rational Western commerce for the patriarchal chaos which he finds in his land, and he puts forward as the first desideratum for Russia a sense of civic responsibility, represented by England, though how this would be possible in an autocracy is not clear.

If Sollogub is not, then, writing as an adherent of either ideology, what if any, is his thesis? Chapters XV and XVI are the most tendentious portions of the work; in them the author speaks in his own person and seriously. They hold the clue to his meaning, and it is not hard to formulate what this is: a totally foreign education once and for all alienates a man from his native roots, and the effects of it with the best will in the world can never be overcome. It unfits its victim for real life and creates a "superfluous man" whose ideas are always ridiculous and who is doomed to be always a useless and pitiable drone. By contrast, no education at all, while hardly something to be recommended, is far preferable to the wrong kind: Vasily Ivanovich turns out to be a solid and relatively useful citizen.

There is no doubt that this is Sollogub's intention, but misunderstanding is built into its very terms. It is easy to misinterpret the relative approval of Vasily Ivanovich's intuitive, patriarchal existence as advocacy of the worst features of the pre-Petrine Muscovite period, a caricature of genuine Slavophile notions. And the author's concession that in all of Ivan Vasilyevich's wildly extravagant and badly based ideas about Russia there is at least a kernel of truth leaves it open to the reader to decide as he pleases what this kernel is; and it appears that in general what results from such a screening fits Slavophile better than Westernizing thinking. Thus in regard to literature, the Russian writer is bidden to eschew Western models and search out his material in the remotest nooks of the country, where relics of antiquity may still subsist; Ivan idealizes the muzhik in the abstract (in concrete reality he finds him repulsive and boring) as the bearer of all the patriarchal virtues of cheerfulness, humility, devotion to his masters, etc. A great deal of this can be readily paralleled by elements of "official nationalism." Yet there always remains the unanswerable question: just how much of Ivan Vasilyevich's discourse is meant ironically, as the product of his imagination working on an atom of reality, and how much coincides with the author's own ideas?

This question becomes particularly important when we come to the final chapter of *The Tarantas*. I think most readers will agree with Yury Samarin that this chapter is very disappointing. One would expect, as Samarin does, to find in Chapter XX a synthesis, a reconciliation, the author's last word on the subject. Yet here too ambivalence is everywhere. After all, "A Dream" is Ivan Vasilyevich's dream, and some elements of it are certainly to be taken as ironical, e.g, the nonsense about the prince's collection of "model paintings of the best artists of the Arzamas school" or his all-Russian library. This is of a piece with the moonshine about Russian literature in Chapter X. But unfortunately there are also elements that just as unmistakably belong to Vladimir Sollogub—thus the equally ridiculous emphasis on the Slavonic character of the architecture in this "brave new world," including even the manor houses, which harks back to the author's own discussion in the chapter on the Pechersky Monastery.

But whether the ideas in "A Dream" are Sollogub's own or his hero's, they are, as Samarin complains, pretty trivial. Everything has been slicked up, all dirt and squalor, even poverty apparently, have disappeared; but just how has such a transformation been accomplished? If the author's principal thesis means anything, it can only be through education; one would expect, therefore, a good deal in this Utopia to be said on this subject. We read that there were schools—evidently church-run, which does not sound encouraging—everywhere, and that they were for "all children without distinction." Fine: but do they dispense only "Slavonic" education? So one would gather. But the whole subject of education occupies such a minuscule place in this picture that one can only conclude that the author sees no way, even in a dream, of reforming it! And what of the other great problems that plague nineteenth-century Russia and constitute the major areas of disagreement among the competing ideologies? Autocracy is evidently as strong as ever—the new order has been initiated by "God's Anointed." What about serfdom? Nothing, of course, could be printed on this subject, but the implication is that the happy, prosperous, clean and well-housed Orthodox people in Ivan's dream are still subject to their landlords, whose stately houses still stand as guardians of law and order. What about the bureaucracy, which has been so much on Ivan Vasilyevich's mind all along? There are still officials, it seems, in the new order, but if "the prince's" example is any indication, they are protected from the temptation to crookedness and bribe-taking by being recruited from the wealthy upper class! But this can only apply to the higher posts in the hierarchy; what about the lowly copy-clerks and stationmasters and their ilk? There would not have been enough gentry to go around, even if one could conceive of a gentleman's assuming such a post. And finally, the all-important question of the vast gulf between gentry and commoners created, or at least exacerbated, by the reforms of Peter the Great. The existence of this gulf and the damage done by it was recognized by both ideologies, and it is the principal theme of Chapter XVII of *The Tarantas*. Does Ivan in his dream see any solution to it? Like poverty and disorder, it has simply evaporated. Samarin's conclusion that this pitiful caricature of a new heaven and a new earth is meant only as a very tasteless joke represents the opinion of an intelligent and influential Slavophile. The expressed conclusion of the Westernizer Belinsky that the whole is intended ironically to discredit the Slavophile position comes to much the same thing: "A Dream" is not to be taken seriously. Unfortunately I am afraid that both critics are only half right; like everything else connected with Ivan

Vasilyevich "A Dream" is ambivalent, and we shall never know for sure how much of it is to be taken seriously. All we can say is that in any case, it is a most unsatisfactory conclusion.

If Sollogub's true thesis in *The Tarantas* is, as I believe, an educational one, the synthesis called for in the last chapter should have been one that demonstrated an amalgamation between the Slavonic tradition and a judicious selection of Western learning. What Ivan Vasilyevich was given was a totally foreign training, inappropriate for any child born outside of France, and not very appropriate even for a Frenchman. Knowing the names and dates of all the Capetian kings is not good preparation for managing an estate of 300 "souls." This does not mean, however, that such Western branches of learning as mathematics, political economy, psychology, philosophy et al. are irrelevant to the life for which Ivan Vasilyevich is destined, and Sollogub does not intend it to be so understood. But in the end he makes no effort to drive home this conclusion, and leaves the reader with a disappointingly unsatisfactory inference: an education such as Ivan Vasilyevich's inevitably leaves its victim a prey to the most chimerical and ridiculous notions, and these are those exemplified by the substance of "A Dream." And yet not all of "A Dream" is chimerical and ridiculous in the author's opinion! The willful ambiguity spoils everything, and suggests, as Samarin sadly remarks, that the author did not, after all, take his idea very seriously. Perhaps, after all, *The Tarantas* was only a "trial balloon," sent up to see which way the wind was blowing, but not meant to carry freight. Probably we shall never know.

Notes

1. V. A. Sollogub, *Tarantas: puteviia vpechatleniia*. Facsimile edition of the 1845 edition, M.: Izdatel'stvo "Kniga," 1982; supplement (A. Nemzer), p. 2.

2. E. A. Boratynskii, *Razuma velikolepnyi pir. O literature i iskusstve*. M.: "Sovremennik," 1981, pp. 165-166.

3. Nemzer in facsimile edition supplement, p. 4.

4. Nemzer in facsimile edition supplement, pp. 1-8.

5. V.G. Belinskii, *Sobranie sochinenii v trekh tomakh*, M.: OGIZ, 1948: review of *Tarantas*, pp. 811-855; p. 814.

6. *Russkaia drama epokhi A.N. Ostrovskogo*. Sostavlenie, obshchaia redaktsiia, vstupitel'naia stat'ia A.I. Zhuravlevoi. M.: Izdatel'stvo Moskovskogo universiteta, 1984, pp. 73-100.

7. Peter Yakovlevich Chaadayev, *Philosophical Letters* and *Apology of a Madman*. Translated with an introduction by Mary-Barbara Zeldin, Knoxville, Tenn.: The University of Tennessee Press, 1969, p. 36.

8. K.N. Batiushkov, *Polnoe sobranie stikhotvorenii*. Introduction, notes and ed. N.V. Fridman, M.-L.: Sovetskii pisatel', Biblioteka poeta, bol'shaia seriia, 1964, pp. 94-102.

9. I.V. Kireevskii, *Polnoe sobranie sochinenii*, M,: P. Bakhmetev, 1861; rpt. Ann Arbor, Ardis, 1983: Vol. I, p. 189.

10. N.A. Nekrasov, *Sobranie sochinenii v vos'mi tomakh*, M.: Izdatel'stvo "Khudozhestvennaia literatura," 1967, pp. 105-117 ; p. 115.

The Tarantas. A Work of Count V. A. Sollogub. Spb. 1845. Review by Yury Fyodorovich Samarin (1846)

Every work that is intended not for a few experts and specialists, but for the whole reading public,—a book that reflects the contemporary state of a whole society—can be considered not only as an expression of the author's personal thought, but also in its relation to the public, in connection with the impressions which it produces, with the sympathy or reprehension, both conscious and unconscious, which it meets with. It is from this point of view that we embark upon a review of *The Tarantas* of Count Sollogub; for works such as this presuppose and evoke a multitude of interpretations and judgments, which despite their seeming diversity, serve as a check on the author's thought, and often act as guides to its significance; the voice of the individual supplements the opinions of the public, both merge into a single manifestation of public opinion, and can be regarded as an indivisible whole. This view, it seems to us, is justified by the very success of the book we are reviewing. It was not hard to foresee this success: it was guaranteed by the author's talent, which everyone acknowledges, by the interest of the content, which everyone can appreciate, by the easy and attractive narrative style, and finally by the superior sketches—animated, intricate, often strikingly true to life. All this is offered in *The Tarantas;* yet in spite of such a rare combination of fortunate conditions, it can be confidently asserted that in the success of such a book, in the interest with which it is read, in the interpretations to which it has given rise, its literary merit has taken only a secondary place. It will be recalled that scarcely had the book been read, than one heard: What does the author mean to show with all this? Which of them is the better, Vasily Ivanovich or Ivan Vasilyevich? If they both are pretty bad, then where is the place between them for the Russian as he ought to be? Some, pointing to Vasily Ivanovich, would say: There he is, the representative of our vaunted national character! Others were delighted with Ivan Vasilyevich and would say: There's what it means to lose touch with one's national character! What some liked, others reprehended, and vice versa. In a word, Count Sollogub's book made its appearance as it were in the very moment of a heated general debate. For both sides the book itself was a secondary matter; each side saw in it confirmation of its own ideas and interpreted it in its own way; the author's own ideas were not noticed or not puzzled out. The dispute grew a great deal more heated *on account of* the book, and the talk to which it gave rise diverted the attention of readers from the book's merits. We do not know whether the author was pleased by this, whether he desired this kind of success. But then, what's to be done, if on his journey from Moscow to Mordasy he met up with those living questions of the present moment which in various forms lie in wait for us at every cross-roads!... What's to be done, if, directing our absent-minded gaze to both sides of the road, he has proved a better exegete than others, and has told in a language intelligible to all some of the singularities and crying contradictions of our reality?

Everyone has met with these and suffered from them, but not everyone has been conscious of them. Of those who have been conscious of them in the years of their fiery youth, many, having settled down with the years, have succeeded in forgetting about them or in getting used to them. Thus, though talented people do introduce them and know that they are doing a good thing, it may be that the time has not yet come with us for a quiet artistic contemplation; but on the other hand the moment has come for mature reflection and a stern judgment upon ourselves.

Let us recall in a few words the book's content. Vasily Ivanovich and Ivan Vasilyevich are riding from Moscow to Mordasy. On their way they encounter what one inevitably encounters over the entire immense expanse of the Russian Tsardom, in whatever direction one might cross it. Stationmasters, officials, muzhiks, merchants, a provincial city, a monastery, a rural village— all this rushes to meet the travellers and flashes rapidly ahead of them, reflected in its own way in the ideas of both. Each of them has his own point of view, his own needs, his own evaluation, his own prejudices. The contrast of these two views of the very same phenomena, conditioned not so much by a difference of years and personalities as by the difference in upbringing, in form of life, and in general in a whole social environment—this contrast constitutes the chief interest and theme as it were of the whole book. An idea, obviously, that is not new. In earlier times works of this sort were written, in which the author would bring into conflict the personified views of youth and age, of prose and poetry; these were colorless and cold. Not such the work of Count Sollogub. In his work the contrast of viewpoint is not a clever invention, not the artificial juxtaposition of bare concepts and abstract extremes of thought, but a living, real fact given by contemporary society. It is one of the countless forms of that fundamental opposition into which all of Russian life falls apart. From a work such as this it is almost impossible to ask for either external unity or strict structural completeness. What we have are not parts, fitted freely into a single whole, but a calculation, a series of pictures, which can be either extended or cut short. But it is essential, first of all, that with all the diversity of content and with all the freedom in arranging this, the fundamental contrast be maintained strictly and to the end, so that, in whatever order or disorder subjects may be changed, a direct and distinctive light may fall upon them from the two chosen points. Secondly it is necessary—and this is not a requirement of art alone—that both views, both attitudes be understood and presented as false in their extremes, in their exclusive one-sidedness. The author must stand above the opposition and the conflict; he must understand it, and consequently reconciliation of the opposites in a higher unity must be within his grasp. If this living reconciliation of what is divided in life is accessible to him, not merely as something possible, as a conclusion of abstract thought, but as the soul's living intimation of something inevitable—then, even though he may not have been speaking from his own person, even though he may not have taken upon himself the role of a juryman pronouncing a verdict after lengthy and one-sided debate—readers will feel in the dispute itself the reality of the reconciliation, will sense the presence of the whole truth even in the discordant interpretations of the one-sided parties.

And so the requirements of criticism have been defined.

What are Vasily Ivanovich and Ivan Vasilyevich? They are two Russians, of whom one is a native product, a phenomenon of a life unillumined by consciousness, impervious to idea: a landowner of advanced years, educated at the dovecote, in a circle of hangers-on and buffoons, who has almost never been outside his village, whose entire activity, all his interests and thoughts are bounded by the tight circle of the management of his home estate. The other is a young man, alienated from the Russian reality by a foreign education and mode of life, who has just returned from abroad with the desire to study his native land. Both persons are taken from contemporary society, they exist in it not as an accidental exception, but as types, under which whole masses of persons are subsumed. And so, in order to study the significance of these types in the present, let us endeavor to trace their historical formation in the past. We shall have to begin far back. It is well known to all that the reform of Peter the Great had different effects in the different constituent strata of our society; it stirred up only the upper stratum and tore it loose from the lower; the reform had no direct effect on the common people: it only changed their relations toward the higher castes, by estranging and as it were distancing them. On the other hand, Peter's idea penetrated deeply into the everyday life, into the convictions, into the habits of the upper caste and turned everything in it topsy-turvy. In place of old forms and such principles as never indeed grow old, but had at that time become choked with underbrush, or of which there was not a sufficient consciousness, new principles and new forms were introduced.

The concept of authority, the activity of service, judicial, administrative and military, the character of education—all was created anew, everything which constitutes an object of interest and is as it were an attribute of the so-called upper caste in contradistinction to the common people. This caste had to accept the reform because it had provoked it.

There was a time—the memory of it has been preserved in our chronicles— when the boyars, the best people (for thus the common people designated them) constituted not a separate self-contained caste, but a select circle of the society of the time and its best flower as it were, freely blossoming upon a single root. Society itself had put them forth from its own midst. They were more cultured than others in this sense that they had a clearer consciousness of the convictions and the needs of all, and accordingly their culture did not tear them away from the life of the common people, did not imbue them with a proud pretension to omniscience, did not hinder their mutual sympathy with the common people, a sympathy which was supported by a constant exchange of ideas. Not such is our conception of the period just preceding Peter I. We call to witness both foreign writers and our own. It is difficult to recognize the descendants of the "best people" in the arrogant and corpulent court officials of Alexei Mikhailovich, who are led about by hand and lifted by hand out of their sleighs, or in the boyars "ignorant of grammar and unpowdered (according to the expression of Koshikhin [i.e., Koto-shikhin]), who sit in the Duma, arranging their beards, and give no opinions."

Their relations with the common people, once open and free on both sides, changed and took on an official character. No longer did they converse with the people, take counsel with them, but only transmitted orders. They went to them only on solemn occasions; their sumptuous processions wound slowly through the city, the crowd looked on them with curiosity; but of the former sympathy, the former lively interchange of ideas and cooperation there is not a trace. The noble features of the great models of a better time were distorted and obscured. The former consciousness of one's own worth turned into arrogance, the power of ancestral memories into a pride in service. Whatever may have been the reasons for this (and among these the influence of the Polish aristocracy takes by no means the last place), the boyar caste of Alexei Mikhailovich's time experienced the fate of every caste that isolates itself in a feeling of egoism and pride: it became weak and degenerate. And so the higher caste provoked the reform by gradually distancing itself from the common people, by its abuse of the people's principles, and finally by that moral stagnation into which it sank. It is clear that on its part there could have been no rational opposition to the transformation, because its standing had been raised only by the forms of the old traditions, the living memory of which it had lost; there could also be none of that blind opposition which Peter I met with in the schismatics and the streltsy. Of course we are speaking of the caste as a whole and do not deny frequent exceptions, which, for the rest, were incapable of altering its fate. Many accepted the reform willingly and casting off, along with Peter, their old hauteur, made their way into learning, towards other nations. A rich activity in service was opened up before them. Others submitted to the transformation out of necessity, without sympathy: they regretted the old habits, the old indolence, the endless banquets and the reposeful ignorance; what was there left for them to do in the transformed society? All the higher spheres of activity in which their grandfathers used to live and revolve, service in the widest meaning of the word, were closed to them; because the needs of the government had changed, because new principles had been introduced which could not possibly be puzzled out by the natural intelligence nor replaced by traditions. It was necessary to begin to learn one's lessons over again; but for this there was neither enough strength or desire. It remained for their lot only to retire to their paternal estates, busy themselves with the management of these and entertain themselves with domestic amusements: with hunting and with fools, male and female.

From this class of people, which on the one hand had long since lost sympathy with the common folk, and on the other was incapable of participating in culture and in consequence was cut off from all the higher interests that ennoble a person and do not allow him to become mired in trivial and selfish concerns, all possible Prostakovs, Skotinins, Sobakeviches trace their lineage, and finally also Ivan Fedotovich, Vasily Ivanovich's father. The author has pictured for us the former's country way of life (XV), his vulgar, idle life and dissolute amusements without exaggeration and without impassioned bitterness. We make mention of this negative merit only because it has become a rarity in our contemporary literature. We have become so accustomed to seeing how avidly writers snatch at anything that may possibly cast discredit on former times, that the tone in Chapter XV struck us pleasantly.

The genetic concept under which we have placed Ivan Fedotovich and Vasily Ivanovich is a creation of circumstance, of the historical destiny of an entire caste; under this concept, it goes without saying, there is place for many ages, characters and personalities. Thus, for example, Vasily Ivanovich differs in many respects from his father. Let us cite the author's words:

> Although he did not do away altogether with the order that had existed in his father's time, he at least changed it in many ways: he sent the jesters off to the carpenter's shop, he seated the coachman on his box, and as for himself, he drank no more than two wine glasses of herb-flavored vodka a day—one before dinner and one before supper. It should not be thought, however, that he had armed himself with the rule of a terrible morality and beat the drum with resounding words—not at all. That which had interested and amused Ivan Fedotovich did not seem detestable to him, only it did not interest or amuse him at all. He understood that it is possible to be a drunkard, only he himself did not care to drink. He understood that it was possible to be amused by fools, only he himself did not find anything laughable in them. In a word, he became a good person not out of conviction, but quite by himself, because otherwise he would have felt awkward and uncomfortable. On the one hand he had a lively memory of the last terrible precept of his dying father, and on the other hand enlightenment, which is spreading imperceptibly everywhere, looking into villages and hamlets, had not passed Mordasy by, but had begun gradually to steal up to Vasily Ivanovich, speaking to him not in empty European apothegms, but in a tongue he understood. Thus he came to understand that his own well-being depended on the well-being of his peasants, and then he busied himself with all his might in the good work which even without this was dear to his softhearted nature... Children were born to Vasily Ivanovich. He began to bring them up not artfully, but no longer as he himself had been educated. A student from the seminary was engaged for them, who taught them history and geography, and a great deal about which Vasily Ivanovich had no conception. His eldest son on reaching his eleventh year was sent first to the provincial gymnasium and then to Moscow University. Vasily Ivanovich realized, himself not knowing why, that in a good education lies hidden not only the real embryo of every man's life, but also the secret principle of the well-being and life of every state.

This natural and unconscious transition from one generation to another is very truly understood by the author. By way of supplement to the characterization of Vasily Ivanovich, a person not new in our literature, I advise one to read Chapter XIII, in which the landowner is idealized.

With all these good qualities, Vasily Ivanovich lacks one thing—consciousness. He loves his peasants out of habit. He makes his son study the sciences because this is the accepted thing. To be sure, the author attributes a higher goal to him; but the whole form of Vasily Ivanovich's thought goes counter to this. In reality it is not so much that he doesn't feel any need based on personal incidents for rising to general concepts—he even manifests a sort of hostility toward them, even a terror. He is afraid of a new idea, a new view, even of a new and too bold word. It seems to him that if an object is not called by the name that he has been accustomed to call it by, the object slips out of his hands; if consciousness penetrates his constricted way of life, this will be destroyed and disintegrated. And so every time his companion, moved by Vasily's own narrative, tries to carry it to the general conclusion that follows from Vasily's own words, he balks, clutches at his own limited reality, renounces his own words, begins a conversation about something else, or pretends to be asleep.

It would be strange to blame Vasily Ivanovich for this, or more precisely, to blame him alone. The distrust of learning, the hostility toward the endeavor of thought to rise and make life better, is explained from one aspect by the fact that learning came to us from abroad, in forms inaccessible to the majority, with a content strange to our national character. It has not yet had time to be converted into our native property, it has not freed itself from a false disdain for life, and in condescending toward life, it frightens it by the boldness of its demands, it repels it by its arrogant pretension to omniscience. Vasily Ivanovich instinctively understands this dissent, and this is the explanation of his mistrust. But this should not be excused; because he is afraid in general of every idea, he is the innocent, unconscious foe of consciousness. This isolated relic of the half-overcome backwardness of pre-Petrine antiquity is mitigated in Vasily Ivanovich by a natural good nature, and is manifested as a scarcely noticeable trait in his whole personality. Sobakevich grumbles to himself more crudely: "Enlightenment, enlightenment, they're always talking about enlightenment!" [N. V. Gogol, *Sobranie sochinenii v shesti tomakh*, M. 1959; Vol. V, *Mertvye dushi*, p. 103]; none the less the basic impulse is the same with both.

Thus Vasily Ivanovich is a victim of the bipartition from which no one can save himself, but he is unconscious of it.

In direct contrast to him stands the other person, one who is completely cut off from Russian reality and has developed in himself an abstract consciousness.

Ivan Vasilyevich belongs to that generation of people which has been educated in foreign fashion: not in French fashion, because a French education demands as an indispensable condition all of France together with its natural world, its institutions and mode of life; not in English fashion, because English education is possible only in England itself, just as German education is possible only in the milieu of German life—but in an abstract foreign fashion, that is, one that is merely non-Russian. Perhaps a Frenchman or an Englishman will not understand this, but we Russians understand it. There is a whole complex of concordant sounds, undefined, but apprehensible to the inner hearing of a child; it is this immaterial and uncorrupted atmosphere of one's native land which is absolutely essential for the first years of childhood. The soul is saturated with this through and through and together with it breathes in a sympathy that is instinctual, and for just this reason not to be subsequently supplanted by anything, toward that world in which it has been fated to live, toward its natural environment, toward the people, toward the sounds of the language, toward all that which is subsumed under the word: native. How a person's spiritual connection with a whole world which is ready to receive him is linked by an invisible bond is impossible to relate or bring under a system. Hence the sympathy we are talking about is not given by education, but is acquired by itself, naturally and simply. Education cannot create it, but it can hinder it. It is possible to lock a child into a tight compartment and shut out living nature from him; it is possible to isolate him from reality, to dissociate him from life and absolutely subject him to an artificial process of education. The fruits of this system are before our eyes; they can be admired in a whole generation of people who are educated, but cut off from their own land, who wander about without a goal, not knowing what to adhere to or on what to base themselves; because that which has taught them to understand everything possible and to sympathize with everything, has deprived them of a native roof, a native earth, a native tongue. Their destination remains an unsolved task for themselves. They speak fluently in three or four languages; but they *have been taught* their own language too, exactly as they have the others, and they have no native tongue. They are capable of acknowledging and appreciating what is fine with all nations, they get along in all the countries of the world; but their relations toward their native land are somehow strange and unnatural. They *have learned* to love it. They know that the honor of a well-educated person is tied up with the honor of his native land, that he is obligated to defend it, and they gladly sacrifice their lives for it. They are capable of being fired with a noble zeal for the public good, they think up a multitude of improvements and a fine future for their native land; they do indeed love, but not so much their native land as the possible realization of their own hopes. They love certain qualities that are laudable in their estimation—that is, they love her just as foreigners might love her. And this is why so many fine impulses and irrevocable votes go for naught. This is what the absence of an instinctive, inborn love signifies, a love of which the beginning is lost in the immemorial years of childhood, a love which does not analyze coldly and distinctly, but embraces a whole nation just as it is, with its light and its dark sides.

Ivan Vasilevich belongs to this generation which is innocently atoning for the sin of a false education. We must add that he has received an education that is worthless in all respects, which has lured his capacities into various directions without contentrating them, has dissociated him from life, and yet taught him nothing. By himself Ivan Vasilyevich, just as Vasily Ivanovich also, is an ordinary person.

We have no complaints that the author picked just such people and not powerful and sharply marked personalities: the native qualities of a generation are expressed more clearly and accurately in such people as these; everyone sees that they are not exceptions, but people of whom there are many. Ivan Vasilyevich has been abroad. Travel is the indispensable supplement of his education; but it has produced an unexpected effect on him, contrary to what it would have produced on his father or grandfather; not that he is better than they, but because a different time has arrived, and independently of people is maturing and developing thought, pushing society upon the path toward consciousness, and pulling after it both strong and weak. In our stories and comedies the Russian who has returned from abroad appears as a sort of buffoon in outlandish apparel; he prattles in French and despises our mode of life. In its time this picture might have been true; but our moralists have fallen behind society and are fighting a chimera. Ivan Vasilyevich has brought back from abroad a respect and love for his own country, a desire to know Russia and grow closer to her. This trait is taken from contemporary reality; it has been caught beautifully, and as far as we know, for the first time. Ivan Vasilyevich is a new person, who belongs to the author. We shall cite a noteworthy passage about the impressions produced on him by foreign lands: [XVI]

> Meanwhile Ivan Vasilyevich was noticing that wherever he turned up, in whatever country he arrived, he was looked at with a sort of hostile, envious attention. At first he attributed this to his personal qualities, but then he divined that Russia occupied willy-nilly all minds, and that he was looked at so strangely solely because he was a Russian. Sometimes at the table-d'hote the most childish questions were put to him: will Russia presently take over the whole world? Is it true that next year Tsargrad [i.e., Constantinople] will be named the Russian capital? All the newspapers that came into his hands were filled with observations about Russian policy. In Germany Panslavism occupied all minds. Every day there issued from the press the stupidest pamphlets and books at the expense of Russia, written with a sort of lackeyish resentment, and demonstrating nothing but the talentlessness of their authors and the fears of Europe. Little by little life abroad made Ivan Vasilyevich involuntarily begin thinking about his own native land. Thinking about her he began to be proud of her, and then he even began to love her. In a word, that which in his native land had not been instilled in him in his education, stole little by little into his soul while in a foreign land. He began to remember all that he had seen and not taken note of in his village, on excursions in the provinces, at the times of his detached duties while in the service. Even though he felt that all these data did not add up to a general opinion, a general whole, yet certain traits he retained quite faithfully, while he filled in the rest with his imagination. Thus he put together for himself particular ideas about officials, about Russian commerce, about our education, about our literature. Then he decided to study his native land thoroughly, and since he undertook everything with rapture, love for his fatherland began to burn in him with a violent fire. Moreover he was delighted that he had given a meaning to his being, that he had found himself at last a goal in life, a beautiful goal that promised him an attractive occupation, useful observations. With such feelings he returned from abroad.

This necessity of a spiritual reunion with one's native land is something that the people of our time are fated to experience. It is manifested in various forms and degrees. With some it is manifested as the consequence of a painful and wearisome consciousness of their disjunction from native life; such suffering, when it is sincere, has a salutary effect upon the soul: it cleanses it from the pride of dead learning, inclines a person before an unconfessed possibility of life, before the simple people, uneducated indeed, but in the simplicity of an uncorrupted spirit preserving a profound sense and a lofty love for truth and goodness. For these people to return to their native land becomes not only an aspiration of the mind, but the task of a whole lifetime, the inner rebirth of their own souls, and they will find the way out. Ivan Vasilyevich is not such. To be sure, he is melancholy and bored; but he is incapable of a cleansing suffering. In his petty soul there is place only for personal grief. He has condemned his upbringing because he has fared badly from it; but he has not realized and lamented in it the crime of an entire society, and so it is natural that the very necessity of a reunion with life does not rise in his soul freely, from within, but is developed upon it from without; it attaches to him as it were accidentally. Scarcely has the sincere thought of a few people been uttered, scarcely has the word "national character" been pronounced, and already the external shell of the thought has had time to become detached from it and to stand forth in the form of a fashion. But this is the way it always is.

From all the preceding it must be clear to the reader in what sense the two persons whom the author presents belong to contemporary society and express its condition. The opposition of their views constitutes the most important phenomenon of the present moment: the rupture of life with consciousness. In this, it seems, is contained the meaning of the book we are reviewing. We do not know whether the author himself understood it so. But then, whether he had this in mind or not, whether he was clearly investing a conscious idea in living figures, or whether these figures took shape of themselves by the accumulation of numerous observations, is not our concern. If the idea penetrated his work without his knowledge, so much the better; this means that it was not dreamed up in idle hours, but inspired by contemporary life. In any case, the gift of observation, the ability to express in a single trait and a single person that which is the property of many, belongs incontrovertably to the author. We note in this connection that the personality of Ivan Vasilyevich is understood more deeply, expressed more strongly and sketched more clearly and fully than the personality of Vasily Ivanovich; evidently because the prototype of the latter could be studied in books, in Fonvizin, Griboedov and others, while Ivan Vasilyevich was created by the author himself, and taken directly from life.

Vasily Ivanovich and Ivan Vasilyevich meet on Tverskoi Boulevard and the following conversation begins between them. V.I. begins:

"And now, if I may ask, what do you intend to do, eh?"

"Why, I'd like to have a look at Russia, Vasily Ivanovich, to get acquainted with her."

"What?"

"I'd like to study my motherland."

"What? What?"

"I intend to study my motherland."

"If you please, I don't understand... You want to study..."

"To study my motherland... to study Russia."

"And how, my dear fellow, are you going to study Russia?"

"In two ways... in regard to her antiquity, and in regard to her national character, which of course are closely connected. By investigating our monuments, our beliefs and traditions, by listening to every echo of our olden times, I shall succeed... pardon! We shall succeed—we, my comrades and I... we shall come to an understanding of the national spirit, character and needs, and we shall know from what source our people's education must come, utilizing the example of Europe, but not taking it as a model."

"As far as I'm concerned," said Vasily Ivanovich, "I've got the best way for you to study Russia—get married. Drop the empty words, fellow, and let's go to Kazan. Your rank isn't very high, but it's that of an officer, you have a gentleman's estate, you'll easily find a good match. And, thank God, we have a good harvest of marriageable girls... Get married, that's right, and go live with the old man. It's time to think about him. Eh, fellow, that's right! You suppose, of course, that it's tiresome in the country? Not a bit of it. In the morning, out in the field, and then a snack, and then dinner, and then a nap, and then to the neighbors... And the name-day parties, and the hunting with hounds, and music of one's own, and the fair... Eh? That's living, fellow! What's your Paris! And the principal thing, you'll be having babies, and your rye will be yielding eightfold, and there'll be so much grain on your threshing-floor that you won't be able to thresh it, and so much money in your pocket that you can't count it, and so, in my opinion, you'll learn to know Russia famously... Eh?"

From this extract it may be judged how the two people whom we already know clash in conversation. I.V. talks not badly and often to the point; but in spite of this he is ridiculous in the extreme. How is it that a genuine and respectable thought takes on a caricatural form when he expresses it? It is because in him there is no sincerity: he blows up to great proportions, but honestly, without the intention of doing so, not others, but himself, imagining that his whole being is permeated by a single idea, that the purpose of his life has been found, whereas he is incapable even of inner concentration or of constantly directing himself. V.I. likewise has faithfully delineated himself. He very much dislikes it that his friend wants to study life; he uses all his weight to draw him into that narrow circle of the household estate manager in which his own experience has been inextricably enclosed.

V.I. and I.V. agree to ride together to Mordasy. The majestic and impossibly overloaded tarantas starts away from the place, and little by little unfolds the monotonous picture of Russian actuality. It can be told beforehand what sort of impression it will make on them. For Vasily Ivanovich everything in it is familiar, and so nothing seems to him worthy of observation. Does his companion begin to annoy him with a question or an inflated phrase—then he closes his eyes, sleeps all the way and directs his indolent mind toward nothing. But as an experienced person and well acquainted with life's external side, he more than once sets Ivan Vasilyevich back, more than once laughs at his air castles, and not without inner satisfaction kills his dreaming with a word to the point or a sly gibe. He is fated to experience the pleasure of a man who is prejudiced against ideas when in his presence an inexperienced youngster gets carried away, and he watches for a moment when he can slip under the other's feet a sharp fact, aptly taken from life. Ivan Vasilyevich affords not a few such moments. Bitter disillusionment lies in wait for him. The reader knows that he is not simply riding from Moscow to Mordasy, but traveling with the purpose of learning to know the national character, and has provided himself for the purpose with a stout bound notebook which he hopes without fail to write full to the last page. In this we recognize Ivan Vasilyevich and all his friends in full measure. A strange combination of childish foresight in trifles with a decided lack of sense in essentials! He has thought about notebook and pencils, but not about whether he will rub his eyes, sharpen his gaze, train his hearing. And here he is, with his book open and gazing all eyes, but not seeing; listening but not hearing, asking and not getting any answers. After two or three unsuccessful tries, here is how he reasons to himself:

> At first I clutched at the antiquities—there are no antiquities; I thought to study provincial societies—there are no provincial societies; they are all uniform, so they say. The life of the capital is a life that isn't Russian, but one that has adopted from Europe small-scale culture and large-scale vices. Where is one to look for Russia? Maybe among the simple people, in the simple day-to-day course of Russian life? But here I've been riding for four days, I keep my ears open and listen, I keep my eyes open and look, and do what I will, there's nothing I can note and write down. The surrounding country is dead: land, land so much land that your eyes get tired looking; an abominable road... Strings of carts travelling in the road... the muzhiks exchange curses, and that's all... and at your destination: now the stationmaster's drunk, now cockroaches are crawling up the walls, now the shchi smells like tallow candles... Can a decent person be interested in such stuff... And the dreariest thing of all is that in the whole enormous expanse a sort of dreadful monotony reigns which fatigues one to the utmost, and gives no respite. There is nothing new, nothing unexpected. Everything is the same, over and over... and tomorrow it will be just as it is today. Here's a station, yonder is the same station again; and still farther on, the self-same station once more; here's a village elder asking for a tip, and yonder again to infinity there are village elders asking for tips... What am I going to write?

This is precisely the way it was bound to be. The inevitability of Ivan Vasilyevich's failure, the impotence of abstract thought and feeling casually set ablaze to comprehend reality, to take possession of life—this fact, full of moral meaning, is clearly understood by the author and beautifully expressed:

> Ivan Vasilyevich was in a most sorrowful frame of mind. The untouched book was wallowing around under his feet next to the cellarette. Russia's instruction as regards her antiquities and national character had decidedly not been advanced. The business, it seemed, was not for the many. Ivan Vasilyevich divined that a good intention alone was not enough for carrying out a great exploit. Placards weren't hung all over Russia on which her life could be read, everything that was, that is, and that will be. One excursion to

Mordasy was somehow too little for such a study. Something else was still needed. Everlasting tenacity was still needed through the course of a whole life. And considerable of this, it seemed. It was necessary to penetrate into the very depths of every subject because from the smooth outer surface nothing was extracted. It was necessary to seek out, as the key to the riddle, the secret, sometimes lofty meaning of every prosaic phenomenon that turned up at every step. But as we know, Ivan Vasilyevich was a person of a weak nature. As he met with difficulties, he made no effort to overcome them, but changed his undertakings. Thus little by little he had renounced, as we have seen, the fine studies the important discoveries for which he was preparing himself with such ardor for the good of humanity.

The first object to which the travellers' attention is devoted is officials. Ivan Vasilyevich in passing declares to Vasily Ivanovich that he heartily loves the Russian muzhik and the Russian nobleman, and hates just as heartily the official and that monstrous nameless caste which has grown up with us out of a vile pretension to some sort of miserable, misunderstood culture:

"But why, my dear fellow, do you hate officials?" inquired Vasily Ivanovich.

"That doesn't mean that I hate people who serve conscientiously and nobly. On the contrary, I respect them with all my heart. But I hate that miserable type of crude culturelessness which one meets with among both gentry and commoners and among merchants, and which I call accordingly by the altogether inexact name of official."

"But why, my dear chap?"

"Because those whom I so designate, for their lack of a solid foundation give themselves only the externals of culture, but in reality are a great deal more ignorant than the simple muzhik himself, whose nature is still unspoiled. Because there is in these people nothing Russian, neither the moral character nor the habits; because with their tavern culture, their self-satisfied ignorance, their wretched dandyism, they not only hold back genuine culture, but often set it on a harmful direction. A monstrous caste has sprung up on the nation's soil, one perfectly foreign to the nation's life. Just look at them: what has become of the noble traits of our people? This class is dirty, it drinks itself drunk, but not on holidays, like the muzhik. It takes bribes, it tries to put down everyone else, and at the same time puffs itself up and puts on airs before the simple folk because forsooth it plays billiards and goes about in a frock coat! Such a tribe is a corrupted tribe, degenerated from a fine beginning."

After this follows a remarkable passage—the genealogy of the official:

A household serf is nothing but the first step toward an official. The household serf is shaven, he goes about in a long-tailed coat of home-made cloth. The household serf serves for the amusement of idle sloth and gets used to parasitism and debauchery. The household serf already gets drunk and steals and puts on airs and despises the muzhik who toils for him and pays the soul-tax for him. Then under favorable circumstances the household serf becomes a clerk, a freedman, a departmental clerk; the departmental clerk despises both the household serf and the muzhik, and studies pettifoggery, and on the sly from the district police officer picks up chickens and ten-kopeck pieces for himself. He has a nankeen coat and pomaded hair. He is already learning stealing of a systematic sort. Then the departmental clerk descends a degree lower, becomes a copyist, a desk supervisor, a secretary, and finally a full-fledged official. Then his sphere is enlarged, then he takes on a different kind of life: he despises both the muzhik and the household serf and the departmental clerk because they, if you please, are uneducated people. By this time he has the highest of requirements, and so is already stealing bank notes. His drink of course has to be wine from the Don, he has to smoke Zhukov tobacco, play "little bank," ride in a tarantas, order caps for his wife with silver spikes of wheat, and silk gowns. For this purpose he assumes his office without the slightest twinge of conscience, just as a merchant enters his shop, and makes trade of his influence as with any ware. One gets caught, and another... It's nothing to him, say his confreres. Take, but take care.

We forget for the moment that it is Ivan Vasilyevich saying this, because this fragment by its sharpness and originality contradicts the general character of his pallid and inflated discourse; and we should forget all this, because the idea by itself is reasonable, and it is good that it has been uttered. And so from the author's words it follows that the household serf is the first step toward an official; consequently, in the descending line, the household serf is the lowest expression of the official. The two then occupy the last rungs on the ladder which with one end is based on the simple people, and with the other rests on what, if not the highest caste, that nobility which Ivan Vasilyevich loves so heartily? The rungs of the ladder correspond to those phases of rapid degeneration which are so wittily depicted in the preceding vignette; they are the steps laid out along the road which every person traverses who strives upward from below. The requirements of this upper level, the character of the goal, naturally determine also the character of the striving itself. If this is so, why attack the official so savagely, when the official has not created himself, but expresses the very natural, even necessary desire of every man to adapt himself to a given, ready-to-hand ideal? Of course, in the select circle into which the official is crawling, many of his vices, for example, the crude contempt toward the lower classes, that arrogance of a supposed culture, are unsuited; but is this because really the vices do not exist there, because the Christian feeling of brotherly love has overcome them, or because it is possible to get used, to accustom oneself to everything; because vice, as it penetrates deeper and deeper into the form of thought, into the feelings, into the whole way of life, loses in doing so its coarse rough exterior, and in time at last puts on it a sort of alluring gloss?

Perhaps only Vasily Ivanovich could have resolved this perplexity; but unfortunately, to Ivan Vasilyevich's question: "what do you think of our aristocrats?" he replied with the words: "I think there won't be any horses for us at the station." Be that as it may, the panegyric with which, after the passage we have cited, Ivan Vasilyevich ends his speech, strikes one strangely: you can't understand how it accords with what precedes it; but this only shows that toward the end Ivan Vasilyevich has begun to speak again. The stern verdict pronounced on officials in the second [*sic*: read "third"] chapter is somewhat mitigated by the depiction of the two persons belonging to this very caste (XVIII: Officials), and who have a definite kinship with Gogol's Akaky Akakievich. We do not mean to compare them, but only want to say that however great the distance between these two works, both are bound to act upon the prejudice which is unfortunately quite widespread in the circle of cultured people, who regard the official exactly as Ivan Vasilyevich does, with a sort of superstitious horror and aversion, imagining that the official is a miserable creation of the evil spirit, whereas he has been very naturally created out of contemporary circumstances. These gentlemen shun encounters with an official, and do not suspect how much moral greatness and humble elevation are encountered in that despised and unhappy caste. The author does a great deal in introducing them to another point of view. But here's the pity: his depiction of the official inspires only compassion, the sort of feeling that gets along with pride, and which, especially with a rapid performanance of any easy act of charity, can be satisfied with the sacrifice of ten rubles. Gogol's work takes a deeper hold on the soul, moves it more beneficially; we have seen how, in reading it, tears have appeared in some eyes... not of sympathy, but of repentance and love. But comparisons aside!

The depiction of the provincial city in Chapter VI is marvelously clear and one-sided. In it is sharply displayed a simple, so to speak, city person's characterization of all provincial towns: their painful striving to be like the capital, to create a sort of artificial community upon existing foundations, a striving that distracts them from the local meaning which is their proper calling. This ridiculous side in them exists, as no one will dispute. But is there not another side? Does not the diversity of localities place particular imprints upon them? Does not the simple knowledge of local needs, to speak of nothing else, connect them by a natural tie with the life and daily round of an entire province? It seems the author himself felt the one-sidedness of his characterization, and so put it in the mouth of a man who has squandered a fortune, ruined himself by petty ambition, and hence is dissatisfied, embittered. The biography of this man, told by himself, is a successfully executed sketch, but unfortunately only a sketch, which might have been a bright, original picture. The hero of the simple and stupid story belongs to the number of people who are not so to say bad, or without talent, but foreign to any content in mind and heart. All their efforts are directed, not toward being something, but only toward seeming so to others. The mainspring of their activity is petty vanity; the talk of the society world takes the place in them of conscience. Having ruined themselves totally, lost their good name, exhausted both spiritual and bodily forces, they acquire a sort of worldly wisdom of cold, barren rationality. The bad side of all social circles is known to them; their criticism is sharp and venomous; but to what purpose is all this, when in their souls there are neither convictions nor love? This person, very successfully contrived, disappears, leaving a painful impression after him.— And here is another person: a Russian nobleman, a person of the same tribe as Ivan Vasilyevich, but a little less advanced than he. This one is a devotee of the West and of Europeanism, and curses his people in the foulest terms; he is accustomed to civilization, to the intellectual life, and he interrupts his discourse with threats and abuse; he declares that he is going abroad, that he needs money, that his peasants are ruined, but that is no business of his—he is a European person who doesn't interfere in his peasants' affairs. In a word, a somewhat dated figure; but whether he belongs to our time or to the past, we shall not take upon us to decide. Now the prince too has drifted past. Around a samovar sit merchants drinking tea and talking about their affairs. Their conversational language is quite successfully caught. I. V. reads them a long lecture on the following theme: in private life you won't take five kopecks from a stranger, but in a business deal you will fleece your own brother unmercifully; honesty with you is divided into two halves—in the first you call deceit deceit, in the second, profit. To this the merchants answer him: "Won't you call, sir, for another cup... with cream?"—And here is a village on holiday. The muzhiks are drunk, the girls trade insults with the young fellows; a schismatic passes the priest without taking off his hat; a serviceman tells of his travels to a crowd gathered around him. This narrative is very lively and original in places, but it lacks unity: you have the feeling that it has been stitched together of selected pieces. I. V. has maintained his character. He has approached the young women; they have made fun of him and called him a slicked-up German; he has tried to question a muzhik about the schismatic whom he has encountered, but he has learned nothing because he questioned stupidly. "A strange folk, an incomprehensible folk," says I. V. to himself; but not the folk, but Ivan Vasilyevich himself is strange, though very comprehensible.

We have pointed to only those sketches which are in some way notable. For supplement and variety are inserted still others: a station, a hotel, gypsies, "A Ring"—a quite unsuccessful imitation of a simple commoner's story; something about literature—an eloquent variation on an old theme; the Monastery of the Caves—a rhetorical exercise in the descriptive genre, dropped into *The Tarantas* for unknown reasons; a landowner; and finally "The East," or more exactly, "The Tatars"; all of this swiftly flashes to meet the traveling tarantas, in light, often graceful sketches, and around them, in fanciful ornamentation, winds the conversation. The author is in full possession of this form of exposition; the talk is free, unconstrained and natural, without flabbiness. It is possible, of course, to reproach him with several incongruities. Sometimes, forgetting himself, the author makes his heroes talk too intelligently and eloquently. We might cite examples of this, but we may better hurry on to the conclusion.

Ivan Vasilyevich tries to understand reality, because he is not living in it; Vasily Ivanovich is to such a degree immersed in it that he doesn't care to understand it. Consciousness and life are in conflict; but they must be reconciled, must understand each other and merge into the unity of a sturdy life, enlightened by consciousness. Having presented us with the limited character of the two views that arise out of the opposition, the author points out to us their reconciliation. Without this the work would take on no integrity, the reader would remain with a powerful feeling of duality. Hence the last chapter was necessary. We approached it with a powerfully aroused curiosity. We wanted finally to listen to the author's own voice, to meet his thought face to face; we were convinced that after such intelligent criticism of the contemporary condition he would reveal to us a comforting vision of the future. Whether our hopes were fulfilled, whether we were able to be satisfied, let our readers judge. We shall present the content of the last chapter. It would be easy to quarrel with its fantastic beginning, the transformation of the tarantas into a bird, with all those phantoms and horrors that do not horrify in the least; but perhaps it was hard to do without this transformation, which, to the author's misfortune, is reminiscent of the last pages of *Dead Souls*. But all this is by the way. With however great a jump, we found ourselves in the future world of a renovated Russia. The tarantas has become a tarantas again.

> The tarantas had become a tarantas again, not clumsy and dishevelled as Ivan Vasilyevich had known it, but polished, lacquered, graceful—in a word, a perfect, dashing youngster. The boxes and the cords had disappeared. The mattings and the bags as it were had ceased to exist. Their place was taken by small chests covered with hide, and tightly attached to the places designed for them. The tarantas had been as it were reborn, reeducated, and made young. In its firm tread there was no trace of its former slovenliness; on the contrary, on it was impressed a kind of confidence, a feeling of inalienable dignity, even of a little pride.

Like the tarantas, nature itself has somehow been freshened anew; rural villages have been cleaned up, straightened up, and dressed in holiday attire.

> On the broad oaken doors were fastened signs which gave token that in the long winter days the master of the house did not spend his time in drunkenness, did not toss idly on the loft-bed, but brought benefit to his brothers with a profitable craft, thanks to the Russian people's capacity for imitating and making everything, and thereby enhanced his own prosperity as well.

An important progress: it wasn't like that before; no doubt the Russian muzhik used to be afraid of the cold and would sit all winter in his own den. It never entered his head to busy himself with a craft. Drunks and beggars have disappeared; alms-houses have been built for old people (which of course didn't exist with us before), and shelters for children (precisely something which our grandfathers didn't know how to create).

> The landowners' houses seemed to stand as guardians of order, as a pledge that the happiness of the realm would not be altered, but thanks to the wise solicitude of its enlightened leaders, all would still strain forward, all would develop still further, glorifying the works of man and the loving-kindness of the Creator.

In a word, there is cleanliness everywhere, everything is picked up, all the people are in their places, there is such order that the heart rejoices.

And in the towns, what improvements! No fences are to be seen at all, nothing but solid buildings, no ruins or tottering walls or dirty shacks... How picturesque must such a city be! Evidently it is so, because looking at it, at this Moscow with its "Slavonic, national, original exterior," I.V. exclaims: "Italy,

Italy, surely we have outdone you in finery!"

It seems that nature, villages, cities have been brought into fine condition. Let us take a look at the people. One acquaintance, the prince whom Ivan Vasilyevich had met on the highway, comes to meet us. But you wouldn't recognize him...

> On his head was a beaver-fur hat, his upper body was tightly held in by a light fabric jacket trimmed with sable fur, and on his feet the yellow morocco boots indicated, according to Slavonic custom, his noble rank.

The prince is all dressed up, his hair is smoothed down in the present-day style, with a part on the side (if one can trust the picture), he has laced himself up in a sort of Hungarian jacket (no doubt this is the way the boyars of old dressed), and he has taken his plumed hat in his hands. For the rest, the prince is convinced "that this costume is perfectly appropriate, and besides, it's our own national one." The prince has grown considerably wiser. He has come to realize that traveling abroad is not at all necessary, because "we aren't children, thank God... it's unseemly for us to concern ourselves with charades and take names for facts," and after this he adds profoundly "that history is nothing but the past's lesson to the present, for the future." The prince expresses himself very well. Here, for example, is how he interprets the reason for Russia's gigantic success: "We separated the human from the ideal." This principle really includes in it a strong incentive to improvement, and will lead far! Later on the prince talks about the equilibrium that is found in love, about humility, etc., so that it seems as though the prince has heard something to the point from some of his friends, but has understood it amiss, distorted it, mixed it up with other, directly contrary principles, and fused all this together in his pompous and colorless speech. According to his words, the Russian people has gone ahead, maintaining strict order, exactly as in a procession, one caste after another, one guild after another. "The nobility went ahead, carrying out the blessed will of God's anointed, the merchant class cleared the way, the army defended the land, and the common people cheerfully and confidently pressed forward in the direction pointed out to it."

But then, perhaps the prince isn't a master at expressing himself; very likely the gift of words constitutes the special property of another caste. It may be that his existence and way of life will explain to us better than any words the renovation of all Russia. And exactly so: first of all, he has many occupations; secondly he goes to the club, which from the English has been renamed the Russian (also an important success for nationalism); finally he is in service as an assessor.

> Because, by being in service, he is not taking away from the profitable occupation or craft of a poor man who might otherwise have had to assume his office. Thus the government is not supporting penurious ignoramuses and conscienceless parasites. Safeguarding the laws is not made a source of law-breaking.

Quite so. The good prince! How grateful the poor man should be to him, whom, thanks to the prince's self-sacrifice, they will finally stop dragging away from his profitable craft! All this seems very touching, but yet one's heart, as it were, doesn't believe the prince. Whether because it's hard to get used to the new order and slough off the old prejudices,—but in these words is heard the old incurable pride of caste. How it is reconciled with that love, that humility about which so much has been said, we are unable to understand. Later the prince invites Ivan Vasilyevich to his old, ancestral castle. Where does this castle come from? In Russia, it seems, there were no such; but then, evidently the prince has built himself anew an ancestral castle in the style of the English ones? But no: he says himself: "My castle stands just as it has for several centuries." Let people suppose what they please. Then I.V. learns that the prince has a gallery of pictures of the Arzamas school, a Russian library almost without any admixture of foreign books; he learns also that in every peasant hut may be found the issues of *The Northern Bee* and a volume of *Notes of the Fatherland*. And why shouldn't one find them? In the ideal Rus, as its author presents it, *The Northern Bee* and *Notes of the Fatherland* are entirely in place. Finally I.V. meets his other friend also, who, thanks to the lectures of certain professors, has become a sage in the style of the ancient philosophers and declares that "unfortunately there can be no equality on earth." I.V. at sight of his family exclaims "there is such a thing as happinness on earth!"

So here it is, the ideal Rus, the Rus that has been the promised land for us and for our much-enduring predecessors, and promised by our own indubitable hopes! We look at it and ask: are all the needs of the present moment really so mean, are the contradictions that we complain of really so trivial, is this duality of life that is to be seen in everything really so superficial that it is only necessary to put a coat of varnish on the tarantas, for the prince to change his overcoat for a Hungarian jacket and to send subscriptions to *The Northern Bee* to all the peasant huts, in order to satisfy our lawful needs and reunite what has been torn apart?

But enough! Is there in all this any unity and true reconciliation, or is this only a parody of reconciliation, a ridiculous masquerade, an imitation of national character, deceptive and harmful: because, in taking upon itself the look of national character, it delays the moment of its triumph?

At the beginning of Chapter IV is presented a remarkable vignette: a Russian peasant hut, provided with a Greek portico. It would have been a good thing to have presented in the chapter depicting the ideal Rus a foreign building concealed behind the facade of a Russian peasant hut.

But then, are we right in talking seriously about what the author himself is giving only as a joke? For this is a vision, these are dreams of Ivan Vasilyevich! Yes—but why has the author, turning to jest a subject by no means amusing, saved himself in advance from too captious criticism? Is it because he has come to hold his idea too dear, and has become afraid for it of a cool, prejudiced judge, or, on the other hand, is it that he doesn't hold it dear at all? To our regret, we are compelled to accept the latter, and it is of this particularly, and by no means in jest, that we reproach the author. The gift of observation is an important matter; but in order to reproduce what one has seen, in order to paint a picture, it is necessary to choose a point of view and maintain it. Criticism of contemporary social phenomena is essential and useful, but it demands not only impartiality, but also a definite and unvarying yardstick. Without unity of thought, without inner concentration of all the spiritual forces in a single basic conviction, an artist will not create a harmonious work, a thinker will not have any effect on society. We are not reproaching the author for not speaking from his own person, with not putting forward his own ideas, but rather that there is no sound of this, that this idea does not exist.

An idea exists in Gogol's works, and if it is not clear to all, this is because Gogol is still too close to us; it exists with Dickens, and with them both it does no harm to their artistry. We find it also in other writers of lesser magnitude, and however one-sidedly false it may be, and however it may disturb the artistic harmony of the writer, it gives him the social significance which is demanded of contemporary art.

The presence of such an idea, or better, its conception in the element of feminine feeling, we find in the author's first works, in that unfeigned sorrow that has arisen from the consciousness of the profound contradiction between the living soul of the artist and the conventional demands of society. But this string is no longer to be heard, and unhappily, nothing has taken its place. Surely the author has not succeeded in becoming reconciled so soon and so easily? We hope it is not so.

Appendix

Sollogub's *Tarantas* was published in full in the spring of 1845. In March of that year Ivan Sergeevich Aksakov, younger brother of the Slavophile theorist Konstantin Aksakov, published a curious work with the title *Winter Journey*, which may or may not have some reference to Sollogub's work. The similarity of structure, in any case, as well as the near coincidence of time (the precise month and day of the *Tarantas* publication are not known) would make it seem likely that Ivan Aksakov had *The Tarantas* in mind in writing his piece.

Winter Journey bears as a genre description the whimsical indication "Licencia poetica." The "poetic licence" applies to the work's synthetic composition: the first part has the outward form of a drama, mostly in verse; but since the "scene" is in a moving vehicle with two occupants. It is obviously a "closet drama." The second part, introduced merely by the words "change of scene," is in prose, and is set inside a peasant hut where the travellers stop. This portion can be regarded as a "dramatic sketch" in the style of the "natural school"; it could actually be staged.

The two interlocutors of *Winter Journey* are the westernizer Yashcherin and the Slavophile Archippov, who are on their way to a name-day party. It is not enough, however, to characterize the two merely with ideological labels: Yashcherin is the practical man, Arkhippov the romantic dreamer. As it turns out in the second part, both are equally unable to understand the peasants, and both are equally classed by the peasants as "gentlemen," and hence of an alien race. A translation of the first part of *Winter Journey*—the only part which is relevant—may allow an interesting comparison with *The Tarantas*.

Dramatis Personae

Peter Semenovich Arkhippov	Young men riding from Moscow to the name day party of a certain land-
Andrei Vladimirovich Yashcherin	owner, a relative of Yashcherin.
Ivan	A servant

The action takes place in the carriage, and partly also at the stations.

(A village on the highroad. Beside the station stands a carriage, harnessed to a three-horse team. Arkhippov and Yashcherin emerge from the station.)

Yashcherin: Well, are we ready?

Ivan: Ready, sir.

Arkhippov: Well then, with God... (*A coachman approaches.*)

Coachman: Master, a tip for an old coachman... (*Arkhippov gives him a tip.*)

Yashcherin: You know, we shall have to turn off on to a country road; we're not far from the place now... (*They take seats in the carriage.*)

Arkhippov (*to the coachman*): How far will it be to the next station?

Coachman: It's reckoned at thirty versts.

Yashcherin: What a bore! I'm not sleepy yet; I had a splendid nap at the last station. Maybe I'll smoke a cigar... (*Another coachman approaches.*)

Coachman: For the headman, master, for his trouble...

Yashcherin: Get out of here! It's enough to have tipped the coachman. What trouble have you been to here?... But why is our coachman dawdling here so long?—Well, are you seated? Get going!...

Coachman (*touching up the horses*): Oh, you... (*The sleigh-bells ring. Ivan jumps up on the box. The carriage drives out of the village on to the highway.*)

Arkhippov: It isn't cold, surely?

Yashcherin: Of course it isn't cold, but a little warmer wouldn't hurt!

Arkhippov: Brother Andrei, you're everlastingly having a chill, but for me it's somehow cheerier in a bit of cold!

Yashcherin: Yes, I know that cheer of yours! Last winter I chanced to be driving to Moscow, to my sister's for a housewarming. In the first place—my back took a hard beating from the jolts; I'll not forget the ruts of that untrammeled winter journey! And in the second place—I'll remember this forever, that I had all I could do to keep from freezing, while my servant didn't come down from the box the whole way—his feet were so frozen, I suppose! That's the kind of trick your "bit of cold" played on us!

Arkhippov: Well, who's talking about such a cold as that! But by the way, how is your family? Will your sister be joining her husband presently? I don't know who it was from, only I heard...

Yashcherin: Yes, her husband lives all the time in the country; he's busy with the farming, will you believe it, day and night and is constantly increasing his yearly income; but their daughter, my niece, her father's capital will soon be bringing to Moscow for an education, with the whole family to live!

(*For some time they continue to drive in silence. Finally the coachman whips on the horses more briskly, and they pass through a small hamlet. Little boys, playing in the road, scatter with shrieks. A peasant woman stands still and gazes.*)

A peasant (*nudges her*): Well, what are you looking at that you haven't seen?

Woman: Aw, the fur coats, the fur coats on them! Just see how gentlemen keep themselves warm!

Peasant: That's why they're gentlemen! But the coachman, isn't he from Semyonovka?

Woman: Yes, from Semyonovka. A little while ago, early this morning, he carried a gentleman yonder, and now he's on his way home with a passenger.

Peasant: Let's go! See, the master is looking at us and laughing... (*The carriage drives on.*)

Yashcherin: Well, there's no use talking, she's not a beauty. What a costume, what a figure! (*He starts to sing a theme from Norma.*)

Arkhippov: You're off key, brother. You can't sing half a word properly and in tune.

Yashcherin: That's just the way it seems to you—it's the deception of your dreaming... You don't understanding singing, but are ready with criticism... But then, right now you couldn't have rightly evaluated my voice with understanding: I'm hampered here by this "gift of Valdai that whistles dolefully beneath the arch." But incidentally: let's sing "Here comes speeding a dashing troika." [Two passages quoted from Fyodor Glinka's poem "The Troika," which had become a popular song]

(*He strikes up the song. Arkhippov chimes in, softly at first, then little by little more loudly, and in this way they sing the song through.*)

Yashcherin (*to the coachman*): Stop! Give me a chance to light a match. You help me, Peter, to shield myself from the wind...

Arkhippov: Certainly, certainly.

(*They stop. They get a flame going under the skirt of a fur coat and begin to smoke cigars.*)

Arkhippov: Well, get long! (*They drive on.*)

Arkhippov: I love a beautiful winter's day! It chases repose and lassitude away, I love to watch when over the virgin snow, so brilliant white, a shadow is lightly spread! Look, how on the edge of the road, here, to the right, the sunlight mirrors us, and our shadow, in giant size, with carriage, with coachman, prances along behind us. The trees are trimmed with a snowy garment, and the blue of the sky is transparent and bright, and the air is pure,—and the breast is full of hope and a feeling of youthful power! You're carried along a level road; instead of wings the smooth runners glide easily, agilely, effortlessly, and the sparks of snow fly to the sides, glittering in the sun. Under foot the frost creaks. And yonder, not far off, over every hut, over every chimney, a column of smoke is blue! At first high up, rising always straight, straight up, and then it changes its shapely course, bends to one side, and merging with a cloud, is lost. The sumptuous vault of heaven, and beautiful nature in her white aspect, and the people's fresh and cheery faces—it all delights me. My God, how happy I am that I can find in simple Russian nature a freer and more beautiful refuge from our artificial, conventional life!

Yashcherin: You fantasize well, but I'm not a fantast. Though I myself at times like nature and verses... But I'm occupied for the present constantly with one and the same thought. My soul carries me farther away than you, I'll tell you here once more by the way: I don't care to sympathize with a single country,—the love in me is more expansive! With Russian nature and Russian man it is impossible, believe me, to be content, for one who follows after the enlightened age! Tell me, can I forget that he [i.e., Russian man] has lived and always will live contemptibly, slavishly... Don't talk to him of the rights of man... He'd sooner understand Arabic than... Nothing but force alone, rude violence—are his guides! But meanwhile, see, everywhere in foreign regions, where the West holds sway, our uncomprehended teacher, what an arena for peaceful labor! How peacefully the seed of social science ripens there! The striving of freedom and love will soon, perhaps, throw off the burden that weighs down the people in dust and blood!

Arkhippov: We like to live with another's mind, to measure what is ours with another's yardstick, and feast at another's banquet; to fuss over and dissemble before one who has no use for us! But if spacious love shall call one in whom an ardent striving agitates the blood, to restore to the oppressed once more all his former importance,—then rather than look to the side, rather than seek intoxication at another's banquet and go along paths laid out, following another's footsteps, and hammer out articles that are not needed,— let him tear the shroud from off himself, let him admit closer to his heart that which shall find a kindred response in him, that which a foreigner will not understand, that which will be strange to one of another faith! Let him feel in himself all the sanctity of his bonds to the people, to the people's lot of suffering; let him consecrate himself to the struggle for the people's profit and freedom! But not upon a path laid out, not in another's narrow footsteps— the people in its development shall walk, believe me, on another path, one independent and Russian. Hear, O Lord, this earnest cry: that the principle of our own way of life may scatter our foes and tear from itself the despised yoke of moral chains!

Yashcherin: Your indignation is ridiculous, your childish dreams are mad! Do you really dare to suppose that your expectation will be fulfilled? Tell me: what was our people doing when other peoples were gathering with heavy labor the fruit cultivated by long ages? They [i.e., other peoples] are moving the world by their own effort, proud of their experience and fame; rich is the noisy banquet of their life, their esteem is magnificent! They will solve the task for us of all the questions of life and striving. But where have you found a foundation for your visions? Where salvation? No! Do not be in a hurry to be bewitched by a mere resounding plaything! Where are those treasures—of the mighty soul of the Russian people? And I do not in the least feel in myself your predilection: where, in what, does *its* principle lie? What is our warranty for it?

Arkhippov: He who has hearing,—let him hear; he who has eyes,—let him see; he in whom a living feeling breathes,—in him let it begin to speak. I shall not give you an answer, I shall not reply! Warmed by the radiance of an inner light, by the heat of a secret fire, by eternal truth, is the life of the people for me!

(*The sounds of the Russian song "Down along little mother Volga" are heard. A big sledge, drawn by a three-horse team, drives up, in which some ten muzhiks are sitting and singing. Coming alongside, they exchange greetings with the coachman.*)

Yashcherin: What people are these, from where?

Coachman: Why, they're from work, from town, and they're hurrying home to a festival. Oh, they had it hard there! This is pleasant, they are having a cheerful ride.

Yashcherin: Well, well, get along!

Coachman (urging on the horses): Hey, you birds of passage!

Arkhippov: What a song, eh?

Yashcherin: Well, it's fine, of course. I'm willing to admit. But I suppose that's all? Permit me now frankly to tell you my judgment about you.

Although there is sincere feeling in you, I see no sort of profit in this! On the contrary, you are living with your dream alone, you've become disused to practical life and you rave about art; doing violence to your soul, you set up nationality as an idol for her. It's labor in vain: she should live freer with the whole world, it's more comfortable and brighter for her there! For this reason you are full of questions and doubts, and your poetical dreams are unwilling to descend into the midst of reality, and be destroyed... this is the truth, you know it yourself!

Arkhippov: In part, I must acknowledge that there is truth in your words. I haven't yet been able to come to terms with life, to be a whole creature, though in youthful years. But I shall contradict you in everything else...

Yashcherin: Stop, who is this rolling along to meet us now?

(*A kibitka drives up: in it is lying an old retired officer, smoking a pipe.*) He looks like the mayor of Belovsk, doesn't he? The similarity of those mugs is striking!

Arkhippov: Why, isn't it the man himself? Just such moustaches, and just such a stubborn look.

Yashcherin: Oh no! I know him intimately...

At this point the two winter travellers lapse into silence, and in a drowsing semi-slumber Arkhippov sees several scenes and hears accompanying "voices." These scenes appear in no logical order and have only a very general relevance to the previous discussion between the two. First "a voice," which seems to belong to the visionary, idealistic side of the ambivalent Arkhippov, describes his mother, praying for the happiness of her absent son. A second voice depicts the bustling social life that the dreamer presumably leads at present, and the impossibility of going back to a life that is past. The voice of Arkhippov's "Muse" interrupts and gives a nostalgic picture of the poet's lost childhood. A "chorus of invisible ones" breaks in with the admonition: "Life is everywhere—it is borne ahead and all around you." At this point a curious episode is introduced: a "stage direction" states: "An old tarantas drives up, set on runners and drawn by six horses, with a postilion." The tarantas sings a five-stanza ditty, which although not related to ideology, is curious enough to quote:

> I live constantly in service and accountability, I have suffered all my days: how many I have carried in this world. I have seen "little mother, Volga-river."
>
> I remember the day when I emerged for the first time from my spacious natal workshop; I had kindred brothers, but they are all scattered about, driving.
>
> Every summer I was on the road, but in the winter I rested by good right; but alas! my owner has ordered runners to be fitted to my foundation-shafts [*drogi*]!
>
> And my household gods have been utterly upset, and I have been illegally harnessed up for a journey! Here I am, dragging along to Saratov. I'm old, it's time for me to rest.
>
> Life for me has long grown cold; in this world the Creator has condemned all things to death! I creak, I creak dolefully now, soon I shall finally break up!"

The tarantas is carrying a beautiful young girl and an elderly landowner's wife; two voices communicate to Arkhippov and the girl her miserable fate, to be hopelessly mired in a dull, stodgy country life. In a brief interlude Arkhippov sees "the mayor of Belovsk," who demands to see his passport; and finally two voices, in alternation, one representing the dreamy, poetical side of Arkhippov (and doubtless of Ivan Aksakov), the other his "social conscience," demanding action to lighten the burden of his oppressed brothers, make their pleas to the dreamer. This inner dialogue is rudely broken off when the carriage hits a particularly bad rut and jolts both travellers awake.

The second part of the piece is set in a peasant hut, into which Yashcherin and Arkhippov invade to eat their lunch. Arkhippov is sympathetic to the peasants, Yashcherin contemptuous and rudely tactless (he talks about them in French and makes remarks that show his utter incomprehension). At the end of the scene the son of the hut's owner, and father of the baby which the women are tending, returns from town with the appalling news that the time for drafting recruits for the army is at hand, and he will probably be drawn. Amid the wails and prayers of the women, the travellers make a hurried withdrawal. As they go, Arkhippov says to his comrade: "Did you hear? Did you see, eh?" Yashcherin replies: "Yes, brother, I saw: but what's one to say? (He throws up his hands.) Let's go." It is evident throughout the scene that of the two gentlemen Yashcherin, the prosaic, practical man is wholly unsympathetic to the peasants, while the dreamer

Arkhippov feels a helpless sympathy for them; but for the peasants there is no distinction between the two: they are both dwellers in another world, and immune to such catastrophes as threaten young Peter and his family.

Bibliography

Aksakov, Ivan. *Stikhotvoreniia i poemy*, L.: Sovetskii pisatel', Biblioteka poeta, bol'shaia seriia, 1968.

Aksakov, Konstantin Sergeevich. *Polnoe sobranie sochinenii*, Vols. 1-3. Spb., 1861-1880.

Aksakov, Konstantin. *Stikhotvoreniia*, in: *Poety kruzhka N.V. Stankevicha*. Vstupitel'nia stat'ia, podgotovka teksta i primechaniia S.I. Mashinskogo. M.-L.: Sovetskii pisatel', Biblioteka poeta, bol'shaia seriia, 1964.

Belinskii, V.G. *Sobranie sochinenii v trekh tomakh*. Vol. 2: Stat'i i retsenzii 1841-1845. M.: OGIZ, 1948.

Christoff, P. *An introduction to Nineteenth-Century Russian Slavophilism. A Study in Ideas*. The Hague: Mouton, 1961.

Hingley, Ronald. *Russian Writers and Society 1825-1904*. New York & Toronto: McGraw-Hill, 1967.

Khomiakov, Aleksei. *Izbrannye sochineniia*, New York: Izdatel'stvo imeni Chekhova, 1955.

Kireevskii, Ivan. *Sobranie sochinenii*. M.: P. Bakhmetev, 1861; rpt. Ann Arbor: Ardis, 1983.

Koshelov, V.A. *Esteticheskie i literaturnye vozzreniia russkikh slavianofilov 1840-1850-e gody*. L.: Izdatel'stvo "Nauka," 1984.

Literaturnye vzgliady i tvorchestvo slavianofilov 1830-1850 gody. M.: Izdatel'stvo "Nauka," 1978.

Lotman, L.M. "Proza sorokovykh godov," in: *Istoriia russkoi literatury*, Vol. 7: *Literatura 1840-kh godov*. M.: Izdatel'stvo Akademii nauk SSSR, 1955.

Pushkarev, S.G. *Rossiia v XIX veke (1801-1914)*. New York: Izdatel'stvo imeni Chekhova, 1956.

Russkaia drama epokhi A.N. Ostrovskogo. Sostavlenie, obshchaia redaktsiia, vstupitel'naia stat'ia A.I. Zhuravlevoi. M.: Izdatel'stvo Moskovskogo universiteta, 1984.

Russkaia estetika i kritika 40-50-kh godov XIX veka, M.: "Iskusstvo," 1982.

Samarin, Iu. F. *Sochineniia*, Vol. I.: *Stat'i raznorodnago soderzhaniia i po Pol'skomu voprosu*. M.: A.I. Mamontov, 1900.

Sollogub, V.A. *Povesti i rasskazy*. M.-L.: Gosudarstvennoe izdatel'stvo khudozhestvennoi literatury, 1961.

Sollogub, V.A. *Tarantas: putevyia vpechatleniia*. Sochinenie Grafa V.A. Solloguba. Spb.: Izdanie Andreia Ivanova, 1845. [With wood engravings by E.E. Bernardsky, after sketches by G.G. Gagarin]; rpt.: M., Izdatel'stvo "Kniga," 1982.

Stender-Petersen, Adolf. *Geschichte der russischen Literatur*, Vol. II. Munchen, C.H. Beck, 1957.

Tsimbaev, Nikolai Ivanovich. *Slavianofilstvo*, M.: Izdatel'stvo Moskovskogo universiteta, 1986.

Index